New York Times bestselling author Elizabeth Chadwick has written over twenty historical novels sold in eighteen languages worldwide. Her first novel, *The Wild Hunt*, won a Betty Trask Award, and *The Scarlet Lion* was nominated by Richard Lee, founder of the Historical Novel Society, as one of the top ten historical novels of the last decade. Elizabeth's nineteenth novel, *To Defy a King*, won the RNA Historical Novel prize in 2011.

Also by Elizabeth Chadwick

ELIZABETH CHADWICK

THE WINTER MANTLE

sphere

SPHERE

First published in Great Britain in 2002 by Little, Brown
Paperback edition published in 2002 by Time Warner Paperbacks
This reissue published in 2018

1 3 5 7 9 10 8 6 4 2

A CIP catalogue record for this book is available from the British Library.

ISBN 978-0-7515-7567-5

Typeset in Horley Old Style by Palimpsest Book Production Limited,
Falkirk, Stirlingshire
Printed and bound in Great Britain by Clays Ltd, Elcograf S.p.A.

Papers used by Sphere are from well-managed forests
and other responsible sources.

Sphere
An imprint of
Little, Brown Book Group
Carmelite House
50 Victoria Embankment
London
EC4Y 0DZ

An Hachette UK Company
www.hachette.co.uk

www.littlebrown.co.uk

ACKNOWLEDGEMENTS

I'd like to say a public thank you to colleagues, friends and family behind the scenes. Since first publication of *The Winter Mantle*, many of the faces and names have changed at my publishers but I want to continue to offer thanks to my then editor Barbara Boote who was always supportive, encouraging and made time to answer my calls even in the midst of a very demanding schedule. My current editor is the terrific Viola Hayden and I want to say a big thank you to her for seeing *The Winter Mantle* forward as it comes out in this new edition. Thank you also to Maddie West who began the process and Thalia Proctor for her work behind the scenes.

Very sadly I lost my dear agent Carole Blake as this edition was being prepared, and I will always remember her wisdom and passion with gratitude and a full heart. I want to thank my new agent at Blake Friedmann, Isobel Dixon, for taking me on and being such a fine mentor, friend and agent and for working so hard on my behalf. The same goes for the other members of the magnificent Blake Friedmann team.

My family are an oasis of steadiness and love in a some-times hectic and fraught world. My husband Roger understands that my writing is my soul and gives me the space I need. He also doesn't mind being tortured by read-outs of the first drafts while doing the ironing, so he is a genuine romantic hero!

I would also like to say thank you to the members of Regia Anglorum, both those I have met in the flesh and those online, who have answered my frequent questions with patience, laughter and astounding knowledge – especially Andrew Nicolson for taking the time to respond to my queries about eleventh-century coffins.

CHAPTER 1

Tower of Rouen, Normandy, Lent 1067

'I wonder what Englishmen are like,' mused Sybille as she helped her mistress to don an embroidered linen shift.

'Judging by the few we've seen, more hair and beards than a flock of wild goats,' Judith replied with disdain. As niece to Duke William of Normandy, now King of England, she was deeply conscious of her own dignity. 'At least with our men you can see what lies beneath, and the lice are easier to keep at bay.' She glanced towards the window, where the sound of the cheering crowds swished through the open shutters like a summer wind through forest leaves. Beyond the lofty tower walls the entire population of Rouen crammed the streets, eager for a sight of their duke's triumphal return from England and his defeat of the crown-stealer, Harold Godwinsson.

Her chamber lady's interest in Englishmen – and her own if the truth were known – was because her uncle William had returned to his Duchy laden with booty and accompanied by highborn hostages – English lords whom he did not trust out of his sight.

'But it is nice to run your fingers through a man's beard, don't you think?' Sybille pursued with sparkling eyes. 'Especially if he is young and handsome.'

'I would not know,' Judith said disdainfully.

'Well, now you have a chance to find out.' Not quelled in the least, Sybille fetched Judith's best gown of blood-red wool from the coffer and helped her into it.

Judith smoothed her palms over the rich, soft wool with pleasure. In the corner of her vision she was aware of her sister Adela being fussed over by their mother, who was plucking and tweaking to align every fold.

'God forfend that there should be a single hair out of place,' Sybille muttered, facetiously crossing herself.

Judith hissed a rebuke as her mother approached. Sybille immediately swept a demure curtsey to the older woman and busied herself with binding Judith's hair in two tight, glossy braids. A silk veil followed, held in place by pins of worked gold.

Adelaide, Countess of Aumale, studied the maid's handi-work with eyes as hard and sharp as brown glass. Her expression remained tight and judgemental but obviously Judith's attire had passed the test of her exacting standards for she nodded brusquely and said, 'Where's your cloak?'

'Here, Mother.' Judith lifted the garment from her clothing pole. The dark green wool was lined with beaver fur and trimmed with sable as befitted her rank. Adelaide adjusted the gold and garnet pin and plucked an imaginary speck from the napped wool.

Judith restrained the urge to bat her mother's hand aside, but Adelaide had clearly sensed the intent. 'We are women of the ducal house,' she said icily, 'and it behoves us to show it.'

'I know that, Mother.' Behind her dutiful expression she was quietly seething. At fifteen years old, she was of marriage-able age with the curves and fluxes of womanhood, but her mother treated her like a child.

'I am glad you do.' Adelaide gave her another hard look, and then, beckoning her daughters to follow, she swept to join the other women of Duchess Matilda's household who were preparing to go out in public and greet their returning menfolk. Not that Adelaide's husband was among them. He was part of the Norman force left behind to garrison England during the new king's absence. Judith had not decided whether her mother was pleased or relieved at the situation. She herself was indifferent. He was her stepfather and she barely knew him for he seldom visited the women's apartments even when at home, preferring life in the hall and the guardroom.

A blustery March wind tumbled around the courtyard, snatching at wimples, and billowing cloaks. Bright silk banners cracked like whips on the tower battlements and above them the clouds flew so swiftly across the blue sky that watching them made Judith dizzy.

Sheltering in the lee of the wall, she wondered how long they would have to wait. Her male cousins, the Duke's sons Richard, Robert and William, had ridden out to greet their father in the city. She would have liked to join them, but it would not have been seemly, and, as her mother was constantly saying, when you were an important member of the highest household in the land, seemliness was everything.

The roars of approbation from the crowd had become a storm and Judith's heart swelled with fierce pride. It was her blood they were cheering, her uncle who was now a king by God's will and his own determination.

To a fanfare of trumpets the first riders clattered into the courtyard. Sunlight glanced on helms and mail; pennons rippled on the glittering hafts of spears. Under the silks of the Papal banner, her uncle William rode a Spanish stallion, its hide the deep black of polished sea coal. He wore no armour and his powerful frame was resplendent in crimson wool, crusted with gold embroidery and jewels. His dark hair beat about his brow and his hawkish visage was emphasised by the way he narrowed his eyes against the buffet of the wind. A squire ran to grasp the stallion's bridle. William dismounted and, landing with solid assurance, turned his gaze on the waiting women.

The Duchess Matilda hastened forward and sank at his feet in a deep curtsey. Adelaide tugged peremptorily at Judith's cloak and Judith knelt too, the ground hard beneath her knees.

William stooped, raised his wife to her feet and murmured something that Judith did not hear but that brought a blush to the diminutive Duchess's face. He kissed his daughters, Agatha, Constance, Cecilia, Adela, then he gestured the other women of the household to rise. His dark gaze assessed them, perhaps with pride in its depths, although his mouth out of long habit and harsh self-control remained straight and stern.

The courtyard was growing ever more crowded as men continued to ride in. Flanked by guards the English 'guests' arrived. Beards and long hair, Judith noted; her words to Sybille had been right. They did resemble a flock of wild goats, although she had to admit that the embroidery on their garments was the most exquisite she had ever seen.

A richly attired priest, whom Judith identified by the ornate cross atop his staff as an archbishop, was talking to two young men whose similarity of feature marked them as brothers. Mounted on a dappled cob was a yellow-haired youth with fine features and a petulant air. His tunic was that rare colour of purple reserved for royalty and his hat was banded with ermine fur. She studied him until her view was blocked by a powerful chestnut stallion, straddled by a young man whose size and musculature almost equalled that of his horse.

He sported neither hat nor hood and the wind beat his copper-blond hair about his face in disarray. Outlining a wide, good-natured mouth and strong jaw, his beard was the colour of rose gold and made her consider Sybille's mischievous comment in a new light. What *would* it be like to touch? Soft as silk, or harsh as besom twigs? The notion both intrigued and disturbed her. He wore his costly garments in a careless, taken-for-granted way that should have filled her with scorn, but instead she felt admiration bordering on envy. Who was he? In the same moment that she asked herself the question, Judith decided that she did not want to know. Her uncle's English hostage was sufficient to her needs. To think beyond that was much too dangerous. She lowered her eyes in self-defence and thus did not see the swift, appreciative glance he cast in her direction.

Turning gracefully on her heel, she followed her mother and sister back within the sanctuary of the great stone tower and did not look back.

He was Waltheof Siwardsson, Earl of Huntingdon and Northampton. That he had retained his lands and titles was because he had not fought against William on Hastings Field. It did not mean that the new Norman king was willing to trust or favour him though.

'It does not matter that William calls us his guests, we know very well that we are his prisoners,' declared Edgar Atheling, who was a prince of ancient English lineage. His fine, almost delicate features were contorted by a fierce scowl. 'Our cage is gilded, but it is still a cage.'

The English 'guests' were gathered in the timber hall that had been allotted to them during their stay in Rouen. Although the doors were not guarded, none of the hostages was in any doubt that any attempt to leave and take ship for England would be prevented on the end of a sharpened spear.

Waltheof shrugged and filled his cup with wine from a flagon standing on an oak chest. Captivity it might be, but at least it was generous. 'There is nothing we can do, so we might as well enjoy ourselves.' He took a long swallow. It had taken him a while to adjust to the taste of wine when he was accustomed to mead and ale, but now he welcomed the acid, tannic bite at the back of his throat. He understood Edgar's chaffing. Many in England thought that this youth should be king. His claim was stronger than either Harold Godwinsson's or William's, but he was only fifteen years old and more of a focus around which to rally men rather than a threat posed by his own efforts and abilities.

'You call drinking that muck enjoyment?' Edgar's light blue eyes were scornful.

'You have to grow accustomed,' Waltheof replied and was rewarded with a disparaging snort.

'So you think that developing a taste for all things Norman will get you what you want?' This was from Morcar, Earl of Northumberland, his tone hostile and his arms folded belligerently high on his chest. At his side his older brother, Edwin, Earl of Mercia, was, as usual, absorbing all and saying nothing. Their alliance with Harold had been tepid, but so was their acceptance of William the Bastard as their king.

Waltheof raised his goblet. 'I think it better to say yes than no.' He met Morcar's stare briefly then strode to look out of the embrasure on the advancing dusk. Torches were being lit in the chambers and courtyards of the ducal complex. The rich smell of cooking wafted to his nostrils and cramped his stomach. It would be too easy to quarrel with Morcar and he held himself back, knowing how the Normans would feed upon their disagreements and take superior pleasure in watching them bicker.

'Have a care,' Morcar said softly. 'One day you might say yes to something that will bring you naught but harm.'

Waltheof clenched his fists, but forced himself not to rise to the bait. 'One day I might indeed,' he answered, trying to make light of the matter, 'but not now.' He returned to the flagon and, refilling his goblet, drank deeply of the dark Norman wine. He knew from experience that after four cups a pleasant haze would begin to creep over him. Ten cups and that haze became numbness. Fifteen purchased oblivion. The Normans frowned on English drinking habits and King William was particularly abstemious. Waltheof had curbed his excesses rather than face that cold-eyed scorn, but still the need lingered – particularly with Morcar in the vicinity.

Waltheof's father, Siward the Strong, had once held the great earldom of Northumbria, but he had died when Waltheof was a small boy and such a turbulent border earldom required a grown man's rule. First there had been Tosti Godwinsson, who had proved so unpopular that the people rose in rebellion, and then Morcar of the line of Mercia, because Waltheof, at nineteen years old, was still judged too young and inexperienced to be given control of such a vast domain. Two years had passed since that time, and Waltheof's sense of possession had matured sufficiently to leave him resentful of Morcar's ownership – and Morcar knew it.

Further into the room, Archbishop Stigand was seated with Wulnoth Godwinsson, who was King Harold's brother and a man who had been a hostage in Normandy for many years. A youth of Edgar's age when he had entered captivity, he was now a young man, with a full golden beard and sad, grey eyes. Quiet and unassuming, he was an insipid shadow of his dynamic brothers Leofwin, Gyrth and Harold, who had died beneath Norman blades on Hastings field. He was no more capable of rebellion than a legless man was of running.

Waltheof downed his wine to the lees and was contemplating refilling his cup again when there was a knock on the chamber door. Being the nearest, he reached to the latch and found himself looking down at a boy of about nine or ten years old. Fox-gold eyes peered from beneath a fringe of sun-streaked brown hair shaved high on the nape. His tunic of good blue wool with exquisite stitching revealed that the sprog was of high rank, probably someone's squire in the first year of his apprenticeship, when fetching and carrying were the order of the day.

Waltheof raised his brows. 'Child?' he said, suddenly feeling ancient.

'My lords, the dinner horn is about to sound and your presence is requested in the hall,' the lad announced in a clear, confident tone. His gaze travelled beyond Waltheof to examine with frank curiosity the other occupants of the room. Waltheof could almost see his mind absorbing every detail, storing it up to relay later to his companions.

'And we must give "King" William what he desires, mustn't we?' sneered Edgar Atheling in English. 'Even if he sends some babe in tail clouts to escort us.'

The boy looked puzzled. Waltheof set a hand on his shoulder and gave him a reassuring smile. 'What is your name, lad?' he asked in French.

'Simon de Senlis, my lord.'

'He's my son.' William's chamberlain Richard de Rules arrived, slightly out of breath. 'I gave him the message and he took off ahead of me like a harrier unleashed!'

'Yes, we must make good sport,' said Edgar, speaking French himself now.

De Rules shook his head and looked rueful. 'That was not my meaning, my lord. My son may be as keen as a hound, but it is his passion that drives him, not his desire to make sport of valued guests.'

Waltheof admired De Rules' way with words – smooth without being obsequious. The Norman's face was open and honest with laughter lines at the corners of his eyes and he had the same sun-flashed hair as his son.

'Ah, so he has a passion for all things English, like most of your breed?' jeered Morcar.

The polite expression remained on De Rules' face, but the warmth faded from his eyes. 'If you are ready, my lords, I will conduct you to the hall,' he said with stiff courtesy.

Waltheof cleared his throat and sought to lighten the moment with a smile and a jest. 'I am certainly ready! Indeed, I am so hungry that I could eat a bear.' With a flourish he swept on his cloak, its thick blue wool lined with a pelt of gleaming white fur. He winked at the wide-eyed boy. 'This is all that's left of the last one I came across.'

'Hah, you've never seen a bear in your life unless it was a tame one shambling in chains!' Morcar snapped.

'That shows how much you know,' Waltheof retorted and cast his glance around the gathering of English nobles. 'I am going down to the hall to eat my dinner because, even if I am proud, pride alone will not nourish my bones and it would be churlish to refuse our Norman hosts.' And foolish too, but he did not need to say so. No matter how much they grumbled at their confinement, they dared not openly rebel whilst hostage in Normandy.

As they were escorted to the great hall, the boy paced beside Waltheof and tentatively stroked the magnificent white pelt lining the blue cloak. 'Is it really a bearskin?' he asked.

'It is indeed, boy,' he said with a smile, 'although you will never see one of its kind in a market place or at a baiting. Such beasts dwell in the frozen North Country, far from the eyes of men.'

'Then how did you come by it, my lord?'

'Morcar's right,' Waltheof grinned over his shoulder at the scowling Earl of Northumberland. 'I have never seen other than the mangy creatures that entertain folk at fairs. But when my father was a young man, he went adventuring and hunted the great bear that once dwelt inside this fur. Twice the height of a man it was, with teeth the size of drinking horns and a growl to shake snow off the mountain tops.' Waltheof spread his arms to augment the tale and the pelt shimmered, hinting at the fierce life that had once inhabited it. 'He had it fashioned into a cloak and so it has come down to me.'

The boy eyed the garment with wonder and a hint of longing. Waltheof laughed and tousled the child's hair.

Attired in their finery for the homecoming of their duke, the Norman nobility packed the trestles set out in the Tower's great hall. The English hostages were placed to one side of the high table with William's kin and the Bishops of Rouen, Fécamp and Jumièges. A cloth of sun-bleached linen covered the board. There were drinking vessels made from the horns of the wild white cattle that roamed the great forests of Northumbria, the rims and tips edged with exquisitely worked silver and gold. Goblets and flagons, decorated candleholders, gleamed in the firelight like the spangled pile of a dragon's hoard. All of it spoils of war, plundered from the thegns and huscarls who had fallen on Hastings field.

Surrounded by such trophies of conquest, Waltheof felt ill at ease, but he was sufficiently pragmatic to know that this was a victory feast and such display was to be expected. He and his companions were here because they were the vanquished and they too were part of that plunder. He supposed that in a way they should be grateful for Duke William's restraint. The legends of Waltheof's ancestors told of how they had toasted their own victories from the brain-pans of their slaughtered foes.

Waltheof had an ear for languages. His French was good, if accented, and he was as fluent in Latin as he was in his native tongue, courtesy of a childhood education at Crowland Abbey in the Fen Country. He was soon engaged in conver-sation by the Norman prelates, who seemed both surprised and diverted by the ease with which he spoke the tongue of the church.

'Once I was intended for the priesthood,' Waltheof explained to the Archbishop of Rouen. 'I spent several years as an oblate in Crowland Abbey under the instruction of Abbot Ulfcytel.'

'You would have made an imposing monk,' replied the Archbishop with a smile as he broke the greasy wing joint off a portion of goose and wiped his fingers on a linen napkin.

Waltheof threw back his head and laughed. 'Indeed I would!' He flexed his shoulders with deliberate pleasure. There were few folk in the hall to match his height or breadth, and certainly not on the dais, where even Duke William, who was tall and robust, seemed small by comparison. 'They are probably glad that they did not have to find the yards of wool necessary to fashion me a habit!' As he spoke he chanced to meet the eyes of the young woman who sat among the other women of William's household.

He had noticed her in the courtyard on his arrival. Her expression then had been a mingling of the curious and the wary, as though she was studying a caged lion at close quarters. That same look filled her gaze now. She was raven-haired and attractive in an austere sort of way, her nose thin and straight, her eyes deep brown and thick-lashed. Her mouth, for all that it was set in a firm, unsmiling line, held a hint of sensuality. For an instant she returned his scrutiny before modestly lowering her lashes. He wondered who she was: it might be interesting to find out. Certainly it would be a diversion to while away the tedious hours of confinement.

Following the various courses of the feast the women retired, leaving the men to the remainder of the evening in the hall. Waltheof watched them depart with interest. In her close-fitting gown of deepest red, the young woman was as lissom as a young doe. Perhaps it was as well, he thought, that fate had not led him to monastic vows of poverty, chastity and obedience. He doubted that he would have been able to keep any of them.

Now that the women had departed the atmosphere grew more relaxed and, although Duke William was morally abstemious, he slackened the reins and allowed his retainers a degree of leeway. Under cover of raised levels of noise, Waltheof took the opportunity of asking Richard de Rules the identity of the girl in the red dress.

The chamberlain looked wary. 'She is the King's niece, Judith – her mother is his full sister, Adelaide, Countess of Aumale,' he said. 'I would advise you to leave well alone.'

'Why?' Waltheof clasped his hands behind his head. 'Is she betrothed?'

De Rules looked uncomfortable. 'Not yet.'

The wine buzzed in Waltheof's blood. 'So she is available to be courted?'

The Norman shook his head.

'Why not?' To one side an arm-wrestling contest had noisily begun and Waltheof's attention flickered.

'The Duke is her uncle, so her marriage will be of great importance to Normandy,' De Rules said, emphasising each word.

Waltheof's eyes narrowed. 'You are saying that I am not good enough for her?'

'I am saying that the Duke will give her to a man of his own choosing, not one who comes courting because the girl has caught his wandering eye when he is at a loose end. Besides,' he added wryly, 'you are probably best to keep your distance. Her mother has the Devil's own pride, her step-father is prickly on the matter of his honour, and the girl herself is difficult.'

Waltheof's curiosity was piqued. He would have asked in what way Judith was difficult, but at that moment Edgar Atheling seized his sleeve and dragged him towards the wres-tling contest. 'A pound's weight of silver that no one can defeat Waltheof Siwardsson!' he bellowed, his adolescent voice ragged with drink.

Men roared and pounded the trestles. Banter, mostly good-natured, flew, although there was some partisan muttering. Coins flashed like fish scales as they were wagered. Waltheof was plumped down opposite his intended oppo-nent, a knight of the Duke's household named Picot de Saye. The man was wide-chested and bull-necked, with hands the size of shovels and a deep sword scar grooving one cheek.

His grin revealed several missing teeth. 'They say a fool and his money are soon parted,' he scoffed.

Waltheof laughed at his opponent. 'I do not claim to be a wise man, but it will take a stronger one than you to separate me from my silver,' he retorted.

Hoots of derision followed that statement, but again they were amiable. Waltheof leaned his elbow on the board and extended his hand to the Norman's. Waltheof's hands were smooth, unblemished by battle, for although he had been taught to wield axe and sword with consummate skill he had never been put to the test.

Picot grasped Waltheof's hand in his own scarred one. 'Light the candles,' he commanded.

Either side of the men's wrists stood two shallow prickets holding short tallow candles. The aim of the contest was for each man to try to force his opponent's arm down onto the flame and extinguish it. In this particular sport Waltheof did have experience, although there was nothing to see. The evidence of his talent lay in the unblemished skin on the back of his wrist.

Waltheof kept his arm loose and supple as Picot began to exert pressure. Resisting the first questing push, he studied the almost imperceptible tightening of Picot's neck and shoulders. Humour kindled in Waltheof's eyes. The smile he sent to Picot was natural, not forced through teeth that were gritted with effort. Picot thrust harder, but Waltheof remained solid. Men began slowly to pound the tables. Waltheof heard the sound like a drum in his blood, but was only distantly aware of the watchers. Focus was all. The pressure grew stronger, and Picot's grip became painful. Waltheof started to exert his own pressure, building slowly, never relenting. He relaxed his free hand on his thigh and held his breathing slow and steady. Now shouts of encouragement pierced the drumroll of fists. Waltheof poured more strength into his forearm and slowly, but inexorably, started to push Picot's wrist down onto the flame. The Norman struggled, his face reddening and the tendons bulging in his throat like ropes, but Waltheof was too powerful, searing Picot's hand upon the candle and extinguishing the flame in a stink of black tallow smoke.

The roars were deafening. Picot rubbed his burned wrist and stared at Waltheof. 'It is seldom I am defeated,' he said grudgingly.

'My father was called Siward the Strong,' Waltheof replied. 'They say he could wrestle an ox to the ground one-handed.' He opened and closed his fist, the marks of the other man's grip imprinted on his skin in white stigmata.

'Cunningly played, Waltheof, son of Siward,' a gravelly voice said from behind his left shoulder. Waltheof turned to find King William standing over him, darkening the light with his shadow. Obviously he had been watching the end of the match and Waltheof reddened, suddenly uncomfortable.

'Thank you, sire,' he muttered.

'A pity there is not much call for ox wrestling in my hall.' Despite the smile on William's lips, his eyes were dark and watchful. Here was a man who did not let down his guard for a moment, and who judged others by his own harsh personal standards.

Although Waltheof had just won the contest, suddenly the taste of victory was not as sweet as it had been.

CHAPTER 2

A week later Duke William's court prepared to depart Rouen and celebrate Easter to the north at Fécamp. Countess Adelaide, suffering from a head cold, had opted to ride in one of the covered baggage wains, its interior padded with feather bolsters and thick furs to cushion the jolting of the cart and keep the occupants warm.

Judith hated travelling this way. The bumping and jarring was wearisome and her sister had an irritating tendency to whine and wriggle.

After much argument she finally persuaded Adelaide to let her ride her black mare instead. 'There will be more room in the wain,' she pointed out. 'I promise to ride where you can see me.'

Adelaide sneezed into a large linen napkin. 'Oh, go, child,' she flapped a weary hand. 'You make my head ache. Just have a care and do not give me anything with which to reproach you.'

Smiling with triumph, Judith curtseyed to her mother, and with a light heart instructed Sybille to tell the grooms to saddle her mare.

Outside there was chaos as the court prepared for the journey to Fécamp. Baggage wains were piled with household items – beds and hangings for the ducal chambers, chests of napery, chairs and benches, cushions, candle stands, all the rich English spoils. Hawks from the mews, hounds from the kennels, a cage of flapping, squawking hens destined for her uncle's table and another of geese. So saturated was the bailey with noise and smell that Judith nearly turned back to the suffocating confines of her mother's chamber.

And then she became aware of the man standing on the open ground where the men practised their weapon play. Waltheof Siwardsson, Earl of Huntingdon and Northampton as she now knew he was named. She had seen him most days among the English party and had studied him covertly, both fascinated and disturbed by his joyful vitality.

As usual the chamberlain's lad, Simon de Senlis, was glued to his side, eyes filled with the boundless adoration of a pup for its master. Waltheof's heavy copper-blond hair was bound back by a braid band and he was showing off with an enormous Dane axe for the boy's benefit and a gathering audience.

Judith gazed upon the effortless whirl and turn of the great blade. This was the weapon that the Norman soldiers had faced on Hastings field – that had held them at bay for hour after punishing hour and almost destroyed them. Watching the grace and power of Waltheof's movement, she had no doubt that God must have been on her uncle's side that day, for how else could he have prevailed against such a weapon?

Waltheof's laugh rang out, as huge and exuberant as the man himself. The axe blade glittered and was still as he grasped the shaft near the socket and presented the weapon to Simon's older brother Garnier to try. A shiver ran down Judith's spine and centred in her loins, filling her with a longing that she had no point of reference or experience to identify, save to know it was dangerous.

They set out for Fécamp as the sun toiled towards its zenith. Approaching Easter, the weather was fine and the roads much improved from their winter mire so that the carts travelled dry shod. Judith enjoyed the gentle warmth on her skin and the pale green tints of spring covering winter's drab blacks and browns. Her mare was frisky and bucked and pulled on the reins, eager for more than just a sedate trot. There were plans to hunt along the way and Judith was looking forward to giving Jolie her head, for she too felt a quickening in the blood, a certain skittishness born of the spring warmth and the need to stretch out after winter's confinement.

A kennel keeper released the Duke's pack of harriers and the dogs snuffled along the wayside, seeking scents to pursue. With one eye on the hounds, Judith did her duty and rode at a sedate pace behind her mother's travelling wain. From within came muffled sounds of coughing and sneezing. Her sister said something in a petulant tone and Adelaide snapped a curt reply. Judith was greatly relieved to have her freedom. She could not have borne to sit within the stuffy confines of that cart with only a limited tunnel view of the passing spring day.

One of the harriers started a hare out of the lush grass growing beyond the rutted road. Uttering halloos of joy, blowing on their horns, the men pulled their mounts out of line and spurred in pursuit. Judith hesitated, but the temptation was too great. Ignoring the belated cry from her mother, she reined Jolie around and dug in her heels. Full of oats, keen to gallop, the mare took off like a crossbow quarrel. Throwing caution to the wind, Judith let her have her head.

She overtook several riders, including her cousin Rufus, who shouted an obscenity, his plump face flushed scarlet beneath his mop of straw-blond hair. The spring breeze filled her open mouth with its cold, pure taste and fluttered her veil like a banner. There were other women riding with the hunt and their high-pitched cries of encouragement spurred her on, although she suppressed her inclination to yell at the sky. That would have been testing the bounds of seemliness.

The hare vanished into a sloping thicket of alder, ash and willow. Judith's mare took the incline in two strong strides but suddenly her gait chopped and shortened, almost jarring

Judith out of the saddle. Clinging to the reins, she struggled to regain her balance while the hunt crashed on through the thicket and into the field beyond, leaving her far behind.

Hampered by her skirts, Judith dismounted and saw that Jolie was favouring her offside hind leg. Without thinking she placed her hand on the injured limb. The mare's skin rippled, and she lashed out. Judith dodged and was fortunate only to receive a grazing blow from the iron shoe, although it was sufficient to rip a hole in the soft wool of her gown and expose her undershift. Jolie plunged away then halted, reins trailing, leg held up off the ground.

'My lady, you are in difficulty?'

She turned in surprise, and saw Waltheof Siwardsson riding back through the thicket towards her, a look of concern on his face.

Judith's heart began to pound and her mouth was suddenly dry. She glanced around but there was no one else in sight. 'My mare.' She directed a stilted gesture at the horse. 'She took the slope too hard.'

Dismounting gracefully for a man of his size, he tied his own horse to the low branch of a tree. Softly, he approached Jolie from the side.

'Be careful,' Judith warned, a quaver in her voice, 'she will attack.'

'No, she will not,' he answered, his voice a low rumble that set up a vibration in the pit of her belly, 'I like horses, and they like me. I have a way with them. Prior Ulfcytel always said that I could have been a groom.'

He took a firm grasp on the mare's reins and stroked her sweating neck with his open palm. Judith had watched him swing a battleaxe with those hands, his precision and control deadly. Now she watched him gentle her horse, and her legs wobbled. He murmured soft love words and breathed his own breath into the mare's nostrils as she had sometimes seen the stable hands do. Slowly but steadily he moved to the mare's hindquarters and eased his hand down her injured leg. Jolie flinched. So did Judith, fearing that he would be kicked and trampled, but after that single recoil the mare stood quietly for him.

'She will not be carrying you to Fécamp,' he said without altering the timbre of his voice. His dark blue eyes were troubled as they found Judith's. 'There is much damage to the leg, I think.'

Judith licked her lips. She looked from him to the horse. 'She will not have to be killed?'

He shrugged. 'Likely not, my lady. Even if she stays lame, she can be used for breeding.' His lips twitched. 'Of course, if it was a stallion it would be a different matter – especially with a hind leg.'

Judith's face flamed at the implication. A stallion could not mount a mare unless he had two sound hind legs to take his weight in the act of mating. She was intensely aware of her vulnerability. She was Duke William's niece. How easy it would be for him to throw her down on the carpet of violets around their feet and rape her in retaliation for his captivity and her uncle's winning of the English crown.

'You need not be afraid of me, my lady,' he said, as though reading her mind.

'I am not afraid of you,' Judith answered boldly, although in truth she was terrified.

The curve of his lips became an outright grin. 'Are you not?' he said. 'I doubt that very much.' And then he sobered. 'I am no ravisher of women,' he said, softly, 'much as I am tempted.' He turned to untether his horse from the tree, swung astride, and held his hand down to her. 'Best mount up my lady if we are to catch up with the baggage train before it arrives in Fécamp.'

She stared at his hand while her stomach churned so hard that she thought she was going to be sick. 'What about my mare?'

'You can send a groom back for her once we reach the others. 'She will have to be rested up in the nearest village until she's fit. 'Come, you cannot stay here, and I promise to restrain myself.'

Against her better judgement Judith gave him her hand, set her foot over his in the stirrup, and let him pull her up. After an initial clumsiness and flurry of skirts, she managed to perch sideways on the chestnut's rump and clutched the saddle's backrest to stop herself from falling off.

He glanced over his shoulder. 'Warn me if you think you are going to fall,' he said. 'I would hate to bring you to your uncle across my saddle like a slaughtered hind.'

'I know how to ride pillion,' Judith snapped, stung by his teasing.

'Then that is well,' he answered, 'for otherwise I should have to dismount and walk at the bridle.' He clicked his tongue and, with a flicker of its ears, the chestnut broke into a smooth walk.

Judith gazed at the farmland and resisted the temptation to glance at her rescuer's broad back. Her mother would be furious. She chewed her lip. It was not her fault – or at least only in the sense that she had pushed Jolie too hard and caused the mare to overreach and stumble.

Waltheof Siwardsson was whistling softly through his teeth. She thought of him swinging that great axe in Rouen's courtyard. 'Did you fight my uncle in the great battle?' she asked.

'On Hastings field you mean?' He twisted in the saddle to look at her. 'No, my lady, I did not.' His smile developed a sour edge. 'Mayhap I should have done.'

'What prevented you?'

'Ah, now that is a long tale, and I am not sure that I know the answer myself.' He was silent for a time, guiding the horse across the field where the wheat was beginning to form a shallow green carpet. Then he sighed. 'I owed neither allegiance nor loyalty to the Godwinssons. They had done nothing to advance my family. They took Northumbria from my bloodline and gave it elsewhere.' He shrugged. 'I do not expect you to understand.'

'But I do,' Judith said, thinking of her mother's constant lecturing. 'A man's birthright is his pride.'

'Well, I never thought that I had much pride, my lady, until I was led in silken fetters to board a ship for Normandy. And now those fetters burn me and I wonder if I was wrong to hold back from Harold's last battle.'

Judith said nothing, for she was out of her depth, but Waltheof answered the question himself with a shake of his head that sent a sparkle of metallic light through his copper-gold hair. 'Even if I had fought, your uncle might still have won. And if by chance Harold had taken the victory, I doubt I would be any closer to having my desire of Northumbria. Morcar is its earl, and Harold was his brother-by-marriage. There is no one to fight for the house of Siward, lest it be Sweyn of Denmark. Sometimes I think that it would be better had I remained at Crowland and become a monk.'

'Indeed, I had heard you were trained for the Church,' she said, but was quite unable to imagine him in holy orders.

'I was, but my older brother was killed in battle, and I was taken from the cloister to be educated as befits the warrior son of a great earl. I had scarce been home two years when my father died too, and his northern lands were given into the hands of Tosti Godwinsson.' He crossed himself and suddenly he was not smiling.

'Would you have liked to take vows?'

'Sometimes I think I would.' He relaxed again. 'There was peace at Crowland and you could feel God's presence. It is harder out in the world to hear His voice – too many temptations.' He turned further to give her an appraising look. 'Richard de Rules said that you were difficult, but I do not think you are.'

She raised her chin. 'I speak as I find. Surely that is being honest, not difficult?'

He bowed his head, conceding the point. 'Indeed, you are much like your uncle, my lady,' he said, giving the horse a gentle dig in the flanks so that it quickened pace.

They reached the main baggage train and a groom was sent back for Judith's mare. Waltheof delivered Judith to her mother. Countess Adelaide eyed him narrowly as he helped Judith into the stifling interior of the covered cart, aromatic with the smell of horehound and sage.

'Fortunate that you were on hand to come to my daughter's aid, my lord earl,' she said, but was plainly not pleased by the turn of events.

'Indeed it was, my lady.' Waltheof gave her a broad smile and bowed. Adelaide inclined her head in frosty acknowledgement and then looked away, indicating that both her gratitude and the conversation were at an end.

'Thank you, my lord,' Judith murmured, feeling that she had to add something since her mother's response was scant recompense. She was aware of the staring maids, and of her sister giggling behind her hand.

'Think nothing of it, my lady. I enjoyed the pleasure of your company.' He bowed, regained the saddle with swift grace and reined away to greet the first of the returning huntsmen.

Adelaide gave her daughter a hard stare. 'The pleasure of your company,' she repeated in a voice nasal with cold. 'I hope that you did not encourage him, daughter.'

'Of course not!' Judith glowered at her mother. 'I have done nothing wrong. Why should I not converse with him when he is my uncle's guest?'

'Converse by all means, but do not encourage,' Adelaide warned. 'He is more and less than a guest, as well you know. You had no choice but to accept his aid just now, but I would rather it had not happened. I do not know what your uncle will say.'

'It is no concern of my uncle's!' Judith said with a quiver of apprehension.

'Everything is a concern of your uncle's. If you seem to favour one man above others, it complicates matters when it comes to settling a husband upon you. Waltheof of

Huntingdon is *handsome* and *pleasant*, but he is not of sufficient rank or quality to make a match with our house.' Her
lip curled on the words handsome and pleasant, making it
clear that such attributes counted for little.

Judith flushed. 'Even though my grandmother Herleve
was a laundress and the daughter of a common tanner?' she
retorted.

Her sister gasped at the blasphemy. Adelaide reared like a
serpent – no mean feat given the deep cushions and the
rocking of the cart. 'I have not raised you to show such disre-
spect for your blood,' she said furiously. 'My mother, your
grandmother, God rest her soul, whatever her origins, died a
great lady and you will not refer to her in such terms ever
again – is that understood?'

'Yes, Mother.' Judith compressed her lips and contained
her resentment, knowing that if she continued to argue she
would be whipped. Her mother was highly sensitive of the
fact that Herleve de Falaise was indeed a tanner's daughter
whom Robert of Normandy had encountered pounding
washing in a stream and brought home to his castle. She had
borne him two children out of wedlock, one of them Duke
William, the other Adelaide, and when the attraction had
paled she had been married out of the way to one of Duke
Robert's supporters, Herluin de Conteville. Adelaide had set
out to distance herself from all mention of laundering and
tanning. As far as she was concerned, only the noble bloodline
existed, and was to be enhanced. Judith knew that her mother
would consider matching her daughter with an English earl
a step backwards for the family name – even if Waltheof
Siwardsson's pedigree was better than their own.

Until her mother's outburst Judith had not really considered the notion of a match with the English earl, but now she
did. She thought of the journey she had just made on the
rump of his horse. The copper flash of his hair against the
soft dark blue wool of his cloak. The warm good humour.
What would it be like to live in a household with a lord who

would rather smile than frown? She was accustomed to a regime of stern words and duty. Would it not be strange and wonderful to throw back her head for once and laugh with abandon?

'He won't give her to you.' Edgar Atheling shook his head at Waltheof in disbelief. It was the second day of their journey to Fécamp and they were close enough to see the smoke from the city hearth fires and inhale the occasional eddy on the sea-salt breeze. 'Not when he has as good as promised his own daughter to Edwin of Mercia. He is not going to marry off all the virgins in his household to English captives.'

'He has not said that he will give his daughter to Edwin, only that he will consider it,' Waltheof responded. 'It is just as likely that he will give his niece to me rather than his daughter to Edwin.'

Edgar snorted. 'Mayhap you are right, Waltheof,' he said. 'Mayhap neither of you is destined for a Norman bride.'

Waltheof twitched his shoulders irritably and wished that he had not spoken to Edgar about his interest in Judith. He was annoyed at the other man's scoffing, which reinforced the warning given by Richard de Rules that William the Bastard's niece was out of reach. She had not been out of reach yesterday afternoon. Edgar and De Rules thought he should forget her and look elsewhere for a bride – a flaxen-haired English or Danish girl who would bear him enormous Viking sons. But it was not what he wanted.

What he wanted was travelling fifty yards behind him in a covered wain, guarded by her mother like a dragon sitting on its precious treasure. What he wanted was to melt the ice and discover the fire.

'Don't be a fool,' Edgar said. 'She is comely, I know, but there are a hundred better women you could consider for a wife.' He made an explicit gesture with his clenched fist. 'And a thousand in Fécamp alone who would welcome you to their private chambers for the price of a smile.'

Waltheof snorted with reluctant humour. The latter notion had already crossed his mind. Wooing and winning Duke William's niece was a matter for the future, albeit that how to do so was occupying much of his time. Meanwhile the tavern girls of Fécamp would go a long way to cooling the heat of his blood – especially if he could find one with long, dark braids and sultry brown eyes.

CHAPTER 3

Sunlight splintered through the shutters and pierced Waltheof's closed lids. Groaning softly he rolled away from the stab of red light and came to rest against the hip and thigh of his sleeping companion. For a moment, he was disorientated by the sensation of another body beside his and then he remembered. He had been drunk, but to the point of neither oblivion nor incapacity.

Outside a rooster was crowing and he was aware that the sound had been threading through his slumber for some time. There were other noises too, the creaking of a passing cart and the gruff bark of a dog, the swish of a birch broom on a beaten floor and two women shouting to each other across a courtyard.

The girl at his side stretched and pressed back against him. Luxurious heat flooded Waltheof's groin. Rolling her over, he parted her thighs and, thinking only with his body, took his pleasure a second time.

She was lithe and petite, with black hair tumbling to her waist and eyes as dark as sloes. It was her colouring that had attracted him, and the sultry way she had looked at him in the tavern. The other whores had made a blatant play for his attention, sitting in his lap, stroking his beard, but he had been indifferent and they had sought customers more eager. Edgar Atheling had disappeared up the stairs with two of them. Edwin and Morcar had plumped for a pair of identical

Flemish twins with plaits the colour of combed flax and complexions of new cream.

The dark girl's initial aloofness reminded Waltheof of Judith, and in his drink-blurred state it had been easy to close his eyes and imagine that the body he was possessing was that of the Duke of Normandy's niece. Now, in the sobriety of the morning light, he saw that apart from her dark hair and eyes, there was little resemblance. The sultry aloofness was contrived, as much a technique of selling herself as was the enthusiasm of the other whores.

She whispered words that he was certain Judith would not know, urging him on, clawing his spine. Waltheof groaned and gave himself up to the surge of climax. The whore gasped and writhed. That too, he thought hazily, must be an act. How could it be any other when her pay was dependent on satisfying her clients?

He rolled off her and lay regaining his breath, listening to the sounds of the city of Fécamp awakening.

'Do I please you?' She eyed him through the tangle of her hair.

'Yes, you please me.' Waltheof sat up and flipped her another silver penny from his pouch.

Clasping her hands at the back of his neck, she kissed him with enthusiasm. 'You will visit again?'

'Perhaps.' Suddenly he wanted to be out of this room with its stale odours of wine, sweat and copulation. Easing away from her, he donned his shirt.

'Have you left a woman behind in England, my lord?'

'Why should you think that?' He sent her a sidelong glance.

'The way you hesitated before you made your choice last night – as if you had a conscience or thought you should not be here.'

He gave a snort of grim amusement and shook his head. 'Little do you know,' he said.

She eyed him questioningly.

Without bothering to lace his shirt Waltheof drew on his tunic. Braies and chausses swiftly followed. 'Are you always so inquisitive about your customers?'

'Only the handsome ones with large pouches.' She stretched sinuously like a young vixen and smiled at him. 'And I have seldom seen one larger than yours, my lord.' Her gaze rested suggestively on his groin.

Despite his irritation, Waltheof laughed. Leaning over, he slapped the girl's rump. 'I am glad to hear it.' Without giving her the chance to ask anything else, he went out of the door and quickly down the outer stairs.

The main room was empty save for a woman scraping old wax from the candle prickets and a couple of William's hearth knights seated at a trestle sharing a pitcher of buttermilk. Waltheof greeted them courteously enough but with a wry set to his mouth. He and his fellow Englishmen might be permitted to roam abroad, but a Norman guard was never far behind, ensuring that no one attempted to escape. The knights were brawny and, although neither of them wore mail, the swords at their hips were conspicuous.

Of Edgar, Edwin and Morcar there was no sign. Waltheof thought about kicking them out of bed but immediately decided against it. The pleasure of the deed would likely not compensate for the ensuing aggravation. Wandering outside he took a long piss in the midden pit beside the stable, and began a leisurely stroll in the direction of the palace.

Another Norman wearing the quilted tunic of a man-at-arms rose unobtrusively from a bench outside the kitchen buildings and followed him into the street. Waltheof glanced ruefully over his shoulder and considered evading his shadow among the warren of lanes leading away from Fécamp's harbour, but it went no further than a thought. Like the notion of kicking his companions awake, the strife it would raise was not worth the bother of the mischief. If he did attempt to lose his guard, doubtless King William would confine him to the palace and double the scrutiny.

As he walked, Waltheof noticed two merchants urging a string of horses towards the ducal residence and cast an appreciative eye over the animals. No common nags these, but livestock bearing the hot stamp of Spanish blood in their sharp ears, arched necks and elegant, compact build. They had lost their plush winter coats and their hides glistened with the polish of spring, bright bay, blue roan, grey and a dun the colour of sunlit sand.

Waltheof followed the traders into the courtyard and watched an official direct them to the stable compound.

'They're for Duke William. My father says so,' Simon de Senlis greeted him, a pile of tack draped over his shoulder. The star designs of worked silver on the buckles and browband of the bridle looked familiar to Waltheof, but he could not recall where he had seen them before.

'I suppose he lost many good mounts at the great battle,' he said.

The boy gave a dismissive shrug. 'Those horses are for riding, not war. Lady Judith is to have her pick because her mare is lame.'

Waltheof met the lad's artless tawny gaze. 'And just when is she to do the choosing?'

'Now.' Simon hefted the tack, which had begun to slip. As the sun dazzled on the silver mountings Waltheof remembered that he had seen them on Judith's black mare on the day of the rescue. Falling into step beside the boy, he was glad that he had not lingered at the tavern. He was also suddenly conscious of his dishevelled appearance. He was not well acquainted with Judith, but already he knew how much store she set by presentation.

He raked his hands through his hair, beat at his tunic and straightened his skewed leg bindings.

Simon eyed Waltheof's hasty attempts at sprucing. 'You don't look as though you've been out in the town all night,' he said kindly.

Waltheof tried to frown but couldn't. His lips twitched. 'And how would you know where I've been?'

'I overheard you discussing it at supper last night. I don't speak English above a few words, but I heard one of you mention Madame Hortense's.'

Waltheof cleared his throat. 'I see.'

'My brother goes there sometimes,' Simon said with a knowing look. 'It's a brothel.'

Waltheof did not know whether to laugh or admonish. 'At your age I did not realise such places existed,' he said, 'But then I suppose I did not have an older brother to corrupt me . . . well I did, but he died.'

'I am sorry.' It was the automatic and polite response, but there was curiosity in the lad's gaze.

Waltheof shook his head. 'I never knew him. He was the son of my father's first wife and almost a man before I was born. He should have worn the bearskin cloak of the house of Siward. My father entrusted my own education to the monks of Crowland Abbey.' He almost smiled. 'So you see I have come rather later than you to the knowledge of brothels.'

'I don't know *everything* about them,' Simon said seriously.

'You don't want to,' Waltheof answered with a grin. 'Keep your feet on the narrow path of righteousness. That way you'll have nothing to regret.'

'Do you regret going then?'

It was with relief that Waltheof saw the stables looming and the tethered selection of palfreys. 'Not at the time, lad, but it is like drinking – the night's carousing has to be paid for by the morning's malaise.' He swatted good-naturedly at the boy. 'Now, stop bedevilling me. You don't need to know the answer to such questions until you're older – much older.'

He watched Simon disappear with the bridle into the stable's dark interior and, shaking his head, went to look at the palfreys that the coper had brought for Judith's inspection.

'I fancy the grey myself,' said a good-natured voice behind him.

Waltheof turned from examining a bay gelding and gazed round at the handsome young man who was leaning nonchalantly against the stable wall, arms folded. Ralf de Gael was a Breton lord whose father had settled in England during the Confessor's reign and acquired the earldom of Norfolk by peaceful means. Waltheof knew and liked Ralf; he was amiable, debonair and had an understanding of English ways missing in most Normans.

Waltheof shook his head. 'It has a mean eye,' he said.

Ralf unfolded his arms and pushed himself off the wall. 'My father was staller to King Edward,' he said. 'He could tell a good horse from bad by a single glance.'

Waltheof grinned. 'That does not mean to say you have inherited his talent.'

'Trust me, I have.' Ralf sauntered to the bay. 'No grace,' he said. 'Whoever sits on this will resemble a sack of oats on a pack pony. The grey has by far the better breeding. Look at the way it carries itself.'

'That may be so, but it still has a mean eye,' said Waltheof, thinking that Judith could ride a woodcutter's donkey and still look like a queen.

Ralf clucked his tongue in disagreement. 'I am sorry to doubt your judgement, but I do.'

The horse coper, who had been half listening to their banter, suddenly dropped to his knees, snatched off his cap and bowed his head. Waltheof and De Gael turned, saw King William approaching with his sons and Judith, and quickly did the same.

'It seems that word has gone ahead,' William remarked, gesturing the young men to rise. His expression was good-humoured but sharp.

'I saw the horses arriving, sire.' Waltheof reddened as he remembered that he had been returning from a brothel at the time. Judith stood with her cousins. She was dressed for riding in a gown of heavy green wool and carried a small whip in her hand.

'And I saw Earl Waltheof studying the horses and joined him, sire,' said Ralf smoothly. 'We were discussing their merits.'

'And do you have an opinion?'

'A difference of. I say the grey, Waltheof says the bay.'

'Reasons?'

As always Waltheof was struck by William's blunt economy with words. Not a shred of time was wasted in getting to the point.

'The grey's got breeding, sire, the bay's a nag.'

'The grey is perhaps the finest animal to look upon,' Waltheof acknowledged, 'but I believe that the bay has a better temper. And none of them are nags.'

'Indeed not,' ventured the horse coper with a bow for Waltheof and a glare at De Gael.

William stepped forward to examine the horses. His sons followed, learning at their father's side how to judge sound-ness and conformation. Judith joined them, listening intently to their conversation, absorbing everything although it was not directly addressed to her. She cast her eyes over the bay, but it was the grey that she clearly favoured. The coper trotted the beast up and down the yard to show off its action, the muscles rippling like water under silk and the mane flowing like a black waterfall on the crested neck. The bay had a longer stride, more of a lope, and it carried itself quietly, without the high pride of the other.

Judith paused at Waltheof's side so close that his elbow almost grazed hers and he could see the individual strands of hair shining in the braids that hung below her veil.

'I admire spirit, Lord Waltheof,' she said. 'I like to ride a horse that knows it is alive.'

'Even if it bucks you off and cracks your skull against the stable wall?'

She slanted him an amused, slightly scornful look. 'I am

as accustomed to riding as any of my cousins.' She indicated the Duke's sons. 'The last time I was thrown I was a babe of three years old upon my first pony. You need not concern yourself for my welfare.'

'It was fortunate that I did a few days since,' Waltheof said quietly.

She lifted her chin. 'I was not in danger.'

'Oh yes, you were,' Waltheof muttered and wrapped his hands around his belt because he was itching to span them at her waist.

'But not from my horse.' She fixed him with a long, level stare in which he read challenge and invitation. Daring him. Holding him off. Then she turned to her uncle.

'I like the grey too,' she said in a clear, determined voice and smiled up at William. 'Can I try him?'

Simon de Senlis fetched the tack and her chosen mount was harnessed. It stamped the yard floor restlessly and kicked at its belly with a sharp hind hoof. Sometimes it was a sign of colic, but Waltheof suspected that in this instance it was irritation at the placing of a saddle.

Young Simon grasped the headstall while Judith set her foot in the stirrup and her cousin Robert boosted her across its back. She drew the reins through her fingers and commanded the squire to let go. The grey took several short, stiff-legged leaps but Judith swiftly brought it under control, using hands and heels to exert her authority. Waltheof watched with keen pleasure. She looked superb upon that champing, spirited horse, and as her eyes met his in triumph he found himself smiling in defeat.

Judith trotted the grey around the stableyard and, returning to the men, drew rein. Simon had caught the bridle and Judith was preparing to dismount when with a sudden frenzy of yowls, two tomcats shot from the stables in a clawing ball of fur.

The coper and his attendant grabbed for the leading reins as the horses started at the commotion. The grey whinnied and reared, jerking the bridle out of Simon's hand. Its powerful shoulder sent the lad sprawling, and as he struck the ground the sharp forehooves came down across his leg. Simon's shriek rose above the noise of the fighting cats. White-faced, Judith strove to control the horse as it reared and plunged around the compound like a demon.

Waltheof was the first to recover from the shock of the moment. Bending, he scooped Simon off the ground and thrust him into De Gael's arms, then ran to intercept the plunging grey. Spreading his arms, he leaped in front of the horse. The shod hooves flashed, threatening death. Waltheof made a grab for the bridle and hung on, wrapping his fist around the leather, bringing the beast's head down and throwing his full weight against its forequarters so that it was unable to rear again.

'My lady, jump!' he roared.

Judith kicked her feet free of the stirrups, set her hands on the grey's sawing withers and half swung, half fell out of the saddle. Ashen with shock, she stumbled across the yard to safety then turned to stare at Waltheof in sick fear.

Slowly, with the same skill and pressure that had won him every arm-wrestling contest in which he had ever competed, Waltheof brought the grey beneath his command. Unable to raise its head, held in the vice of the man's grip, the fighting turned to the trembling, wild-eyed sweat of surrender and the grooms raced out to secure the horse with stout halter ropes.

Waltheof released his grip. The bridle had scored red weals across his palms and his sleeve was smeared with foam from the grey's muzzle. Wiping his hands on his tunic he hastened across the yard. 'My lady, you are unharmed?'

She swallowed and nodded. 'I am all right,' she whispered. 'Thank you . . .'

'You acted swiftly, my lord,' William said with a curt nod. 'My family is in your debt.'

Waltheof cleared his throat. 'It is a debt I do not acknowledge, sire,' he muttered, feeling awkward now that the heat of the moment was cooling. 'I acted without thought of gratitude or reward.'

'You might not acknowledge it, but I do.' William gave a wintry smile. 'My niece means a great deal to me.'

To me as well, Waltheof wanted to say, but dared not. Head lowered, he strode to the stall where Ralf de Gael had laid young Simon. The boy's complexion was as pale and shiny as new cheese and his fists were clenched against the surge of pain.

'Broken leg,' De Gael said, looking somewhat green himself. His eyes told Waltheof a tale that he would not speak aloud in the child's presence. 'I'll bring his father.' He ducked out into the daylight.

Waltheof knew it was an excuse. De Gael could have sent one of the grooms to seek out Richard de Rules. Removing his fine cloak, the English earl crouched to drape it over the shivering boy. 'I know it hurts,' he said gently, 'but help is coming.'

William's presence shadowed the doorway. 'You saved his life too, Lord Waltheof,' he said. 'I have sent for my chirugeon. Let us hope that he can mend the leg.' Entering the stall William crouched across from Waltheof and lightly touched Simon's arm.

'Courage lad,' he said, the harshness of his voice softer now and holding a rumble of compassion.

'Yes, sire,' Simon answered through a throat corded with pain. Tears brimmed in his eyes and he blinked them fiercely away.

William nodded with brusque approval and stayed until the chirugeon arrived, with him an anxious Richard de Rules. 'Be a good soldier,' he said to Simon as the chirugeon began to cut away the boy's torn chausses in order to inspect the damaged leg.

Waltheof grimaced to himself. The lad was but nine years old and however brave and courageous, he was still terrified and in pain. Mercifully, William rose and departed. The moment he had gone, Simon let out the breath that he had been holding on a long groan.

Richard de Rules leaned over his son. 'It will be all right, I promise you.' He smoothed the fair-brown hair. 'Once the bone is set, all will be well.'

'Yes, Papa.' Simon's eyes were huge and so filled with trust that Waltheof could not bear it.

'Move aside from the light,' commanded the chirugeon, a grumpy young man, prematurely grey of hair. He scowled at Judith, who was standing in the doorway, her complexion little brighter than the boy's.

'Will he be all right?' she asked.

'My lady, I cannot tell until I have been able to see how much damage has been done – and for that I need the light.'

Gnawing her lip, Judith backed out of the stable. Waltheof rose to his feet and, murmuring an apology, went after her.

She was standing with her back against the wall, pleating her riding gown between her fingers. 'It is my fault,' she whispered. 'If I had not been so determined to prove that I could handle that horse, it would never have happened.'

'You take too much on yourself, my lady,' Waltheof said. 'The horse bolted because it was startled, not from your mishandling. The rest is misfortune – or perhaps good luck, since both you and the boy are still alive.'

She looked at him, then down at her busy hands and shook her head. 'I should have listened to you and chosen the bay.'

'It has happened; there is no sense in lamenting over what cannot be undone.' He had wanted to comfort Simon. By the same impulse he wanted to pull her into his arms, smooth her braids and tell her that everything was all right, but such familiarity was impossible – as matters stood.

'That is easy to say.' Challenge and bitterness clogged her voice.

Waltheof took a step towards her then stopped. 'Is not blaming yourself for everything a great arrogance when you should be accepting that it is God's will?'

A flash of anger sharpened her features. 'How dare you!'

He shrugged. 'Because I have very little to lose, and everything to gain.'

She stood her ground, and then, like the horse, the fight went out of her and she began to tremble. Uttering a gasp she gathered her skirts and ran from him. Waltheof watched her out of sight and then heaving a deep sigh, returned to the fusty dark of the stable and sat with the injured boy and his father while the chirugeon did his best to set the broken leg.

Damn him, damn him! Judith could not remember the last time she had wept. Her father had died and her eyes had stayed dry. Her mother had whipped her for childhood misdemeanours and lapses and she had not cried. So why now? Why should the gentle reproach from an English hostage undo her? Judith wiped her eyes with the edge of her wimple and leaned against the wall, trying to compose herself, knowing that if she went within looking like this her mother would wring her dry with interrogation.

'What's wrong?' Her sister Adela had come looking for her. 'Why are you weeping?' She eyed Judith with astonishment.

'I'm not weeping,' Judith snapped. 'The dust from the hay barn affects my eyes, that's all.'

'Have you chosen your horse?' Adela could not give a fig for riding. She much preferred to stay with their mother in the bower and sew. The fact that Judith was to have a new mount, however, had roused a certain amount of jealousy. She had already begun to wheedle their mother for a new gown to compensate.

Judith shook her head and controlled herself. 'Simon de Senlis has been kicked by one of the new horses and broken his leg,' she said, and was relieved to hear her voice emerge in its usual measured tones. 'He's being tended by Uncle William's chirugeon.'

Adela gasped with pity. 'The poor boy!'

Remembering the suffering in the lad's expression, the twisted angle of his leg, Judith knew that, no matter what Waltheof of Huntingdon said, the blame was hers to shoulder whilst young Simon de Senlis paid the price.

CHAPTER 4

Ducking under the door arch, Waltheof entered the small wall chamber where Simon lay. There was space only for a narrow bed, a stone bench with cushions and a niche in the wall for placing a candle. A thin window slit let in a waft of cool air and an arch of powder-blue sky.

Richard de Rules sat on a stool at the bedside, watching his son's restless slumber with paternal anxiety.

'How does he fare?' Waltheof asked softly.

The Norman sighed. 'Well enough for the moment. The chirugeon set the leg as best he could . . . but it was a bad break.'

'He has the best of care,' Waltheof said, trying to impart reassurance. 'God willing he will mend.'

De Rules' expression remained worried. 'God willing.' He sighed and rubbed his face. 'Jesu, he is but nine years old. He was to be trained to arms. What will become of him if he is crippled?'

'That will not happen, he is too tenacious. Even if he is lamed, he will still be capable of riding a horse, won't he? The injury will not affect the capacity of his mind.' He was aware of over protesting, as if his words would somehow make the situation more positive.

'That is what I keep telling myself.' The Norman offered his open palm to Waltheof. 'Whatever happens, I am indebted to you for saving his life. If you had not pulled him from beneath those hooves . . .'

'I only wish that I had been able to act more swiftly.' Waltheof clasped De Rules' hand, released it and stood up. 'I will come again when he is awake.'

'I will tell him that you were here.' De Rules gestured to the folds of fur-edged blue fabric on the bench. 'Your cloak, Lord Waltheof. Thank you for its borrowing.'

Waltheof took the garment and draped it carefully over his arm. 'I'm glad it was of service,' he replied and left the room, sombre and troubled. If William's chirugeon said that the break was bad, then what chance did that give the boy? Waltheof had not lived a soldier's life, but he had seen enough wounds treated at Crowland Abbey to know all the permutations.

Some broken limbs healed with nary a scar or discomfort, save to trouble their owners in damp weather and old age. Other times, however, the injury would swell and turn green, sending streaks of poison through the patient's body, harbingers of an agonising death. Or the bone would heal, but in a manner twisted and deformed that left the victim crippled and in constant pain.

Suddenly conscious of his own sound limbs, Waltheof descended the stairs to the great hall. As usual it was churning with activity. Scribes wrote industriously at lecterns, their business dictated by senior officers of the Duke's household. Petitioners and messengers arrived and left, or waited on the long benches edging the hall to be summoned. Two boys were stacking fresh logs by the hearth and replenishing the charcoal baskets for the braziers. A servant from the butler's retinue was decanting wine into flagons ready for the main meal later in the day, and nearby a young woman was transferring new candles from a wicker basket onto wrought-iron prickets.

'Lord Waltheof.'

He turned at the imperative note in the woman's voice and

found himself looking down at Judith's mother, the formidable Adelaide of Aumale. The dragon guardian.

'Countess,' he bowed and regarded her warily. Judith had a darker version of her eyes and similar autocratic features. In Adelaide the bone structure was almost hawkish and he could see how Judith might look twenty years from now.

'I have heard what happened in the stableyard this morning,' she said stiffly. 'It seems that yet again I must thank you for coming to my daughter's aid.'

'I am glad I was there,' Waltheof replied graciously. 'I hope that she has taken no harm?'

'None – although I understand it might have been different without your intervention.'

Waltheof thought that her face might crack if she smiled. He could see that she was doing her duty by thanking him – and hating every moment. He had often heard married companions make wry jests about their mother-in-laws, and had thought them rather harsh. Now he began to understand.

Adelaide inclined her head and moved on, her spine as straight as a mason's rod. Her husband, Eudo of Champagne, was in England, keeping the peace. Waltheof wondered uncharitably if Lord Eudo had chosen to remain there rather than returning to his glacial marriage bed.

One of the maids attending Adelaide paused at Waltheof's side for an instant. 'Mistress Judith is in the abbey chapel praying for the boy's recovery,' she said swiftly, giving him a meaningful look before following the Countess.

Waltheof gazed after her in bemusement. Then he began to smile. Turning on his heel, he left the hall and walked purposefully towards the Abbey Church of the Holy Trinity.

The decorated arches had a pleasing symmetry and the pale slabs of Caen stone possessed a warm, butter colour in the sunshine. Tonsured holy brethren in their dark Benedictine robes were everywhere, their air proprietorial. Pilgrims crowded the front porch, their dusty appearance and travelling satchels marking them out from the general population.

Some were here because of the Duke's presence in the town, but most had come for Easter week and to view the miraculous phial of the Holy Blood of Christ.

Waltheof joined their number and entered the incense-soaked greatness of the abbey's nave. He had worshipped here before at Easter Mass, but still the beauty of the carved and painted pillars filled him with delight and awe. He loved churches in all their forms, from the small wooden edifices no more than huts that served many of his Midland manors, to the towering dignity of great cathedrals such as Westminster, Canterbury, Jumièges and Fécamp. He could find God in any of them and tailored his worship to the surroundings. In the small churches he was humble and reflective; in the cathedrals he praised God in pleasure through the rich colours and ceremony. At Crowland in the Fens he yielded himself completely and received peace in return.

But today, although he was aware of God's presence, his seeking was of a different kind. Leaving the pilgrims, he walked down the great nave. Votive candles burned by the hundred on prickets and candelabra, tended by monks from the abbey. Before the altar knelt yet more pilgrims, praying, paying their respects, reverently touching the ornate box containing the phial of the Holy Blood of Christ that was being held by a watchful priest.

Waltheof sought among the gathering of bowed heads and found her kneeling at the edge and a little apart. Self-contained as always. Her head was bent towards her clasped hands and her eyes were closed, revealing smooth lids lined by thick dark lashes. Squeezing amongst the pilgrims, Waltheof knelt in the space she had left between herself and them.

She opened her eyes at the intrusion. The haughty stare she had been about to give him widened into one of recognition and then grew wary. Waltheof responded with a smile and bowed his neck, attending to the letter of worship if not giving the task his full concentration.

For perhaps a quarter candle notch they knelt side by side.

Several pilgrims rose and departed, their places taken by others. The sound of suppressed coughs, of shuffling footsteps and the murmur of worship echoed against the stone vaulting.

'One of the maids told me where you were,' Waltheof said to his clasped hands.

'I came to pray for the recovery of Simon de Senlis,' Judith answered stiffly.

'Indeed, that is my own reason for being here.' Waltheof was selective with the truth, sure that God would understand.

Silence fell between them again, but it was one of exchange rather than isolation. Waltheof felt as though there was a high wall separating him and Judith, but somehow he had managed to pull a slab out of the centre and could now glimpse her through the ensuing gap.

When she rose to leave he rose with her and escorted her out, one hand lightly beneath her elbow. It was indicative of the breach in the wall that she accepted his touch and did not draw away, but in the wide sunlit porch she turned to him. 'What you said earlier today, about God's will,' she said, 'you made me feel ashamed.'

'I am sorry, my lady, that was not my intention.'

'I know it was not. You were trying to offer comfort . . . and in a way, you did – after I had the time to think.'

Waltheof wanted to pull her against him and kiss her, but he clenched his fists at his sides and reminded himself that he wanted to live. 'I often speak my mind without thinking at all. Abbot Ulfcytel always said it was my greatest failing and my saving grace.' He fell into step beside her, reluctant to let the moment go. He sensed a similar mood in Judith, for as they left the abbey precincts she did not seek to distance herself from him, although there were many witnesses to see them walking together.

'There has been one matter I have thought about ever since that first day in Rouen, though,' he murmured. 'And I have kept it inside my head until sometimes I feel my brains will burst with the effort of holding back.'

She lifted her head to him and he saw that she understood his meaning, for her cheeks grew pink. 'If it is so important to your wellbeing, then you must approach my uncle and my stepfather for guidance,' she said.

'That I know, but perhaps it is better to bide my time until my feet are on more solid ground.' He paused in the shadow of a wall, aware that they were almost at the palace and in a moment he would lose her to the public space of the great hall. 'And before I make my bid, I need to know that I am not embarking on a fool's errand.' He sought her hand and heard her sudden intake of breath.

'I want you to wife,' he said, and covered her cool, fine fingers in his powerful grasp. 'Are you willing?' Lust licked through him. One gentle push and her back would be against the wall. That was all it would take.

He could sense the wildness in her and the control, pushing it down. 'I can give you no encouragement without the consent of my family,' she said breathlessly.

'But if your family were to give their consent – would you have me?'

Her throat worked. 'I do not know,' she said and pulled away. For the briefest instant he tightened his grip, but before panic had time to flare in her eyes he let her go. She had not refused him, and if she did not know, then it was up to him to help her and her family to decide in his favour.

Simon stared at the wall beyond the end of his bed. It was a sight to which he had grown accustomed over the past fortnight. He knew every flake of plaster, every line of stone. He played games, making pictures out of the marks, a dog, a tree, a castle, until his eyes blurred with strain and he had to look away. The window embrasure yielded a cool draught and a narrow column of sky. Sometimes there would be the distraction of passing clouds, but today his window was the blank blue canvas of a perfect spring day.

What he would give to be able to throw aside the covers,

leap out of bed and hurtle down the twisting stairs to the glorious morning outside his prison. But he suspected that he would never hurtle anywhere again. When people came to see him they smiled and said loudly that he would soon be better, but their eyes told a different story. And he had heard them mutter among themselves when they thought they were out of his hearing.

The break was bad. Even without the overheard conversations of his visitors, he knew that. The chirugeon had dosed him with syrup of white poppy before setting the limb, but the agony had been terrible – like white-hot teeth biting into his shin. The limb was now held rigid with ash splints bound tightly to his leg and wrapped with linen bandages soaked in egg albumen. His task was to lie abed and allow the bone to knit.

The searing pain had been replaced by a dull, steady throb. For the first few days he had been feverish and he knew they had feared for his life. That stage had passed and it was now evident that whether the limb healed straight or crooked he was going to live. Thus he lay on his bed and waited out the never-ending minutes, hours and days of the long healing.

Early in his convalescence Lady Judith had brought him a box containing a sweetmeat made from crushed walnuts boiled in honey. She had sat with him for a while, doing her duty, assuaging her guilt. Then Lord Waltheof had arrived, bringing a tafel board and gaming pieces and the Lady's face had grown as radiant as a sunrise. They visited him often. One would arrive and the other would follow like doves homing to the cote. Simon had swiftly realised that they were meeting each other rather than comforting him, but was glad of the company and enjoyed being a party to their conspiracy. Sometimes too Waltheof would send his personal skald, Thorkel, to entertain Simon with sagas of faraway lands inhabited by fierce Vikings, giants and trolls, and those occasions were magical for the lad.

All that, however, was finished. As from today he was alone. Apart from affording him a glimpse of sky, the window embrasure also yielded up sounds from the courtyard below. The rumble of cartwheels, the shouts of soldiers and drivers, the clatter of hooves as William prepared to leave Fécamp. By noon the last of the baggage wains would have rolled ponderously out of the gates, leaving the palace to its garrison and resident retainers. A fortnight ago he had been part of that vast, energetic tide; now he was debris, tossed above the water line. The thought brought a lump to his throat and filled him with tearful misery.

Footsteps sounded on the stairs and he hastily wiped his eyes on a corner of the coverlet. It would not be manly to be caught crying, and he did not want any of them to think he was a snivelling infant.

Waltheof flourished aside the chamber curtain and ducked into the room, his height and vitality immediately diminishing the small space. In the spring warmth he wore a linen tunic and had tied back his abundant copper hair with a strip of leather. Simon could smell the freshness of the outdoors on his clothes and wanted desperately to go there. 'You've come to say farewell, haven't you?' he demanded.

'Yes lad, I have.' Waltheof looked uncomfortable, but did not shirk the question. 'Where William goes, unfortunately I must go too.'

Simon scowled glumly at the coverlet, utterly miserable. Even if the English earl had conducted his courtship with Lady Judith in this room, he had still stayed to play tafel once she had gone, had still made time to talk.

'I promise I will visit as often as I can while we are within riding distance.' Waltheof clasped his large, warm hand over Simon's on the coverlet. 'I won't forget.'

Simon gazed at the rings flashing on Waltheof's fingers. One was of gold wire, twisted into a rope, the other bore a large, blood-red stone and looked a little bit like one of the rings he had seen Bishop Remegius wear. The lump of despondency grew in his stomach until it was as heavy as a small boulder.

'As soon as you're better I'll take you out riding,' Waltheof said cheerfully.

'But that's weeks away!' Simon could not contain his furious disappointment. 'And I might not get better!' He thumped the bedclothes and felt a sharp pain stab through the centre of his broken leg.

'Of course you will.' Waltheof fixed him with a piercing blue stare, forcing Simon to meet his gaze and not look away. 'It was a bad break, I know it was, and I would not belittle your suffering, but you will not be confined for ever – I promise you.'

'It seems like for ever,' Simon said mutinously.

'Yes, if I were your age I suppose that it would feel like for ever to me. Indeed, I think that I would feel the same now,' he said with a rueful smile. 'I cannot bear to be cooped up.' Ferreting beneath his cloak, Waltheof produced a bone flute carved from a goose's wingbone. 'Thorkel fashioned this for you,' he said. 'We thought perhaps you would enjoy making music.'

Simon thanked him, trying to sound more enthusiastic than he felt. It was not that he did not appreciate the gift, but it was no compensation for being abandoned by his hero.

Waltheof also presented him with several sheets of parchment bound in a roll and tied with a ribbon. This was followed by a leather pouch containing the ingredients for making ink, a small, sharp knife with a bone handle, several goose quills, and a small wax tablet and stylo. 'You can lessen the distance by writing to me,' he said cheerfully.

Simon flushed. 'I . . . I'm not well lettered,' he mumbled.

Waltheof spread his hands. 'Do you have anything else to do except lie here and mope? Duke William himself barely reads his own name but he values greatly those who are literate. It would be much to your advantage to learn, and besides, I would like to send you messages and receive them in return.'

Simon nodded rather dubiously. 'I will try,' he said, speaking more out of a desire to please Waltheof than out of any enthusiasm of his own.

'Good lad. I . . .'

More footsteps trod on the stairs, lightly this time. Simon knew them, and so did Waltheof, for eagerness blazed in his eyes as he turned expectantly to the door. The boy wondered what Duke William would say if he knew about these meetings between his niece and the English earl. Now that the court was moving on it would not be so simple for them to be alone.

'I cannot stay,' Judith said more breathlessly than the stair climb warranted. 'My mother is waiting below, but I came to bring Simon a parting gift.' She approached the bed. Waltheof moved aside, deliberately brushing past her so that her long, dark braid touched the back of his hand. She shot him a swift look and her colour heightened.

Simon looked down because Lady Judith made him uncomfortable. She did not have Waltheof's easy manner. When she spoke to him it was always as if she was struggling to know what to say and her movements were stilted and unnatural. He knew she felt guilty about his injury and all that really brought her to visit him was the lure of being with Waltheof.

'We were packing the chests to leave and I found this.' She gave Simon a rolled-up band of linen a little less than a foot wide. 'I thought that you might find it preferable to looking at the bare wall all day and we are not going to miss it among all the others.'

It was a hanging embroidered in wool and depicting the story of how the Normans had arrived in France and claimed the land for their own. Warriors and horses came to life in gold and green, scarlet blue and tawny. As he unfolded it, Simon was astonished and delighted. The first smile in days spread across his face as he touched the procession of figures and the scenes they created. He looked at Judith with genuine pleasure in his eyes, all resentment gone. 'Thank you, my lady.'

Her own lips curved in a stiff but no less genuine response. 'You are pleased?'

'Oh yes, my lady!'

'Then I am glad, and it was the least I could do. Next time I see you, I hope you will be walking.' With a nod, she went to the door.

Gesturing to Simon that he would return in a moment, Waltheof hastened after Judith.

The boy gazed upon the colourful pictures spread across his bed. He could almost smell the crisp autumn day of a boar hunting scene, imagine the clash of spears as Frenchman met Viking, hear the hiss of the sea beneath a longboat's keel. It did not make up for being left behind in Fécamp, but suddenly life was slightly more bearable.

Waltheof caught Judith on the narrow walkway to the stairs. 'That was kind of you,' he said, his voice melting with pride and tenderness.

Judith faced him, her chin bearing a defensive tilt. 'It was the voice of my conscience,' she said.

He shook his head in exasperation. 'Why can you never admit to tenderness?' he demanded. 'Ah Judith, you're as fierce as a goshawk.' He raised his hand to stroke her face. 'I have never known a woman like you . . .'

'You should not . . .' she began to say, but he set his forefinger to her lips.

'I know what I should and should not,' he said, 'but knowing is not always the same as doing, is it? You realise this is the last time we will be able to meet as freely as this.'

'Perhaps that is a good thing,' she said. 'It cannot be right without the consent of my uncle. If my mother knew . . .' Her words were cut off as he pulled her against him and lowered his mouth to hers.

Twin strands of heat and cold prickled along Judith's spine

as he kissed her. She ought to struggle, slap him, scream for help, but she did none of these things. She was intoxicated by the scent of him, by the strength and gentleness of his hands, and by the disturbing but pleasurable sensations engendered by his kiss.

The tip of his tongue lightly brushed her lips encouraging them to part. One hand slipped from her waist to lightly cup her buttocks and pull her in closer. Waltheof groaned softly and the sound filled her mouth, enhancing her sensations. Her arms slipped around his waist and for a glorious moment she lost herself in him.

The kiss finally broke, leaving them both gasping for breath. Judith hastily took a back step, knowing she had to put distance between herself and Waltheof while she was still capable.

'Perhaps it is time your mother did know,' he said, his eyes bright and narrow. 'I must have you, Judith.'

She licked her lips, tasted him there, and felt a mingling of fear and pleasure. 'I do not know if that can be,' she whispered.

'I will make it be,' he said in a tone that was no longer light with laughter.

They both stiffened at the scrape of feet on the steps below. 'Judith?' Her mother's voice was querulous with impatience.

Judith gave a single, frightened gasp then steadied herself. Gesturing Waltheof to stay back and remain silent, she started down the steps. 'I am here, Mother,' she called. Her hands were shaking, her lips felt swollen. As she descended the steps, she was aware of a dull ache in her loins, reminiscent of flux pains.

'Where have you been child?' Adelaide snapped. 'Anyone would think that you had had to stitch the hanging from the start instead of just giving it to the boy.'

'I stayed to speak a few words of comfort, Mother,' Judith said more calmly than she felt.

Somewhat awkwardly, Adelaide turned on the narrow stair

and descended to the courtyard. Once in open daylight, she fixed Judith with a gimlet stare. Reaching out she pressed one hand to Judith's brow. 'You look feverish,' she said with sudden concern in her eyes. 'I hope that you are not ailing.'

Judith jerked away from her mother's touch, feeling flustered and guilty. 'There is nothing wrong with me.'

Adelaide pursed her lips. 'Even so, it might be wiser if you travelled in the wain with me. As a precaution.'

'Mother no!' Judith protested but Adelaide was adamant.

'Do not seek to argue,' she snapped. 'These past few days you have been granted more freedom than a girl of your status is usually allowed. You will travel with me, and you will be content.'

'Yes, Mother.' Knowing that argument was futile, Judith held her tongue, but behind her silence, she imagined lashing out in rebellion. Suddenly she wished that she had not bade Waltheof remain out of sight until it was safe to come down. Suddenly she wished she had yielded to him. Waltheof had said he desired her to wife. Even if she was not sure that she wanted him, she was positive that life with him would be ten times better than dwelling beneath her mother's joyless rule.

CHAPTER 5

Judith threaded her needle with a single, fine strand of red-gold wool and, leaning over her embroidery frame, began to sew with swift, neat stitches. The design she was embroidering had been carefully sketched onto the linen ground in fine charcoal and depicted a scene of men and women riding out to hunt. Intended as a horizontal strip hanging to decorate a wall behind a dais, it was already about a third completed. The women of Duchess Matilda's household would work on the hanging when not occupied by other tasks. Judith was an excellent embroideress and since Adelaide had been keeping a close eye on her these past two months, much of the needlecraft was hers.

An unconscious curve to her lips, she worked upon the hair of one of the riders. It was long, unlike that of his companions who wore the shaven style of the Normans. She had outlined the man's beard in pale gold, and given him a gown of soft blue. The darker blue cloak flying from his shoulders showed a lining of white. At his side, a hawk perched on her wrist, rode a woman on a black mare.

'You like him, don't you?' Agatha, Duke William's middle daughter, joined Judith at the embroidery bench and tipped a silver needle from her ivory case. She was small and rosy with fine, fair hair and dainty features – so dainty that Judith thought them like the sketch on this fabric – nothing without the added boldness of colour.

Judith did not pretend ignorance of Agatha's meaning. It was obvious to the most casual observer that the figure was Waltheof. 'He saved my life,' she said, 'I want to remember him . . . and yes, everyone likes him.'

Agatha poked among the threads, finally selecting a dark green. 'Not everyone,' she sniffed. 'Edwin says he should never have been allowed out of the cloister.'

Judith took several swift, controlled stitches. It was no secret that Agatha and Edwin of Mercia were conducting a courtship. William openly encouraged the couple to sit together in the hall of an evening, and he had dropped several heavy hints about a betrothal, but the deliberateness of the suggestions had led Judith to wonder. Her uncle was not usually so forthcoming with his designs.

'Edwin would say that,' she sniffed. 'He does not want Waltheof claiming Northumbria from his brother.'

Agatha began to outline one of the horses with neat stitches, revealing that she too was an accomplished needlewoman. A tip of pink tongue peeped from the corner of her mouth. 'Waltheof is not strong enough to displace Morcar,' she said with a toss of her head. 'He's untried and knows nothing of governance.'

'That does not mean he is incapable,' Judith objected, 'and he is the heir by blood.'

Agatha flushed. 'My father is content to let the house of Leofric keep its lands.' Her eyes glittered with malice. 'He will agree to my match with Edwin of Mercia long before he agrees to a match between you and Waltheof of Huntingdon.'

Judith returned Agatha's look with a cold stare. 'Your father desires to keep Edwin of Mercia dangling on his hook. 'You would be foolish to read too much into his suggestions I think.'

'I am more than just bait on a hook,' Agatha said proudly. 'Edwin's well born. My father will give me in marriage to him.'

Judith said nothing but raised one eyebrow in a way that

said Agatha was entitled to believe as she chose but was deluded.

'Anyway, Edwin said that Waltheof should have stayed in the cloister because he hasn't got the wit to be out in the world. He's a big, dumb ox.'

In and out went Judith's silver needle, stab and draw, stab and draw, filling in the marigold brightness of her horseman's hair. 'A dumb ox who can read and write and cipher,' she said quietly. 'A dumb ox whom our Norman courtiers like well, and who has proved his worth twice over. I have yet to see Edwin do more than pose in his fine clothes and show off.'

Agatha scowled. 'You won't be allowed to have him,' she said.

Judith shrugged, pretending she did not care. 'I may sew his image in an embroidery, but that does not mean I am ready to become his wife.'

'Are you not?' Agatha's gaze was hard and shrewd. 'I have heard it whispered that your mother keeps you closeted in the bower because you grew too familiar with him in Fécamp.'

'Then you must listen to whispers in some foul corners,' Judith snapped and set her needle aside, afraid that her anger would spoil her stitching. 'I have done nothing to cause reproach.'

It was Agatha's turn to raise a knowing eyebrow. 'You have never been so charitable towards the sick before,' she said. 'You seemed very concerned for the wellbeing of Simon de Senlis.'

'He was injured in my sight. Of course I was concerned for him,' Judith said, but could feel her face growing hot. 'I still am, for I do not think he will ever walk a straight course again.'

'And it had nothing to do with the English earl's visits to the boy.'

Judith sprang to her feet, unable to bear being near Agatha a moment longer. 'Of course it didn't.' Her sudden movement dislodged the silk basket, spilling a riot of colourful

hanks on to the floor. With a hiss of exasperation she stooped
to pick them up and untangle them.

Agatha was silent for a while but there was a satisfied curl
to her lips. 'Waltheof has a mistress in Fécamp you know,'
she said at last. 'She's a brothel whore from Madame
Hortense's near the harbour.'

'I suppose Edwin told you that too,' Judith said neutrally
and kept her back turned so that she would not have to bare
her expression to her cousin's predatory eyes.

'No he didn't, as it happens. It was my brother Robert.
He went there with some of his friends and saw Waltheof
with her. He says she's got the reputation of being willing to
consider all manner of unnatural deeds for a silver coin . . .
and that she has long dark hair just like yours.'

Judith carefully set the basket of silks back on the bench.
'I think that you would say anything just for the pleasure of
casting a stone in a pool and watching the ripples,' she said.
'The Earl of Huntingdon's private affairs are of less interest
to me than they are to you, Agatha. You weary me with your
prattle, and I will listen to no more.' Head held high, she
walked across the room to join her mother and sister who
were sewing a tunic for her absent stepfather.

Adelaide gave Judith a thoughtful look but said nothing
and merely handed her a seam to stitch. Judith was glad of
the silence while she composed herself. Agatha's gossip was
unsettling. Men seldom made permanent mistresses of girls
they met in brothels, she knew that, but they did make
regular assignations. Judith wondered if Waltheof's choice
had been deliberate. Did he imagine that he was bedding her
when he paid for the whore's services? The thought left her
torn between embarrassment, anger and shameful feelings
of lust.

Adelaide sighed and laid down her sewing. 'You may as
well know that a messenger arrived from your stepfather this
morning,' she said, her light brown eyes full of anxiety. 'I was
wondering whether to tell you, but there is no point in keeping

it to myself. It will be common knowledge soon enough. There is trouble in England.'

'Mother?' Judith's needle poised between stitches. Adela looked up. Judith was not close to her stepfather, but he was family, and she felt a jolt of fear.

'Lawless thieves and rebels are banding together and causing dissent. Your stepfather says that the men your uncle William left to govern the country are hard pressed to keep order. He says it is like sitting on the lid of a boiling cauldron.' Adelaide pressed the palm of her hand over the fine linen fabric of the garment she had been sewing, as if by smoothing it she could make everything well. She would not say aloud that she feared for her husband's life, but Judith could sense her alarm.

'Uncle William will send aid,' Judith said quickly.

Adelaide nodded. 'He is already making plans to cross the water and put an end to it once and for all.' Fierceness glittered in her eyes. 'He will make them pay dearly.'

Judith bit her lip. 'Will my uncle take the hostages with him?'

'That I do not know, although I hope so. They do naught but drink us dry and live lavishly off our tables. I for one am tired of the sight of them, and their habits are a bad influence on our own young men.'

Judith bent her head over the needlework so that her mother would not see her expression. 'When is my uncle to leave?'

'As soon as he can gather troops and ships,' Adelaide said. 'Your stepfather has heard a rumour the Northerners have been appealing to the Danes . . . The English cannot be allowed to join with them.'

Waltheof was half Danish. Judith wondered where his loyalty would lie if it came to the crux. With the rebels, or with her uncle at whose feet he had knelt in homage. Was he aware of the news, and if so what would it mean to him? A chance to raise rebellion, or the opportunity to prove himself a loyal vassal and then mayhap ask her uncle for a Norman bride? She did not know which way he would step, because despite their meetings at Simon's bedside in Fécamp she did not know him.

The rumours of a return to England received a mixed response from the hostages. There was pleasure at the notion of going home, furtive hope that the rebellion would succeed, and continued resentment at the knowledge that they would be bound closely to William's side and watched like naughty children.

'If William does not give me Agatha to wife by the end of the year, then I will find a way to join the rebels,' Edwin muttered, sloshing another measure of wine into his cup and passing the flagon along. 'I am not a tame dog to trot to heel for the promise of a bone that is never produced.'

Waltheof refilled his cup with wine. No one was sober and the talk had turned dangerous. He had no doubt that whatever was said would get back to William, but for the moment no one seemed to care.

'You think you can fight William?' he asked. 'You think you are a better warrior than Harold Godwinsson?'

Edwin's pale complexion darkened. 'I am still alive,' he slurred. 'Harold chose the wrong time and the wrong place.'

Morcar nodded in vigorous agreement, as did Edgar Atheling, who had been listening to the fighting talk with bright eyes.

'All of the North Country will rise up,' he declared, striking a pose. 'William has never set foot across the Humber. If Sweyn of Denmark sends a fleet then we can shake off the Normans like a dog shakes water from its pelt.'

Waltheof had held aloof from the fighting talk thus far, but the mention of the Danes brought him into their circle. He was half Dane and the tie of blood was strong. What would he do if Sweyn of Denmark sailed into the Humber – join him, or profess his allegiance to William? The wine buzzing in his head made it difficult to think. Kinship and belonging were important. Often he felt that he possessed neither. Parents and a brother he had scarcely known before death took them, lands that had been snatched from beneath his boyhood feet. All he had were the tales of his father's great deeds, and in strange contrast the quieter chanting of monks, drawing him through simple faith into the heart of their community. The way of the warrior or the way of peace: he had a foot in each territory and knew that he was in danger of falling down the chasm between.

He staggered to the coffer and picked up a fresh flagon, knowing that if he could down it to the dregs he would find the comfort of oblivion. He would not have to listen to the plans of his companions or the contradictory voices arguing back and forth in his mind. He gulped the potent red brew, felt the overflow trickling through his beard, and thought of Judith. If he took the cowl she was lost to him, the same if he chose the Danes. Only by becoming William's man did he stand a chance – and that was a slim one.

He knew that everyone liked him because he was good-natured and always prepared to laugh at his own expense. Never angry, always patient. Unfailingly polite despite his rustic English manners and his propensity for drink. Oh yes, he knew his worth in the eyes of other men. But tonight, in the murky light of dark plans and sour wine, the laughter had deserted him and he felt dangerously close to tears.

'I've brought you another gift,' Waltheof said, his breath steaming in the dank November air.

Simon watched Waltheof produce a walking stick from beneath the bearskin cloak. It was made of ash wood – a cut-down spear haft by the look of the thickness and length, fantastically carved with a sinuous design of hunting dogs pursuing a stag towards the smoothed and polished top. Man and boy sat on a bench in the courtyard of the palace at Fécamp where King William was making final preparations to sail for England.

Simon hated the stick, but forced a smile. 'It is very fine, my lord, thank you.' Very fine if you were an old woman, but not a boy of ten years old desiring to run across the sward with the fleetness of a wild deer.

Waltheof looked pleased. 'I thought it would help you now you are able to bear weight on the leg.'

Simon nodded. 'Indeed it will,' he said tonelessly. To prove it he took the stick, levered himself to his feet and walked several steps across the courtyard. Fog was rolling off the sea and smothering the town. Heavy, damp, clinging. Waltheof's coppery hair was hoar-grey and a cobwebby mist dewed his cloak.

There was biting pain every time Simon set weight on the leg. The break had healed reasonably well, considering the seriousness of the original injury, but the limb was still twisted out of true. His walk was no longer an unthinking bounce but an awkward lop-sided progression. Lying abed for weeks on end had caused his muscles to waste and he had no strength to support the damaged limb.

He had seen the beggars at the abbey gates with all manner of wounds and deformities, had watched men pity them and toss a coin, or walk past in the arrogance of their own power and manhood. He had observed them beg crusts and other leavings from the monks who came to dole out food at vespers. Now, but for the grace of his noble birth and his father's position at court, he would be one of their number.

Waltheof studied his progress with folded arms and a slight frown. 'You should do this every day,' he said. 'And go further each time. Only then will you build up your strength.'

'It hurts,' Simon answered, knowing that he sounded churlish but unable to prevent the all too familiar black misery from flooding over him.

'I know.'

'But you don't feel it.' Simon tightened his fist around the carved stick. Suppressing the urge to cast it across the bailey he continued to limp towards the open ground where the squires trained. It was empty this morning, the straw archery targes standing like ghosts beyond the quintain post that reared out of the mist like a gibbet.

'Perhaps not, but I see it.' Waltheof walked beside him, shortening his own long stride to accommodate Simon's. 'If you do not fight, lad, it will destroy you.'

Simon compressed his lips petulantly.

'You are not short of courage,' Waltheof said, 'but it will be to no avail if your self-pity is the stronger.'

Waltheof's words goaded Simon across the practice ground until he stood at its centre. The pain stabbed through his damaged leg in excruciating waves and he clenched his teeth so hard that his jaw began to ache too.

'Much better.' Waltheof clapped an approving hand on his shoulder. Simon staggered, as the accolade almost felled him. Waltheof made no move to steady him, but left him to find his own balance.

'Come the spring you'll be walking three times as fast, riding a horse, and back in full weapons training – I mean what I say. I am not feeding sops to an invalid – or at least I hope I am not.'

Simon jutted his jaw. Waltheof's words had stung his pride. Even if he died of the pain, no one was going to accuse him of wallowing in self-pity. Pivoting on his good leg, he made his way back towards the hall. Half smiling, Waltheof accompanied him.

They were halfway across the courtyard when Ralf de Gael joined them, his eyes bright with the relish that always lit in them when he had gossip to impart.

'You're doing well,' he said with a pleasant nod to Simon.

Simon nodded gravely in return. Many folk disliked Ralf de Gael. They said that he was smooth and shallow and not to be trusted. But then Normans frequently disparaged men of Breton birth. Simon liked him because he was amusing and he took the time to speak to him without being superior. That

De Gael was Waltheof's friend was also no small part of the boy's approval.

'Very well, considering the severity of the break,' Waltheof said with a wink at Simon.

The gesture warmed a smile from Simon. He strode out a bit more, showing off despite the increased pain.

'There's news from England,' De Gael said.

'Oh yes?' Waltheof's tone was suddenly cautious.

'The trouble has escalated. Exeter is in full revolt and there is a rising in the West Country that has spilled beyond containment. We're sailing on the morrow's tide. You had best hone your battleaxe – for whichever side you choose.'

'You know for sure we are to sail?' Waltheof demanded.

De Gael nodded. 'I look through the right keyholes,' he said with a feline smile. 'And listen at the right doors.' With a pleasant nod and a ruffle of Simon's hair, he moved on.

Waltheof halted and stood gazing into the fog, his head turned in the direction of the harbour. Simon thought that he looked like a hound testing an elusive scent.

'What is England like?' he asked.

Although Waltheof smiled in reply, the expression was wry and sad. 'I am not sure that I know any more,' he said, and after a moment began slowly to walk. 'Changed for ever. Nothing will ever be the same again – no matter how we wish it to be.'

Limping along beside him, pain stabbing through his leg, Simon knew exactly what he meant.

Judith crossed herself, rose from her knees, and with downcast eyes and modestly folded hands left the church. Sybille followed a few paces behind, her pose echoing that of her mistress.

From the edge of her eye, Judith was aware of Waltheof rising too, signing his breast and following her out. His presence loomed behind her, large as a bear in the porch. Without looking round she stepped out into the swirling, dank air. The fog had thickened as the day progressed and now it was like wading through a fleece.

She heard his footfall and shivered with the instinct of all creatures to fear shadows from behind. Then he fell into step beside her and the threat changed its form.

She had seen little of him since their encounter on the stairs. Her mother had been suspicious and shrewd enough to confine her to the bower. Although Judith had chafed she had also found relief within the safe walls of the women's quarters. Rules were rules, and, while she was tempted to break them, the orderly domesticity of her surroundings and her own strict sense of duty kept that temptation within bounds.

Only in church and beneath the eyes of others in the great hall had she and Waltheof exchanged words. He had made no approach to her uncle concerning marriage or even courtship. She would have heard. Perhaps he did not have the strength of will or courage to take the necessary steps. Perhaps he was all words and no intention.

She slanted him a glance, aware that she should not be speaking to him. 'So you are to sail to England with my uncle?' Her breath clouded in the air and mingled with his.

'I do not have a choice, my lady,' he replied. 'Where he goes, so do I – until he chooses to release me.'

'Will you help him put down the rebellions of your countrymen?'

'I will act as my conscience dictates,' he replied evasively.

'If you are not my uncle's ally, then you are his enemy. There can be no middle path.'

'I would rather make friends than enemies,' Waltheof said, 'but it is difficult to know which is which.'

'Is it?' Decisive herself, Judith felt a surge of impatience. 'If you cannot see what is before you, then you might as well be blind.'

'Stumbling in the mist you mean,' he said with a grin to which she did not respond.

'You are foolish to make light of the matter. My uncle can

fulfil your ambitions, or he can cast you in the abyss. But the road you choose is your responsibility.'

He looked taken aback, chagrined almost, and it was a strange expression to see on the face of so large and vital a man.

He cleared his throat and stooped slightly, bringing his height closer to hers. 'Judith . . . are you angry that I have held off from asking for you?'

She tightened her lips. 'Why should I be angry?'

'Because perhaps you thought I was reneging on a promise.'

'In truth the matter has dwelt little on my mind,' she said. It was a lie, but pondering the matter had led her towards her mother's viewpoint. 'I may be innocent, but I do know that a man's words are often driven by his lust.'

'Not mine!' He was indignant.

'Indeed?' She gave a scornful toss of her head. 'And what have you told your dark-haired whore at Madame Hortense's who will do whatever you desire for a silver coin?'

She expected him to bluster and deny her accusation, but although his complexion grew as red as his hair he answered her candidly. 'Nothing of late,' he said gruffly. 'I have not seen her in many months. Besides, Edwin has her now.'

Judith was taken by surprise. 'Edwin?'

He spread his hands in an open gesture. 'I lay with her no more than two or three times, so she had to find custom elsewhere.'

Judith almost smiled, imagining Agatha's expression could she hear this now. 'I was given to understand she was your permanent mistress.'

He made a face. 'No. I went to her in lust and the aftertaste was bitter because she wasn't you.'

Judith inhaled sharply. She was affronted, but his words excited her too.

'I meant no insult,' Waltheof said quickly. He reached for her hand. 'If I have not asked your uncle for permission to be your suitor it is because I have been waiting the right moment.'

'Then perhaps you are one of those men who will wait for ever.' She snatched her hand from his for they were close to the ducal apartments and could not afford to be seen thus.

'It is not that . . .' He gnawed his lip. 'I am afraid that he will refuse me . . . and then the matter will be finished.'

'Unless you ask, you will not know, and he will bestow me on someone who does have the courage to approach him,' she said, jutting her chin.

He drew back as though she had struck him. 'I may lack many things, my lady, but do not missay my courage,' he said stiffly.

She saw that she had wounded him but lacked the ability to conciliate. The words stuck in her throat, refusing to come. 'Then do not insult my pride,' she said instead and swept on into the women's apartments.

Usually after attending prayer she felt calm and refreshed, but now she was flustered and out of sorts.

'You were harsh with him, my lady,' Sybille said.

Judith rounded on her maid. 'When I want your opinion I will ask for it!' she spat. 'You think I was harsh? You do not know the meaning of the word.'

'Neither does he, my lady,' Sybille murmured, not in the least set down by her mistress's fury. She had long since grown impervious to the cold words and hauteur, aware that there was a softness concealed within Judith's brittle shell. 'He is truly gentle, and such men are as precious as gold. You should treat him with more care.'

Judith's eyes narrowed. 'Hold your tongue if you would keep your position with me,' she snapped. 'That is a command.'

'Yes, my lady,' Sybille said in a tone that told Judith precisely what she thought of such tactics.

Judith turned her back on her maid and paced swiftly into the hall. Someone had put damp wood on the fire and the billows of smoke seemed no less thick than the fog she was leaving behind, but Judith walked with relief into the pungency. Waltheof disturbed her. She wanted to lay her head on his broad chest and listen to the thud of his heart, and the rumble of his soothing voice. At the same time she wanted to repudiate him and not have to deal with the dangerous turmoil of emotions he raised within her. Better to forget him. With the decision came a feeling of relief, coupled with a sudden, inexplicable urge to weep.

CHAPTER 6

Exeter, Winter 1067–1068

Waltheof handed Osric Fairlocks a cup of mead. 'Drink this,' he said with sympathy. 'It will warm your blood.'

The young man took it hesitantly and raked his free hand through his flaxen hair. He was not old enough to grow a beard and his face had the tender smoothness and bloom of late adolescence. His eyes were fearful although he was doing his utmost to be brave. That afternoon he and eleven other hostages had been brought to the Norman camp in token of Exeter's promise to acknowledge William as king and cease hostilities. Osric, whose father was a prosperous merchant, was the youngest hostage and Waltheof had taken him under his wing.

Outside the tent the January day was raw with cold. Nightfall was closing on the horizon and rain spattered in the wind. 'William is harsh, but he treats his hostages well,' Waltheof reassured the youth and led him to a large brazier burning in the centre of the room. 'You will not want for anything.'

'Except my freedom,' Osric said, his complexion reddening.

Waltheof nodded, 'There you have it. That is indeed the hair shirt we all wear. But if the city yields on the morrow, you at least will be free to go home to your kin.'

The young man regarded him with doubt and even a little scorn in his pale blue eyes. 'Are you free to go home, my lord? Could you leave here on the morrow and not be hunted down?'

Waltheof twitched his shoulders as if shifting a burden that chafed. 'No,' he said, 'but I hope to do so very soon.' William had bestowed on him the full titles of Earl of Huntingdon and Northampton and confirmed him in his lands before the entire court at the Christmas feast. The freedom to take charge of those estates had not been forthcoming, though. Instead William had bidden him join this campaign in the West Country. It was the same for Edwin and Morcar; they too had been confirmed in their lands and then forced to stay at William's side. Edgar Atheling had been left in London under guard, but he had no lands from which to rally support and he was still little more than a boy.

He gave Osric a glance filled with warning. 'No one crosses the lines that are drawn by King William.'

'And if they do?'

'I have never met a man so sure of himself, or so ruthless.' Waltheof finished his mead and replenished his cup. 'He is feared, and rightly so.'

'You know that King Harold's mother and his sons are in the city?' Osric said with a defiant look.

'I had heard the rumour. If they have their wits about them they will make shrift to leave tonight before the gates open on the morrow.'

'And if the gates remain closed? What then?'

Waltheof shook his head. 'You do not want to know, lad,' he said grimly.

'My father and the elders say we should open the gates to William rather than see the city burn, but others say we should resist.' Osric stood tall with pride. 'We have stout walls, good fighting men and plentiful provisions. William may find he is king in London, but not king here.'

'Yet, knowing the danger, you agreed to be a hostage?'

'I had no choice,' Osric said with bravado. As my father's firstborn son, it was my duty.'

Waltheof said nothing, for there was no point in frightening the lad and he knew from his experience with Judith how powerful a sense of duty could be. He hoped desperately for Osric's sake that sense prevailed and the citizens of Exeter opened their gates on the morrow.

Swirling the mead in his cup and watching the reflections break and shimmer on the surface he wondered what he would do if this were Northampton or Huntingdon. Would he yield to the invader, or fight to the last drop of blood in his body? 'I am William's man now,' he said aloud, the remark intended to bolster his own resolve rather than make a bold statement for the pale-haired youth at his side. 'For better, or worse.'

In the morning the Norman army gathered before the walls of Exeter in full array and William demanded that its citizens yield their town into his hands. Upon the Roman walls, outlined in the red winter dawn, a soldier lifted his tunic, turned his exposed backside towards the Normans and waggled his hips. As William's jaw tightened, missiles began to fly over the battlements – cabbage stalks, clods of dung, rocks and stones. Horses skittered and shied. The Norman ranks developed ragged holes as men fought with their mounts and drew back out of range.

'Ut, ut, ut!' surged the English battle roar, a sound not heard since the October confrontation on Hastings field. 'Ut, ut, ut!'

Amidst the chaos William sat as still as an effigy on his black Iberian war horse. He stared expressionlessly at the walls, and the more the volume of the shouting increased the greater became his control. At last he tugged on the bridle and urged his horse out of danger's way.

Watching from the back of the line with Edwin and Morcar, Waltheof swallowed. Something bad was going to happen. He could feel it all the way down his spine.

'A pity one of their slingers didn't get him while they had the opportunity,' Morcar said softly.

'Hold your tongue, fool,' Edwin muttered, glancing round.

'There is no one to hear except sympathisers,' Morcar growled. 'Is that not so, Waltheof?' His eyes gleamed with challenge and malice.

'Indeed, I have great sympathy for the people of Exeter,' Waltheof said grimly. 'Judith told me a story about William as a young man. The people of Alençon taunted him by waving hides from their walls, reminding him that his grandsire was a common tanner. Some lived to rue the day and the rest were butchered.' He lowered his voice. 'That slinger could not afford to miss, any more than that fool on the battlements could afford to bare his arse.'

He drew back as a dozen Norman soldiers arrived and shoved their way through the ranks. Their mail gleamed like dull water, reflecting the steely dawn. Waltheof's gut clenched. Moments later the men returned, escorting the hostages that had been given by the city's elders in token of their good faith.

'Dear, sweet Christ,' Waltheof whispered and crossed himself. There were ten men, including Osric who was the youngest and yet to reach his majority, and five women, high of rank and gowned in deep-dyed wool, rich with embroidery.

Waltheof nudged his horse forward, intending to follow, but more Norman soldiers barred his way.

'No, my lord earl,' said one of them and grasped Waltheof's bridle close to the headstall. 'You cannot go.'

It was Picot de Saye, the Norman whom he had defeated at arm wrestling on that first evening in Rouen, and it was obvious from the look on his face that he was enjoying the moment. Waltheof was tempted to dig in his heels and ride the man down, but knew that he would not live much beyond the deed.

'But you can watch,' Picot added lazily and shifted his fist to the cheekstrap, the force of his grip preventing Waltheof from wrenching his horse around and riding away. 'So are all traitors brought to justice.'

Waltheof swore in English at the Norman. De Saye absorbed the insult without a flicker. 'Watch,' he said, his lip curling. 'Watch and learn your lesson.'

King William was staring dispassionately at the clutch of hostages. Raising his mace, he pointed it with brutal decision at Osric. 'Bring him before the walls and put out his eyes,' he commanded.

Without demur, two of the escort plunged among the Saxons, seized the youth and manhandled him towards the towering city defences. Osric's expression was pale with fright, but he knew no French and thus did not understand the portent of William's words.

De Saye might have had a tight grip on Waltheof's bridle, but he had no control over Waltheof's voice. 'No, my lord king, you cannot!' he roared. 'In God's name, have mercy, I beg you!'

William turned his head. The sharp eyes appraised Waltheof and they were impassive. Neither pity in them, nor anger, nor irritation. Nothing but a brown so dark that it was almost black and merged with the pupils. 'Save your pleading, Lord Waltheof, and be thankful that I have not ordered the blinding of all,' he said icily and, reining away, rode off to see the sentence carried out.

Osric screamed like a hare in a trap. The sound, high-pitched and keening, went on and on until it wound itself permanently into the coils of Waltheof's brain. His gorge rose and it took all his will not to unman himself and spew over his mount's withers. From Exeter's walls came a response of angry yells and a renewed barrage of missiles. The two Normans sheathed their bloody knives and retreated out of range, leaving Osric to groan and writhe in the wet, reddening grass.

The sound of Osric's moans continued long after the early winter dusk had fallen, growing gradually more sporadic and faint as blood loss and cold took their toll. Finally, not long after Compline, the sounds ceased. Waltheof had spent the time on his knees in prayer for Osric's soul. There was nothing else he could do for William was as implacable as granite. No one was to go to the hostage's aid. Any breach of William's command and a second hostage would be blinded too. 'Not so fine now, your Norman lord,' sneered Morcar in passing. 'What price now your desire to be a Frenchman?'

Waltheof's hands clenched on his prayer beads as he fought the desire to round on Morcar and use his fists to pummel away his grief and anger.

'Leave me be,' he said raggedly. 'I cannot pray to God while you disturb me.'

'You think prayer is the answer?' Morcar mocked. 'Truly you should not have strayed from your cloister, "Brother" Waltheof.' Wrapping his hands around his belt, Morcar sauntered off to join his brother.

Waltheof bowed his head and whispered the Psalter over and over, seeking the path through and between the words towards communication with God. But tonight the way was stumbling and strewn with lurid, bloody images that tripped and felled him.

The morning dawned and still the citizens of Exeter howled defiance at the Normans. Under cover of darkness a handful of them had crept out and brought Osric's body back into the town, leaving only a depression in the grass and dark bloodstains on the pallid winter blades.

William summoned Waltheof and brought him before the walls. In the early light, sappers were toiling to undermine a section of the massive stone battlements. Screens of wattle hurdles protected the men and Norman archers kept the defenders on the walls pinned down. William's half-brother, Robert, Count of Mortain, was supervising the activity, the harshness of his voice carrying on the frosty morning air.

Waltheof bowed stiffly and then stood at William's side to watch the industry. 'They did not open their gates, sire,' he said, making oblique reference to yesterday's atrocity. He wondered why William had requested his presence. Was he going to be forced to view another blinding in order to 'learn' his lesson?

'They are stubborn,' William replied. 'It is because they are harbouring the remnants of the Godwinsson family. They would not be so ready to defy me if they had naught but their own hides to defend.' He slanted Waltheof a dark look. 'You think me harsh, Earl Waltheof?'

'I could not have done as you did, sire. It would fester on my conscience.'

William gave a contemptuous grunt. 'A king cannot afford to have a conscience when his lands are threatened. Sometimes a single act of savagery saves time. I destroy one man for the sake of saving others. If the people of Exeter had opened their gates yester eve, they would have spared themselves a deal of pain.'

Waltheof could not prevent a shiver of foreboding. 'What will you do when you have broken down the walls, sire?' There was no doubt in his mind that Exeter would eventually fall. There was not an Englishman left in the land who could match William's iron discipline and military leadership.

'You suspect I am going to order a massacre?' William said dryly.

'It had crossed my mind, sire.'

'That depends on how swiftly they learn their lessons. What I did yesterday was not from anger but necessity. If I had let their defiance go unpunished they would have seen it as a weakness and it would have bolstered their resolve.'

'But they did not open their gates to you, sire.'

'That would have been a weakness on their part. But when the sappers bring down their wall and my soldiers ride through the breach I doubt their boldness will continue. No one wants to see their child maimed, blinded or trampled beneath the hooves of a war horse.'

Waltheof could not prevent the shudder that rippled down

his spine. Remembering Osric's screams he was filled with a revulsion so strong that he felt sick.

'This is the way of a leader, Waltheof,' William said, nailing the young earl with a shrewd and ruthless stare. 'You have to make harsh judgements and overrule all other men with your will. Even if your choices burden your conscience, you do not cry out but shoulder them without sign of weakness.' He took up a bullish stance – planting his feet wide and folding his arms. 'I am not justifying myself to you, but explaining the role of a leader in wartime.'

'Why should you do that, sire?' Waltheof asked stiffly.

'Because you are an earl and the son of an earl. Because you have never been blooded in battle or had your abilities tested to the limit.'

Waltheof flushed. 'I have been your hostage for a year. How can I be tested when I kick my heels at court?'

William looked at him steadily, his eyes obsidian dark. 'It is all a matter of trust, is it not? If I take my fist off the leash and let you go, will you be loyal, or will you muster an army and make war against me? I have little doubt that your companions would whet their swords the moment they were out of my sight.'

'You would release me, sire?' A note of eagerness entered Waltheof's voice.

'I did not say that. I said that it was a matter of trust. How trustworthy are you, Waltheof?'

'I gave you my oath at the Christmas Gemot in Winchester, sire.'

'As did the others. I did not ask about your oath, but about your trustworthiness.'

Waltheof set his jaw. How loyal was he? Could he follow a man who would blind a youth for political expedience? If he couldn't, then he faced worse than blinding himself. If he could, then perhaps William might let him have Judith. 'I am trustworthy, sire,' he heard himself croak. 'Only let me go from court and I will prove it to you.'

William rubbed his palm across his jaw, considering. Finally, he nodded. 'Stay with me until Exeter is taken, and then I give you leave to depart until the Easter feast at Westminster.' Elation coursed through Waltheof, sweeping aside all other considerations. It was only later that he remembered Osric and felt ashamed that the gift of his own freedom should so easily have overwhelmed his revulsion at William's deed.

Exeter fell, the mined walls rumbling down and an initial charge of Norman cavalry pouring through the breach to terrorise the citizens into capitulation. Following hard upon that first warning assault, William sent in his most disciplined troops. There was to be no looting, no burning, no harassment. A Flemish mercenary caught in the act of rape was summarily hanged.

Waltheof watched the masterly taking of Exeter, the way the population now pleaded with William for mercy and how he gave it. Not only that, but the orderliness of his troops and his implacable attention to discipline gave the people an anchor. They were not going to be butchered in their homes, everything was going to be all right. William might be a Norman conqueror, but he had won the right to be their king.

The remnants of Harold Godwinsson's family escaped by boat at the last moment, but William was sanguine about the matter. There was no one to truly challenge him from that clan. Their best had died on Hastings field.

He gave instructions for land to be levelled and a castle to be built. That this involved the destruction of several English houses and garths was the only damage wrought on Exeter apart from the broached wall.

True to his word, William gave Waltheof leave to depart the city and return to his lands. Edwin and Morcar were furious, but impotent. Threats to leave William of their own will were met with courteous but firm counter threats. The promise of marriage to Agatha was dangled before Edwin's eyes together with the insinuation that Mercia would suffer if William had to go chasing north in pursuit of renegades. Perhaps later, he hinted; perhaps after the Easter feast.

'You must have had to lick his arsehole all the way to his throat for this,' Morcar sneered as Waltheof mounted his chestnut stallion and prepared to leave the city. He had a safe conduct in his pouch from William and an escort of Norman knights and English mercenaries.

'My lands are not as great as yours,' Waltheof answered. 'He risks less in letting me go than you or Edwin. Besides, this is only a trial. If I renege, William will throw me in the deepest dungeon he possesses.'

Morcar fixed him with a look of utter loathing and turned away. Edwin stepped forward and looked up at Waltheof through sun-narrowed eyes. 'Enjoy favour while you may, son of Siward,' he said with a curled lip. 'It will not last.'

There was nothing more to say. Waltheof knew that if he extended the hand of friendship, he would be shunned. Clicking his tongue to the horse, he reined about, heading for Exeter's city gates and the road home.

He had to pass the remnants of the burned-out houses that were being flattened to make way for the castle. Under the watchful gaze of Picot de Saye, English labourers toiled with shovels, their expressions wearing a blank neutrality that Waltheof was coming to know too well. More eloquent than resentment, more subtle than resignation. He averted his head from the sight and the acrid stink, fixing his gaze instead on the ragged blue sky and the pale sun, forerunners of the spring. He promised himself that in his own earldom no man should ever look upon him thus.

CHAPTER 7

Dawn streaked the sky and sea with pearl and silver. A brisk wind mined the seams of light and bellied the sails of the Norman fleet, thrusting it towards the smudge of England's shoreline.

Simon stood on the deck of his galley and watched the land drawing closer. His leg was aching, but he was so accustomed to the sensation by now that it only bothered him when his mind was unoccupied. For the moment, he was too full of exhilaration to give the pain much heed. He had scarcely slept at all during the night – just a couple of hours rolled in his cloak. Mostly he had lain awake, gazing at the stars as they appeared and vanished behind fine tresses of cloud. His mind had turned with the turning of the heavens, dwelling on the adventure to come.

Duke William had put down the rebellions in England; the Danish threat had been avoided by diplomatic negotiation, and he had summoned his family to come to him. This Eastertide Duchess Matilda was to be crowned Queen of England in King Edward's great abbey of Westminster. Simon had pleaded with his father to be allowed to make the crossing as part of the entourage, promising vehemently to be a help, not a hindrance. He could walk, he could ride, he never complained. When his father had frowned doubtfully, Simon had started making plans to stow away on a supply vessel, but it had not come to that; his father had finally agreed to let him come. 'If only to prevent my ears from being nagged off,' he had said with a reluctant smile.

De Rules had found Simon light fetching and carrying duties within the household. When his leg grew tired he was made to sit and keep tallies of the goods being transported, or given employment greasing armour and mail ready for the voyage.

Yester eve they had sailed from the port of Dieppe and headed out into the Narrow Sea. Simon had been boarded on the Duchess's galley, its strakes painted a moon white and rows of overlapping kite shields protecting the deck from the exuberant salt spray. The ladies had recourse to a canvas shelter and had spent most of the time inside it, the flaps pulled tight. Duchess Matilda was not fond of journeying across water, although for her husband she would have braved sailing over the edge of the world itself.

It was Simon's first sea voyage. His stomach was queasy, but he had not succumbed to outright seasickness. On the galley that held the Duke's sons he had several times seen Rufus puking over the side. There was no mistaking the pale sandy hair and thickset body. Simon felt sorry for Rufus and was glad that he was not sailing on that particular ship. Jeers from the Duke's older sons and their companions floated on the wind, laced with the malice of too much wine. The ringleader, however, was not of William's brood, but Robert de Bêlleme, a son of the great Earl Roger of Montgomery. The youth was extraordinarily handsome and outwardly of a charming and debonair mien, but Simon knew from bitter experience that De Bêlleme's deeper nature was twisted and cruel. Inflicting pain and humiliation were favourite pastimes of his, and Simon, with his damaged leg, was often on the receiving end of pranks and taunts. Today he was safe, but Rufus, with his lack of grace and his stammer, was not.

Simon inhaled the salt tang in the air and watched the band of dawn widen and spill across the sea like the glitter from an open treasure chest. Turning, he saw the Lady Judith had emerged from the women's shelter. She nodded to him without speaking and went to look out on the approaching land.

Simon knew that she did not like him much. He would always be grateful to her for giving him that hanging when he was confined to the tiny wall chamber in Fécamp, but he knew she had done it from guilt, not kindness.

Lord Waltheof was smitten by her. She seldom laughed or smiled, and Simon thought that the Earl pursued her in the hopes of making her do those things. He was hoping Waltheof would be at court. He wanted to show him how far he had progressed since their last encounter. From halting steps to strides, from blotted scrawl to fluent script, and from uncertain notes on the bone flute to twinkling tunes.

He had been standing in one place for too long and as he moved vicious pain stabbed through his leg, making him stumble. He stifled the instinctive cry of pain and managed to grab a stay rope and remain upright. Lady Judith half glanced, then swiftly averted her head.

Turning his back, pretending he had not seen her look, Simon limped stiffly towards the red-faced sailor at the steerboard. The man greeted him with a grin and let him try his hand at operating the large wooden rudder. Simon's discomfort immediately diminished as he tackled the challenge. The wind tangling his hair, a mist of salt droplets narrowing his eyes, he became a bold sea-reaver with the blood of the Vikings surging in his veins.

Judith hated crossing the Narrow Sea. The knowledge that all that lay between her and fathoms of drowning green water was a flimsy layer of wood was terrifying. She would not disgrace her blood by showing her anxiety, but within her, that blood ran as cold as the ocean beneath the keel.

She wished that Simon de Senlis had not been assigned a place on the women's vessel. The sight of his stiff gait was a permanent reproach to her conscience, and the way he looked at her with those knowing fox-coloured eyes made her want to shout at him to go away and leave her alone. She wanted to bury that moment in the stableyard and forget it had ever happened. And she could not do that with the evidence always before her eyes.

Judith was relieved when the boy went to join the steersman and left her line of vision. She made an effort to banish him from her thoughts by concentrating on the matters uppermost in her mind. England and Waltheof.

Her mother muttered privately and out of the Duchess's hearing that England was occupied by a gluttonous, uncivilised rabble and that given a choice she would rather remain in Normandy. Even the grand prospect of a coronation had not sweetened the vinegar of her mood.

Judith turned her thoughts to Waltheof. In the three months since his leaving, her memory of him had both faded and clarified. She could not recall his features clearly, but his vibrancy and vitality had stayed with her as surely as the memory of his glossy red-gold hair and the feel of his lips on hers. Those things were indelible, no matter how she strove to obliterate them.

There had been no word from England to indicate that he had pursued his declaration to have her. Judith knew that for her own sake she should stay as far from the fire as possible. Only a fool stepped too close and risked being burned.

The fleet docked in Southampton and, after the royal entourage had rested there overnight, they travelled on to Winchester and thence to London. Gazing upon the April landscape as they rode, Judith thought that England was not much different from Normandy. The same pastoral scenes in the countryside; the same industry in the towns. The only signs of unrest and struggle were sporadic – charred marks on the ground where a building had burned, a farmstead worked solely by women whose husbands had not returned from the great battle, the rising earthworks and palisades of motte and bailey castles, dug by the English and supervised by the Normans.

She could almost see the peace, laid down as heavily as slabs of stone between lines of mortar. No one dared rebel lest they were crushed beneath a mailed Norman fist, but Judith could feel the resentment. It was there in the way that folk bowed to her, concealing their hostility beneath downcast lids and making obscene gestures under the cover of their doffed hoods. She rode past with a raised chin, her shield one of Norman hauteur, but it was not sufficient to protect her from the pierce of their side-cast glances.

They arrived in London just before dusk of the second day and travelled by barge up the Thames from the wharves at Queenhythe to the royal palace at Westminster. Sequins of sunset dazzled on the water and turned the sky to molten gold beyond the towers of King Edward's abbey. Judith folded her arms within her cloak, glad of the fur lining, for the river wind was bitter.

'Are we almost there?' Agatha demanded petulantly. 'I feel sick.'

Judith regarded her cousin with dislike. Agatha was convinced that her parents were going to announce a betrothal between her and Edwin of Mercia at the coronation celebrations. Throughout the journey to England she had been insufferable, primping and preening and setting herself above the other women.

The barge bumped along the side of the wharf and the bargemaster secured his craft with a stout mooring rope. Willing hands reached down to steady the passengers as they disembarked.

'My lady,' Waltheof said and, taking Judith's hand in a sure, warm grip, he pulled her onto firm ground. The sunset burnished his hair to fire. He was wearing a tunic she had not seen before, of sky-blue wool richly embroidered, and the famous bearskin cloak was clasped at his shoulder by an enormous ring-brooch set with chips of amber and garnet.

'My lord of Huntingdon!' Her greeting was a gasp.

'Why so surprised?' He flashed her a smile. 'We are all

here to swear our oaths of fealty and witness the coronation of Duchess Matilda. I thought I would be the first to bid you welcome.' Leaning in closer, he breathed against her ear. 'I also intend to ask your uncle for you in marriage.'

His words shook her, as did the danger of being so close to him in public. She took a back-step.

So did he, and at the same time he bowed. 'Countess,' he said.

Judith's mother inclined her head in a brusque response and as she swept past him beckoned Judith with a terse forefinger.

'Waltheof!'

He turned at the cry and Judith saw his smile widen until it split into a broad grin.

'Well look at you, Simon de Senlis!' Striding forward, he clasped the lad in an exuberant embrace. 'I told you that you could do anything if you set your mind to it. How's the leg?'

Adelaide swung to look at the scene and gave a cluck of irritation. 'I am reminded of the dogs your father used to keep,' she said contemptuously. 'Huge, enthusiastic and tiresome.'

Judith looked down. She dared not tell her mother that Waltheof was intending to ask for her in marriage – at least not while Adelaide's mood was tetchy from travelling. Glancing over her shoulder, she saw that Waltheof and Simon were walking together, the former tailoring his pace to the latter's uneven gait. The boy was chattering and Waltheof was leaning to listen with every indication of interest. Her mother had disparagingly compared Waltheof to one of her father's dogs, but Adelaide had omitted to mention the unconditional love and loyalty of which such animals were capable. Such traits, surely, were worth their weight in gold.

The evening meal served an hour after their arrival was a relatively casual affair. No one had known the precise hour at which the Duchess would arrive at Westminster and so no formal arrangements had been made. Agatha and Edwin were permitted to sit side by side and share their portions of pigeons in wine sauce. Their blond heads leaned close and Judith could almost hear them cooing like lovebirds.

Judith was seated next to her mother, her sister and her stepfather, Eudo of Champagne. He was stocky and robust, balding, but still handsome with a determined cleft chin, high cheekbones and shrewd blue eyes. Adelaide had married him out of political expediency. There was little love or attraction between them, but there was pride and unity of purpose, and the ever-present bonds of duty.

Waltheof sat at the same trestle but at some distance from Judith, separated by various magnates and their families. Judith noticed how confident he was amongst them and thought she perceived a change in him. To say that he seemed more responsible or more of a man was wrong. His ready laugh still rang out with too much exuberance and his tongue still ran away with him, yet something was different. Assurance? Authority? Perhaps it was because he was now on his own soil instead of being a hostage in a foreign land.

The meal finished, the company broke up into smaller groups, men gathering around friends and acquaintances to exchange news, play dice and tafel, or listen to the bards sing tales of praise for whichever lord they served. Her mother prepared to retire to the small chamber that Eudo had secured for them, but Judith begged permission to linger awhile and listen to the tales.

Adelaide raised her brows. 'You are not usually so fond of song,' she said suspiciously.

'The English music is different, and I'm not tired.'

Her mother frowned and began to shake her head.

'Yes, stay,' spoke up her stepfather with a brusque gesture. 'And your sister too. I scarcely think that listening to a few tales in the open hall will compromise your virtue.'

'I don't—' Adelaide began, but her husband squeezed her hand in his strong, swordsman's fist.

'Peace, wife,' he said brusquely. 'Let the girls have their pleasure, and let us have ours.'

Adelaide's face flamed at his implication, made all the more obvious as he began tugging her purposefully towards the stairs. 'Do not be too long,' she said somewhat desperately to Judith.

'But not too soon either,' Eudo said with an eloquent eyebrow and a swift smile. 'Your mother and I have much to talk about.'

Judith's own complexion reddened. She knew that their activity would not involve much talking. At least if she and her sister were in the hall they would not have to lie on their pallets and listen to the sounds of coupling coming from the main bed.

Sybille chuckled. 'It is not often that your mother is bettered,' she said.

Judith sniffed and pretended not to hear.

The maid considered her with knowing eyes. 'I wonder why you want to stay, mistress,' she said. 'I do not think it is out of consideration for your mother and stepfather, and you no more enjoy listening to bards than I'm the Duchess of Normandy.'

'You are impertinent,' Judith snapped.

Sybille shrugged. 'I speak the truth as I see it.' She fell into step behind her mistress, her grey eyes sparkling with mischief.

Ignoring her maid, Judith glanced around the hall. Adela had darted off to join her royal cousins Agatha and Constance, who were in the company of Edwin of Mercia. Waltheof, by his height and the brightness of his hair, was easy to locate. He was standing beside Ralf de Gael and young Simon de Senlis, listening to one of several bards in the hall. Judith's brows twitched together at the sight of him with the boy, but her hesitation was a brief one and she went forward to join the group, but made sure to maintain a formal distance.

Waltheof gave her a smile of welcome. Judith nodded

briefly and then fixed her gaze on the bard, pretending to give him her full attention, although she could not understand a word that he was singing. The English tongue was foreign to her, and the man's pronunciation was different again from the English she had heard Waltheof speak.

With the smirk of a conspirator Sybille stepped aside, making room for Waltheof next to her mistress.

'What do you think of my skald?' he asked.

'Your skald?' The rumble of his voice sent a shiver along her spine.

'My bard,' he gestured to the singer. The man's hair was the dull gold of new pinewood and his beard was striped with the silver of early middle age.

'I did not know that you had such a man in your retinue.'

He shrugged his wide shoulders. 'I did not take him to Normandy with me. Why should I clip his wings as well as my own? He is a free spirit and he serves me for pleasure, not duty.'

Judith eyed the man who was accompanying himself on a small but beautiful lyre. Whether or not the sound was true she could not tell for she had no flair for music. 'His accent is strange.'

'Thorkel comes from Iceland. He speaks English well, but it is not his mother tongue.' He looked at her. 'It is the same with me for French.'

They stood in silence for a while and listened. Waltheof seemed to be enjoying the ballad, whatever it was about. There was a gleam in his eyes, and his lips were parted in pleasure. 'It is the story of a great warrior who held a bridge singlehanded against all comers,' Waltheof said. 'And through his action his country was saved, even though he died of his wounds.'

Judith was less than impressed. Most songs were of that ilk. She had nightmares sometimes about the tedium of the Song of Roland, which was a favourite of her uncle's own bards. The songs were all for men, she thought, but then she was not sure that she would have the patience for love ballads either.

The skald finished his lay on a haunting cry and a rippling shiver of notes. Judith guessed that the hero had tragically died, surrounded by a massed heap of enemy corpses.

Applauding loudly, eyes moist with a suspicion of tears, Waltheof drew a gold bracelet off his arm and presented it to the musician. 'Well sung, Thorkel,' he said gruffly.

'Your belief in my craft is worth more than gold, my lord, but I thank you for the gift,' the Icelander said graciously. His dark grey eyes flickered between Judith and Waltheof and he coaxed a gentle, stepping stone of notes from his lyre.

'Perhaps a tune for the lady?' he suggested.

Judith started to refuse, but Waltheof overrode her. 'Yes, Thorkel, a tune for the lady.'

The skald nodded and eyed Judith thoughtfully. 'A wood in springtime,' he announced. His gaze went past Judith to Sybille and he drooped his eyelid at the maid in what might just have been a wink. Then he started to play. No words, just sweet chords and cascades of notes that mimicked bird-song and the rill of meltwater down a hillside.

Judith surreptitiously moved her feet as they began to grow heavy with standing. She knew that many folk found music almost as essential as breathing, but she was not one of them. The skald's head was bent over his lyre but now and again he glanced up. His eyes pierced Judith as if he could see through her and she wanted to squirm, but after the first couple of looks he turned his attention to Sybille, and it soon became obvious for whom he was playing.

The tune ended on a clamber and fall of notes reminiscent of a skylark's song. 'That was beautiful,' Sybille sighed, her eyes misty. 'I could feel the leaf dapple on my eyelids.'

Thorkel smiled with pleasure. 'You have a rare imagination, mistress. It is not given to everyone to be so gifted.'

Judith narrowed her eyes, but the musician's attention was upon her maid and there was no sign of mockery in his expression. 'You are very skilled, Master Thorkel,' she said.

He bowed and she met a glint of caustic humour in his

eyes. 'I am pleased you think so, my lady.' He excused himself to fill his drinking horn. Sybille lingered, obviously smitten.

Waltheof laid his hand on Judith's sleeve. 'Thorkel is not the only man of my retinue here at Westminster,' he said, and proceeded to introduce her to some of the other warriors who had been listening and whom she had earlier seen seated at one of the lower benches in the hall. Their names all ran one into the other, harsh and guttural: Hakon, Toki, Guthrum, Siggurd, men of Huntingdon and York, whose grandfathers had been Danes, tall and square-boned with the same vital air as their lord. She felt engulfed by their presence and was glad when Waltheof drew her out of their company and into a quieter corner.

'Your uncle released me to my lands after Exeter fell,' Waltheof said. 'And for that I have been grateful.'

Judith's gaze sharpened. 'He truly let you go?'

Waltheof nodded. 'He said he put his trust in me to return to court for this feast, but otherwise I have been my own man, free to deal with my estates as I see fit.'

The implications of his words sent a jolt through her. 'But he did not release Edwin of Mercia or his brother,' she said.

Waltheof looked almost smug. 'He released neither of them. They and Edgar Atheling have been held in London ever since our return from Normandy.'

'So, he favours you.'

Waltheof pondered. 'I hope he does, because after the coronation I am going to ask him for you in marriage.'

'You said you were going to ask him before.'

He grimaced and rubbed the back of his neck. 'I know I did, but I could not. Your uncle confirmed me in my lands on the feast of Stephen. After Exeter, he let me return to them. To have asked on top of that would have seemed greedy.' His expression brightened. 'Now I have brought the men of Huntingdon to court and fulfilled my vow to come to him at the feast of Pentecost I am in a better position to make an approach. My loyalty is proven.' He stroked her cheek and his voice softened. 'I want you, Judith, never doubt that.'

She smiled, but drew away, aware of how many eyes there were to see and report. 'You have been spending too much time in the company of your bard.'

'And you in the company of your mother,' he retorted.

'My duty is to her . . . until you make it differently. I must go.' She made to push past him and he caught her hand in his.

'Is that all you want? If I gain the consent of your uncle, you will be content to wed with me?'

She was aware of the danger, that people would see and they would both be compromised. The urgency in his voice spoke to her, the language exciting, dangerous and frightening. Giving him a stiff nod, unable to dare further, she snatched her hand out of his and hurried away.

CHAPTER 8

In the great abbey church of Westminster, William's duchess Matilda was crowned Queen of the English before a vast array of witnesses, both Saxon and Norman. At William's coronation two winters since, the English had rioted outside the church, resulting in the burning of several houses and many English deaths. This time all was peace and decorum, if not love and harmony.

Waltheof had been present at both ceremonies, the first time as a full hostage, his breath emerging as white vapour in the stark winter chill and his blood freezing as the houses burned. Now, still under Norman scrutiny but free of his leash, he witnessed the transformation of William's duchess into a queen. The green scent of May filled the air and touched his heart with optimism. Spring was burgeoning around him. Matilda herself was fecund, her belly swelling with the child conceived in Normandy shortly before William's departure. Perhaps now all would be well. He imagined Judith as his wife, her own womb ripe with a child of their mingled blood, English, Dane and Norman. The thought warmed him and he glanced to where she stood in attendance behind the new queen, her eyes modestly downcast. Her dark braids were glossy, reflecting the candle flicker, and crowned by a veil of gossamer silk. She would be his own queen, he thought, and he would cherish her all of her days. She would lack for nothing, least of all his love.

As if sensing his scrutiny, she looked up. The slightest flush tinged her cheeks and the almost curve of her lips sent a flash of desire through him. His own smile in return was bright and warm.

'You seek audience with me, Waltheof?' William beckoned his visitor to enter his private chamber and with another flick of his fingers dismissed the guard.

'Sire.' Waltheof bowed and advanced into the room, his footfalls crackling softly on the new green rushes that strewed the floor. William was seated in a chair before a charcoal brazier that had been lit to take the evening chill from the room. Two fawn hunting dogs lay at his feet. Both had been dozing, but now they raised their heads to watch Waltheof's approach.

Queen Matilda sat across from him, some embroidery in her lap. Here in the private chamber she had removed her wimple and her sandy-blonde hair hung to her waist in two thick braids woven with ribbons of blue silk. Her rounded belly pushed against the fabric of her gown.

'Sit.' William indicated a folding stool with a leather seat. Waltheof did so. The stool was too small for his great frame and he hunched over uncomfortably. Matilda looked at him and he thought he detected a gleam of sympathy in her gaze, perhaps even a twitch of humour. He fondled the head of the nearest dog and it beat its tail on the rushes.

'Wine.' A clap of William's hands brought a lad from the corner of the room where he had been burnishing the Duke's helm.

'Sire.' With a show of great dignity Simon de Senlis poured wine into two drinking horns and offered the Queen a daintier goblet.

Although he felt sick with apprehension, Waltheof managed to find an encouraging wink for the boy and something approaching a smile. 'I see that you are training your chamberlain's son to follow in his footsteps,' he said.

William grunted. 'He's a good worker,' he conceded. 'I

take on merit as much as breeding.' He nodded to Simon in dismissal and the boy returned to his work. The limp was noticeable but controlled. 'I know that you take an interest in him, my lord. Be assured that his talents will grant him a permanent position in my service.'

'I am glad, sire.' Waltheof took a swallow of the wine and almost coughed as it slipped down his parched throat. William was looking at him expectantly. Waltheof knew how impatient he was with petitioners who did not come straight to the point.

'Sire,' he began, paused to cough again into his clenched fist, and made himself speak. 'You have shown much favour to me in vouchsafing my lands and granting me permission to dwell on them . . .'

'But you want more . . .' William said. His dark stare was hooded and impassive.

'Sire, I . . .' Stumbling would not help his cause. William would see it as weakness. Waltheof thrust out his jaw. 'Sire, I ask your permission for the right to take your niece Judith to wife.'

William neither spoke nor moved but studied him with the eyes of a hawk. Beneath the scrutiny, Waltheof felt as vulnerable as prey in the grass.

It was Matilda who broke the terrible silence. Leaning forward, she fixed him with a gaze no less piercing than her husband's. 'Has my niece endorsed your suit, Lord Waltheof?'

'She has, madam . . . but within the bounds of propriety,' he added hastily as he saw her expression grow pinched.

'One contradicts the other, my lord,' Matilda said severely. 'If my niece has given you encouragement of any kind, she has been very foolish.'

'No more encouragement than to say that I should seek your permission if I desire to court her.'

'And why should you "desire" to court her?' William's voice was quiet but terrifying. 'Because the sight of her inflames your lust, or because the thought of marrying into my bloodline inflames the lust of your ambition?'

Waltheof's complexion darkened. 'It is naught of lust or ambition,' he declared in a congested voice, furious that William was making his motives sound obscene and grasping.

'Then you should have been a monk indeed,' William retorted. 'All men are driven by their lusts and their ambitions. All men,' he repeated, thumping his chest to emphasise the point. 'It cannot be love, since you do not know the girl well . . . unless of course you are lying to me, and you and she have been conducting a liaison behind everyone's back.'

'I do not lie, sire,' Waltheof said, feeling increasingly angry and humiliated. 'I came to you in honesty and good faith to seek your permission.'

William's eyes narrowed. 'I have given you much, Waltheof Siwardsson. Do not strain the bounds of my generosity. You have my leave to go.'

'Will you tell me why you will not give your consent?' Waltheof's voice was hoarse with the effort of control. A red mist edged his vision.

'You would be wise not to push me,' William growled. 'Suffice to say that I have already been more than generous to you, my lord. You ask for too much.'

'So seeking your niece in marriage is too much?' Waltheof's upper lip curled back on a sneer. 'Is my English blood not to your taste?'

William looked him coldly up and down. 'It is naught of blood,' he said. 'But of merit and suitability. That is my last word on the matter. I hope I do not have to summon my guards.'

Waltheof clenched his fists. Some final thread of self-preservation prevented him from using them. Turning on his heel he managed to leave the room with a modicum of tattered dignity, but once outside in the cold corridor he smashed his knuckles against the wall, tearing the skin, bruising to the bone, and let out a roar of anguish and rage so wild that it might have belonged to the white bear whose pelt lined his cloak.

'Last word!' he snarled in English. 'I will ram his last word down his throat until it chokes him!'

He strode into the hall where folk were preparing to bed down for the night. Waltheof should have been amongst them; he had his own sleeping space near the dais. Already members of his retinue were rolling out cloaks and blankets. 'Do not bother,' Waltheof snapped. 'We are not staying.'

'My lord earl?' His shieldbearer Hakon looked up at him in surprise.

'Go and tell my grooms to saddle our horses. We're leaving.'

'But . . .'

'But nothing!' Waltheof snarled. 'Do it!'

Waltheof's behaviour was so out of character that Hakon stood his ground. 'My lord, there is a curfew. No man may go abroad after dark, and the horses are bedded down for the night. Should we not wait until dawn?'

'I have William's leave to go,' Waltheof ground out. 'I will not stay a moment longer than I must.'

Still Hakon hesitated. He was almost twenty years older than Waltheof and had known his father well and served him with loyalty. Such credentials gave him the leeway to ask, 'Does this bode ill for us? Have you quarrelled with him?' He looked pointedly at Waltheof's bleeding knuckles.

Waltheof swallowed, his restraint precarious. 'No to both questions,' he said in a choked voice. 'I'll tell the grooms myself. See that everyone else gets the order.'

Without giving Hakon further opportunity to argue, Waltheof strode out.

The air was moist and mild, a night for lovers. A night for fools. Cursing, Waltheof drew deep breaths filled with the almond scent of May blossom. Perhaps at the back of his mind he had known that William would refuse. Perhaps that was what had made him hold back for so long. Without having the brutality of the answer, it had been possible to dream. He knew in his heart that Judith would not fight the decision. Her uncle's word was the rule by which she lived, and, although she was strong-willed, that will was devoted to serving her family.

The red tide of his fury and disappointment dissipated in the gentle, scented air, leaving a weight of dull misery. Sucking on his grazed knuckles, Waltheof turned towards the stables. The grooms came sleepily from their loft, and with looks askance and much wordless grumbling kindled lanterns and set about the task of harnessing the mounts belonging to Waltheof's entourage.

Waltheof set about saddling Copper, his chestnut. It gave him something to do other than wallow in dark thoughts. His work was interrupted by the sound of rustling from a nearby stall, and on investigation, he discovered his skald and Judith's maid Sybille lying in a lover's nest of piled straw. Her light brown hair tumbled around her shoulders in disarray and her lips were red and kiss-swollen.

Usually Waltheof would have laughed, but tonight all humour had flown. 'Does your mistress know where you are?' he demanded roughly.

Sybille faced him squarely. 'No, my lord, and there is no reason to tell her since it is no concern of hers.' She tugged her gown back over her shoulders.

'It would be if she knew. You do her reputation no good by sullying your own.' He scowled at Thorkel, who was looking at him with wounded astonishment. 'I am going home to Huntingdon tonight. Go or stay as you choose.' He led his chestnut out of the stall into the open air. Christ, it was so easy for them, the minstrel and the maidservant. Envy was a crimson wire in his chest.

The grooms were swiftly harnessing other beasts and his men were beginning to arrive from the hall with their travelling satchels and accoutrements. No one spoke, but their expressions were eloquent.

From his eye corner, Waltheof saw Thorkel murmur to Sybille before the girl slipped away through the darkness.

'William refused you then?' the skald asked, coming to Waltheof's side.

'It is none of your business.'

'When you are an earl, it is everyone's business,' Thorkel contradicted, his words dovetailing with Waltheof's thoughts of a moment since. 'Whatever has caused your anger, it will be all over Westminster come the morrow.'

'Well, I won't be here to listen,' Waltheof snapped. He glared at Thorkel. 'William says that he has shown me enough favour. He says that I fail on merit and suitability.' He spat the last word as if it were poison.

'Ah,' said Thorkel.

'And since he is of that opinion, I am not inclined to stay.'

'You do not believe he will change his mind in time?' Thorkel asked. 'Sometimes when men have surprises sprung upon them, they react as though they have been thrown a live rat.'

'I doubt that William will change his mind between night and day,' Waltheof said bleakly. 'Better for us both if I leave.' He glowered at the Icelander. 'Stay if you wish. I am sure that Lady Judith's maid will continue to give you all the "comfort" you need.'

Thorkel shook his head and smiled wryly. 'Mistress Sybille is indeed engaging, but I have no mind to stay at court. Doubtless Earl Edwin or Morcar would offer me places in their retinues, but I would rather ride with you to Huntingdon than dwell in lust and luxury here.'

Slightly mollified, Waltheof gave a brusque nod. 'As you wish,' he said and swung into the saddle.

Overlooked in his corner, Simon had hardly dared to rub the oiled cloth over the surface of the helm lest the slight sound recall his presence to William and Matilda. Moments ago the King had summoned an older squire and sent him to fetch Judith. The air bristled like the atmosphere on the edge of a thunderstorm. Something bad was going to happen.

'Did you know about this attraction?' William demanded.

His wife shook her head. 'If I did, I would have quashed it at once,' she said. 'And I am sure that Adelaide would have done so too. I know she was in Earl Waltheof's debt for saving Judith from that bolting horse in Fécamp – we all were – but it went no further than that.'

'Quite obviously it did,' William contradicted grimly.

'Certainly not in my sight,' his wife said on an indignant note. 'Adelaide is the most conscientious of mothers – you know she is. It could be that Waltheof has overstated his case – perhaps mistaken a word in passing as proof of a deeper interest.'

William grunted and chewed on a thumbnail. 'Perhaps,' he said sceptically.

In his corner Simon remembered the clandestine meetings that had taken place between Judith and Waltheof in Fécamp. The tales he could tell if he chose. Almost as if fearing the words would spill out of their own accord, he tightened his lips.

'So you would not consider a match between Waltheof and Judith at all?' Matilda asked into the heavy silence. 'Do you truly believe that he is unsuitable?'

William stared into the brazier and said nothing for a time. Then he looked at his wife. 'Waltheof is young and rash – acts before he thinks. I like him, but he is untried in battle and in diplomacy. His heart rules his head, and that is not a good trait for a man of authority.'

'Indeed not . . . my lord.' Matilda's voice held a note of amused irritation and Simon was surprised to hear William chuckle gruffly in response.

'I do my best to hide my single weakness,' he said. 'And I am glad that you aid and abet me.'

'And if I did not?'

'I think you know the answer.'

There was another silence, ended by a knock on the chamber door.

'Enter!' William raised his voice to command, thereby sparing Simon the need to rise and show himself.

A guard opened the door and ushered Judith, her mother and her stepfather into the room. Judith was as white as a new cheese. Adelaide looked impatient and irritated, Eudo of Champagne bewildered.

'Why have you sent for me at this late hour?' Adelaide demanded of her brother, and gave him such a perfunctory obeisance that it was almost an insult.

William gestured her to a bench positioned near the brazier. 'Perhaps you should ask your daughter that question.'

Adelaide refused the offer of a seat and her gaze darted between William and Judith. 'I do not know what you mean.'

Leaving her mother's side, Judith knelt before her uncle. 'Waltheof of Huntingdon has asked your permission to seek me in marriage, hasn't he?' she said.

'What?' Adelaide's voice started low and finished on a new octave. Her eyes widened. Leaving her astonished husband, she crossed the room and stood over her daughter. 'Have you been conniving with him behind my back?'

'Peace, Adelaide.' William raised his right hand, palm outwards. 'Since it has reached my ears, let me be the one to deal with it now.'

Dusky colour heated her cheeks. She prided herself on running an orderly household and her brother's terse comment suggesting that she had been lax was galling. 'If you have brought shame on this house, I will see you confined to a nunnery,' she hissed at Judith.

Judith swallowed and raised her chin. 'I have done nothing of which to be ashamed.'

William narrowed his lids. 'And yet you knew without my speaking of the reason why I have sent for you. Does that not suggest that you and the Earl of Huntingdon have already made your own arrangements?'

Judith held her uncle's gaze. It was the hardest thing she had ever had to do. She knew that if she relaxed her spine for one moment, she would melt in a boneless heap of terror.

'There were no arrangements, sire,' she said, and wondered what Waltheof had said to William. Waltheof had no skill at dissembling. She could only pray that he had not mentioned that interlude in Fécamp.

'So why should he come to me with hope in his eyes?' William demanded.

Judith gazed at him mutely, not knowing what to say.

'Answer me, or by God, I will indeed do as your mother suggests and see you closeted in a nunnery!' William thundered, slamming his fist on his thigh.

'I . . . .' She chewed her lip. 'I know that Waltheof had a certain regard for me, but I did not encourage him. He . . . he did broach the subject of marriage and I said that he would have to approach you . . .'

'And how long ago was this?'

'He first spoke of the matter in Normandy. I thought perhaps he had forgotten, but when I saw him again he said that he still intended to seek your permission . . .' She clasped her hands together until the knuckles showed white. 'I have kept my distance and obeyed my duty.'

William grunted. 'And if I had agreed to his request, what would you have said?'

Adelaide spluttered, the sound declaring without words what she thought of the notion.

'I would have been bound by the decree of your will, whatever your decision, sire,' Judith murmured and felt herself wilting beneath the blaze of his stare.

'So you have no especially fond regard for Waltheof of Huntingdon?'

She bit her lip. 'I am grateful to him for saving my life.'

'But it goes no deeper than that.'

'No, sire.'

There was a long and thoughtful pause. 'It seems then,' William said at last, 'that the young man was building a mountain out of no more than a heap of soil. I do not doubt your virtue, niece, but I hope you will not make a habit of sending me young men with whom you have passing acquaintance to ask for you in marriage.'

'I did not know what else to do,' Judith said.

'Well, the dilemma is easily solved,' Adelaide spoke out angrily. 'From this day forth you do not leave the confines of the bower lest I be at your side.'

Judith was not quite swift enough to conceal a grimace and Adelaide seized upon it. 'Yes, my girl, I have clearly been too lax with you, and that slut of a maid is no protection.'

'I have done nothing wrong,' Judith reiterated, and pushed from her mind the remembrance of being kissed and kissing back at the foot of the stairs in Fécamp.

'Let matters rest, Adelaide,' William said. 'Waltheof has either left the court or is leaving on the morrow, and I made the situation plain to him. He knows I will grant him no further privileges above those that he has. Judith has received her warning. I know she will be more cautious in future.'

'So will I,' Adelaide said grimly, and Judith's heart sank.

As Judith followed her mother and stepfather to the door there was a clatter behind them. Whirling round Judith saw young Simon de Senlis picking up the banner that his elbow had dislodged and sent tumbling. Judith met the youth's fox-brown eyes and saw the knowledge in them. If he spoke even half of what he knew the scandal would burn her alive. She thought that she could trust him, but she was not certain. At least he was fond of Waltheof. Blurting out his knowledge would not help his hero's cause. She could only hope he was more discreet than she had been.

As the door closed, William beckoned to Simon. 'I have no need to tell you that what goes forth in these chambers is not to be discussed outside that door,' he said tersely.

'No, your grace.' Simon returned William's dark stare before looking down as custom demanded. 'I know when to hold my tongue.'

William's mouth twitched. 'And when to be as quiet as a mouse so that you are overlooked,' he said.

Simon flashed a glance from beneath his brows, so innocent that William's almost-smile became a grunt of
amusement. 'I hope that you have not been paying so much
attention to your ears that you have neglected your other
duties,' he said and held out his hand. 'Bring me that helm.'

Simon duly fetched the King's helm from the corner where
he had been oiling and burnishing it. The metal shone with
all the colours of the forge, an iridescent bloom of blue-gold
on the iron surface.

William examined the work and nodded with thoughtful
satisfaction. 'Large ears, quick hands, a close mouth. It seems,
young man, that you will go far.'

Simon reddened with pleasure.

'The trick is, of course,' William said, still turning the
helm in his hands, 'to know when to stop.'

'Who is Waltheof of Huntingdon?' Eudo of Champagne
demanded of his wife. His stepdaughter had retired to her pallet,
pleading a headache, and Adelaide had let her go without demur
– more, he thought, from wanting her out of the way than from
compassion. They were standing together in a corner of the hall.
It was draughty away from the braziers, but relatively private.

'You must have seen him,' she said impatiently. 'The tall
one with the red hair and white bearskin cloak.'

'Ah, yes.' Eudo nodded with a slight narrowing of his eyes.
'A friend of Ralf de Gael of Norfolk to judge from the manner
they were laughing together.'

Adelaide sniffed disparagingly. 'They are of an ilk,' she
said, 'and neighbours.'

Eudo's lips twitched. His wife obviously had a wasp in her
wimple over the Earl of Huntingdon. 'Whoever knew a tall
man who was wise or a red-haired one who was faithful?' He
flippantly quoted the old proverb.

'Precisely,' Adelaide snapped. 'And it is no cause for
amusement.'

Eudo grimaced. His wife had brought him the prestige of

an alliance with the house of Normandy but she was a shrew of the highest order. Putting her in her place was not an option when her brother was Duke of Normandy and King of England.

'Has Judith truly been indiscreet with him?' he asked.

'Enough to form an attraction, but not sufficient to cause a scandal. However, I should have been more vigilant. There are always foxes prowling around the henhouse in search of a victim.'

'I do not doubt your vigilance.' Eudo gazed across the hall at William's three sons, who were chasing each other boisterously in and out of the aisles of the hall. Queen Matilda was swelling with yet another pregnancy. All he had thus far of his own marriage were two stepdaughters resembling their mother and the prestige of the bond with the house of Normandy. It would be a fine thing to set a son in his wife's womb. She was not barren, just reluctant. Perhaps a new child would lessen her intensity over her daughters too.

'What of this Waltheof's lands? If he is an earl, might not the match be suitable?'

'You would see your stepdaughter wed to an ignorant Viking?' Adelaide's bosom heaved with indignation.

Eudo shrugged. He was not going to remind his wife that her own mother was the daughter of a common tanner. That would have been tantamount to treason. 'I would see her content,' he said.

Adelaide gave him a scathing look. 'I doubt that Judith could be content with such a man,' she said glacially. 'He has no sense of what is fitting.'

'But she would be a countess. Mayhap we should investigate how large and prosperous his earldom is.'

His wife raised a scornful eyebrow. 'We can do better for her than Waltheof of Huntingdon.'

Eudo nodded, appearing to concede the point, but he was not taken in by her dismissal of the notion. There had definitely been a spark of interest in her eyes. He was a patient man and the notion of adding an English earldom to his family's concerns was an attractive one.

Across the hall there was a loud commotion as William's eldest sons Robert and Richard caught their brother Rufus, flung him to the ground and sat on him while Robert de Bêlleme attempted to stuff floor rushes into the victim's mouth.

Eudo watched the ensuing struggle with folded arms and did not attempt to intervene. He was fond of the older boys, who were high-spirited, boisterous youths, but he had never been able to warm towards the third son. William was considering Rufus for the Church and the boy was being educated at Saint Stephen's in Caen, although he had been released from his lessons to come to England and see his mother made queen. Rufus was a plump, unprepossessing child with sandy-white hair and lashes that put Eudo in mind of a pig. He seemed to squeal like one most of the time too.

'Christ, someone send that boy back to the cloister,' muttered Robert of Mortain, coming to join Eudo and Adelaide. 'He screams like a girl.'

Eudo gave a pained smile of agreement. Robert of Mortain was a maternal half-brother to William and Adelaide. Eudo did not particularly like him, but he respected him, and they shared antipathy towards their youngest nephew. Both were content to stand by and watch his brothers bounce on him as though he were a cushion while De Bêlleme attempted to prise open Rufus' tightly clenched jaw.

However, someone else was willing to step in. One of William's senior pages, who was passing through the hall carrying two sharpened spears, approached the fracas, stooped, and murmured to the bullies. Looking irritated and petulant, they got off Rufus and let him go, although De Bêlleme gave him a sharp kick in the ribs. The older youths swaggered from the hall, leaving their victim choking and blubbering on the floor. The page stooped to comfort Rufus and after a moment helped him to his feet.

Mortain lost interest and turned away. 'If he cannot fight his own battles now, he will never amount to anything,' he growled.

Eudo nodded agreement and turned away too. He had promised to buy Adelaide some gold strap ends for a girdle she was weaving, and he could tell from the look in her eyes that she was growing impatient.

Gasping for breath, his complexion blotched, Rufus looked up at his saviour. 'Did my father really want to see them?'

Simon shook his head. 'No, my lord, but it seemed the best way of stopping them without provoking a fight.'

'You should have st . . . st . . . stuck them in the ribs,' Rufus said, his grey-flecked eyes bright with vehemence and tears. 'They'll be after y . . . you when they realise you've tricked them.' He dragged his sleeve across his nose, leaving a slimy trail on his cuff.

Simon shrugged. 'I can take care of myself,' he said with more confidence than he felt. He had no particular fear of William's older sons, but Robert de Bêlleme was a different cauldron of pottage entirely. 'Best not linger here though. I'm going to the armoury to get these spear tips honed – if you want to come?'

Rufus nodded. 'Thank you,' he said. 'I won't forget this.' Giving another loud sniff he extended his hand to Simon. His fingers were heavy and soft to the touch, still clammy with the cold sweat of fear and struggle, but Simon betrayed not a twitch of distaste. He knew what it was like to be viewed as flawed. Rufus might stammer, might be an ugly and clumsy child, but for all his awkwardness he had a swift brain and a generous heart. If he said that he would not forget, then it was true – both in matters of friendship and enmity. His elder brothers, for all their outward strength and boasting, did not have the staying power of a pair of grasshoppers.

Companionably, side by side, one lame, the other walking with his customary wallow, they headed towards the armoury, and Rufus insisted on carrying one of the spears.

CHAPTER 9

The fenland stretched away to the horizon, grasses bleached to shades of gold by the blaze of the early September sun, the meres and pools glinting like eyes as they caught the light. The song of reed warblers drenched the air and flies hovered in the ripples of heat rising from the reeds and sedges. Through the shimmer Waltheof watched Crowland Abbey's herd of white cows graze the rich pasture. Autumn might be on the horizon, but it was still no more than a distant speck and the sun still had power to burn.

'You are content, my son?'

Sweeping his hair off his brow, Waltheof studied the small monk standing at his side. Abbot Ulfcytel looked no older than he had done fifteen years ago when Waltheof had entered the noviciate, but he must be at least three score by now. The monk's skin was still smooth, and, although the existing lines had deepened with time, there were remarkably few new ones.

'I wish I could say that I was,' Waltheof said. 'Indeed, I sometimes wish that I were one of those cows with naught to concern me but grazing the meadow.'

'You would still be bedevilled by the flies, my son,' Ulfcytel said, 'and before winter you would likely face the poleaxe.'

Waltheof sighed. 'You are right,' he conceded. 'I do not suppose that life as an ox would be much different to the life I lead now . . . although perhaps less knowledge would be a boon. I know I should have the grace to accept what is to be, but recently I have found it hard to come by.'

Ulfcytel said nothing and turned back the way they had come, following the dusty path towards the cool, grey stone of the abbey. Waltheof paced beside him. Usually a visit to Crowland and time spent with Ulfcytel would settle his restlessness – like the hand of a ploughmaster on the yoke of a favoured ox, he thought wryly. But today there had been no such peace. News had arrived that precluded such a possibility.

Since returning to his lands, he had visited the monastery often, a part of him yearning for the spiritual grace that had been his as a young oblate learning his Psalter at Ulfcytel's knee. That yearning was strong today. For two pins he would have exchanged his rich tunic for a simple Benedictine habit.

'All around me I see people struggling beneath William's yoke,' he said as they toiled along the path, the late summer's blaze making their limbs heavy and bringing a glisten of sweat to their brows. 'And I do nothing. I bury my head, I feign ignorance.'

Ulfcytel made a sound of acknowledgement and doubt. 'Has your own lot been difficult?' he asked. 'Are your people not contented and your lands peaceful?'

Waltheof grimaced. 'It is true that my lands are peaceful,' he said, 'and that my lot has been easier than many. But the King's hand is heavy. It seems to me that he takes all and gives very little back.'

'But if you rise against him and you fail, it may be that he will take all and give nothing at all back,' Ulfcytel warned. 'Others have tried and failed this last year, have they not?'

Waltheof paused to look at the abbey buildings. The church was dedicated to Saint Guthlac, and had been raised above the marshy ground on oak pilings with additional soil brought from Upton, nine miles away. While his gaze admired the toil of man in the cause of God's glorification, he pondered the Abbot's cautionary words.

Filled with discontent, Edwin and Morcar had fled the court and tried to raise rebellion but William had dealt with the uprising as easily as swatting a couple of flies. Once again the brothers were hostages at court and castles were being built in the English heartlands to quash any further notions of revolt. Edwin was still being promised a royal bride, but Waltheof thought the Earl of Mercia had little chance of seeing that promise kept. The Normans appeared to think that English husbands were not good enough for their daughters – or nieces.

'Edgar Atheling has made his escape to the Scots court with his mother and sisters,' he said.

The older man exhaled heavily. 'And so could you, if that was your desire, but I do not think that it is. If you stay here then you must accept the burdens laid upon you by the Normans. Complaint will only turn you sour.'

Waltheof's lips twitched. 'You mean either shit or leave the privy.'

A down-to-earth, unaffected man, Ulfcytel was unperturbed by the robust language. 'That is exactly what I mean. It is no use bemoaning your lot. Either accept it or change it.'

Waltheof experienced a rush of affection for the small monk. 'That is why I came to speak to you. I have had news today and I do not know what to do with it. I need your advice.'

'Ah,' said Ulfcytel, rubbing his jaw where tiny spikes of silver stubble glinted in the sunlight. 'I thought there was more to this visit than the spare time a man has when the harvest is all but gathered in.'

'A messenger came to Huntingdon two nights ago,' Waltheof said. 'From Earl Gospatric in the North Country.'

'Ah,' said Ulfcytel again, rubbing hard enough to make a rasping sound.

'King Sweyn of Denmark has sent his fleet into the Humber – two hundred and forty ships filled with warriors ready to fight the Normans.'

'And you want my advice whether to join him or abstain?' Ulfcytel saw the eagerness and doubt written clearly in the young man's deep blue eyes and was troubled.

Waltheof folded his arms, tucking his hands into his armpits as if resisting temptation, but a moment later he lowered them and clutched at the hilt of his dagger. 'It is perhaps the last chance Englishmen will ever have to be rid of the Normans. My father was a Dane; I have blood ties with the men in those ships. I do not believe I would have stirred from my lands for the sons of Harold Godwinsson, but this is different. I can almost smell victory on the air.'

'To a man of the Church, victory and defeat both smell suspiciously of blood and burning,' Ulfcytel said, turning round to look at the peaceful scene they had just left.

Waltheof turned too, but his gaze looked inwards. 'If I go north and lend my arm to the uprising, perhaps I will be able to regain all the lands that my father held and that the Godwinssons denied to me.'

'Morcar might have something to say about that,' Ulfcytel said.

'Morcar does not have the advantage of my tie with the Danes.'

Ulfcytel shook his head. 'I think, my son, that whatever I say will make no difference to you, for you have set your mind, and rather than asking me for advice you have come to tell me of your intention to join this uprising.'

'You disapprove?'

'I disapprove of all warfare,' Ulfcytel replied. 'The Norman king has proven himself repeatedly in battle. You came to me with your nightmares of what you witnessed at Exeter. Has it all faded from your mind so swiftly?'

'No,' Waltheof said grimly. 'It has remained with me every waking moment.'

'Then why risk the same happening to your own lands?'

'Because I stood back at Hastings. Because the Danes and the English are my people – not the Normans. Because . . .'

He made a gesture to show that he could not explain what he was feeling.

'Because your heart rules your mind,' Ulfcytel said almost sorrowfully, 'it has always been so.'

'Surely a man must be guided by what is in his heart?'

'But curbed by the rein of his reason,' Ulfcytel said, feeling deeply saddened. The young man would join the Danes whatever he said, and march with them because they were 'his people', because kinship mattered when kin were few.

'Father, will you give me your blessing?' Waltheof went down on his knees in the dust before Ulfcytel and bowed his head, his copper hair falling forward to expose the tender white nape of his neck. The sight reminded the Abbot of how much a boy Waltheof still was – and likely would be all of his life.

Gently, with a paternal ache in his heart, Ulfcytel laid his hands upon Waltheof's sun-hot hair. 'God be with you,' he said softly, 'and bring you through all trials with grace.'

Fires twinkled in the night, hundreds of them, lighting the spread of the Danish army and the English who had flocked to their banners. The surface of the River Humber seethed with longships, lanterns lighting the carved prows and sending shimmers of gold across the dark water.

Drunk on mead, camaraderie and hope, Waltheof feasted with the sons of King Sweyn of Denmark and roared death to the Normans with the rest of them. These men were his kin. He recognised himself in their joyful fierceness. Here he did not have to be abstemious and guard his tongue. Here he did not have to curb his laughter. He arm-wrestled with Danish warriors and his strength was acclaimed. He was a true son of Siward Digerra, accepted, fêted and treated as a hero, not a green boy.

Come the morning the Danish army, its ranks swollen by Northumbrians and Scots, by the men of Holderness and Lindsey, by English rebels from every corner of England, would march on York, the old Norse capital of England. Hopes were high, and increased with each swallow of mead. The Normans would be driven from the land and their hated castles torn down.

Waltheof ceased drinking before he reached a state of helpless intoxication. He did not want to go mead-witted into battle on the morrow. While such a state might enhance his courage and daring, it would numb his responses. To go up against a sober Norman would be intense folly. The Danish leaders seemed to think the same way, for they curtailed the feasting early and commanded men to seek their slumber so that they would be ready to advance with the dawn.

Waltheof slept with his axe for company and thought that, had matters been different, he would be lying in a feather bed at Huntingdon with his dark-haired Norman wife at his side – perhaps even a child of their mingled blood in the cradle. The notion was too sweet and sad for a battle eve. He closed his eyes and prayed, the Latin words filling his head in drink-muddled snatches, echoing as if they were being chanted in a church.

He dreamed of battle, but instead of the physical effort of wielding his axe he was trying to muster arguments in his head. He found himself engaged in a contest of wits, but the more he racked his brains, the closer he came to defeat. He could hear himself shouting, and a woman's voice shrilling in furious reply. She had all the strength; he was powerless. As the argument drained him, she forced him to his knees and he saw that they were in a courtyard, surrounded by accusing faces, none of them friendly. On the edge of the crowd a child gazed at him out of solemn, dark-blue eyes. As he looked at her, she turned away and Waltheof knew that in some way he did not understand, he had failed her. He bent his head; there was a scything pain and then nothing.

He awoke in a cold sweat, his heart thundering and the sharpness of the pain transmuted into the dull assault of a drink-induced headache. The shouting continued outside of his dream, but there was no anger now, just the exhortations of men eager to march on York and drive the Normans out.

As the massed English and Dane army approached the city the smell of smoke gusted at them, reminding Waltheof of Exeter and turning his stomach. The scouts who had gone ahead reported that the captains of the Norman garrison had burned down the houses immediately in front of the castle so that the English would have to cross open ground in order to lay siege to the keep. The flames had spread from the initial burning and had engulfed much of the city, including the cathedral itself.

Waltheof gripped the haft of his axe and prayed as they advanced into York. Those townsfolk who had not fled hastened to join the invading army, cheering, waving brooms, pitchforks, or spears that had been kept well hidden in the rafters. Elation and pride roiled in Waltheof's belly and tears prickled his eyes, some the result of wind-blown smoke but most caused by the enthusiastic welcome. He was entering the city that had been the Norse capital of England for over two hundred years, a settlement that had been familiar to his father as Earl of Northumbria, and to his dead brother. Now their mantle was his and pride coursed through him with each beat of his heart.

A thick drift of smoke gusted across the advancing army and suddenly the cheers became screams and shouts of warning. The Norman commanders were sallying from the keep using a charge of cavalry and heavily armed soldiers to try to scatter the invaders.

Without warning, without time to realise and assimilate, Waltheof's section was confronted by a conroi of mounted Normans. Hakon screamed and went down beneath the trampling hooves and the thrust of a lance. The razored steel punched through his throat, killing him instantly. The knight withdrew the lance with a jerk of effort and turned on Waltheof.

Waltheof's mind ceased to function and instinct took over. As the spear thrust at him he brought up the axe, whirling it round and down to chop off the haft beneath the socket. The knight groped for his sword and Waltheof struck again, and again, his lungs filling with a howl of rage and denial. Horse and knight went down, and so did the footsoldier who ran to defend them. Waltheof licked his lips and tasted the saltiness of blood. The edge of his axe ran red, and he felt a terrible exhilaration. No more demonstrating his skills and strength for the paltry entertainment of his Norman captors. This was the reason why he had sweated on the training ground. This was *his* entertainment now, and when he had finished there would not be a single Norman left in the city of York.

Morning mist wove between the trees of the Gloucestershire forest in milky ribbons and a red sunrise filtered through the turning leaves. Simon rode his mount along the edge of the woodland, glad of his cloak, for although the day was set to be fair there was still a chill in the air this early. The King had decided upon a day's hunting and the court was gathering in preparation. He could hear the shouts of the kennel keepers calling the hounds to order and the boisterous laughter of men keen for a day's sport.

Simon was eager too. Since breaking his leg and enduring months of convalescence followed by the painful struggle to return to his duties, he valued such days as these. They allowed him to test himself to the limit, to force his will through the pain and keep up with or even exceed the other squires. In the saddle his handicap was minimal. He had to ride with his left foot at an odd angle in the stirrup, but he had learned to adjust to that, and the high pommel and cantle on the saddle gave him additional support. He was never going to make a jouster, but that did not matter. His slight, wiry build was meant for reconnaissance and scouting, for nimbleness and travelling light. Besides, to be a good battle commander Simon knew it was better to have an overview of the fighting rather than be in the thick of it.

He slackened the rein and let his pony pick its way along

the edge of the trees until they came to the track that led back
to the hunting lodge. William would want him soon to carry
his spear or hold his cloak.

Two gossiping women walked down the track towards the
lodge, carrying baskets filled with freshly picked fungi. Simon
eyed the bounty as they drew level. He was very fond of the
mushroom pasties that William's cook made when the ingredients were available. Served with wheaten bread and tart
blackberry sauce, there was no finer dish in the world.

Remembering the English that Waltheof had taught him,
he greeted the women pleasantly in their own language.

They looked at him, startled, muttered a response, and
heads lowered, wimples drawn across their faces, hurried past.

Simon was wounded, but not surprised at the rebuff. The
English had acknowledged William as their king, but grudgingly – because they were forced to do so. They yielded
deference with hatred in their eyes and it was not going to
change for the sake of a single greeting.

He turned his pony to follow the women. Behind him,
hooves thundered on the track and a messenger hurtled
towards the lodge on a sweat-foamed courser. The man
bellowed at the women to get out of his way and they leaped
for their lives with screams of shock. A basket went flying,
scattering mushrooms far and wide. One of the women shook
her fist at the horseman's dust and cursed him. Then her gaze
fixed on Simon and her voice fell to a low mutter.

Abruptly Simon reined his pony about and galloped in the
messenger's wake. He could feel the women's glares burning
his back and knew that they were calling him a Norman
whoreson.

The messenger had dismounted outside the hunting lodge
and was on his knees before William. Simon arrived in time
to see the King's brows draw together and his colour begin
to darken in response to what was being said. In the three
years since Simon had come to court he had never seen
William in a rage. Angry on occasion, but always a cold

anger, held down with iron control. William was scorching now, though, his complexion purple.

'It is true, sire,' the messenger panted, his head bowed and sweat dripping from his forelock. 'The North has risen against your rule. The Danes have anchored in the Humber and marched upon York. Lord Malet begs that you come with all haste.' He coughed and someone stepped forward with a cup of wine that the hunters had been drinking. The messenger took several grateful gulps.

'All the North?' William repeated. His own voice was dry and husky, but when he too was offered wine he waved it aside.

'Maersweyn, Gospatric, Edgar Atheling,' the messenger said, 'and Waltheof of Huntingdon. It was he who led them into York, and he and his men who caused the most damage. North of the Humber there are naught but English and Danes.'

Simon's stomach plummeted. He had been hoping to visit Waltheof in his earldom. He had thought that Waltheof liked the Normans, that he was prepared to be part of their rule . . . but perhaps he too was like those women with their mushrooms, serving because he was forced and filled with secret hatred.

William's eyes had narrowed at the mention of Waltheof's name. 'Splendour of God!' he growled. 'Once and for all I will show the English who is their king, and I will write the lesson so large and in so much suffering that no one will be in any doubt!'

The hunt was abandoned; the hounds were returned to the kennels but the horses remained saddled. The messenger was ordered to change his mount, refresh himself and prepare to take to the road again with instructions to William's commanders.

Simon helped to load baggage wains with William's effects, which were to follow in the wake of the rapid cavalry advance. No concessions were made to Simon's disability and he fetched and carried with the rest of them. Stools, hangings, caskets, lamps and candle prickets, trestle legs and boards, spare cups and flagons, a set of gaming counters and a tafel board. Then he aided the grooms harness the cobs to pull the wains and the pack ponies to carry more immediate supplies such as food and bedding and the royal tent. His leg ached ferociously, but he forced himself through the pain. If he stopped, he would have to think. Toiling like a demon helped to keep his anger and distress at bay.

As he struggled to load a sack of oats onto a pony's back, his arms burning with effort and his legs in danger of collapse, the load was taken from him by his father, who heaved it the rest of the way across the pack saddle.

'Ants work together,' said Richard de Rules, 'so why should you think you can do it all on your own?'

'I can manage,' Simon said defensively, but the exhausted tremor of his limbs gave his words the lie.

'So can we all, but a little help makes things easier. I've been watching you from a distance and you've been working like a slave with a whip at your back.' From his shoulder his father unslung a small leather costrel and handed it to his son.

Simon pulled out the stopper and drank. It was the King's best wine, potent and smooth. Usually the nearest he got to it was pouring it into goblets when he was on duty in the private chamber. The warmth of the drink burned into his stomach and fortified his limbs.

'What's wrong?' De Rules placed a perceptive hand on his son's taut shoulders.

Simon shook his head. 'Nothing.'

His father's gaze remained steady. 'It's Earl Waltheof, isn't it?'

Simon's eyes began to burn. He turned away to fiddle with a buckle on the pack pony's bridle. 'I thought that when Lord William refused him Lady Judith he would turn against us, but he didn't . . . he just went and stayed on his lands. So then I began to think everything was all right . . . and that I could go and visit him . . .'

De Rules sighed. 'Perhaps everything would have been all right if the Danes had not arrived,' he said. 'Even if the King had given Lady Judith to Waltheof, I do not know that he would have remained loyal. He is half Dane after all, and his father is buried in the city of York. His heart must surely lie in that direction.'

Simon shook his head. 'He is our enemy now.'

'Yes,' said his father gently. 'I am afraid that he is.'

CHAPTER 10

It was the shortest day of the year, and the darkest. Lowering clouds and heavy drizzle had drawn a dark curtain across the land, so that the space between dawn and dusk was little more than twilight.

In the antechamber of the Queen's apartments in Winchester, Judith directed a maidservant to lay more charcoal on the brazier. Rain spattered against the shutters like tiny stones. Over the hills of the North Country it would be falling as snow, she thought. They heard sporadic reports of the hard-fought skirmishes between her uncle's troops and the English and Danish rebels. Bitter, bloody, no quarter given. Reports said that all the land north of a town called Stafford was now a smoking, ravaged waste, that wherever her uncle went fire and sword were his terrible companions. There were rumours about Waltheof too. How he had slaughtered a hundred Normans single-handedly at York in a battle frenzy the equal of any berserker in a Norse saga. She had known that he had grudges to settle, but the depth and wildness of his rage had frightened her. Perhaps it was as well that she was not to be his wife.

From behind the closed door of the main chamber, Judith heard her mother give another low moan. The soothing voice of the midwife followed, with the sound of water splashing from pitcher to bowl.

'Surely the labour should not take as long as this.' Her

sister Adela moved from the window embrasure where she had been standing, supposedly spinning fleece, although there were scarcely two yards of thread wound onto the drop spindle from the distaff stuffed through her belt. 'Queen Matilda only took from matins to prime to birth Prince Henry, but Mama's been labouring twice as long as that.'

Judith shrugged. 'I know not,' she said, her tone short because she was worried. The infant her mother was struggling to birth had been conceived during the coronation festivities, the result of deliberate strategy. Eudo had said that he was entitled to try to beget an heir. Adelaide, a stickler for duty, had been forced to agree, and in her forty-first year, with daughters old enough for marriage, had found herself with child again. Throughout the pregnancy she had been ill. Judith and Adela had done as much fetching and carrying as the maids, massaging their mother's swollen legs and feeding her slivers of expensive imported ginger to aid her querulous digestion.

'What if she dies?' Adela's lower lip quivered.

Judith rubbed her hands together. In spite of the fresh building of charcoal, the sealed shutters and the two gowns she wore over her undershift, she was cold. 'She won't die,' she said. 'The midwives would have sent for the priest by now if that was the case, and Sybille would have been out to us. Don't you dare start snivelling!'

'I'm not.' Adela inhaled deeply and folded her arms beneath her breasts in a defensive gesture.

Judith folded her arms too, keeping herself to herself, even though she could tell that Adela wanted the comfort of a hug.

A fresh burst of rain peppered the shutters and the wind rattled the catch so hard that for a moment it seemed that the wild afternoon would burst into the room. The wind died, and in the lull that followed a baby's wail pierced the heavy wooden door between the main chamber and anteroom. Thin as a reed, sharp as an awl.

The girls stared towards the sound, transfixed. Judith's stomach churned. The door flung open and Sybille came out to them, her face flushed as if she had been labouring too and her sleeves pushed back up her wrists. 'You have a brother,' she announced with a wide smile. 'A fine boy.' She stood aside so they could enter the birthing chamber.

Adelaide was propped against a pile of bolsters in the great bed. Her dark brown hair, usually secured in two tight braids, was loose around her shoulders, since to have any bindings or knots in the birthing chamber might have impeded the delivery. A statue of Saint Margaret, patron saint of women in labour, stood in a niche, candles burning either side of her image. Swaddled in Adelaide's arms was a small, pucker-faced bundle with a quiff of golden hair.

Adelaide looked up at her daughters. There were bruised smudges beneath her eyes and her lips were bloody where she had bitten them in her attempt not to give vent to her pain. But beneath the suffering there was glittering triumph and a love that was as fierce as fire, a love that had never kindled for the labour of bearing female children. Seeing that look, Judith was filled with a huge and jealous resentment. It took every ounce of her determination to approach the bed and look at the newborn intruder.

'How is he to be named?' she asked.

'Stephen – it is one favoured by Eudo's line,' Adelaide said. 'Let the best wine kegs be broached and let everyone drink a cup to honour his birth. I trust you to see to it.' Her gaze swept briefly over Judith then dropped again to the new treasure of her son.

Adela leaned over her baby half-brother and extended a forefinger so that he curled his minute hand around it. 'He's beautiful,' she said, her expression utterly besotted.

Judith's stomach heaved at the betrayal. 'I'll do it now, Mother,' she said in a choked voice, and fled the stench of the birthing chamber before she was sick.

Seated on his campstool, Waltheof listened to the mourning of gulls and drew his bearskin cloak around him, seeking warmth and knowing that the gesture was fruitless. The cold came from within and had little to do with the bone deep-chill of the January morning outside his tent. No longer did the fire of battle burn through his bones. The conflagration had been too fierce, too intense to last, and Waltheof did not have the nature for coddling a flame once the initial blaze had died down.

York had fallen. That part had been bright and glorious, although he could remember little enough of the battle. They said that he had fought like a hero; that it was as if the great Earl Siward himself had returned to wreak vengeance on the Normans who had dared to violate his slumber. Thorkel had composed stirring battle songs to honour Waltheof's prowess: there had been huge rejoicing, and every man, woman and child in York had rushed to tear down the hated keeps that the Normans had erected to control the city. Those moments had been dazzling – a great blaze of triumph and exultation. The Norman usurpers would be driven from the land. Waltheof had been so certain, so sure, so filled with burning enthusiasm. Now it was all ashes blowing in the wind.

Rising from the campstool, he swept his lank hair off his brow and went outside into the chill morning air. A fine drizzle was falling, so cold that it was almost sleet and the land was lost in a misted grey haze. They should never have torn down the castles at York, he thought. It had been a mistake. They'd had no fortifications to bolster their position when William came raging to the North.

Allies had melted away like butter off a hot griddle. The Scots, the Northumbrians had plundered and scattered. The Danes had returned to their ships, feeding off the land like migrant geese but showing small commitment to stay and fight.

Toki brought him a cup of hot mead and Waltheof took it gratefully, holding the cup in his hands like a small heart. There had been no stopping William. Organised, determined, cold as iron, he had pushed northwards, destroying everything in his path. Waltheof was still ashamed that he had retreated, but there had been no alternative. The fortresses were burned, their army of its own volition scattering to gorge on the delights of victory and plunder. Whatever was visited upon them was their own fault.

They had heard terrible tales of William's wrath. That entire villages had been destroyed – the livestock slaughtered, the young men executed, so that never again would the North be able to rise in rebellion. On Christmas Day William had sent to Winchester for his regalia and had worn it in York's devastated ruins, setting the stamp of his rule upon the city.

Now, too late, Waltheof understood the true power of the man to whom he had given his oath of allegiance and then reneged. The ruthless, single-minded determination, the skills of leadership were beyond anything that the rebels could match. What use was personal courage against the inexorable force of disciplined Norman troops?

A figure emerged out of the mist – Earl Gospatric, lord of lands on the Scots borders. He and Waltheof had retreated together with each advance of William's army until now they were camped on the banks of the Tees, unsure of their next move. Toki brought mead for Gospatric too. The Earl took the cup, drank deeply and gazed morosely into the drizzle without speaking.

'We could take the road to Chester,' Waltheof volunteered after a moment.

'We could,' Gospatric said, but without any great enthusiasm. He knuckled red-rimmed eyes.

'Likely we would be safe there for the winter at least. I am told that the walls are well manned and strong.' The safety of Chester also happened to lie on the other side of the Pennine Mountains. A January crossing of the passes was a prospect that neither man relished, but it had to be considered. They did not have the resources to fight the Normans at this point unless they could muster their scattered army. And the likelihood of that was the same as the drizzle ceasing this side of the morrow.

They needed someone to tell them what to do, to imbue them with the fire and confidence they had possessed at York. He didn't have it; neither did Gospatric.

Their brooding was interrupted by the arrival of one of their scouts, who had been out reconnoitring the Norman position. Behind him, bearing a banner of truce, rode Richard de Rules and his two sons, Garnier and Simon.

Waltheof stared. Then he leaped to his feet and strode forward. His heart was hammering like a fist against his ribcage.

'My lord, I bid you welcome,' he cried and gestured a hovering soldier to take their horses.

De Rules dismounted. Although Waltheof had smiled at him, the Norman did not return the gesture, just inclined his head gravely, as did his eldest son. Simon's face was expressionless and he looked not at Waltheof but at the ground. Waltheof noticed that the boy dismounted smoothly and balanced himself well. A space at the back of his mind found time to wonder how many hours of practice that move had taken.

'You will drink mead?' Waltheof gestured towards his tent.

Again De Rules inclined his head. 'I am sorry to greet you in such circumstances,' he said as Waltheof led them into the relative dryness of the canvas shelter. Gospatric followed and dropped the flap.

'And I am too,' Waltheof responded. 'We hear grievous tales of the harm being visited upon the people of the North Country.' He turned to Simon and pointed to the cups and mead jug standing on the chest at the side of his camp bed. Wordlessly, eyes still downcast, the boy set about pouring drinks.

'A harm that they have brought upon themselves by giving succour to Danes and rebels,' De Rules said sharply.

Waltheof flashed him an angry glance. 'But Danes and rebels have more in common with these people than you Normans ever will. My own father is buried in Jorvik under the care of Saint Olaf, and its people abhor your keeps and your fortifications. They are symbols of captivity.' He had clenched his fists. Looking down at the skin stretched taut across his knuckles, he saw again the battleaxe in his hand and remembered the mingling of exhilaration and revulsion as he wielded it.

'They are symbols of the order that King William would bring to the land,' De Rules said softly. 'He will brook resistance from no one. You stand in his way not only at your peril, my lord, but at your death.'

Waltheof took the cup that Simon gave him and saw that despite his attempt at a neutral visage the boy was on the verge of being overwhelmed. He felt much the same way himself. 'I am not afraid to die,' he said.

De Rules' look pierced straight through the bravado. 'Then you are a fool, Waltheof of Huntingdon, and I speak as a friend now, and a man who is grateful for the gift of his son's life, not as my king's messenger. You should be afraid to die because you will be squandering more than just your life. You say you have heard what is happening to the people of the North because of their defiance. What then will happen to the people of your earldom? Under whose yoke will they be put to labour if you die? Your responsibility is to them first, not your own selfishness. You cannot hold out against William. He will cross the river with his army and you will retreat – where, to Chester?'

Waltheof stared at De Rules, his blood turning to ice.

'It is obvious,' the Norman said with an impatient gesture. 'The last English resistance is gathered there. William will advance and break it as surely as he has broken all defiance. Do not make the mistake of believing it impossible at this time of year. He is capable of moving mountains, let alone crossing them.'

'So what are you offering?' Gospatric spoke for the first time, his voice a dry whisper. He remained standing near the tent flap, as if ready to take flight.

De Rules took a drink of mead then rested the cup on his knee. 'The King will give you your lives and allow you to retain the lands you held when you swore your first oath of allegiance,' he said, 'but you must surrender to him now, and your surrender must be absolute.'

Waltheof exchanged glances with Gospatric.

'You will not find succour with the Danes,' De Rules added. 'William has bought their loyalty with gold. Those who have not taken it and sailed away are pinned down and dying even now beneath the swords of Mortain, Taillebois and Eudo of Champagne.' He shook his head. 'The Danes came like kites for plunder, and they mind not whether it comes from English or Norman pouches.'

'That is not true!' Waltheof was stung to retort.

'True or not, they are no longer here to back your cause. They have had their victory of battle and they have their plunder. Why should they stay to face a hard winter fighting the Normans when they can go home with their booty and feast in their own mead halls with their wives and bedmates?'

Waltheof rubbed his beard and suddenly felt as weary as an old man. Their cause was hopeless. The only spark of light was the fact that William had sent Richard de Rules to the parley and that he should have brought the lad with him – a sign that the road to discourse was still open.

'You can go home too,' De Rules murmured. 'All you need do is surrender to the King.'

Waltheof smiled grimly. 'This is my home,' he said. 'And William may indeed be the King, but that does not mean that this land will ever truly belong to him.'

The Normans took their leave shortly after that. Gospatric had departed to his own tent, but Waltheof accompanied De Rules and his sons to the horse lines. Simon had still not spoken beyond a monosyllable and his eyes had not met Waltheof's once.

'I know the reasons why you took up arms against the King,' De Rules said.

'Do you indeed?' Waltheof folded his arms across his body like a shield.

'Mayhap in your position I would have done the same.'

'And what would you do if you were in my position now?'

The Norman set his foot in the stirrup and swung his leg across the saddle. 'I would throw myself on the King's mercy and renew my oath of allegiance.' Gathering the reins, he rested his hands upon the carved pommel. 'William knows your reasons too,' he said. 'If your yielding is complete, he may be prepared to change his stance on certain matters.'

The words hit Waltheof like a punch in the gut, taking his breath. For a moment he could only stare, then somehow he managed to gather his scattered wits. 'And dangle me like Edwin of Mercia?' he snarled. 'You think I am so cheaply bought and sold?'

De Rules' horse plunged and circled and the knight swiftly shortened the rein. 'You saved my son's life. I may be William's messenger but I am my own man and would not say you false. The King is camped across the river and you have fourteen days in which to make your surrender.'

'And if I do not?'

'Then God have mercy on your soul,' De Rules said sombrely. He extended his hand in a pleading gesture. 'In the name of Christ, my lord, I ask you to make your peace with William before it becomes the peace of the grave.'

Waltheof's jaw tightened. 'I doubt if I made my grave now that I would lie in any kind of peace,' he said. 'Tell William that I will come when I am ready.'

De Rules nodded. Simon swung up into the saddle and took the lance of truce into his hand.

Waltheof looked up at him. 'How is your leg?' he asked.

Finally the boy's eyes met his and Waltheof saw that they were filled with wariness and reproach. 'It serves me well, my lord.'

His voice had deepened, although it still bore the pure bell tones of boyhood and it would be a while yet before it broke.

But much of the eager innocence had gone and Waltheof was saddened, not least because he suspected he had a part in it. Heroes were not supposed to be traitors, and explaining the motivation was too difficult when he did not understand the half of it himself.

'It is good to see you again, and you have certainly grown,' Waltheof said, taking refuge in the mundane.

Simon's gaze was direct now, his eyes the shade of Baltic amber. 'Do you not hate us?' he asked.

'Hate you?' Waltheof was nonplussed. 'God's love child, of course I do not hate you! Why should you think that?'

'Because of York . . . because of what has followed.' His voice faltered. Waltheof wondered how much of the devastation Simon had seen. Probably more than he could stomach, given that he was squiring in William's household. And in York, in the heat of battle, Waltheof had personally slaughtered an untold number of Normans. Walking among the corpses in the aftermath, he had emptied his belly at the sight of so much blood and destruction. He had confessed his bloodlust, had been absolved, but it felt as if the taint still remained on his soul and would never wash clean.

He shook his head and grimaced. 'Ah lad,' he said, 'you always bring me questions I cannot or should not for decency's sake answer. There are many things I might hate about Normans, but you are not one of them . . . and never will be.'

Simon pondered this, a slight frown knitting his brows. 'Does that mean I can visit you . . . if you are pardoned?'

Waltheof found a pained smile. 'You and your father will always be welcome at any of my manors,' he said. 'Whatever has gone before, whatever comes afterwards, I would never turn you away.'

Simon's expression gentled in response, the frown vanishing. 'I hope it is soon,' he said.

'So do I,' Waltheof replied, and meant it. If there was one good reason among all the less noble ones for bowing his head to William, then the boy's trust was it.

*

The Norman camp was orderly and disciplined. Riding into it with his troop, Waltheof felt like a brigand or a common pirate. His white fur mantle, the gold bracelets on his wrists, the rings on his fingers seemed garish in comparison to the spartan garb of the soldiers who watched him ride through their ranks. Their short hair and clean jaws added to the impression. Waltheof had washed his hair and combed his beard before setting out to the parley, but still he felt like a barbarian at the gates of Rome.

The drizzle of two days ago had been replaced by a bone-deep cold and the ground had begun to freeze. Waltheof had stuffed his boots with extra fleece and wore his quilted gambeson as much for warmth as protection. Any last shred of hope that the Norman army might turn back from a serious winter campaign was destroyed as he rode through their camp. Seeing the industry and discipline, he realised how naïve he had been in ever thinking that he could pit his abilities against William's. Waltheof dismounted and handed the reins to his groom. Richard de Rules arrived to escort him to William's tent. 'I am glad you came, my lord,' he said with relief in his eyes.

Waltheof shrugged. 'I had no choice, did I?'

De Rules cleared his throat. 'I must take your sword and your knife,' he said. 'They will be restored to you when you leave.'

Waltheof handed his belt and scabbard to the chamberlain and turned to lift his axe from its strap behind the saddle. 'That too,' De Rules said, eyeing the weapon sidelong.

Waltheof shook his head. 'That I will yield only into the hands of the King.'

'You cannot go into his presence so armed. I have seen your skill with that thing, and heard of your prowess at York. One blow and no one could stop you.'

Waltheof flushed. 'You doubt my integrity?'

'No,' De Rules said quietly, 'I do not, but I would be failing in my duty if I did not see foremost to the safety of my liege lord.'

Waltheof clenched his fists around the smooth ash wood of the haft. He had spent hours cleaning the blade and honing out the pits and nicks scarring the steel from its contact with wood and mail and bone. Now the edge gleamed with silver fire. 'I will yield this only to the King in token of my surrender,' he said. 'It is my pride. I will let no other man do so.'

Richard de Rules had not become the King's chamberlain by chance alone. Quick wits and tact formed a large part of his usefulness. 'I understand your reluctance, my lord,' he replied. 'But you must understand my responsibility. Perhaps for your pride you will let no other man carry your axe – but what of a boy?'

'A boy?' For a moment Waltheof was nonplussed, but then he saw Simon standing in the background and took De Rules' meaning. 'Very well,' he said. 'Let your son be my axe bearer.' He beckoned Simon forward. Wide-eyed, the lad came to him, his stride awkward but controlled.

Waltheof presented him with the weapon. 'Bear this as if it had been in your family since the time of your grandfather's grandfather,' he said.

Reverently Simon gripped the haft, holding it as Waltheof had shown him, one hand immediately beneath the socket, the other halfway down. His fingers were thin and fine but possessed a tensile strength that made them competent to the task. 'I will not let you down, my lord,' he promised, and set his mouth in a resolute line.

'I know that you will not,' Waltheof said. Drawing a deep breath to sustain himself, he gave his attention to De Rules. 'I am ready.' He gestured Simon to go before him like a standard bearer. It seemed entirely fitting to Waltheof that his axe bearer should be lame, for the entire campaign had been flawed from the start.

William's tent was little different from the others pitched along the banks of the Tees. It contained only a camp bed, a trestle table and a travelling chest. Austere, functional, like the man himself. A ceramic hanging lamp was suspended on chains from the wooden support running across the top of the canvas and the ground was covered in a thick litter of clean straw.

William sat at the trestle table, his broad shoulders swathed in a scarlet cloak lined with sables, and beneath that a quilted, gambeson. Surrounding him were his senior battle commanders and they were obviously in the midst of planning their campaign.

On seeing Waltheof, William rose to his feet and pushed aside the wax tablet upon which he had been sketching diagrams. Men turned and stared, eyes narrow in speculation and hostility. Feeling as if he had stepped into the lair of wolves, Waltheof fell to his knees in the heavy yellow straw and bowed his head. 'My liege, I yield myself to your mercy,' he said formally. 'And in token of this, I give to you the axe that was my father's and his father's before him. My life is yours.'

Beside him, Simon knelt too and held out the weapon on the palms of his hands. Waltheof imagined himself seizing the axe and arcing it round and down to cleave William from crown to breastbone like a flesher splicing a bacon pig. The vision held such clarity that he was sure the others must see it. His palms were suddenly slick with sweat and his breathing shallow; nausea churned his gut.

He was on the verge of breaking, of snatching the axe and leaping to his feet, when William stooped and took it from the boy, setting his own firm, square hands to the haft and taking up the stance of an executioner.

'You yielded once before,' William replied coldly, 'and you swore me your oath of loyalty. When a man puts his hands between mine and promises to serve me, the vow is binding unto death.'

Waltheof swallowed. 'I know that, sire.'

'Then why did you turn oath-breaker, Waltheof Siwardsson? It seems to me that all of your countrymen are faithless.'

'I had no choice but to take the oath to you,' Waltheof said, a hint of resentment creeping into his voice. He wasn't faithless, no matter that it seemed that way to William.

'But you had the choice to hold to it or break it,' William said silkily. 'And you chose the second way.'

'The Danish people are my kin. I have no blood in common with Normandy. I thought . . .'

'You thought that if you could shake off my rule that the Danes would embrace you as one of their own and give to you the lands and riches that were your father's,' William said scornfully. Hefting the axe, he turned it contemplatively in his hand.

'No!' Waltheof's eyes flashed. 'It was a matter of kinship . . . of belonging. You made it clear that you desired no such bond with my blood.'

'And if that were to change?'

Waltheof met the hard, dark eyes. Devoid of warmth, they probed him and he dared not ponder their purpose. 'Sire, a blood bond is the most binding of all.'

William continued to grip him with his stare. 'How long will your loyalty last this time?' he demanded. 'If I bid you renew your homage, how do I know that you will keep the faith?'

Waltheof bowed his head. 'I have seen the way you lead your men, sire. To go against you is futile. If Sweyn of Denmark had truly desired the North Country, he would have come himself rather than send his sons.'

'Perhaps he thought that the taking would be easy. Like you, he knows differently now.' William raised one fist and clenched it on the statement. His upper lip curled with contempt. 'At least you had the courage to come to me and submit to me yourself. Your companion Gospatric has chosen the Danish way and sent proxies to submit in his stead.'

If he had hoped for an indignant response, he was disappointed. Waltheof knew Gospatric's shortcomings, even as he knew his own.

'I have no intention of giving an opinion when I have my own lacks,' Waltheof said quietly. 'What Gospatric does is for his conscience and manhood to decide.'

William gave a disparaging snort. 'What manhood?' he said, and thrust the axe into Waltheof's surprised grasp. 'Go in peace, Waltheof Siwardsson. Tend your lands, stay out of trouble . . .' He paused to give his next words significance. 'Mayhap I will after all consider that bond of blood.'

Waltheof's breath caught. He did not know whether to be filled with joy or irritation. How often had Edwin of Mercia had the promise of 'good news' dangled before him without a royal match ever materialising? Waltheof had just sworn to be William's man whether he was rewarded or not. But if that choice should bring him Judith . . .

He saw wintry humour light in William's eyes, as if the King could read his thoughts.

'Thank you, sire,' he said, and bowed out of William's presence into the raw January morning. The ashwood haft of his axe felt warm under his fingers. He had his lands, he had his life, and the hint of more than such sustenance to come. He felt wildly euphoric and deathly sick and it was all he could do not to vomit against the side of William's tent.

De Rules emerged, a paternal arm curved around Simon's shoulders. When the baron made to approach him, Waltheof thrust out a hand to ward him off. 'Let me be,' he said in a choked voice. 'For the moment, I can stomach neither your comfort nor your company.'

'I think I would feel the same,' De Rules said, and then, mercifully, walked away, his arm firmly guiding his son.

Simon looked over his shoulder at Waltheof, his stare filled with question and anxiety.

Waltheof swallowed. 'That does not mean I hate you,' he said. 'But my wounds are bloody and you would only rub salt into them.' He spun on his heel and strode towards the horse lines.

Simon watched him leave, then looked up at his father in perplexity.

De Rules' fingers tightened upon the curve of his son's narrow shoulder. 'Let him be,' he said. 'If we were in his place and he in ours, do you think we would desire his companionship of this moment?'

Simon's dark tawny brows drew together. 'No,' he said doubtfully. 'But I wish it wasn't like that.'

'It is the way of the world,' De Rules said, and when Simon looked up into his father's face he saw that his expression was grim and tired.

'So, you will give him Judith?' asked Eudo of Champagne, rubbing his thumb across the cleft in his chin. The notion of bringing an English earldom into the family gnawed at him, the more so since his son had been born. His own lands were negligible, for although he was the son of the Count of Champagne he was living in exile on his brother-in-law's sufferance.

'I am considering it.' William drew the wax tablets towards him again and turned the bone drawing tool end over end. 'He is young and malleable still. If I can anchor him to me, then well and good.'

'And yet before you would not have him.'

William shrugged. 'He burst in upon me with the demand when I had already given him more rein than any other Englishman. He was like a child begging for one more sweetmeat . . .'

'And who then had a tantrum when you refused,' pointed out Robert of Mortain with a scowl.

William pushed his thumb against the side of the stylus and looked at his half-brother with a brooding dark stare. 'Perhaps that was part of his rebellion, but not the whole I think. Nor do I believe that his request for Judith was one of overweening ambition.'

Mortain snorted. 'A man who follows his cock is unreliable.'

'Perhaps,' William nodded, 'and again perhaps not. I bind men to me with the tools I have. Judith is of an age to wed and Waltheof harbours as much desire for her as he does for her connections. She has a strong will to compensate for his weakness and powerful family ties to bolster her. I may have denied him before, but it would be folly not to reconsider.'

'And dangerous,' said Mortain.

'No more dangerous than letting him run loose.'

'Why let him run at all?' Eudo asked. 'Why not confiscate his lands and bestow them elsewhere?'

William gave him a piercing look that made Eudo check and hold his breath, wondering if he had been too eager.

'That would only cause more rebellion and we are stretched enough as it is. Chester is my goal, and ridding the land of the last of Godwinsson's supporters. I do not want to chase my tail back to Huntingdon, and I need your presence here, Eudo. For the granting of a small grace, I have peace with Waltheof. His lands are prosperous. Judith will be a countess and you will be Waltheof's father-by-marriage. I cannot give you Huntingdon outright. I hope you understand that.'

Eudo nodded stiffly and swallowed his disappointment. He had not really expected William to give him Huntingdon, but it had been worth planting the idea. And as William said, he would be Waltheof's father-by-marriage. Likely he could bring some influence to bear.

CHAPTER 11

Caen, Normandy, Autumn 1070

Judith sat near the embrasure so that the light spilled onto the hem of the wine-red tunic she was embroidering. It was to be a Christmas gift to her uncle William from his wife. Since Matilda was acting ruler of Normandy in her husband's absence and did not have the time for embroidery, the task fell to the other women of the household.

Judith's needle flew in and out, laying down a lozenge pattern in shades of emerald and sapphire on the background of Flemish twill. An hour since, a messenger from England had arrived and was now closeted in the Duchess's private chamber unburdening his news. Judith wondered what tidings he had brought in his worn leather satchel.

There had been several uprisings in England during the past year, all of them swatted down by her uncle like bothersome flies. The most serious had been the rebellion in the North around the time that her brother was born. Waltheof had been amongst the leaders. She had braced herself to hear that he had fallen in battle, but learned instead that he had surrendered to her uncle and had been pardoned. Her relief had sharpened the knife-edge along which she trod until it was impossible to be at peace with herself.

She and her mother had returned to Normandy with the

Queen. Waltheof, so Judith gleaned, had stayed firmly on his lands whilst fresh surges of unrest disturbed the country. Agatha had been inconsolable when Edwin of Mercia had been killed whilst hiding out with rebels in the fenlands. His brother Morcar had been captured and thrown into prison. Waltheof, however, remained free.

Sometimes she would think of him while engaged in needlework. She would wonder what he was doing, how he was faring. Was he the same? Had he found an English wife to complement his estates – her uncle's conquest must have left many bereft heiresses – or did he remain unwed? She had knelt with a distraught Agatha to pray for Edwin's soul, and had been ashamed to discover a secret well of hope. Now that Edwin was no longer a contender for a Norman wife, perhaps there was a chance for Waltheof.

The notion unsettled her. Suddenly the sewing, which she usually enjoyed, was tedious. Setting the needle in the fabric, she rose and went to the open shutters. Outside it was cold and overcast, the window arch yielding a vista of dull, grey cloud. Placed where he could obtain the best of the light, but out of the draught, her small half-brother Stephen gurgled in his cherrywood cradle. He had Eudo's cleft chin and blue eyes and all the women doted upon his plump rosiness. All but herself. She turned from his gummy smile with tightening lips, refusing to be wooed. In the eleven months since his birth it had become clear how much more value Adelaide set upon her son than she did on her daughters.

The curtain rings clattered vigorously across the doorway and her mother stalked into the room. She was breathing heavily and her fists were anchored so tightly in the fabric of her gown that her knuckles were bleached.

'Cease your daydreaming,' she snapped. 'There is news from England and your aunt Matilda wishes to speak with you.'

Judith touched the sudden swift pulse at the base of her throat. 'What about?'

'That is for your aunt to say,' Adelaide replied stiffly. 'I am only your mother. My word evidently means nothing.'

Judith made a deep curtsey to her aunt, who sat on a cushioned bench before a glowing brazier. Nearby a nurse was dandling Matilda's youngest child, the two-year-old Prince Henry, in her lap.

Matilda patted the bench, indicating that her niece should come and sit beside her. The Queen's fair complexion wore the flush of recent anger, making Judith wonder what had happened between her and her mother, who were usually such firm allies.

'Child, you are to go to England.' The Queen placed her hand over Judith's in a proprietorial gesture that subtly excluded Adelaide.

'England?' Judith's gaze widened. 'Has the Du . . . King sent for us?' They were to spend Christmas at the royal court, she thought. That was why her mother was so agitated; she loathed sea crossings. It also meant she would have to join her husband, whom she tolerated much the better for the distance between them.

Matilda shook her head. 'Not for all of us, child,' she said, 'but certainly for you and your mother. Your uncle has arranged for your marriage to Waltheof of Huntingdon on the feast of Saint Stephen.'

Judith was aware of staring at her aunt and being unable to move. 'My marriage?' she repeated in a stunned voice. 'But I thought . . .' she swallowed. 'I thought Earl Waltheof was considered an unsuitable match.'

'Your uncle has changed his mind,' Matilda said neutrally. 'He wishes to reward the young man's loyalty.'

'Loyalty!' Adelaide spat. 'After what happened in York?'

'He has not been involved in the uprisings since – and some of them were perilously close to his borders,' Matilda said flatly with a narrow glance at her sister-in-law that warned her against speaking out. 'The King feels that

Waltheof is owed a reward – that binding him more closely to our house will ensure his future co-operation. Your step-father is in full agreement.'

Adelaide made a strangled sound that told without words what she thought of such an endorsement.

'If William deems this match with Waltheof of Huntingdon to be provident, then nothing will stand in his way. Neither you, nor I, nor a winter sea crossing,' Matilda said with iron finality. She looked at Judith and her expression softened. 'I do not think your daughter will be displeased by her uncle's decision.'

Judith shook her head, certain that she was going to wake up and discover that this was all a strange dream induced by eating too many cheese wafers close to retiring. What was she supposed to say? What was she supposed to feel? Marriage to Waltheof. Once she had dreamed of it, but now the memory was as distant as summer on this raw November morning. 'It is my duty to do my uncle's will,' she heard herself say.

'Pah!' Adelaide folded her arms tightly beneath her bosom. 'Your uncle thinks that wedding you to an English earl is a worthy ploy, but he will live to rue the day he did not marry you to a Fleming!'

'Adelaide!' Matilda said in terse warning.

Judith's mother compressed her lips. 'You will need cloth for a wedding gown,' she said without pleasure, 'and warm robes to keep out the winter chill. I suppose you will have to take linen for sheets and napery too.' The tone of her voice suggested that she thought Judith would be living a primitive existence bereft of all comforts.

'I will send for the mercer this very day,' Matilda soothed. 'As Judith says, it is our duty to do my lord's will, and we must fulfil it to the best of his expectations. Let her go in the full array due to the niece of a king and the daughter of a countess. She shall have the best of everything, and you must have new robes too.'

Adelaide's lips remained pursed but some of the stiffness went from her posture.

Judith looked at her aunt. 'Did . . . did Earl Waltheof say anything?'

Matilda reached to the ivory casket on the coffer beside her and threw back the lid. 'Your uncle says that Earl Waltheof agreed readily to the contract. He awaits your arrival in England with eagerness and in token has sent you this ring.' She held out to Judith a small circlet fashioned from plaited gold.

With shaking hands, Judith took it from her aunt. Waltheof had one the same; she had often seen it gleaming on the middle finger of his right hand. Aware of the older women's scrutiny, she slipped it on her own right middle finger. It fitted perfectly and shone with a dull lustre against her skin.

Matilda nodded and smiled. 'He has chosen well. My own betrothal ring hung off my finger like a quintain hoop.'

'We shall see,' Adelaide said darkly. 'Rings that fit a young girl at the start often grow too tight in the wearing.'

Matilda frowned at her sister-in-law. 'Making doom-laden predictions serves no purpose,' she said with irritation. 'We must be practical. Travelling chests need to be packed and arrangements made.' Leaning over, she gave Judith a dry kiss on the cheek. 'I am happy for you, niece.'

Adelaide made no move to embrace her daughter. Instead she swished over to one of the clothing chests, banged open the lid and began to sort through the linens within.

Matilda gave Judith's newly adorned hand a sympathetic squeeze. 'All will be well,' she said. 'A little time to grow accustomed is all that is needed – for us all.'

Judith nodded and finished the wine. The first numbness of shock was beginning to wear off. It was true. She was going to England. She was going to marry Waltheof and become Countess of Huntingdon and Northampton. But the thought that blossomed most brightly amongst the several that began to chase around her mind was that she was no longer going to be ruled by her mother but would be able to make rules of her own. She would be mistress of the household and able to do as she pleased. Without stifling, without censure.

A tinge of colour returned to her cheeks, and her eyes began to sparkle as she realised that this news meant her freedom.

Chapter 12

S hears in hand, Waltheof's chamber attendant Toki hesitated. 'You are sure about this, my lord?'

Waltheof grimaced. 'I am not sure at all,' he said, 'but
do it. It is not as though the results will be permanent if I
change my mind. Make haste. It would be unseemly to be
late for my wedding,' he said with a shaken laugh. He could
still not quite believe that William had granted him Judith in
marriage. For a month he had been pinching himself. But it
was true. This morning was the feast of Stephen, and before
the hour of prime, their marriage was to be blessed by
Lanfranc, Archbishop of Canterbury, and celebrated with a
mass inside the abbey church of Westminster.

Behind him he heard Toki sigh heavily and felt the crunch
of the shears as they came together. Seated on the bench, his
hands braced on his thighs, his head held very still, Waltheof
watched the locks of hair fall around him like tongues of
flame. His father had been flax-white of hair, his mother
plain brown, but the copper trait had run in her line and she
had bequeathed it to him. Perhaps tonight he would in turn
bequeath it to a child of his own. The thought made him shift
on the bench and caused Toki to swear.

'If you do not remain still, my lord, you will go to your
marriage with a missing ear and a resemblance to the Earl of
Norfolk's dogs,' he said, referring to Earl Ralf's deerhounds,
which had recently been affected by a serious attack of mange.

Waltheof laughed, then swallowed the sound and was still.

'You're going to feel the cold,' Toki warned as he started on the beard.

It was a statement already borne out by the truth. Waltheof's bare neck did indeed feel the draught from an ill-fitting shutter. His beautiful golden beard, which had grown stronger over the last two years, had caused him more agony of decision than his hair. As an Englishman it was an immediately identifiable sign of his manhood, something to toy with in times of anxiety, to hide behind, and a symbol of authority. Without it his face was naked to the world.

Toki stepped back and eyed his handiwork dubiously. He stroked his own thick beard as if for reassurance. 'Splendour of God,' he declared, using King William's favourite oath. 'You surely do look like a Norman, my lord.'

Waltheof ran his hand over his smooth jaw and then through his cropped hair. Toki had sheared it in the Norman style, baring the entire back of the neck and up the scalp so that the hair began on a level just above Waltheof's ear lobes and was shaped above the ears and round to a fringe. 'I want to do Judith proud,' he said softly. 'I want to surprise and please her.'

Toki clucked his tongue. 'You'll do that for certain, my lord.'

Waltheof looked hard at Toki but the manservant's expression was blank. He wondered if he had done the right thing. It was too late to worry.

The bath was the next order of proceedings, to remove the tickle of cut hair and ritually cleanse himself for the coming marriage. The wooden bathtub was somewhat small for his large frame and he had to bend his knees and keep his elbows in. Although the water was hot, it quickly began to chill and Waltheof did not linger at his ablutions.

He had just stepped from the tub and another manservant was drying him with linen towels when there was a knock on the chamber door and Simon de Senlis entered the room. The lad wore a tunic of russet-coloured wool that enhanced his fox-gold eyes and dark tawny hair. A beautiful tooled sheath hung from the belt at his waist and a hilt of cunningly worked antler stood proud of the top.

Waltheof flashed a grin at the sight of him. 'You're not supposed to outdo the bridegroom!' he said.

Simon did not respond to the jest for he was staring at Waltheof in open-mouthed astonishment.

'What do you think?' Self-consciously, Waltheof rubbed his shorn scalp. 'Do you think Lady Judith will approve?'

'You look very different,' the boy said.

Waltheof made a face. 'You're as diplomatic as your father.'

Simon frowned. 'No . . . It suits you, but you no longer look like yourself. But I think that Lady Judith will be very pleased indeed . . . and Countess Adelaide too.'

Waltheof snorted. Young Simon was as sharp as an awl. 'Come, help me dress,' he said. 'I presume that your father knows where you are.'

'Yes. He said not to linger if you wished to be alone.'

Waltheof shook his head. 'No, lad. I like my solitude for prayer, but I need company as some men need bread.'

While Toki set about emptying the bath water Simon helped Waltheof to don his wedding clothes. First came the shirt of soft embroidered linen, then braies of the same, held up by a waistband of plaited cord. Hose of dark blue wool were fastened to the braies with leather ties. Kneeling at Waltheof's feet, Simon carefully wound decorative braid from ankle to knee. Filaments of gold thread twinkled amidst the red and white wool. Waltheof's tunic was of a lighter blue than his chausses, a summer-sky colour with the same red and white braid trimming the hem, cuffs and deep neck opening, the latter pinned by a large gold brooch. The sword belt came next, the solid gold buckle cunningly worked in the shape of a serpent coiling round to swallow its tail.

Waltheof hesitated over donning his gold bracelets. His

father and brother had always worn them, using them as gifts for songs well sung and services performed. The Normans, he knew, saw the habit as barbaric and outmoded. 'Yes, or no?' he said to Simon.

The boy considered. 'You cannot give up everything of you that is English,' he said. 'Everyone will be too busy looking at your naked face to have time to notice your wrists.'

Waltheof grinned at the lad's perception. 'Aye, you're right.' He slid the bracelets onto his arms, but all the same pushed them a little beneath his sleeves. The final touch was the bearskin cloak. He had thought about discarding that too, but had swiftly quashed the notion. More than anything this was his heritage, a symbol of who he was. No one else owned a cloak lined with the fur of an Arctic bear.

'So,' he said, 'will I do?'

'You look magnificent, my lord.'

There was more than just diplomacy in the boy's tawny eyes. The gleam of admiration bolstered Waltheof's courage. Turning to a coffer, he took his battleaxe from its waxed wrappings and presented it to Simon.

'Here,' he said. 'You were my weapon bearer when I surrendered to William. Now be so again in pride as I go to my marriage with his niece.'

Simon flushed with pleasure and he took the weapon reverently.

With heart beating fast, Waltheof went to the door. For a moment his hand seemed stuck to the latch. He had deliberately made his men wait outside while he took the traditional bath and the less than traditional drastic barbering. He knew there would be consternation. What he hoped would carry him through was the approbation of his bride. It mattered that Judith should be proud of him and show to all that she was marrying a man worthy of her love.

Jutting his naked chin, he raised the latch and stepped outside. The gold bracelets jingled on the movement and slipped down over his wrists to lodge at the base of his thumb.

*

Seated in the great hall, granted a place at the head of the high table because it was her wedding feast, Judith glanced at her new husband. She could not believe the transformation that the barber's shears had wrought. He had been handsome before, in the unkempt way of the English, but now his features were clear and sharp, etched in Norman austerity. So changed was his appearance, she was unable to keep her eyes from him; quite simply, he was stunning. Women, who had ignored him before, now cast him languishing glances. Men, who had disapproved of his English abundance, clasped his hand in gruff approval. Even her mother had been impressed by Waltheof's changed appearance. Since his French was so fluent, she said, one could almost mistake him for a true Norman. If only it weren't for those vulgar bracelets jangling on his wrists.

Judith had noticed them too, and dismissed their presence as a matter of small importance. She would have care of his clothes and his dressing now that she was his wife. It would be a simple enough matter to persuade him to set them aside.

Some of the English guests had been less fulsome in their praise of Waltheof's shaven looks, but they were common thegns and counted for little. Any Saxon with a grain of sense these days was doing as Waltheof had done and adopting Norman ways.

Waltheof caught her looking at him and smiled. It was an open expression, full of honest joy. Judith blushed and looked down, conscious that everyone was watching them and judging their every response.

'I am the most fortunate of men,' he said huskily, laying his hand over hers, his thumb caressing the two bands of gold that now sat side by side on her middle and ring fingers.

'And I am the most fortunate of women,' she replied, her voice barely audible.

Ralf de Gael noticed Waltheof's gesture and raised a rowdy toast. Judith set her lips at his conduct. He behaved like an Englishman, always the first to disappear under the table, but not before making himself sick and objectionable with drink.

'Then our children will be doubly blessed,' Waltheof leaned close to murmur, his breath scented with the spiced wine that had been served with the last course of honeyed figs, cheese wafers, and small crisp, flat cakes cooked on a hot griddle.

The mention of children made Judith's breath catch. She was trying not to panic about the wedding night, but with little success. She was not ignorant about the act of procreation. Her mother could not confine her to the bower all the time. She had seen dogs in the hall, cats in the stables, and had once come across one of the grooms taking a kitchen maid in the heaped straw beyond Jolie's stall. At the time she had stared at the heaving white buttocks and straddled thighs with a mingling of shock and fascination. Sybille, on being told of the incident, had chuckled knowingly and assured Judith that the groans she had heard were of pleasure, not pain. Now, tonight, she and Waltheof would adopt that same position and she would find out. The notion of crying out beneath him was one that made her shiver with shame and curiosity, eagerness and fear.

'Are you cold, my heart?' Waltheof asked, 'or does the notion of our children unsettle you?' He raised a playful eyebrow.

She forced a smile. 'A little of both,' she admitted. 'Last night I slept in the women's hall, as I have done for all the years of my life. Tonight I must lie in a different bed and perform the duties of a wife.'

'Ah,' said Waltheof. A smile lit in his eyes. 'So bedding with me is going to be a duty?' His voice was warm and teasing as he signalled the attending squire to refill his horn.

'That depends upon how drunk you become,' Judith said with a pointed look at the brimming vessel. 'What price your dignity and my pride if you have to be carried to your wedding bed?'

Waltheof's smile broadened into a white grin. 'Not twelve hours wed and already you are scolding me.'

Judith blinked and bit her lip. 'You make light of the matter, but everyone's eyes are upon us. If you are drunk they will remember and think less of you.'

'And that matters to you?' The humour left his face.

'Of course it does.'

Waltheof shook his head gently. 'You have enough pride for both of us, my love,' he said. 'But rest assured I will not tumble it in the mire. I sheared myself close as a May sheep for you this day. Remaining sober is small enough coin compared to that. Besides,' he added, his smile returning with an incorrigible glint, 'I have no intention of ruining my wedding night with a surfeit of wine. I want to remember this occasion for the rest of my life.'

The couple had been allotted a fine chamber on the upper floor of the hall, with arched windows looking out over the moonlit glint of the River Thames. Fresh rushes had been strewn on the floor and scattered with aromatic herbs so that each footfall aroused the scent of lavender, rosemary and cinnamon. Charcoal braziers burned in each corner of the room, keeping the cold at bay, and a jug of wine had been set on a cover over one of the braziers to warm through.

Judith sat in the bed where the women had placed her and watched Waltheof bolt the door after the last guest, predictably Ralf de Gael, who at one point in the merry jesting had offered to take Waltheof's place in the great, fur-covered bed. The notion had nauseated Judith. Once she and Waltheof were more familiar with each other she thoroughly intended discarding certain of his friendships along with those garish bracelets.

There were small, damp spots on her chemise where Archbishop Lanfranc had sprinkled her with holy water as he blessed the union between her and Waltheof. Waltheof's shirt was damp too. At least they had not been made to strip totally naked, as sometimes happened. She could not have borne the thought of standing before the entire court clad in naught but her hair.

Waltheof turned from the door he had just barred. 'I would not put it past Ralf to listen outside and then burst in on us at the crucial moment,' he said with an embarrassed laugh and rubbed the shorn back of his neck, which had turned a rich pink.

'Neither would I,' Judith replied with asperity, 'although I think that my uncle and my stepfather will keep him in hand.'

'I suppose so, or your mother will know the reason why.'

Judith did not want to talk of Adelaide. The closing of the door marked a barrier between her former life beneath her mother's roof and her new one as Waltheof's wife and countess in her own right. No longer was she subject to her mother's rule, although she knew there would be some struggles on that score. Adelaide was nothing if not tenacious. 'Do you remember your own mother?' she asked to divert her thoughts.

Waltheof went to the heated jug of wine, poured a scant measure into one of the cups set to hand, and came to the bed. 'Only a very little,' he said. 'She died when I was small. I remember that she wore her hair in long braids twined with red ribbons. She was very fond of her garden and would spend hours tending the plants. She was much younger than my father – she was his second wife, and it was not a match made for love.'

'Matches never are.'

Waltheof looked at her and the expression in his eyes melted the flesh from her bones. 'Maybe not,' he said softly, 'but sometimes the spark is there. Sometimes men and women are fortunate enough to make an arrangement that brings them their heart's desire.'

Judith swallowed. Her throat was dry. As if sensing her need, he handed her the cup of wine. Their fingers touched and he raised his index one to rub it gently along her knuckles until she shivered at the sensation.

'I desired you from that first night in the hall at Rouen when I asked Richard de Rules who you were,' Waltheof said.

Folding his hand around hers, he brought the cup to his own lips and drank from the place where hers had touched. 'And now I have you and I swear that for the rest of my days I will want nothing and no one else.'

'You are not ambitious, my lord?'

'I have seen what ambition does to men . . . and what you do to me is far more important.'

Judith licked her lips. Waltheof moved closer, angled his head and kissed her. She was passive, struck by fear and uncertainty. His mouth tasted of wine and sweetness. He pulled gently away and looked at her.

'Drink,' he said, returning the cup to her keeping. She shook her head. 'I have had enough.'

'Trust me, you have not,' he said.

Her tone took on a waspish note. 'You mean it will be easier for me if I am insensible?'

Waltheof laughed, and bouncing from the bed, went to refill the cup. 'No, I didn't mean that at all. You would be missing a deal of pleasure, and you would suffer so thunderous a headache in the morning that you would wonder why you had not chosen to be aware.'

Judith slanted him a look. 'My mother says that coupling is a duty,' she said.

Waltheof returned to the bed, took a single swallow from the brimming cup, then returned it to her. 'Your mother sees everything in the world as a duty,' he said wryly. 'Coupling is a pleasure.'

'But is it not a sin to enjoy it?' Judith said doubtfully and drank the sweet, strong wine.

'Some priests say that it is,' Waltheof admitted, 'but I think that God gave us the means for pleasure as well as pain. I am no scholar, and I leave it for others more knowledgeable to debate. Perhaps it is better to be continent, but without procreation there would be no children . . .'

'But it is not the reason that men go to brothels – to procreate children.' Judith's tone was acerbic.

Again Waltheof laughed. 'No,' he agreed, 'it is not. And that is why we go to confession.'

The wine was beginning to spread through her limbs, bringing lassitude and a feeling of wellbeing. 'But if you confess and then sin again . . .'

Waltheof took the cup from her hands and set it to one side. 'I have no intention of ever sinning again in my life,' he said. 'Well, at least not in matters of the flesh. If we are to speak of duty, then let us speak of your duty to keep me on the straight path.'

'You are mocking me.'

'No, teasing you. There is a difference.' Raising the sheets, he got into bed beside her. 'Your hands are cold,' he said. 'Lie down.'

Somewhat cautiously Judith complied. Waltheof drew the crisp linen sheet, the striped blanket and beaver fur coverlet over their bodies. Taking her hands in his and raising his shirt, he laid her palms against the heat of his breast. She felt the dry warmth of his flesh, the thump of his heart.

'That's it,' he said softly. 'Just for warmth . . .'

She knew it wasn't true. How could it be when the bloody sheet of her taken virginity was expected to be displayed to the entire court on the morrow as proof that any child born nine months from now would be of Waltheof's begetting? However the lie was soothing and she relaxed against him. He rested his head on one hand and used the other to caress her spine in gentle, rhythmic strokes.

To Judith the sensation was entirely new and blissful. Waltheof's hand wove its magic, now gentle and slow, now sweeping and firm. Imperceptibly he moved lower until his fingertips swirled the small of her back. Judith gasped softly and pushed her hips forward. Waltheof continued caressing her, murmuring gently, reassuring. One hand trailed up her ribcage and feathered over her breast. It was the lightest of touches, but rather like a leaf falling into a pool the small ripples spread from the contact and drew a response from all

of her body. Her loins were meltingly sensitive. His palm
found and lingered upon her nipple, slowly rubbing through
the linen chemise until her breath caught in pleasure. When
he replaced his hand with his lips and the flick of his tongue,
Judith arched and gasped.

Waltheof pulled on the lacing at the top of her chemise
until it came undone, and then she felt his touch on her naked
skin. His breathing had changed, no longer quiet and even,
but ragged and swift. Now he kissed her throat, her jawline,
and reclaimed her lips. This time Judith was less passive. She
moved her mouth beneath his, and shivered when he explored
her lips with his tongue. Her arms encircled his neck and she
pressed against him. Thus far he had kept his lower body
away from hers, but now he set his arm across her waist, drew
her in close and rocked his hips against hers.

She felt the heat and strength of his body, his hardness and
virility. Imagining him within her body had been something
to shy away from, but she was drugged with wine and pleasure
now. He continued to kiss her and his hand stole beneath her
chemise, drawing the linen upwards, baring her legs, her
thighs. And the fondling continued, stroking, lulling, leading
her onwards. He knew exactly where to touch and she began
to writhe and whimper.

Waltheof sat up and removed his shirt. In the dim light
from the night candle his hair was the colour of flame and
the scattering of hair on his chest sparkled like gold wire. His
muscles gleamed with health; his belly was as flat as the
planking on a new shield.

'Your chemise,' he said hoarsely, 'take it off.'

'I . . .'

'It will bunch between us and be uncomfortable.' He drew
her up and tugged the garment off over her head. She watched
him cast it to one side, careful even in the intensity of the
moment not to send it in the direction of the candle.

The cold night air struck her flesh and raised small goose
chills. He combed his hands through her unbound black hair

and watched the tresses slide against his skin. Pulling her down, he began the slow, stroking process again, until Judith was hot and breathless. The wine and the slow seduction had done their work. Now she gasped openly and made small sounds at each new assault on her senses.

He parted her thighs and began to rub with slow insistence. Judith clenched her fists. She would have bitten her lip too, but he was kissing her, thrusting kisses of his tongue now, moving in time with motion of his hips. A tight sensation was growing and building in Judith's loins, each stroke of his finger bringing her closer. She raised herself against him, wanting to cry out for him to stop so that she could catch her breath, wanting him to go on. Nearer and nearer. He was groaning and she could feel the vibration of his voice through their joined mouths. The sound added to the maelstrom of sensations and excited her further. She was on the brink of discovering something so overwhelming it would shatter her.

He took his hand away and she made a sound of frustration. He cupped her buttocks. Once, twice, she felt the hot jab of flesh, and then he steadied, and thrust into her. Judith cried out at the intrusion. There was a jagged flash of pain, but there was pleasure too. He withdrew a little way and pushed forward again, holding himself still at the deepest point of the surge and pressing his hips flat against hers, then he withdrew, and pushed and held again. Judith whimpered softly. Each time his hips surged, she would feel a flash of pain and then a stab of swollen pleasure. And as he moved faster, the two became joined until she did not know where one began and the other ended. She began to thrash and gasp.

'Please . . .' she entreated, not knowing whether she was asking him to stop or go forward. 'Please . . .' Her body was rigid with tension as she held back from the edge.

Without breaking rhythm he reached down between them and stroked. It was the final stimulus to send her crashing into the first climax of her life. She arched against him, her fingers like claws, her teeth clenched, and in the wildness of the moment she threw back her head and screamed. The sound brought an answering roar from Waltheof and his weight came down on top of her and where their bodies were joined she could feel pulsations like a heartbeat, throbbing strongly, then flickering and ebbing away.

Silence fell except for the sobbing gasps of their breath. Judith began to struggle up from the deep well of pleasure into which she had been cast. She became aware of Waltheof's weight pinning her to the bed. Her thighs were stretched causing a cramping discomfort, and there was a raw burning in the softness between them.

Slowly Waltheof eased from her body. She clenched at the pain, and wondered how in the world she had just accepted him with cries of delight. Was this the nature of lust against which the priests counselled?

Waltheof drew her against him and stroked the tangled hair away from her face. 'I love you,' he murmured. 'If it hurt, I am sorry. In time it will grow better.'

In time? Judith swallowed. 'I will lose myself,' she said in a shaken voice.

'That is no bad thing for a while,' Waltheof said. 'I want to see you smile. I want to see beyond the face you show to the world. When you cried out in my arms just now . . .' His own voice shook with tenderness.

Judith hid herself against his chest. She had been unable to help herself, and now she was chagrined.

'Come now,' Waltheof said softly. 'We should rightly sing praise for what gives us delight.' Tilting up her face he kissed her. Judith responded, but with reserve now. She needed time to assimilate and recover.

'Truly – did I give you pleasure?'

She heard his need for reassurance and bit her lip. 'Yes,' she whispered, 'you gave me pleasure. I had not imagined that it would be like that. Now I understand why the priests are so often ignored when they exhort people to celibacy.'

Waltheof snorted. 'More than half the village priests in

England have wives and children,' he said. 'It is only of late that the Church has taken a different stance. I can see that fornication is a distraction to the spiritual life of monks and nuns, but a common priest should live with his parishioners as they live with him.' He yawned. 'I am glad that you found as much joy in your duty as I found in mine.'

A few moments later he was heavily asleep. Judith eased out of his arms and surreptitiously pushed down the covers. Her inner thighs were stained with blood and there were streaks and smears on the sheets too – proof of her virginity. She pulled the sheets back up and turned on her side away from Waltheof, keeping her distance.

In the morning, he made love to her again, once more coaxing a shattering response that left her dazzled, disorientated and sore. He told her he loved her, that she was his life, and gave her a gift of a gold and garnet brooch and jewelled fillets to thread on the ends of her long dark braids.

The bloodied sheet was displayed in the hall before the entire court as proof of Judith's virginity and the successful wedding night. Adelaide wore an expression compounded of pride for her daughter's bravery and mild distaste at the evidence of what Judith had been made to suffer.

Sybille, ever practical, quietly handed Judith a small pot of soothing salve. 'Until you grow accustomed,' she whispered. Having spent the night rolled in the cloak of Toki, Waltheof's shieldbearer, her own complexion was rosy from the burn of his beard and the satisfaction of being well loved.

Judith took the salve and wondered if she ever would grow accustomed. The sensations roused in her by Waltheof were as disturbing as they were glorious. 'I wish I was like you,' she said to her maid. 'I wish I was like my husband.' Her glance flickered to Waltheof, who was devouring bread and honey with gusto while he engaged in buoyant conversation with Richard de Rules and her stepfather.

'No use wishing to be like other folks,' Sybille said shrewdly. 'You have to learn to live at peace within your own skin.' She squeezed Judith's arm, a gleam of sympathy in her eyes. 'Lord Waltheof's a good man. Just trust in him and you will be all right.'

Judith said nothing. Trust was the last thing she would yield to anyone.

CHAPTER 13

Summer 1072

Simon rode into Huntingdon on a warm evening in June. He passed townspeople hoeing their garths, women gossiping as they worked distaff and spindle at lightning speed to weave thread from fleece. Others were eating their suppers over outdoor fires. The smell of food and smoke mingled with the green scents of summer and an underlying but not overpowering whiff of midden pits and latrines.

People glanced up as he passed and then ignored him. Simon wondered if they would scowl in hostility behind his back, but he thought not. There was nothing to mark him as overtly Norman unless he opened his mouth. A hood of green linen hid his cropped hair, and his tunic was a sober russet colour with only a narrow trim of decorative braid.

At fourteen years old, Simon was as slender as a birch twig. No matter how much he ate, none of it remained on his wiry frame except by way of stretching his length. His father had jokingly commented that someone must have put manure in his shoes to judge by the speed of his growth. His features were changing too, his nose and jaw lengthening and a smudge of hair downing his upper lip.

A patrol of soldiers came towards him from the direction of the new castle and he turned his roan cob aside to let them pass. Their mail glinted in the evening sun and he heard the rapid French and Flemish of their speech. One of them drew rein and glared at him from beneath the brow ridges of his helm.

'Soon be curfew, boy,' he growled. 'What are you doing out?' He eyed the horse and Simon felt a jolt of fear. He knew that good animals such as this were targets for requisitioning. After the inroads that Hastings and the Northern campaign had made on saddle horses, demand for remounts was ferocious.

'I am travelling to the hall of Earl Waltheof of Huntingdon with messages from the King,' Simon answered more boldly than he felt. 'My name is Simon de Senlis and I am a royal squire and the son of his chamberlain.'

The soldier's eyes narrowed. 'You are young to be entrusted with so important a matter.'

Simon shrugged. 'The King has entrusted me with letters before.'

'Let me see your messages.'

For a moment Simon thought about rebelling, but decided that six against one was not fair odds. Keeping his eyes firmly fixed on the soldier, he reached in his saddle pack and drew out the vellum packet. The man took it, turned it over in his hands, studied the dangling red seal and, with a grunt, thrust the documents back at Simon.

'On your way,' he said gruffly and wafted his arm as though batting at a fly.

With clammy hands and thundering heart, Simon dug his heels into the roan's flanks and made haste to put distance between himself and the soldiers. He knew how intimidated the English must feel with such a watch on their activities. Prisoners in their own land.

In passable if not fluent English, he asked directions to Waltheof's hall of a man returning from the fields, his hoe over his shoulder, and was pointed towards a long building with a roof of wooden shingles and a stockade of pale ash stakes. A soldier guarded the gateway, the westering sun shimmering on the rivets of his hauberk. Seeing Simon approach, he stood to attention.

'Toki,' Simon greeted him with a smile. 'It's good to see you.' The warrior shaded his eyes with his palm and a sudden grin spread over his face. 'Master Simon! I didn't recognise you!'

'I've brought letters for the Earl. Is he here?'

'Aye, he's here.' Toki held the cob's bridle while Simon dismounted. 'Saint Winifred's bones, you've grown!' He gave the boy an exaggerated head-to-toe scrutiny.

'I know. I have to duck under the stable lintel at home,' Simon laughed. As he took the weight on his left leg, the familiar pain struck through him, but he had learned not to flinch or grimace. He wanted neither pity nor gentle handling: the less reaction he gave to his pain, the more men treated him as one of their own. Toki summoned a groom to take the horse and Simon told him about the knights he had encountered on the town street.

The smile fell from the Saxon's face. 'They'll be the sheriff's men from the castle,' he growled. 'And the bane of Earl Waltheof's life. King William might have given my lord his own niece to wife, but he has saddled him with a Norman keep and a Norman sheriff who has about as much notion of fair play as a starving wolf has of compassion for a tethered sheep.'

Simon gazed at him, but Toki compressed his lips. 'I've said too much, lad. Go on to the hall. The Earl will be right glad to see you . . . and his lady too,' he added as a diplomatic afterthought.

Simon forced a smile. He was looking forward to seeing Waltheof, but Lady Judith was a different prospect. Nor did he think that she would be overjoyed to greet him.

The arched windows along the length of the great hall were thrown open to admit spars of evening sunlight, gilding the floor rushes and trapping filaments of smoke from the central hearth. Simon caught glimpses of retainers busy assembling trestles for the evening meal and his mouth watered at the tantalising aroma of some kind of meat and onion stew.

On entering the building, he saw that the walls had been recently daubed with white limewash and as yet there were no layers of smoky residue to darken the brightness. Painted Saxon round shields were arrayed down the length of the hall, interspersed with crossed spears and battleaxes. At chair height, several narrow panels of embroidery colourfully divided the expanse of white wall. A lively young soldier by the name of Hrolf escorted him to Waltheof. Although the Earl had no private chamber separate from the hall, there was an area screened off by heavy woollen hangings that served as both apartment and bedchamber.

'Lady Judith likes to keep the curtain across,' said Hrolf. 'She would rather stay at Northampton because they have a private hall of their own, but my lord prefers Huntingdon – he says it is more homely.' Pausing, he raised his voice and craved admittance.

Waltheof answered in a cheerful bellow and, parting the curtain, Hrolf ushered Simon into the private chamber.

Waltheof was seated at a table, poring over a chessboard. One hand was braced on his thigh, the other rubbed his jaw. Judith sat opposite him, her dark braids glossy in the light from the window embrasure, her brow marred by a slight frown that Simon suspected had been caused by his intrusion.

'Simon!' The Earl sprang to his feet in a surge that made the table shake and knocked over several pawns. Beaming from ear to ear, he strode to Simon and swept him into a bone-crunching embrace. 'What brings you to Huntingdon?'

'I have letters from King William, my lord,' Simon replied. 'I asked if I could take this duty.'

Waltheof released him with a hefty slap on the shoulder that almost sent Simon to his knees. 'I'm glad that you did. Judith, look who's here!'

She did not rise but gave a thin smile from her place at the chessboard. 'You are welcome,' she said, her tone holding none of Waltheof's warmth.

Waltheof laughed broadly. 'Pay no heed. My wife is annoyed because she was beating me and you have spoiled her pleasure!'

Dutifully Simon made his obeisance to her. Earl Waltheof's jest had caused Judith's frown to deepen. Simon thought she was lovely, but petulant. He bowed over her shapely, ring-adorned fingers and saw that the hand she did not offer him was laid upon the ripe curve of her belly.

'Our child is due on the feast of Saint Cuthbert,' Waltheof announced, gazing proudly at his wife.

Simon looked blank. He knew many of the saints' days, but he was not familiar with all of them, especially English ones.

'In about two months' time,' Waltheof said with a wave of his hand. 'My lady desires the babe to be born at Northampton, so we are travelling there for the lying in.' Although he spoke with a smile, there was a certain tension at his eye corners, which suggested that the decision was not entirely of his making.

'You said you had letters,' Judith prompted, a flicker of impatience in her tone.

'Yes, my lady.' Simon delved in his satchel and, although Judith was nearer, handed the vellum packet to Waltheof in a show of masculine solidarity.

A look of amusement on his face, the Earl broke the seal and, unfolding the vellum, went to the window where he could read by the light of the westering sun.

'What does my uncle say?' Judith demanded. Her fingers twitched as if longing to snatch the missive from him.

Waltheof shrugged. 'William desires my pledge of assistance in his campaign against the Scots. I am to join him as soon as I may.' He handed her the vellum.

Judith took it and scanned the lines with an avid expression.

Waltheof stroked his beard and sighed. 'This comes at a bad time. I had hoped to be with you for the birth of our first child.'

Judith raised her head from the vellum and gave him a narrow look. 'You must do as my uncle requests. If you show reluctance, then you will displease him. There is nothing you can do at the birthing except pace outside the chamber door and get underfoot. It is not as though your presence will affect the outcome.'

Simon felt the tension coiling in the atmosphere, invisible but potent as the heat from a brazier.

'You would rather I went to war?'

'I would rather you did your duty to my uncle,' she said stiffly.

'What about my duty to you and the child?'

'Attending my uncle *is* that duty,' Judith replied tersely. 'You would not want him to seize your lands for your failure to perform your obligations.'

'No . . . but I care about you first . . .'

'Then do as my uncle bids. He is, after all, the King.'

Waltheof glowered and bit the side of his thumb. Judith stared back, her implacable will beating his down.

'Women.' The Earl gave a forced laugh and clapped his hand across Simon's shoulders. 'You never know whether you're going to burn or freeze when you go near them, only that either way you'll lose your ballocks.'

Judith averted her head and Simon could tell by the thrust of her jaw that her teeth were clenched.

Waltheof propelled Simon from the chamber and into the hall. 'Best to let the dust settle,' he murmured. 'My lady can be difficult to handle, but I would not change a hair on her head.'

'Only your own, my lord,' Simon said.

Waltheof ran his hands through his severe crop and smiled rather sheepishly. 'Aye, well, that's of no matter,' he said. 'Tell me what you have been doing.'

So Simon told him about his duties as a squire, about his training and how it was developing apace. Waltheof listened with the genuine interest and concern that made him so well liked by his soldiers, his retainers and the ordinary people of his earldom. Pride he might possess, but unlike his wife there was not an arrogant bone in his body.

'And the leg?' Waltheof glanced down.

Unconsciously, Simon had been putting his weight on his right side to ease the ache. 'It pains me sometimes,' he admitted. 'When I have been standing awhile, or when it is late at night and I have been on duty the day long.' He looked quickly at Waltheof. 'I am not complaining, my lord.'

'I know you are not. It was I who asked.'

'Mostly I do not notice.' It was both the truth and a lie. Simon was always aware of the injury. He was determined that he would not be different, but the path that was straight for others was often more hazardous for him because of the very nature of his handicap. Sometimes he felt bitter and resentful, but he tried to keep such feelings in check. A squire who was surly and uncommunicative received far more kicks and blows than one who was cheerful and swift to please. To avoid the subject of his leg, he told Waltheof about his meeting with the sheriff's men in the centre of Huntingdon.

Waltheof's expression clouded. 'The sheriffs of my lands,' he said in a voice that was now devoid of charity, 'are a thorn in my side. Why the King should give the offices to such wolves as Robert Ilger, William de Caghanes and Picot de Saye is beyond my understanding.'

Simon frowned. A vague memory came to him. He had been a junior squire collecting empty wine jugs in the hall at Rouen on the first night that the English hostages had arrived. He remembered the arm-wrestling contest and Waltheof's prowess against one of William's favoured mercenaries. 'Picot de Saye is a sheriff?' he asked.

'Of Cambridge.' Waltheof bared his teeth. 'And the worst

of them, although they are all painted with the same brush. They line their purses at the expense of the people and come down upon them with a mailed fist for the slightest transgression. I may as well not be earl here for they treat me with the utmost contempt.'

'Can you not speak to the King?'

Waltheof shook his head. 'I begin to think that William knows very well how his sheriffs behave and that it is his personal intention to hem me around with such men.'

'I have heard nothing at court,' Simon said, frowning.

'I do not suppose you would. Even you are not permitted into every corner of the King's life.'

Simon shifted uncomfortably, unsure how to respond. At court no one was ever open about their motives or thoughts. 'I think he is pleased to have you for a nephew,' he said diplomatically.

Waltheof smiled bleakly. 'He is pleased to have me where he wants me.'

Simon was spared from finding another reply as Judith's maid Sybille came towards them. A tiny baby was bound in a linen sling at her shoulder.

'Simon!' She embraced him with the side not occupied by the infant and kissed his cheek. 'Saints, boy, you are taller than me now!'

'And you seem to have acquired a baby.' Simon nervously eyed the rosy little face within the depths of the bundle.

'This,' said Sybille proudly, 'is my daughter, Helisende, born on the feast of Saint Winifred.'

Simon murmured congratulations, not quite sure of his ground. He could not ask outright if Sybille had a husband now. Her affections had always been peripatetic in the past and he could think of half a dozen candidates. He was also wary of small babies. For creatures that looked so innocent, they had the ability to make a fearsome noise and even more fearsome smells.

'Do you want to hold her?'

Simon wondered how to decline without seeming churlish.

'He will when she comes of age,' Waltheof rescued him with a twinkle and took the baby expertly into his own brawny arms. 'In the meantime I have to practise.' He smiled at Simon. 'Helisende is my god-daughter,' he said. 'Sybille married Toki last year.'

'Congratulations, mistress,' Simon murmured.

Sybille gave a little preen of her neck like a swan. 'I'm a goodwife now,' she said proudly. 'A fine lusty husband, a baby in the cradle and a mistress about to bear a babe of her own.' She gave a wry chuckle. 'They serve to keep me well out of mischief!' Plucking her daughter from Waltheof's arms, she bustled on her way.

'She and Toki are very happy together,' he murmured, and for a moment his expression was wistful. Then he shook himself like a dog shaking off water, and the look was gone. Simon did not dwell on the moment because at fourteen years old such matters were beyond his experience and of little interest. Besides, the steward had just sounded the dinner horn and Simon was ravenous. Everything but sustenance was suddenly unimportant.

It was a sweltering day at the beginning of August. In the women's bower at Waltheof's hall in Northampton the windows had been thrown open with the view that it would help the woman labouring on the birthing stool to expel the child from her womb.

Judith had begun her travail in the cool of the previous evening's moonrise. Now the sun blazed at its zenith and still the child had not come. Soaked in perspiration, her shift clung to her body, her swollen breasts and distended belly. They had unbraided her hair so that it would not bind the child in her womb, and it hung in sweat-soaked rat-tails to her hips.

Not in her darkest nightmares had Judith imagined the agony and the indignity that childbirth was visiting on her body. Surely this must be akin to the tortures suffered by damned souls in hell. The pains had grown steadily worse as her labour progressed. It was hours since her waters had broken in an enormous gush of fluid that had soaked the floor rushes and the skirts of the two midwives in attendance.

'Not long, my lady, not long now,' encouraged one of the women, making Judith sip from a cup of honey and water.

Judith's hands tightened on the cup as another pain built to an excruciating pitch and crashed over her. She clenched her teeth and forced down the scream that rose in her throat, her whole body rigid.

'You must not fight it, my lady,' said the other midwife and patted Judith's brow with a cloth soaked in lavender water. 'Let it come.'

The pain receded. Judith sagged on the birthing stool. She wanted to weep, but she would not do so in front of these women . . . and especially not in front of her mother, who was watching the proceedings with a critical eye. Adelaide had already reminded her several times that she was the niece of a king and the wife of an earl and that to scream like a fishwife was unseemly.

She was glad that Waltheof was absent at a parley with her uncle, laying the ground for the campaign against Malcolm of Scotland. Had he been present he would have been pacing outside the room, demanding every few moments to know how she fared. She could not have borne his anxiety on top of her own. Besides, Waltheof and her mother were tepid with each other, and the less they had to share company the better for all concerned.

Another contraction gripped her in its pincers and made her its prey. She writhed and called out to Saint Margaret, protector of women in childbirth. At least by exhorting the saint she could give vent to her pain.

'That's it, my love,' encouraged the senior midwife and knelt beneath the birthing stool to examine how matters were progressing. 'At the peak of the next pain you must begin pushing. We'll have the babe in your arms before the light fades.'

Judith dug her fingernails into her palms at this news and swallowed the sob in her throat. She did not know how much more she could endure.

'You are doing very well, my lady,' the woman encouraged with a smile. 'The child is large and robust.'

'Not too large?' Adelaide queried tersely.

'Oh no, my lady,' the midwife hastened to reassure. 'Just a good size. Your daughter's hips are wide enough to accommodate him, but he is taking his own sweet time to be born.'

'Hah, lazy like his father,' Adelaide sniffed.

Despite her mother's words, Judith founded the slightest glimmer of satisfaction. A healthy boy, she thought. An heir for Huntingdon and Northampton. That would silence her mother, whose first two children had been daughters.

She clung to the notion as the pains surged and she toiled to expel the infant from her womb. He would be named William for her uncle. Waltheof might want to call him Siward, but Waltheof was not here, and the say was hers.

The candle clock had burned down two more notches before the baby's head finally crowned between Judith's thighs. Panting, almost spent, she lolled against the midwife supporting her.

'One more effort, my lady,' the woman crooned. 'One more push.'

Judith heard the words from a distance and summoned her strength for a final thrust. If the child was not born on this last surge, she knew that she would die.

The pain ripped through her in a tearing surge. Judith bore down, the tendons in her throat standing out and her face flushing red as wine. The second midwife cried triumphantly as the baby's head was born. Adelaide moved swiftly to the side of the birthing stool.

'What is it?' she demanded eagerly, looming like a crone over a cauldron.

'Can't tell, yet, my lady. One more little push . . .'

The baby slithered from Judith's body into the swathe of linen that the midwife was holding ready.

'A boy . . .' said Adelaide triumphantly. Her eyes were narrow as she sought to focus.

The baby spluttered, raised a tentative wail, hesitated, then bawled full force.

Looking discomfited, the midwife unwound the bluish, pulsing cord from between the infant's legs. 'No, my lady, your daughter has a girl child,' she said in a subdued voice.

'A girl?' Adelaide's lips pursed.

'Yes, my lady.' Snicking the cord with a small pair of shears, she swaddled the baby tightly in bands of fresh, soft linen. The bawls subsided to kitten mewings and snuffles.

Judith closed her eyes. She squeezed them tightly shut, but still tears of weakness and disappointment leaked out from beneath her lids. All that effort, all the squalor and pain for a girl child, not the heir of her longing.

'Do you want to hold her?' The midwife brought the wrapped baby to the bedside.

'No.' Judith turned her head aside and refused even to look. 'Take her away. I can bear no more.'

Sybille glanced at Adelaide, and when she did not move stepped forward herself. 'My mistress is exhausted,' she murmured to the midwife. 'I'll hold the babe for now.'

The woman put the infant into Sybille's arms. 'It takes them like that sometimes,' she whispered. 'They sets their heart on a lad, and when the labour goes hard and the child is female they're mortal disappointed. She'll come around soon enough.'

In spite of the lowered voice, Judith heard what the midwife was whispering to Sybille. She did not think that she was ever going to come around to taking joy in the child. All she wanted was for everyone to go away so that she could sleep and forget.

Adelaide came to the side of the birthing stool. 'Look at

me, daughter,' she said. It was no coincidence that the last word was emphasised.

Judith gazed at her mother through the spikes of tears and sweat clogging her lashes.

'I know how much the bearing of a girl child is a disappointment. I suffered it myself, twice over, but it is something with which you must learn to live. A daughter will be a companion to you as she grows, and useful in making marriage alliances. Be thankful that the child is strong and safely delivered.' Awkwardly, she pushed a sticky tendril of hair off Judith's brow. 'It is perhaps not the time to talk of such matters, but you might be more fortunate on the next occasion. You can see that I was when I bore Stephen.'

Judith clenched her teeth as her loins cramped and the second midwife set about dealing with the delivery of the afterbirth. 'You are right, Mother,' she choked. 'It is not the time to talk of such matters.'

Adelaide let out her breath on an exasperated sigh and went to turn down the bedcoverings.

Through a haze of pain, misery and exhaustion, Judith was aware that on a certain level her mother was relieved. If Judith had borne a son, the balance of power between them would have shifted subtlely in Judith's direction. For the moment, Adelaide continued to have the upper hand.

Sybille jogged the baby gently in her arms. 'Just wait until your papa sees you,' she crooned. 'You'll be the sun and moon to him.'

Judith was assaulted by a vicious pang of jealousy, swiftly followed by remorse. How could she be jealous of her own child? Tears filled her eyes and swelled in her throat until it ached fiercely with the effort of holding the dam.

'Come, my lady, let us make you more comfortable.' Soothing her as though she were a small child, the senior midwife helped Judith from the stool to the bed while the other dealt with the afterbirth, which was to be blessed by the priest and buried. A maid set about clearing up the bloody rushes beneath the birthing stool. The stool itself was removed for scrubbing and storing until it should be needed again.

The smooth, lavender-scented sheets and feather mattress felt like heaven beneath Judith's sore body. Her stained and sweat-soaked shift was thrown on the laundry pile. The women washed her in scented warm water, tidied her hair into two long, dark braids, and gave her a fresh shift to wear. Judith's tears retreated as her dignity was restored and she felt the familiar mantle of control begin to settle back around her shoulders, cocooning her from harm.

Sybille approached the bed, the baby snuffling gently in her arms. The look of tenderness on her face made Judith feel guilty and a little resentful.

'Here,' said the maid as if reading her thoughts. 'You hold her.' Gently lowering the baby, she arranged Judith's arms so that they supported the delicate skull. 'Doesn't she look like her father?'

Judith stared into the crumpled features, unable to see any resemblance at all, except perhaps to a wizened turnip. Its face was red and its eyes had a strange, shiny appearance. The tuft of hair sticking out from beneath the edge of the blanket was stiff with birthing fluid, but the underlying colour shone through – copper gold, like Waltheof's. She had heard women speak of overwhelming love at first sight, but no such emotion resided in her breast. She was surprised; she was curious in a detached sort of way – could not believe that this creature had come from her body. And she was so disappointed that she had failed to bear a son. The baby, who had been settled in Sybille's embrace, began to fret. The red face grew redder and the little face screwed up. A hole opened in its face and an enormous noise emerged.

Judith panicked and pushed the baby away. Leaning over, Sybille swiftly gathered the bawling bundle in her arms and cradled it until the roars subsided into angry hiccups. The infant turned her head and made rooting motions at Sybille's breast.

'I think that she is hungry,' the maid murmured. 'Perhaps if you were to feed her.'

Judith looked horrified. 'I cannot,' she whispered. 'You ask too much. She has taken too much from me already.'

Sybille bit her lip. She turned to Adelaide for guidance. Looking peeved and anxious, the older woman waved her hand. 'You are a new mother yourself, you have milk in your breasts. It will be no hardship to feed the child for now. Your mistress is too distraught.'

'My lady.' Cradling the baby tenderly in her arms, Sybille carried her out to the antechamber. She unpinned her gown, unlaced the drawstring of her chemise and put the child to suckle. As the little jaws worked, she touched the copper bronze curl with a gentle forefinger. Tears of compassion filled her eyes, and love. How could Lady Judith reject such a beautiful, vulnerable little thing? When she had borne her own daughter, she had been unable to wait to hold her in her arms. Regardless of the pain and the exhaustion, she had wept with joy, not chagrin.

Perhaps it would be different when Lady Judith had slept. Her labour had been long and difficult and she was clearly at the end of her endurance. 'Never fret, little one,' Sybille whispered to the baby. 'I will make sure you do not lack for love, and your papa will adore you. I know he will.'

It was late when Waltheof returned to Northampton from his parley with William. Tired and hungry, he rode into the courtyard, dismounted from his horse and handed the reins to the youth who came running.

'Any news, Brand?' he asked, finding a smile despite his weariness.

'Yes, my lord,' the stable lad said. 'The Countess was safely delivered of a daughter before Compline this very eve.'

Waltheof stood still while he absorbed the news, and then, forgetting his exhaustion, he ran.

'Judith is sleeping,' Adelaide said, standing across the

bedchamber doorway as fiercely as any armed guard. 'The birth was difficult and she is very tired.'

Waltheof struggled with his impatience and the urge to swipe his termagant mother-in-law out of his way. 'Nevertheless, I would see my wife and my child. If Judith is sleeping, I promise I will not waken her.'

With obvious reluctance, Adelaide stepped to one side. Her nose wrinkled. Waltheof looked at her censorious expression, sniffed his armpit, and asked her politely if she would arrange for a bathtub to be prepared. With tightly pursed lips Adelaide stalked away to summon the maids and Waltheof laid his hand to the latch.

There was no sound in the room. Judith was as fastidious in sleep as she was awake. He had never heard her snore or mumble. She lay on her back, the woven coverlet rising and falling as she breathed. Waltheof tiptoed to the bedside and looked down at her in the light from the thick wax candle. The dark shadows beneath her closed lids spoke not just of weariness like his own but sheer exhaustion. Her hair had been neatly braided, reminding him of a child. She looked so vulnerable that he wanted to sweep her into his embrace and protect her from everything. He had to fold his hands in his belt and force himself not to touch her.

He peered cautiously into the cradle at the side of the bed, but it was empty. Indeed, it had never been used, the linen coverings smooth and unrumpled. A slight sound in the doorway caused him to turn.

Sybille was standing on the threshold, a bundle in her arms. Laying her finger to her lips, she beckoned him from the room. 'If she cries, it will disturb her mother,' she whispered.

Waltheof stepped out into the antechamber, his arms already held out to receive the child.

Sybille did not have to tell him how to hold his tiny daughter; he had a natural instinct. His large hand supported her tiny fragile skull and her body lay along the length of his powerful forearm. Tears filled Waltheof's eyes and spilled down his cheeks. He had never set eyes on anything as beautiful, or as moving. A part of himself, a part of Judith, mingled in this perfect, tiny creature. The baby's eyes had been closed, but now they opened and studied him with such owlish solemnity that he laughed through his tears.

Sybille sniffed too and wiped her cheeks. 'She's been christened Matilda in honour of the Queen,' she said.

Waltheof stroked a tender forefinger upon the soft little cheek. 'The King and Queen are to be her godparents,' he said.

Sybille hesitated. Waltheof looked at her. 'What is it?'

'Nothing, my lord. Perhaps it is better that you know that my lady was disappointed not to bear you a son. Countess Adelaide has appointed me as a wet nurse for the moment.'

Waltheof glanced through the crack of the door into the room where his wife slept. 'She will come around,' he said. He knew how much store Judith had set on bearing a boy. But how could she fail not to fall in love with the enchanting baby daughter they had made between them?

The infant snuffled. Waltheof nestled her more securely in the crook of his arm and set off towards the outer chamber door.

'Where are you going?' Sybille's voice rose on a worried note.

Waltheof paused and swung round. 'To show her off to her people,' he said with an exalted smile. 'I want everyone to see her, from the steward to the stable boy.'

'Will the Countess Adelaide approve?' Sybille looked anxious.

The relaxed muscles in Waltheof's face grew taut. 'I do not give a grain of sand whether the Countess approves or not,' he growled. 'For the moment, this child is my heir, and I want my people to see her, and all the pride and love I have for her.' With determined tread, tear streaks shining on his face, he carried his newborn daughter into the public domain of the great hall.

CHAPTER 14

Abbot Ulfcytel leaned over the cradle and studied the small baby gurgling on the coverlet of soft lambskin. She waved her arms at him and kicked her legs.

'My wife says she should be swaddled to make her limbs grow straight, but it seems a pity to me not to let her feel the joy of using them,' Waltheof said. 'I cannot see that an hour's freedom will ruin her for life.'

Ulfcytel smiled. 'Nor I,' he said, 'but women are ever protective of their offspring, especially the firstborn.' He prodded the infant with a gentle forefinger and was rewarded by a crow of response and an animated flail of limbs.

Waltheof suspected that Judith's protectiveness stemmed from a desire to order the world as she chose rather than from maternal devotion. His mother-in-law had departed to her own lands in the south a week ago and Waltheof had quietly thanked God for that particular mercy. Judith was always worse when Adelaide was at hand to aid and abet.

He and Ulfcytel were standing in the garden at Northampton. A last flourish of summer had swept the herb beds with sunshine and pointed the sundial to the hour of sext. Nearby the gardeners were harvesting marigold seeds and tidying the straggle of herbs that were tiring as a hot summer wilted towards autumn. On the morrow he was to take his troops and ride north to join King William on the campaign against Malcolm of Scotland.

Waltheof was apprehensive. Edgar Atheling was sheltering at the Scots court and he had no desire to meet his
former ally and companion on the battlefield.

Ulfcytel wrapped his gnarled brown hands around his
staff. 'I am pleased to see you settled with lands and a family,
my son,' he said. 'I feared for you when you joined the Danes
in the North and King William took his revenge.'

Waltheof smiled uneasily and looked away. 'I am going to
the North as a Norman now,' he replied, and thrust his fingers
through his short, coppery hair as if hoping to discover that
its former abundance had grown back. 'It will be hard, but
as Judith tells me . . . it is my duty and I have no other choice.'

Judith was polite to Abbot Ulfcytel but vexed by his presence
at their table. He spoke very little French, and Judith had no
intention of learning the coarse, guttural tongue of the
English. There was soil beneath his fingers from tending his
garden; the cuffs of his alb were patched and the only possession that reflected his rank was his staff with its beautiful
carved ivory head.

Waltheof, however, was so fond of him that he treated the
rotund, coarse little abbot as one of his family. Ulfcytel dined at
their table more frequently than any other guest, much to Judith's
irritation. When she was not enduring Ulfcytel's presence she
had to suffer the company of the Breton Ralf de Gael, Earl of
Norfolk, whose smooth, bland manner and sly ways she disliked
intensely. She could not understand why Waltheof favoured the
man other than their shared capacity for drink. Her husband's
judgement of others was unsound and a cause for worry.

Making her excuses to Waltheof and Ulfcytel, Judith
retired to her chamber. She yearned for the refinement of the
Norman court, just as once she had yearned to escape from
its stultifying confines. To hear French spoken as a matter of
course, rather than mangled haltingly through an English
accent. To be accorded the full deference due to her rank.
Here she was aware that people bowed to her face and gave

her resentful looks behind her back. She was their beloved earl's Norman wife, an intruder, a burden they had to shoulder for their lord's sake. She knew that without her presence in the hall men would be slackening their belts and reaching anew for the ale. The laughter would grow raucous and bawdy, Waltheof's retainers gladly abandoning the notion that they were constrained by Norman rule.

Tomorrow Waltheof would leave for the North and she would become responsible in his absence for the welfare of the earldom. The notion was pleasing. She would have work to keep her occupied, even if it was an uphill struggle to deal with the recalcitrant English. She enjoyed the duties of administration and dealing justice. Waltheof was not so fond of such toil and left much of it to his officials, but Judith would often linger in the hall to observe them at work and provide the necessary overseeing of authority.

Sybille sat in a seat near the brazier, suckling baby Matilda at her breast. Judith thanked God that her maid had sufficient milk to feed two infants, for the notion of suckling a baby at her own breast disturbed her. Some folk said that giving a nobly born baby sustenance from a baser source would coarsen the child. Others said that, providing the wet nurse was of good character with abundant milk, it made no difference. Sybille's character had given cause for concern in the past, but since wedding Toki she had settled down and there was no denying the quality of her milk. Little Matilda was thriving and growing plump.

'She's a greedy one,' Sybille said with a laugh. 'I think she is going to be as big as her father when she's full grown.'

Judith winced at the notion of a woman the size of Waltheof. Certainly, Matilda had his hair. The fine wisps on the baby's skull were like threads of gold caught in the light of the setting sun, her complexion the pink and white of dog roses. Folk cooed over her daughter and said that she was beautiful, but to Judith she looked like any other baby. Sometimes she would stand over her and try to find some spark of maternal devotion, but it was as if a barrier stood between her and the child. It might have been different if Matilda was a son. At least then she would have had pride.

Waltheof doted on the baby and would often fetch her from her cradle and carry her around in the crook of his arm, talking softly to her, showing her the world. Judith had felt emotions then, but none of which she was proud. Indeed, she had prayed on her knees in the chapel for them to be expunged.

Sybille gently prised the baby's jaws off her nipple. 'Asleep,' she said softly, a tender smile on her face that made Judith feel mean and unworthy. She watched the maid expertly change the baby's wet linens then place her snug and replete at the head of the fleece-lined cradle. Little Helisende, Sybille's own daughter, occupied the foot. 'They won't waken again much before the second matins bell – prime if fortune smiles,' Sybille said. Rocking the cradle with a tap of her foot, she removed her wimple and began loosening her thick brown braids.

Judith looked at her askance.

'You have to send your man away to war with a fond fare-well,' Sybille said knowingly. 'I don't want Toki getting randy with some red-haired Scottish wench.' Taking her cloak down from a peg set in the wall, she went to the door. 'Besides, you'll be wanting some time alone with your lord.' Winking, not waiting upon a dismissal, the maid left the room, her step light and swift.

Judith flushed. She and Waltheof had not bedded together since Matilda's birth. Her body had needed time to heal, and a man was not supposed to lie with a woman within forty days of childbed, the Church said so; indeed, some Church teachings went further than that. It was six weeks since Matilda's birth. Two and forty days. She went to look down at the sleeping children. The next one would be a boy. That's what everyone told her – as they had told her that Matilda would be a male. And before a child could be born, it had to be begotten, and then forced into the world through a travail of pain.

Shivering, Judith turned away from the cradle and went beyond the curtains into the chamber that she and Waltheof shared. The large bed was the centrepiece of the room, its sides carved with a strange interlacing design of serpents chasing and swallowing each other. It had belonged to Waltheof's father, the legendary Earl Siward, and to his father before him. The hints of pagan religion in the carving filled Judith with unease. Waltheof, however, had grown intractable when she suggested they be rid of it, and had sworn that while he lived it would remain.

Piled around the room were items of baggage that on the morrow would be loaded onto pack ponies. His mail hauberk, neatly wrapped in a waxed bundle and greased with pig fat to prevent it from rusting; his round shield, which he still preferred over the Norman kite design, the terrible rune-engraved axe, again handed down from his father. She shuddered as she looked at the edge, shining in the candlelight like rippled water. He had killed Normans with that weapon. She was seldom fanciful, but she thought that if she peered too closely in the reflection of the steel she might see scenes from its bloody past flowing across the mirrored surface.

Averting her head from the axe, she sat gingerly on the bed with its coverlet of silver fox pelts and summoned one of her other tiring maids to help her disrobe.

Waltheof arrived a short while later, slightly loquacious with drink but almost sober. She heard him stop in the curtained-off antechamber and knew that he had paused by the cradle. He never passed it at night without looking upon his daughter. Judith felt the familiar pang of jealousy, followed by one of guilt. With an irritated gesture she dismissed the maid and sat up in bed, her chemise firmly laced at her throat, her hair combed and smoothly rebraided.

Waltheof parted the door curtain and entered the room. Judith gazed upon her husband and her breath caught with that strange fluttering of panic and desire that she had never been able to reconcile. How could she be so attracted to him, and feel such impatience at the same time?

'Ulfcytel sent me,' he said with a smile. 'He said that I should not be spending my last night before a campaign in the company of an old priest but in the warm arms of my wife.'

Judith raised her brows. 'So you could not come to that conclusion yourself?'

'Well, yes, I was preparing to be polite, but his perception was the swifter.' Waltheof sat down on the edge of the bed and began removing his clothes. 'Besides,' he added softly, 'sleeping in the warm arms of my wife when I cannot make love to her has been a bind beyond endurance these past weeks.'

Judith fiddled with the neat lacing of her shift. There was an immodest heat and heaviness in her woman's parts. It was lust, she thought. No matter how she battled to subdue it, her need was the stronger.

'Some priests say that a woman is not clean to lie with until eighty days have passed from the birth,' she procrastinated.

'Eighty days!' Waltheof looked at her in consternation. 'I have not heard that one before!'

'It happens if the child is a girl. I think it is to do with the sin of Eve.'

He snorted down his nose. 'I would say that "some priests" must hate women beyond all charity, but if the notion of coupling with me disturbs you, I can always fetch Ulfcytel to bless our bed. I am sure he will be delighted to do so.'

Judith shook her head. 'That will not be necessary,' she said in a choked voice. She could imagine nothing worse than having the small, earthy abbot with his ragged tonsure blessing their union. 'I too think that forty days is sufficient.'

'I think it is too long.' Waltheof's voice was heartfelt. He finished undressing and turned to her. Already he was magnificently erect. 'Ah, Judith,' he said softly. He reached to unpluck the laces of her chemise. 'You cannot know . . .'

But she did know, and whilst a part of her was shocked another part welcomed him with open arms and wide-parted thighs, and as he lifted her buttocks and thrust into her she coiled her legs around his hips and dug her nails into his broad back. The bed became a Viking ship, rocking on a stormy sea, and she was a slave, tied to the mast and ravished by its seawolf master. The imagery tore through her, heightening her lust. She was helpless; what was happening was not her fault, and she was not to blame. When she climaxed she muffled her scream against the polished curve of his shoulder and heard with fierce pleasure the roar of his release and felt the pulse of his seed within her. The next child would be a boy. No girl could possibly be born of such a wild and vigorous mating.

Simon's jaw cracked as he did his best to conceal a yawn. The dawnlight was a low flush on the eastern horizon, but he had been awake and on duty for most of the night. He wondered how the King could be so indefatigable. William had not retired until well past midnight and had risen long before prime. Simon had staggered blearily around the campaign tent, fetching him a ewer of warm water to bathe his hands and face and assisting him to dress. He had attended mass with William in the chapel tent, had knelt among the other battle commanders, barons and squires to receive the body and blood of Christ. Waltheof had been present, looking as bleary as Simon felt, his coppery hair in need of a trim and his stubble thickening into a corn-coloured beard. He had managed a wink at Simon and by swift, silent gestures had intimated that too much ale the night before was the reason for his malaise.

Now Simon was burnishing William's helm. He could have delegated the task to one of the junior squires, but ever since entering the King's employ the duty had been his and it had become a ritual that he guarded jealously. Helm in one hand, cloth in the other, he went to the tent flap, where his gaze was met by ranks of canvas shelters. Soldiers stood around the haze of their morning fires dining on flat bread and ale, and through the wreaths of smoke there was a heather-scented nip in the air. The grooms were readying the horses and Simon could hear the snap of the banners in the stiff breeze that had risen with the dawn.

The Norman army had been on the march for several days, prepared for war but progressing unhindered. No Scots army came raging from the heather to prevent William from entering Lothian, crossing the Forth and marching on into King Malcolm's domain.

Hooves thudded outside the tent and a large chestnut stallion blocked his light. 'I have just been speaking to the King, and he says that you have his permission to ride out awhile,' Waltheof leaned down from the saddle to announce. He looked more awake than he had done an hour since. He had obviously dunked his hair in the burn, for it was sleeked back from his forehead and gleamed like wet rust. His grizzle of beard remained; he had not seen fit to barber it off.

Simon gave the helm another polish. The notion of riding out was a lure too tempting to resist. 'If you but wait a moment while I finish this. It has to be right.'

'Of course it has,' Waltheof said with a straight face, although Simon was sure he detected a twinkle in the deep blue eyes. 'It would not do for King William to greet the King of Scotland in anything less than royal splendour.'

Simon finished burnishing the helm and set it carefully to one side on a wadded linen cloth. Telling the junior squire to check over the other equipment and make sure that the wine pitcher was full and fresh bread to hand, he left his post and approached the horse line where his roan cob was dozing. Waltheof followed, his huscarls Toki and Siggurd riding a few paces behind with swords at their hips and round shields slung at their backs.

Untethering his mount, Simon grasped a handful of mane and vaulted nimbly across the saddle, showing off a little in front of the men. Waltheof's lips twitched.

'Not only a trusted messenger, but a fine horseman, I see,' he teased.

Simon gave him a self-conscious grin. Then he sobered. 'There was a time when I thought I might never do such a thing,' he said.

'I never doubted it. You have a will the equal of my wife's – formidable.' Waltheof tugged on the reins and set his heels to the chestnut's flanks.

They rode past the sentries and away from the Norman camp, following the rutted cart track through the hardy sheep pasture – although no sheep grazed the turf. All livestock had been spirited away by the locals so that it would not end up as dinner for Scots or Norman soldiers. The nearest settlement was the town of Abernethay, which their scouts had reported as three miles distant and where the Scots army was mustering behind its defensive palisade.

The wind gusted. Waltheof's sleek hair turned wild as it dried and beat around his face. Their horses climbed away from the Norman camp, muscles straining, ears pricked. Simon opened his mouth and let the air blow into him until he felt as though he could take off and scud across the sky like a cloud.

On the crest of a hill they drew rein to let their horses regain their breath. Below them the land spread out like an elaborate embroidery, moors and mountains, russet and purple, clean scented with heather. Here the bones of the earth felt close to the surface, no padding of well-fed flesh to conceal their beauty. The ride and the wild scenery exhilarated Simon, but after a moment he found himself wondering what the blue smudge of the horizon concealed. What lay beyond the ability of the eye to perceive? If only he could climb and see all with the eyes of an eagle.

'The King said to me earlier that it will not come to a fight,' Waltheof said, gazing into the distance. 'We are too strong for Malcolm.' He smiled sourly. 'Men begin to think that William of Normandy is unstoppable.'

Simon said nothing. He heard a great deal, being William's squire of the chamber, but he never spoke of the matters discussed therein. His discretion was a matter of pride, discipline and honour; no one would ever accuse him of braying confidences abroad. Representatives from King Malcolm had arrived shortly after mass bearing messages for William. Simon already knew what was going to happen. He glanced at Waltheof, wanting to speak, constrained not to.

'It isn't true,' Waltheof said softly into Simon's silence. 'We could have stopped him in York if only we had acted together instead of squandering our advantage. I am not advocating treason,' he added quickly, as Simon drew a sharp breath. 'The Danes have gone home and there is no one who possesses the same skills of leadership as William. Edgar Atheling is a weak reed, the sons of Harold are pirates, and after York I know that my own abilities are not up to the task.' He gave a self-deprecatory smile. 'A man should know his own weaknesses. Besides, a child of my blood is William's own great-niece.'

Simon wondered uneasily if there was a crumb of bitterness festering within Waltheof. It was likely, but then from what he had also heard that morning William had a possible cure for it. 'The Scots are coming to parley,' he said, pointing towards a party of horsemen who had appeared on the track below. The new morning sun slanted over their armour and spears, making a brave glitter. A standard-bearer carried aloft the banner of King Malcolm of the Scots and close behind him, riding a white horse, was a thickset man of middle years who resembled a peasant but wore a crown at his brow.

Simon reined his horse around. 'I'll be needed for chamber duties, and King William will want you present, my lord.'

Waltheof gave Simon a thoughtful look. 'Will he, indeed?'

'Yes,' Simon answered. 'I can say no more, save that it will be to your advantage.'

Malcolm of Scotland was a little over forty years old with sandy hair turning silver at the temples and narrow light blue eyes.

Last year he had set aside his first wife and married Margaret, the sister of Edgar Atheling, thereby binding his own house of Dunkeld to that of the ancient West Saxon line.

The fact that Margaret desired to enter a nunnery had been ignored. Margaret herself, after some protest, had finally agreed to the marriage. It seemed that she had swiftly become reconciled to her change of direction, for she was already great with child. It was rumoured that her fierce, rambunctious husband doted upon his faery-blonde wife and that he was warm clay in her hands. It was also rumoured that she had embarked on the task of taming and civilising the Scots court. If she was not going to be a nun, then at least she could dwell in an atmosphere conducive to harmony.

There was, however, small sign of that harmony in William's campaign tent. Malcolm of Scotland, known as Caen Mor or Big Head by his own people, was bullish and opinioned. Even if he had come to yield to William of Normandy, he had small intention of doing it with grace.

Simon poured wine and unobtrusively handed it around. Malcolm took the proffered goblet, sniffed suspiciously and then drank. His lips twisted. 'I've tasted better cat's pee,' he said, speaking French but in such a mangled, guttural accent that although the meaning was clear the words themselves were difficult to decipher. Simon was fascinated. Waltheof looked both amused and bemused. William's face wore its customary blank expression, giving nothing away.

'Is ale more to your taste, Lord King?' Simon asked politely. Malcolm's shrewd warrior's eyes met his. 'Aye,' he snapped. 'Give me ale, although I doot that any o' your Sassenach muck will taste good on my palate.'

'And yet you have put aside your first Scots wife to take a "Sassenach" bride,' William said with deceptive mildness. 'And I understand that congratulations are in order now that she is with child.'

Malcolm scowled and dug his fingers into his beautiful,

gilded belt. 'Ye'll nae mock me,' he growled.

'Far from it,' William said smoothly. 'I was merely pointing out that a ruler must act on expediency before instinct – or why are we both here?'

Malcolm continued to glower. Simon returned with a brimming stone cup. 'It is heather ale, Lord King,' he said, 'of your country's own brewing.'

'Hah, and stolen by Normans,' Malcolm sneered, but he took the cup and sank a long mouthful. 'It will dae,' he said with an irritated wave of his hand.

Simon bowed and retreated. Ever curious about the ways of other peoples, he had sampled Scots fare in the form of a sort of meat and barley pudding boiled in the membrane of a sheep's stomach and served with a thick bread cooked on an open griddle. Compared to the fare of the Norman court it was coarse and strange, but it had been hot and nourishing and had kept out the bitter evening chill. He had to agree with Malcolm that heather ale was preferable to their Norman wine, which had not travelled well. Waltheof seemed to think so too, because he was eyeing Malcolm's cup with a covetous gaze. Simon poured another measure of the ale and unobtrusively exchanged it for Waltheof's wine, thereby earning himself a quick smile of gratitude.

The negotiations went forward in fits and starts, mostly caused by Malcolm's mangled accent and his determination to be cantankerous even though he was here to surrender. He had with him his eldest son, a twelve-year-old who was to be given as hostage for his father's good behaviour. The lad, quiet and dark-haired, was a slender contrast to his thickset overbearing father.

'Ye'll treat him well,' Malcolm growled, 'else I'll make garters of every pair o' Norman guts between here and Durham town.'

William inclined his head. 'Providing you keep to your side of the bargain, your son will come to no harm,' he replied.

Malcolm scowled and blustered, but finally agreed to the

terms. However, neither he nor William were yet prepared to seal them by the ceremony of making the kiss of peace. Both men still had points to settle. William desired the removal of Edgar Atheling from the Scottish court.

'I canna dae that, the man's my brother-in-law!' Malcolm's eyebrows bristled and he folded his arms belligerently.

'The man is a thorn in my side who persists in fomenting rebellion. In yielding to me, you are accepting me as your overlord and you cannot harbour my enemies at your court. Your brother-in-law or not, Edgar Atheling goes.' William spread his hands on the trestle and leaned on them to emphasise his point.

There was a long silence but only one outcome. Everyone knew that Malcolm had no choice. It was one of the prices to pay for peace and the only way that the Norman force was going to withdraw back across the Forth.

'If I do that for you, then you mun dae something for me,' Malcolm said.

William raised his brows.

Malcolm glared with triumphant malice at Earl Gospatric. 'I'll no have that blethershite Gospatric facing me o'er the border. There'll be more bloodshed than ye've ever seen if he stays.'

Gospatric leaped to his feet, his complexion fire-red and his hand going to his empty scabbard, all swords having been prudently left outside. 'You dare to make such demands!' he spat. 'You're naught but a murdering, primitive heathen with sheepshit for brains!'

'And you're nae more than a runty wee arsewipe who I'll nae entertain as my neighbour.'

Gospatric launched himself at Malcolm and got such a grip on his throat that it took three men to haul him off and then pin him back against the side of the tent. Choking, Malcolm fell to his knees, and Waltheof went to his assistance. With cold fury in his eyes William gestured two guards to carry Gospatric outside.

'Ye see?' Malcolm wheezed. 'What chance is there for peace wi' him on my borders?'

William did not look best pleased. 'You force my hand,' he said, 'and that is something that I do not like.'

'Hah, well I don't like yielding to you, but I mun do it to survive,' Malcolm rasped.

William swung round to pace the short length of the tent. Simon watched him. Outside Gospatric could be heard wrestling with the soldiers. There was indeed a bitter enmity between Gospatric and Malcolm. The former had plundered the Scots lowlands last year, serving a warning that Scots raids on English territory must stop. In retaliation Malcolm had brought devastating fire and sword across the border, his attack so savage that William had come harrying north to deal with the situation.

'Very well,' William said, swinging round. 'I will appoint a new earl, and raids on both sides will cease.'

'That depends on who ye appoint,' Malcolm said.

William rubbed his jaw as if deliberating, but Simon knew that his mind was already made up and had long been so. 'I have in mind Earl Waltheof of Huntingdon,' he said. 'He has a natural entitlement to the position, and although he has a Norman wife he is without Norman blood.' A wintry smile curved his lips as he made the last observation.

Waltheof's breath hissed through his teeth and Simon saw astonishment widen his eyes and brighten his complexion.

Malcolm turned his gaze on Waltheof and eyed him craftily. 'I suppose needs must when the De'il drives,' he pronounced, but he was clearly not displeased by the choice. Why should he be, Simon thought. Waltheof might be a fine warrior in his mid-twenties with an enhanced reputation from the Danish invasion of York, but as yet he was no Siward the Strong, the very mention of his name to be feared. Doubtless the King of Scots thought that he could run rings around him.

Looking dazed, Waltheof first stood up then knelt at

William's feet and bowed his head. 'It is a great honour that you do me, your grace.'

'It is indeed,' William said. 'Make sure you honour the position as much as it honours you.' Stooping he took Waltheof's hands between his own and gave him the kiss of peace on either cheek, thereby conferring on him the earldom of Northumbria that had once been held by his father.

'And what of Gospatric?' Malcolm demanded with a contemptuous jerk of his head. 'What will ye do wi' him?'

William stood straight. 'He can be escorted to the nearest shore and put out of these isles with your outlawed brother by-marriage,' he said curtly.

Malcolm nodded, accepting the fact, then turned to Waltheof, who was slowly easing to his feet, a beatific expression on his face. 'Watch yoursel', laddie,' he said. 'Your king uses men like food. Eats them up and spits out the bones when he's had the sustenance.'

Simon frowned. Malcolm had it wrong. William did indeed devour men, but if he discarded them it was not because he had no more use for them, but rather that they were unable to live beneath his harsh codes and demands for unquestioning loyalty.

'Since I have never gained so much goodwill from being anyone else's man, I'll take the risk,' Waltheof answered, inclining his head in courtesy to the King of Scots. 'I am sure that you are a gambling man yourself, sire.'

'Aye,' Malcolm said sourly. 'And look where it got me.'

Two weeks later William prepared to leave for Normandy where a border war was brewing with his neighbours in Maine. Waltheof returned home to Judith, bearing with him the momentous news that now, as his father had been, he was Earl of Northumbria.

Judith's pride in his accomplishment glowed out of her eyes. When he kissed her, she kissed him back. In bed her responses were almost feverish and he brought her to pleasure twice before he reached his own. It was as though his new status was a powerful love potion that she was unable to resist.

'Now you are truly a man of influence,' she declared as they lay together in the breathless aftermath of lovemaking, her fingers gently tugging on his coppery chest hair. He had shaved his beard and had the barber return his growing locks to the harshness of a Norman crop in consideration of his wife.

He was aware that his new title meant a great deal to her, but he had not realised how much until he saw her incandescence at the news. He was amused, and also, if the truth were known, a little uneasy. His love for Judith was not bound up in her status as the Conqueror's niece, yet it seemed that her regard for him was powerfully influenced by his social standing. But he said nothing. To have done so would have exposed aspects of their relationship that were better kept buried. Besides, he was very tender of her, for she was again with child. The infant had been conceived on the night that he'd departed for Scotland. At the most there would be eleven months between the new babe and its sister.

'This time it will be a son, for our lands,' Judith said fiercely, and taking his hand, laid it upon her smooth belly. 'I feel it as strongly as a river flowing.'

'Son or daughter, it matters not,' Waltheof murmured, spreading his hand over the pale curve of her flesh. 'There is time enough for both. King William has an equal number of each.'

'No,' Judith said stubbornly, 'it will be a boy.' Her lips became mulish and a little folded inwards, the way they did when she was determined to have her own way.

Waltheof shrugged and smiled, indulging her. 'Very well,' he said with a yawn. 'It will be a boy.'

In the midsummer heat of the following year, Judith gave birth to their second daughter. She wept bitterly and refused to be consoled when the midwife hesitantly delivered the unwelcome news along with the squawling, dark-haired bundle. 'If I had married a Norman,' she hurled at Waltheof, 'he would have given me sons!'

'And if I had taken an English wife, I would not have to suffer the unseemly lash of her tongue!' he had retorted. Shocked at the clash of their mutual bitterness, hurt and angry, Waltheof stormed from their bedchamber and proceeded to get roaring drunk, because apologising was more than he could bear to do. Early on in the session, before he lost his wits in the cool depths of a firkin of ale, Sybille brought him the new baby, still damp from her birth and wrapped tightly in linen swaddling. Holding her in the crook of his arm Waltheof saw his wife clearly in her tiny seashell features and the puff of black hair on her brow. It made him want to weep.

'How is she to be named, my lord?' Sybille asked gently.

Waltheof swallowed. 'For her mother,' he croaked. 'Mayhap it will recall her to her duty.'

Sybille said nothing, although she privately thought that naming this second child thus was a bad idea. Every time she looked at the baby, Judith would be reminded of her failure to produce a son.

Waltheof gazed at Sybille. 'How is it possible to begrudge a child its life because of its sex?' he asked in a torn and bewildered voice.

Sybille did not have an answer. Biting her lip to stop it from trembling, she took the baby back into her own arms. 'I'd best go and take her to the new wet nurse,' she said gently. 'I would have nursed her myself, but I don't have enough milk for three.'

Waltheof nodded a dismissal and turned back to the jug of ale with a vengeance.

CHAPTER 15

Palace of Northampton, Spring 1075

The apples had been stored over winter and were slightly wrinkled, but their sweetness was wonderfully concentrated. Sybille peeled one with her small, bone-handled knife, cut it into slivers and divided it between her daughter Helisende and the ladies Matilda and Judith. Lured by a warm flood of April sunshine, she had brought the girls into the garden. Their mother, as usual, was at her prayers. Recently she had been speaking of founding a nunnery on her lands at Elstow near Bedford.

Matilda lingered at Sybille's knee, her eyes on the core.

'You want it, *chérie?*'

'I want to make a tree,' Matilda said. Each word was firm and clear. Everyone agreed that the child was advanced for her years, in both stature and intellect. Already she topped Helisende by a head. Caught back in a blue ribbon, her hair was a mass of coppery-bronze curls, slightly less red in tone than Waltheof's. Her creamy skin was peppered with freckles and her eyes were the same dense shade of blue as her father's. 'A tree, my love?'

Matilda took the core in her chubby hand. 'You put it in the ground,' she said patiently to the maid, 'then you water it, and a tree grows.'

'Ah,' Sybille nodded. 'And who told you that?'

'Edwin.' She announced the gardener's name loudly and looked at Sybille as if she thought her dim-witted. Taking the core, she marched over to a bed of recently dug soil and set about planting her treasure. Sybille thought that she had better inform Edwin about Matilda's endeavour lest he had other plans for the newly turned bed.

Helisende and little Judith came to watch the ceremony of the planting. The latter decided that the soil itself might taste nice, and Sybille had to grab and apprehend the child before she could cram her mouth.

A spectacular tantrum ensued. Helisende looked on admiringly while Matilda ignored the shrieks completely, save to increase her concentration in the burying of the apple core.

'Now water,' she said. While Sybille's back was turned and her fingers busy separating little Jude's mouth from the soil she had managed to put in it, Matilda ran over to the well. A heavy wooden lid was held fast to the opening by an iron draw bar. Matilda scowled at the decorative wrought-iron bands securing the oak sections and put her hands on her hips. The gesture was an unconscious imitation of Sybille, whom Matilda regarded as her mother. Her true mother was a distant, frowning person who seldom smiled and in whose presence the little girl felt distinctly uneasy. *Her* hands were always clasped in an attitude of prayer. She was always speaking about something called 'duty', and seemed to think that Matilda should know what 'duty' was. Something not very nice, the little girl had decided.

Since the well covering simply would not budge and she needed the water, she looked around for Edwin the gardener or one of the other men who tended the herb and wort beds. Then her eyes lit on someone even better.

'Papa!' Her feet flew on the path and she launched herself at the large man coming towards her from the wattle gate in the garden's side entrance.

He swung her up in his arms and whirled her around until

she squealed with delight. Clinging fiercely to his neck, she nuzzled her cheek against the wiry softness of his golden beard.

'What are you doing out here alone, chicken?' he asked. He spoke in English, and she answered him in the same tongue – something else of which her mother disapproved. Norman was the language of somewhere called the 'court' and nobody there ever spoke English.

'I'm not alone,' she said. 'I'm with Sybille. I want to plant a tree to make apples, but I have to water it.' She pointed to the well cover. 'It's stuck.'

'For a good reason. Someone your size might trip and fall down the well.'

Setting Matilda on her feet, he went to the cover. She watched the strong surge of his muscles as he drew back with ease the bolt that she had been unable to move. Her papa could do anything! He slid the heavy wooden disc aside and pulled on the hemp rope to draw up the wooden bucket from the depths. Matilda peered over the edge into the hole. He watched her with amusement and pressed her gently away when she began to crane too far.

'Here,' he said, and pressed half a silver penny into her hand. 'Throw it to the water elf.'

She looked at him huge-eyed. Sybille often told her stories about the elves and spirits that occupied their world but were seldom seen. Her mother would scold and say that such tales were un-Christian and not true, but that didn't stop Sybille telling them when Lady Judith was not around.

'Is there really an elf?' she demanded.

Her father nodded, seriously. 'Oh yes,' he said. 'And occasionally he has to be paid in silver to keep the water sweet. But he is very shy. He will not come out while the cover is off.'

Enchanted, Matilda tossed the coin. It clinked on the clay and wattle lining of the well, bounced off, and plinked into the black water far below.

Her father nodded approval, smile lines crinkling around his eyes. 'So,' he said, 'where's this tree of yours?'

Solemnly, her little hand engulfed in his huge paw, she took him to the place where she had buried the apple core. Sybille came running towards them with her other two charges in tow. The maid scolded Matilda for running off and Waltheof greeted little Judith and Helisende. However, he seemed to realise Matilda's need and having curtailed both greeting and scolding with a smile and a word, he gave his attention to the moist churn of soil by his boot.

Crouching, he scooped a handful of water and carefully trickled it over the spot where the core was buried. 'Saint Fiacre of the Holy Furrow, I entreat your guardianship of this seed,' he intoned. 'May it grow into a mature tree as my daughter grows, tall and strong, and bearing many branches of fruit . . . amen.' He crossed himself and Matilda did her best to imitate his gesture before sprinkling her own palmful of water over the patch of soil. She might not yet be three years old but she felt the solemnity of the occasion and knew that something greater than the planting of an apple core had just taken place.

From that moment forth Matilda took to planting seeds with a vengeance. Figs and raisins disappeared off the dining trestle to be buried under mounds of earth, as did costly almonds and peppercorns. She would accompany Edwin the gardener on his rounds, and talk to the elf in the well. She also prayed regularly for her tree and watched anxiously for the first shoots to appear.

'You are as bad as Sybille,' Judith snapped at Waltheof, 'telling her all that nonsense about "elves in the well". What kind of Christian example is that to set to your daughters?'

'Did you have no sense of fun or imagination as a child?' Waltheof countered, then shook his head and sighed. 'No, I do not suppose that you did – or else that it was "dutied" out of you while you were still very little.'

'It is all nonsense.' She folded her mouth inwards.

Waltheof raised his eyes heavenwards and, without a word, went to the window embrasure to gaze out on the soft glow of a late summer evening.

She looked at his turned back, his forearm braced against the wall, his fist clenched. Lately the gulf between them had grown wider. He seemed to go out of his way to irritate her. She could not bear his ebullient personality, the way he clapped folk on the back whether they were noble or peasant. It was inappropriate to both. His drinking, his loud laughter and childish sense of humour, the way he took nothing seriously and seemed unable to concentrate on any task for long enough to see it through: all of these traits annoyed her to the point of screaming. But looking at him now, quiet, brooding, she could feel his masculinity and her body responded as it had done the first time she set eyes upon him. And when they were in bed, he knew how to make her scream too.

Waltheof sighed and paced back into the room, then crouched at her feet and took her hands in his. 'I don't want to quarrel with you,' he said softly.

Judith swallowed. 'Nor I with you,' she unfolded enough to admit.

He grimaced. 'There are worse things in this world than elves, believe me.'

They went to bed and made love. She muffled her pleasure against his wide, straining shoulder and dug her nails into the smooth, flexing muscles of his back. As usual he pushed her beyond reticence and for a blinding moment she did not care. Then self-awareness returned and she scuttled back into her shell, feeling ashamed.

He withdrew and rolled over on his back, breathing harshly.

'What did you mean about worse things in this world than elves?' she asked after a moment.

Waltheof turned his head on the bolster. 'I meant trolls such as Picot de Saye and the other sheriffs of my counties. This morning Tigwald the currier came to me with a complaint that Picot de Saye had misappropriated a cowhide and three goatskins to his own use.' Waltheof bared his teeth. 'He comes to the market place with his soldiers and he seizes what he wants. If my people protest, they are thrown in gaol or beaten. He's not a sheriff, he's a common thief.'

'Is there nothing you can do?'

Waltheof snorted impatiently. 'Picot de Saye has been appointed by your uncle. I have complained to William on several occasions but without joy. It seems that a common thief is tolerated when he is a tough and brutal soldier into the bargain. I have spoken to Picot myself, but to no avail.' His lips curved in an arid smile. 'I could, of course, take my axe to them, as I took it to their fellows in York, but even I can see the consequences of such an action, and my poor people would be made to pay the price in silver and blood, although what they are paying now is scarcely less.'

Judith said nothing. She knew that De Saye was acting beyond his jurisdiction and that Waltheof's complaint was justified, but she misliked the bitterness in his voice. How easily it could spill out to encompass all Normans. Against her will, she felt defensive.

'I have compensated Tigwald from my own coffers for the price of his hides,' he said, 'but compensation is not justice and I cannot afford to pay everyone from whom De Saye steals.'

'Perhaps you should have complained to my uncle with more vigour,' she suggested.

Waltheof laughed bitterly. 'He would not listen. Picot de Saye is his most trusted servant, and he would see me as a troublemaker. No, he has me where he desires. Earl of Northumbria, Northampton and Huntingdon – mighty titles brought to nothing by the power of his sheriffs.' He punched the bolster.

Judith bit her lip. 'He would listen to you if you made a good enough case.'

'So you think my case not good enough?'

'You are too soft,' she said. 'You melt from argument into anger without standing your ground, and your reasoning comes from the heart not the head.'

'What is wrong with that?' he snapped.

'Nothing,' she said, 'but my uncle is a man who reasons with his head. He has little time for matters of the heart – as well you should know by now.'

'And God forbid I should ever follow that path.' Waltheof rose from the bed and, drawing on his shirt, padded beyond the hangings that separated their bedchamber from the rest of the long room to look down at his sleeping daughters. 'Innocence,' he said softly. 'What price innocence?'

From the bed Judith watched him. Her appetite sated, she felt only weariness now. A chill draught from the half-open shutters made her shiver and pull the fur coverlet up around her shoulders. 'A price you cannot afford,' she responded in a murmur that disappeared on the air of her breath. He looked around as if he had heard her, but she knew that it was impossible.

Judith laid her hand to her belly. Her flux was a week late, but it had been so on several occasions and she attached small significance to the fact. Perhaps a son would change him, she thought, give that extra bite of iron to his character. Or perhaps he was only capable of siring girls because of the softness at his core. Whatever. She knew that when the time came to choose husbands for their daughters she would be exacting in her selection, and tenderness of manner would not be a consideration.

CHAPTER 16

For Matilda's third year day, Waltheof gave her a pony, bought on his northern lands from a Lothian horse trader. The small beast was little bigger than a large hunting dog, with a shaggy black mane and tail and a hide that was the same golden colour as the sands stretching along the shore by the great keep at Bamburgh. Tiny little bells were stitched around the edges of the red saddlecloth, and the buckles on the bridle were decorated with a pattern of thistles. For Matilda it was love at first sight. She hugged her father, who laughed and swept her up in his arms to receive two smacking kisses. Even her mother wore a smile. Learning to ride was apparently an important part of becoming a lady.

'She is yours to name,' Waltheof said as he set her down and brought her to the pony. It extended its nose towards her and she felt the sweet gust of its hay-scented breath in her face. Her father produced a crust of bread and placed it in her hand. Steadying and guiding her movements with his own, he offered it to the little mare. She lipped the bread off Matilda's palm with great gentleness, but devoured it greedily and looked for more. Waltheof laughed. 'Small wonder that she's so plump!'

Matilda laughed too, thoroughly enchanted. Her father lifted her up and set her on the pony's back. She felt the cool leather of the saddle against her thighs and the pressure of the stirrups across her instep as he secured her feet.

'Well,' Waltheof said, 'can you think of a name?' Clicking

his tongue, he led the mare around the yard at a gentle walk. Matilda laughed in delight and looked proudly around.

'Honey,' she said after a moment, 'because she's that colour.'

Her father smiled in that special way he had that was only for her. 'Very fitting,' he said, 'and much better than "Glutton".'

Matilda screwed up her face at the word and he chuckled deep in his throat, a lovely warm sound that made her feel bubbly with pleasure.

For the next few weeks he continued to teach her to ride. It was a golden time, steeped in honey like the name of her pony, and its memory was to tantalise Matilda for the rest of her life. Everything was perfect. She basked in her father's warmth and attention. Saint Fiacre, aided by the water of the well elf, ensured that her apple tree began to grow, thrusting a single green shoot through the soil. She collected poppy and marigold seeds with the gardener, ready for sowing next year. She played with her little sister and Helisende, and the days seemed to stretch for ever, warm, shining, secure. Nor was the idyll spoiled by her mother, who left the tending of her daughters to Sybille even more than usual. When the reason was revealed, it only added to Matilda's pleasure.

'Your mama is to bear you another sister or brother,' Waltheof told her as he took her out on Honey, a leading rein attached between his mount and the mare like an umbilical cord. 'In the winter time.'

Matilda frowned. It was harvest now. Her papa had promised to take her to his manor at Ryhall on the morrow when he went to oversee the reaping. Winter came after harvest; she vaguely knew that. There were other things she vaguely knew as well. Only last week she had watched a goat drop two kids in the enclosure by the kitchen garden. Sybille had explained that young ones grew inside their mothers until they were ready to be born . . . unless they were chickens, of course . . . or trees.

'I see I have silenced that busy tongue of yours.' Her father's voice was warm with amusement but held the hint of a question.

Matilda looked up at him. Since she was constantly told that she was a gift from God, she assumed that it was God who put the babies inside the mothers to grow. 'Mama will want a boy,' she said.

Her father's eyelids tightened but his smile remained. 'It matters not,' he said. 'It is God who chooses and we should be thankful for his gift of life.'

Matilda nodded, her notion of how babies arrived in the womb reinforced by his words. She liked babies. One of her favourite toys was a doll made of leather, its limbs stuffed with lambs' wool. She would wrap it in linen scraps for swaddling and croon to it, as she had seen the women of the household croon to their own infants.

'Are you pleased?'

Again she nodded. She did not feel as delighted as when she had been given Honey, but the sensation inside her was happy. When they returned from the ride, her papa had visitors. Matilda recognised his friend, Ralf de Gael, because he often came to visit. They would go away to hunt and play chess and drink a lot of ale. She knew that her mama disliked Ralf de Gael, and Matilda agreed with her. The attention her papa paid to his friend meant he had less time for her. Although De Gael always brought her a present, she had the instinct if not the intellect to understand that she was of no consequence to him – indeed perhaps a nuisance.

Her father flung himself down from his own horse, lifted her carefully from Honey, then strode to embrace his friend and slap him heartily on the back. Matilda watched the greeting with resentful eyes and a pouting lower lip.

'I see your eldest is growing into a pretty little wench,' declared De Gael. He stooped to Matilda and a white grin flashed across his thin, handsome features. 'Looks like her mother at the moment, though, eh?'

Her papa laughed and lifted her in his arms. Matilda clung to him fiercely and scowled at De Gael.

'Heaven preserve us from jealous women!' De Gael chuckled. 'Never mind, sweetheart. I've brought you a pretty brooch, all the way from Denmark . . . and since you have Dane blood, I thought it fitting you should wear it.'

Matilda turned her face into her father's warm, strong neck, rejecting the visitor. Against her cheek, she felt him tense, but he did not rebuke her for her rudeness. 'You have been talking to Danish traders then?' he asked in a strange, flat tone that she had never heard him use before.

'You could say that.' There was a cautious note in De Gael's voice too. Matilda wanted him to go away. She clung like a leech to her father, knowing with a growing sense of dismay that already she had lost him.

'They bring news that you might find interesting,' De Gael added as they walked towards the hall.

'I have plenty to interest me these days already,' Waltheof said, 'and my wife is with child again.'

'Congratulations,' De Gael replied, but not as though he meant it.

In the hall Waltheof sent a servant to summon Sybille and inform Judith of De Gael's arrival. 'Although you will excuse her if she does not attend on us,' he said ruefully. 'She is at the stage where she is constantly sick.'

De Gael gave a knowing grin. 'And I would only make her worse,' he said.

Sybille arrived. She curtseyed to the men and reached to take Matilda from Waltheof. Matilda tightened her arms around her father's neck until she was almost throttling him and screamed as Sybille attempted to prise her off.

'Come,' Sybille cajoled, 'your papa will play with you later.'

'No!' screamed Matilda. 'No!' She kicked out, her emotions so overwhelming and raw that even had she wanted she was powerless to stop the tantrum.

De Gael winced and looked astonished, as if a flower had bitten him. Waltheof unhooked her arms from around his throat and handed her to the maid. Sybille tucked the threshing, screaming Matilda under her arm and struggled out of the hall. Taking her to the stables, ignoring the stares of the grooms and attendants, she threw Matilda down in the clean straw of an empty stall and there let her flail out the storm.

Matilda's voice gave out and the wildness of her emotion drained her body of all its energy, leaving her limp and tearful. Crouching in the straw, Sybille gathered Matilda in her arms and gently rocked her back and forth, smoothing her flushed brow and shushing her. Matilda's eyelids drooped and she fell into an exhausted slumber, her dark-gold lashes spiked with drying tears. Tenderly, Sybille lifted the child and bore her back to the women's chambers, where she laid her on a pallet near the window and covered her with a light blanket.

'What is wrong with her?' Judith demanded. 'She looks feverish.'

'She is all right, mistress,' Sybille said quickly to dispel Judith's concern. 'The Earl of Norfolk is here and Mistress Matilda did not want to be parted from her father.'

Judith pressed her hand to the slight curve of her belly. 'Ralf de Gael,' she sniffed, her tone leaving no doubt as to her opinion of their guest. 'Is it just me and my daughter? Does no one else see through his posturing to what he is?'

Sybille lowered her eyes and fiddled with the strap end of her belt. 'He and Lord Waltheof have long been friends.'

'Lord Waltheof does not need "friends" of that ilk,' Judith snapped. 'There are men of considerably more character whose company he could seek. If he did as much drinking with my uncle's sheriffs as he does with Ralf de Gael, then he might conduct better business with them.' Turning away, she went to lie down on her own bed. 'My head aches,' she said, closing her eyes. 'I am indisposed – and I believe the malaise will last until that man leaves.'

*

Ralf de Gael studied the golden liquid in his cup. 'English ale,' he said. 'I have never understood why men have a preference for wine when they could drink nectar like this.'

'It depends on the alewife, and the freshness of the brew,' Waltheof replied, 'but our Wulfhild is the best brewster in the entire earldom.'

Ralf toasted him, then reaching to his tunic, unpinned a fine circular brooch set with irregular globs of polished amber like new, clear honey. 'The brooch for your eldest lass,' he said with a rueful smile. 'I do not think that she was best pleased to see me.'

Waltheof smiled too, albeit with a more pained expression. 'She likes me to herself – not that I mind if I have nothing else to do.' He turned the brooch over in his hand. The Danish silverwork was superb; this would have cost more than a half penny at a huckster's stall. 'Whenever you visit, it is always to take me away for several days' hunting. You cannot blame her for the association.' He pinned the brooch to his own cloak so that he would not lose it.

Ralf drank his ale and replenished his cup from the pitcher set to hand. 'Are you not going to ask me about my news from the Danish trader?'

Waltheof frowned. 'I have small interest in my Danish cousins these days.' It was not entirely true. He could still feel the surge within him like the wash of a wave against a longboat prow, but he held back. There was too much at stake, and the Danes had proven unreliable allies in the past. 'I cannot see what you would gain from intriguing with them either.'

Ralf gave a shrug that was slightly too nonchalant. 'It is better to be informed on these matters than to hide your head beneath the sheets – or under your wife's skirts – and pretend that they do not exist. King Sweyn of Denmark is dead and it is said that his son Cnut intends to send a fleet to England. If we hear these things in Norfolk, then just as surely you must hear them in Huntingdon.'

Waltheof turned his head aside, but he could not ignore the words. 'They are of no interest to me – save that perhaps I should keep my men in readiness should the King have need of them.'

Ralf gave him a long, thoughtful stare.

Waltheof swallowed. The hair on the back of his neck prickled. 'What are you saying?'

'Nothing.' Ralf spread his hands in an open gesture that to Waltheof rang false. 'My mention of Danish traders was premature and not the reason why I am here.' He forced a smile.

'Then why have you come – to hunt?'

De Gael shook his head and a more natural smile lit his features. 'I came to invite you to my wedding and to a week's feasting and sport afterwards in celebration of my nuptials.'

'Your wedding?' Waltheof's gaze became one of astonishment. 'Jesu, Ralf, I did not realise that you were courting a bride!'

'Ah, well it has not been a long courtship,' he said, 'but the match suits all parties. I am to marry Emma, sister of Roger of Hereford.'

'Congratulations!' Waltheof clapped his friend on the shoulder. 'What's the lass like?'

Ralf laughed and described a curvaceous shape in the air. 'Fair-haired, generously endowed and good-natured. It will be no hardship to do my duty.'

The mention of 'duty' caused Waltheof to wince, for it was the word that most frequently soured his own marriage. He and Judith were miles apart on its meaning. He would see it as his duty to attend his friend's wedding, and he knew that Judith would say that his duty was to remain with her.

'You will come?' asked De Gael, prompted by Waltheof's hesitation.

'Of course I will,' Waltheof said with overdone heartiness and beckoned for another pitcher of ale. 'You danced at my nuptials. It is only fitting that I should dance at yours.'

*

'You should not go to this wedding,' Judith said when Waltheof joined her in their chamber that evening and told her of his intentions. 'No good will come of it.'

Waltheof's brows drew together. 'What is wrong with the match? Surely, Ralf and Emma FitzOsbern are well suited?'

'Too well suited,' Judith snapped. 'I know that my uncle does not approve of the friendship between their families.'

'Do you?' Waltheof sat down on a bench set against the wall and folded his arms. 'I have heard no rumours. Has William moved to ban the wedding?'

Judith shook her head. 'No,' she said irritably, 'but my mother says that he does not trust De Gael.'

'Your uncle trusts no one whose blood is not Norman,' Waltheof said curtly. 'He gives me honours then hems me around with his own men; he makes sheriffs of his common mercenaries and turns a blind eye to the brutalities that they perpetrate.'

Judith had been lying on the bed. Now she rose and drew a bedrobe over her chemise. Her hair hung down her back in a dark silk curtain. Waltheof loved to run his fingers through its heavy masses, but tonight he knew that it was out of bounds. The flesh around her eyes was puffy and, despite the glow cast by the candlelight, he could see that her complexion was wan and drawn. She was not carrying this child well, and he felt a stab of guilt run through his exasperation.

'I grant that De Gael is of Breton stock and that your uncle has been at war with Brittany, but that is not reason enough to be suspicious of a man.' He narrowed his eyes at her. 'In truth, you have never liked Ralf.'

Going to the small prie-dieu standing in the corner of the room, Judith lit the wax candles either side of the oak statuette of the Virgin Mary. Kneeling on the embroidered prayer cushion, she clasped her hands. 'There are men of far better character whom you could make your friends,' she said. 'And more suited to your standing.'

'Hah!' Waltheof exhaled bitterly and, going to the flagon

on the coffer, poured himself some of his wife's wine. It was always wine in the bedchamber. If he wanted ale, he had to send a servant to fetch him some and then suffer Judith's scowling disapproval. 'My standing. Sometimes I think that is all you care about.'

'Someone has to care, because you do not,' she said, flashing an angry look over her shoulder. 'You demean your rank by jesting with grooms and gardeners and kitchen maids. How will folk respect you when you cannot behave fittingly?'

The disdain in her eyes kindled a glowing coal of anger in his belly. 'When I cannot behave like a Norman, you mean?' he threw at her.

'When you cannot behave like a man of noble blood!' she retorted. 'Our daughters are born to high station and yet you bring them to the stables and the outhouses; you encourage them to speak to servants and soldiers as though such people were of their rank – and in English!' She made a gesture of contempt.

Waltheof drew himself up, but even his full height was not large enough to contain his fury. 'So greatness of stature lies in ignorance,' he bit out. 'You are condemned out of your own mouth, my lady. You are nothing. While you are kneeling at your pious devotions, perhaps you might do well to dwell upon the fact that our Lord Jesus Christ came from a family of humble carpenters!' Turning on his heel, he stormed out. He would have been within his rights to strike her, and that made him walk away all the more swiftly. It was common knowledge that William of Normandy was not averse to beating his own wife when she overstepped the bounds of his tolerance. He knew of men who kept hazel switches poked in the thatch for just such a purpose, and others whose belts bore the bloodstains from the welts they had raised on the flesh of their wives and children. But he was not one of them. Even now, he told himself through clenched teeth, he was not one of them.

In the bedchamber Judith closed her eyes and swallowed,

fighting the nausea of her pregnancy. She drew slow, deep breaths until her thumping heart slowed and her belly settled to a queasy churn. Turning her attention back to the prie-dieu, she tried to take solace in prayer but was thwarted by Waltheof's words about the Saviour being a common carpenter. Finally she genuflected, rose, and retired wearily to bed.

Matilda watched her father prepare to ride out. It was a cool, September morning with low mist wreathing the ground and dew making clear jewels of the spider webs strung in the eaves and across the wattle fencing that divided the stable yard from the garth. But Matilda had no eyes for the beauties of nature this morning. Only for her papa, who was going away with his friend and leaving her behind.

He gathered the reins, set his foot in the stirrup and swung his leg across Copper's broad back. His thin-legged black hunting horse, Jet, was tethered on a leading rein and there was also a fat, bay packpony laden with baggage. The soldiers of his retinue were mounting up, laughing and talking amongst themselves in close male camaraderie. Ralf de Gael was resplendent in a tunic of flamboyant crimson wool edged with metallic braid. Across his chest he wore a baldric and attached to it was a polished hunting horn, chased with silver.

'Your papa will not be gone for long,' Sybille said soothingly, but her grip was tight on Matilda's hand, ensuring that the little girl did not dash out among the horses.

'I want to go too.' Matilda's lower lip trembled.

'When you are older, *chérie*.' Sybille gently brushed her hand over Matilda's copper-bronze curls.

Waltheof collected his reins. Matilda thought that he was going to ignore her but he raised his glance and his eyes lit upon her and Sybille where they stood against the stableyard entrance. Heeling Copper's flanks, he rode across to them.

'I will take her,' he told Sybille. Leaning down, he scooped Matilda in his arms and drew her onto his saddle before him. For a wonderful moment, Matilda thought that she was going with him. From the back of the horse her view was altered and she could see everything without having to crane. Her father's arm was strong and warm, holding her in the saddle, and she could smell the sweet, herbal scent emanating from his blue tunic. Leaning back, she nestled her bright head against the thick white fur lining of his cloak.

'I promise to be home soon, sweetheart,' he said, giving her a light squeeze.

'I want to come too,' Matilda pouted.

'This time you cannot, but when I return I promise on my oath to take you out on Honey as often as you want.'

'Now,' Matilda said, and the horrible feeling began welling up in her again as it had done yesterday when she had started screaming and been unable to stop.

'Shall I take her, my lord?' Sybille hastened to the saddle, holding out her arms, her eyes filled with anxiety.

Waltheof shook his head. 'It is all right,' he said. 'I will ride a little way down the road with her. One of the men can bring her back in a moment.'

Sybille nodded and, although she was chewing her lip with anxiety, stepped away. Waltheof clicked his tongue to the horse and urged Copper to a trot that took him away from the other riders. When De Gael moved to catch up, Waltheof gestured him back.

'Now then,' he said softly to Matilda, leaning over so that his beard tickled her ear, 'whether you scream or not, I must go. I know that you want me to stay, but I cannot. I am not going to ask if you understand, you are only a baby but . . .'

'I'm not a baby!' Matilda cried and wriggled round in her father's arms to give him an indignant glare.

He smiled and gave her a whiskery kiss on the cheek. 'No indeed, you are a big girl,' he said, 'and I want you to be a big girl now and wait patiently until I come home.'

Matilda wrinkled her brow. The dreadful feeling of unrequited rage still lurked in the background, but her father's talk of her being a 'big girl' had given her a device to control it. She folded her soft pink lips together in unconscious imitation of her mother and managed a nod. The reward was another hug and kiss from her father, and she rode on his saddle all the way through the town. People stood at their doorways to watch them go by. Women curtseyed; men bowed or tugged at their hair. There were several cries of 'God bless you my lord and the young mistress!' and her father replied by shouting a response in English and throwing a small change of silver to the recipients. The warm feeling returned to Matilda's stomach. The silver-throwing ceased as they rode past the castle and the dour-faced guards in their rivet mail hauberks. The salutes were grudging and unfriendly. Her father turned his face away and, even though she had no understanding of why, Matilda knew that something was wrong.

Behind them Ralf of Norfolk had been bowing to the townsfolk and flirting with the women. Now he rode up alongside her father.

'You should do something about those soldiers of De Saye's,' he said. 'I would wring respect out of them with my hands to their throats if I were you.'

Her father's complexion darkened. She knew that he was angry, but she did not know why, or at whom. With a warning look at Ralf, he shook his head. Then he leaned over Matilda. 'Time for you to turn back now, *deorling*,' he murmured. 'Sybille will be wondering where you are, and your mother will be growing anxious.' Lifting her in his strong arms, he handed her across to one of the following escort.

Matilda's chin wobbled but she didn't scream. Her reward was her father's smile. 'There's my brave girl,' he said. 'I'll be back before you know it . . . I promise.'

Matilda craned her head around her escort's strong arm and stared after her father until he was lost to sight. On the way home, although she waved to people and they waved back, it was not the same.

CHAPTER 17

It was late, but Judith was restless and unable to sleep. Leaving the bed, she knelt at her prie-dieu and clasped her hands before the figure of the Virgin, but tonight the motions of ritual and prayer had no power to soothe her troubled mind. Waltheof had been gone for ten days, intent on celebrating the marriage of Ralf de Gael to Emma FitzOsbern. He had sent no word, and Judith had sent none to him. For a while the silence had been a blessed relief, but now she was beginning to worry. His nature was such that he had to touch and talk. For him not to communicate at all was unusual. It was true that they had argued before he left, but they had argued before and always he had returned, contrite, bearing gifts, seeking her forgiveness. However, at the back of her mind lay the niggling fear that her approval no longer mattered to him. During the last few months, he had ceased to crop his hair and shave his beard – indications that her influence over him was waning.

Sighing, she rose from the prie-dieu. The statue of the Virgin was just that – a statue carved of oak and painted by the hand of man. Tonight the spirit of the Holy Mother of God chose not to descend and blanket Judith in a silent blue cloak of peace. She poured herself a cup of wine from the flagon on the coffer. One sip caused her lips to pucker. Summoning a maid, she thrust the flagon into her hand. 'This wine is sour,' she snapped. 'Fetch a fresh flagon, and I will have words with the steward in the morning.'

'Yes my lady.' Bleary-eyed, clumsy with sleep, the girl stumbled off on her errand.

Judith paced the chamber, lighting candles in the corner, chasing the shadows from their hiding places. In the ante-chamber she heard one of the children cry out in her sleep. Matilda, she thought, with impatience and guilt. Since Waltheof had gone the child had not been sleeping well – and in the daytime she was quiet and withdrawn. Sulking, Judith had thought, and had been sharp with her. Yet, as she scolded her, she had felt a disturbing awareness of repetition. Thus had her own mother done to her.

A masculine voice crooned softly to the child. Judith set her hand to the curtain but before she could part it to inves-tigate it was drawn aside by Waltheof, the refreshed flagon held in his hand.

'I met the girl on her way to you with this,' he said. Entering the room, he drew her after him and dropped the hanging. 'Matilda's settled back to sleep; I don't want to wake her.'

Judith eyed him in growing consternation. She would not have expected him to ride in at such a late hour unless there was trouble. His look said there was. Purple shadows ringed his eyes and his jaw was tightly grooved above the beard line. He seemed to have aged ten years in as many days. 'What have you been doing?' she hissed. 'What's wrong?'

'I should have expected no less a welcome,' he answered bitterly. Flagon in hand, he went to the coffer and poured the deep red wine into a goblet. 'I have been doing nothing,' he said as he took a long drink, 'and I very much suspect that it will be my downfall.' Abruptly his legs gave way and he sat down on the bed.

'Meaning?' Judith's hands went to her hips. An unpleasant smell of stale wine and sweat rose from his body. His tunic was badly stained and could have stood up on its own.

'I fear,' he said, 'that I have committed treachery against your uncle.' He drank down the rest of the wine and put his head in his hands.

'What?' Judith's heart began to pound.

Waltheof swallowed. He started to look at her, but he could not hold her eyes and his gaze slipped like a footstep on ice. 'Ralf de Gael and Roger FitzOsbern are planning to welcome Cnut of Denmark to our shores and offer him the prize of kingship,' he said. 'They have turned their backs on William for what he has done to the English and Breton people.'

'Jesu!' Judith stared at him in growing horror.

'Even now, there is a Danish fleet assembling to sail to England. Ralf and Roger have overwhelming support from the Bretons both in England and in Brittany.' His throat worked. 'They have asked me to bring my own force to the endeavour.'

'It is treason!' A cold knot tightened in the pit of Judith's stomach.

'I know.' Waltheof groaned. 'Roger has gone home to assemble his troops, and Ralf is mustering his. I am supposed to gather my huscarls and join them.'

Judith could not help herself. So great was her anger that she lost control. Snatching up her cup, she dashed the wine in his face. 'You fool!' she shrieked. 'You stupid, stupid fool! What in the world possessed you? What is going to happen to us now?' He had recoiled instinctively as the wine splashed over him. Now he looked at her, red lines trickling down his face and throat, dark droplets trembling in his hair. 'I thought . . .' His voice cracked and she was horrified to see tears glittering in his eyes. 'You are the strong one. I thought you would know what to do . . .'

The urge to hurl the cup after the wine was almost over-powering. With unsteady hands she set it down on the coffer. Her stomach ached as if he had punched her in the softness beneath her ribcage. 'Just what did you promise?' she asked in a voice tight with revulsion.

'I do not know . . .' He wiped the back of his hand across his eyes, leaving a grubby smear of tears.

'You do not know?'

'I . . . I was drunk.'

Judith closed her eyes and swallowed. She could imagine the scene. A raucous wedding feast. Copious amounts of wine and ale. A gathering of men possessed of similar interests. Amongst silver-tongued plotters such as Ralf de Gael and Roger of Hereford, Waltheof was as well armed as an infant amidst a pack of wolves. She should have prevented him from going. But 'should have' was too late.

He sniffed loudly. 'I believe I said I would not stand in their way . . . and that if that way went well, then I would join them.'

'So another attempt is to be made on wresting my uncle from England's throne, and you have implicated yourself in it.'

Waltheof nodded. 'It was against my will. I tried to argue against it, but they would not listen.' He gave her a pleading look. 'If I had not agreed to their plan, then Hereford at least would not have let me leave the feasting alive. I was trapped.'

'If you had ridden out the moment that the talk began, you would not be in this predicament,' she snapped. Her upper lip curled back from her teeth. 'Or perhaps you liked the idea. After all, you colluded with the Danes last time, did you not?'

'It wasn't like that!' His complexion darkened with anger and chagrin.

'Then what was it like?' she spat, knowing she had hit the mark. 'You have always been obsessed by your father's people. We lie in a pagan bed because of it, and you wear that damned cloak all the time as though it is a second skin. It matters not all the honours and greatness that my uncle has bestowed upon you. You would yield it all for some Viking pirate because of his Dane blood. And . . . and for a scheming Breton who has tangled you up in the silken threads of his spider's web.'

He had put his head in his hands as she lashed him. Now he sprang to his feet. 'Hold your venom, you bitch!' he roared, raising his clenched fist.

She winced and flinched, but the blow did not descend. In the silence that fell as the ring of his voice faded, a look of pure horror crossed his face. His fist opened, extending instead in supplication. 'Judith, please . . .' he whispered. '*Deorling*, I did not mean . . .'

She stepped away, whisking her gown aside as though his merest touch on herself or her clothing was anathema. 'I wash my hands of you,' she said hoarsely. 'It is finished between us. I may be your wife, but I no longer wish to live as such.' She folded her hands in front of her like a nun at her devotions. 'On the morrow I will go to my manor at Elstow and you will not follow me.'

'Judith, don't leave me . . . I need you . . .'

She tightened her lips and drew herself up. 'You left me first, when you went to Ralf de Gael's wedding in order to plot treason. Go to him for your succour. Doubtless he will furnish you with some willing Danish or Breton whore to slake your lusts. If you are plotting treachery then the last thing you need is a Norman wife.' Her voice trembled as she fought hysterical tears. Unable to face him any longer, she went to her coffer, threw back the lid and began sorting through her gowns, as if choosing those that she would take to Elstow. But it was a ruse. Hand and mind were not co-ordinated.

'I am not going to join them, I swear it.'

His tone was pleading, like a child's begging forgiveness for a prank that had gone wrong.

'If you do not go to my uncle immediately and tell him what is afoot, then you are damned,' she said without looking round. Her hands crumpled a veil of light gold silk, uncaring of the delicate fabric.

'I . . . I gave my word to De Gael . . .'

'You gave your oath to the King!' Nausea churned her belly, rose up and surged. She only just reached the slop pot in time and hung over it, retching until she thought her gut would tear.

'Go away,' she gasped. 'Go away, you make me ill. I loathe you!'

She heard him stand up and the slow drag of his feet across the chamber rushes, as though they were bound by shackles. Then, mercifully, he was gone. Judith huddled over the bowl, gagging and weeping. There was pain in her stomach, pain encircling the base of her spine in a tight girdle, and then a sudden gush of water and blood. She had rejected Waltheof. Now her body was rejecting his child.

As she screamed for her maids, Judith found herself hoping that she would die.

'What do I do?' Waltheof asked of Ulfcytel. It was a fine autumn morning and they were sitting in the Abbot's parlour, drinking ale and watching the white clouds scud past the open shutters.

The monk sighed and shook his head. 'I wish I could tell you, my son,' he said. 'Doubtless others have already told you how foolish you have been.'

'Only my wife. I have spoken to no one else. A few of my men are aware, but I trust them without reserve.'

Ulfcytel gave Waltheof a severe look. 'Trusting without reserve appears to be part of the reason for your predicament,' he said. 'Only the Lord God is worthy of such faith.'

Waltheof grimaced. 'I know that, Father.' Sighing, he rubbed one hand over his face. 'I gave my oath to William, I married his niece, and my own children carry the blood of Normandy in their veins . . . but . . .' He did not complete the sentence.

Ulfcytel sighed too. 'But you let a distant dream, the weakness of drink and the power of another man's tongue lead you away from reality. I know you better, lad, than you know yourself.'

'I should have remained in the cloister and taken holy vows,' Waltheof muttered. 'I do not think I have ever been as content in my life as I was here at Crowland.'

'Yes, perhaps you should have stayed with us,' Ulfcytel

said gently, and laid a compassionate hand on Waltheof's shoulder. 'But since you did not, you have to face the storm you have conjured.'

Waltheof tugged at his beard. 'How?' he asked. 'What should I do?'

Ulfcytel was silent for a time. 'It is a matter for your own conscience. I cannot choose your direction.'

'Then advise me.' He gave the Abbot a pleading look. 'I know that my weakness lies in indecision and lack of foresight. What would you do if you found yourself in my position?'

Ulfcytel's grip on Waltheof tightened. 'I would ask myself what mattered most to me in the world. And then I would ask myself how I could best serve and protect it.'

'My children. They are what matter.'

'And how will you safeguard their future?'

Ulfcytel's voice was gentle, but its power was like the smash of a war axe. How indeed was he going to protect his daughters? Already he had lost one. In the aftermath of their argument four nights ago Judith had miscarried of a third little girl. He had seen it before they took it away and buried it – a scrap without a soul, but already its transparent little body perfectly formed. He thought of all the oaths he had given to different men. All of them under duress. And the unspoken promise he had given to his little daughter. That was more important than any oath.

'I . . . I will go to William,' he said. 'I will ask his mercy – beg if necessary.' His expression twisted at the thought.

Ulfcytel's shoulders rose and fell in a sigh of relief. 'It is your decision, but I am glad you have made it,' he said. 'But I would counsel you not to go directly to William of your own accord. You need a mediator. Seek out Archbishop Lanfranc, make your confession to him, and ask him to intercede.'

'You think me incapable of stating my own case?'

The Abbot gave him a steady look beneath which Waltheof was humbled. 'Aye, you are right,' he said. 'I do not have the subtlety of mind to find my way safe.'

'I will write to the Archbishop and tell him of your plight – remind him that you were once intended for the Church and that you have no evil in you – only folly.'

'Great folly,' Waltheof concurred. 'I should have remained in the cloister.' It was not the first time he had said so. At every crisis of his life the cry went up, and he had never meant it more than now. He rose to his feet, but only then to kneel at Ulfcytel's.

A surge of great tenderness and apprehension swelled within Abbot Ulfcytel as he laid gentle hands upon Waltheof's head. The young man was too vulnerable for the wider world, and he feared greatly for him.

Matilda was in her garden examining the small shoot of her apple tree when her papa returned. She heard the creak of the gate, and turned to see him striding towards her. His expression was grim and she thought that he was going to deliver a scolding, but as he drew closer his lips stretched into something that looked like a smile and she realised that he was not angry. Matilda hesitated for a moment and then ran to him, as she had always done. He swung her up in his arms and hugged her so tightly that her breath left her body and she began to struggle with fear. He let her go then and crouched to her level.

'Why are you crying?' She touched the wet streaks on his face. 'Are you sad?'

'A little.' Taking her hands in his, he rubbed his tears off her fingertips. 'I have done something foolish, and now I have to try and set it to rights.'

She frowned at him.

'Ah, you do not understand, and perhaps it is for the best.' He smoothed her tangled curls.

'Do you want to see my tree?' she asked, wanting to break his strange mood. Curling her grip around his thumb and first two fingers, she tugged him to the bed where the small green shoot was growing sturdily.

He admired it, but his eyes filled again and he had to turn

away to wipe them on his cuff. 'It will grow into a fine, strong tree, even as you grow up into a fine and beautiful woman,' he said. 'I am proud of you, and always will be.'

Matilda looked up at him. Something was definitely wrong, but as with most adult behaviour she was at a loss to understand.

'Tomorrow I have to visit an important churchman, and then I must travel to Normandy to see King William, your great uncle. I may not be home for some little while. I want you to think of me when you tend this tree. And when your mama and Sybille bring you to church, I want you to remember me in your prayers.'

Matilda nodded. 'I always pray for you, Papa,' she said solemnly. This time she did not scream and throw herself on the ground in a drumming of heels. Tomorrow was as far away as the stars and she had his attention and company now. 'Can we go and throw a coin to the water elf?'

'Yes, why not,' he said tremulously, and engulfed her small hand in his, a tender pain bursting in his heart.

CHAPTER 18

Rouen, Normandy,
Autumn 1075

Simon's new falcon was a gift from William in recognition of his squire's exemplary service both in the battle camp and at court. Being pleased with the man emerging from the chrysalis of boyhood, the King had displayed his approval, as was his wont, in a practical fashion.

The young peregrine's wings shone with a slate sheen and her breast was mottled with soft cream and blue herringbone feathers. Simon had called her Guinevere, for to him she was a queen. He was training her to fly as a game hawk rather than to the lure, and for the moment she was taking up all the time he did not spend on duty. She had to be gentled to his fist and so he took her out with him, familiarising her with the sights and sounds of the court, to the presence of dogs and horses and the noise of men. At first she had bated her wings in panic and struggled to be free of her slender leather leashes, but gradually she had grown accustomed to the world outside the mews. Now she perched silently on his wrist, gripping the leather falconer's glove with shining talons like small scimitars of blued steel.

Sabina, the head falconer's daughter, stood beside him at Guinevere's perch. In the sharp-scented dark, her eyes sparkled like black glass. She wore a kerchief for decency over her raven braids, but he could remember the feel of her hair beneath his fingers when he had cozened her into loosening it yester eve. Soft and black and deep. The dreams that had visited him later as he lay on his pallet outside William's chamber had been the sort to take to confession.

Crooning softly to the hawk, calling her my love and my beauty, caressing her with his fingers, he lifted her to the perch. All his movements were slow and measured. Swiftness of any kind was forbidden in the mews, where even a stumble or a raised voice could disturb the highly strung birds of prey. She stepped from his fist to the perch, and only briefly bated her wings.

'She does well,' Sabina murmured. 'Soon you will be flying her.'

Simon smiled and agreed. He wanted to say that all the time he had been stroking the bird's breast he had been thinking of Sabina's, but he bit his tongue. It was the sort of trite statement he had heard the other squires make in their efforts to impress the younger women of the Duchess's retinue.

'I wish you could stay.' She looked at him through her thick, black lashes.

Simon glanced around. They were alone, and there was no sign of her father. 'Why should you think I cannot?' he asked and boldly drew her against him, mouth to mouth, hip to hip. He lost himself in the sweetness of the kiss and the heat that rushed from their joined lips to suffuse other parts of his body. He grew as hard as a quarterstaff. Painfully, wonderfully hard, and frustrated; last night's dream had done nothing but vent the overspill. He reached to the softness of her breasts and wondered how they would feel without the barrier of gown and chemise. Sabina made an enthusiastic sound and arched against him, but after a moment disengaged from the embrace and gave him a little push. 'I think you cannot because the King has a guest,' she said. 'You will be sought to serve at the table. They say that there is no one in the King's household who can carve meat like you.'

Simon drew her close again and pressed his lips to the soft pulse in her throat. 'They will find someone else,' he said, nipping flesh, but he knew he was deluding himself. He was one of the senior squires and the junior ones would be looking to him for help and advice, whilst William would indeed expect him to carve at table and serve the food. Of course, that depended on the guest. If it was someone of minor standing, then one of the other young men could see to the task. 'Do you know who it was?'

'Yes,' she said. 'I saw him many years ago when I was a little girl and the English hostages were at court. I cannot remember his name, but he has hair like beaten copper and a yellow beard.'

Simon stiffened. Now it was he who drew away and looked at her with narrowing eyes. 'Earl Waltheof?'

'Yes, that's him . . . what's wrong?'

Simon grimaced. 'Nothing,' he said, 'I thought this would be the last place he would come.'

'Why?'

'Because there has been some trouble in England.'

'And you would not tell me what kind even if I tied you to a hawk perch and brought the King's eagle to threaten your eyes,' she said, smiling and frowning at the same time.

Simon gave a reluctant chuckle. 'No, I would not,' he agreed. 'Rumours enough abound at court and I make sure I am not the one who starts them – unless I'm ordered. There is power in knowing what happens in the King's chamber, but I will not smirch my honour or the trust the King has in me by spreading tales.' He kissed her cheek and made to depart.

She folded her arms and smiled at him. 'Come back soon,' she said.

'As soon as I can,' he promised over his shoulder in parting. Whenever that would be.

Making his way towards the tower, Simon's limp was scarcely noticeable. He was well rested, the weather had yet to turn cold, and the muscles he had developed in training and on campaign supported the damaged limb. As he walked, he wondered what Waltheof was doing in Normandy.

William had received letters from Archbishop Lanfranc informing him of the rebellion by the Breton contingent in England, led by Ralf of Norfolk and Roger of Hereford. The letters had assured William that the rebellion was being contained and that there was no immediate cause for the King to return to England. Messengers had continued to arrive at regular intervals. Ralf of Norfolk had fled the country to Denmark to plead for rapid help from the Danes, leaving his young wife under siege at his keep in Norwich. Earl Roger had been captured and flung in prison to await William's pleasure. It seemed that Earl Waltheof, although not participating in their rebellion, had known of their intent and had stood back to let their armies gather. Lanfranc wrote that Waltheof bitterly regretted his action, but Simon wondered if bitter regret was atonement enough. He did not know how he would feel when he saw Waltheof. The man who had saved him from a bolting horse, the man who had sat with and encouraged him, who had pulled him through his darkest days. It seemed ungrateful to call him a fool and a traitor, but those sentiments haunted Simon's mind.

He paused at the entrance to the great hall to wash his face and hands at the laver then made his way unobtrusively along the side of the room towards the dais. William was presiding over the high table surrounded by nobles and officials. Waltheof sat beside him and, although the atmosphere was somewhat strained, the men appeared to be talking amicably enough. Waltheof's hair was Norman cropped again, although he wore a beard, trimmed close to his jaw emphasising the strong Danish bone structure. Two junior squires were serving the lords with wine and dried fruit.

'I have never known a man as brave or as foolish as Waltheof

Siwardsson,' muttered Simon's father, pausing briefly beside his son. 'I clearly admit that in his shoes I would have fled to Denmark with Ralf de Gael, not come seeking forgiveness in the lion's den.'

Simon eyed the gathering on the dais. 'Has it been granted?'

His father shrugged. 'I think that William cannot make up his mind. For the moment he bides his time, but again, if I were Waltheof, I would tread carefully.'

Simon made a face. 'He does not know how to do that.' Advancing to the dais, he took the flagon and linen napkin from the lad who was serving and proceeded to the task himself. As he leaned to replenish Waltheof's cup, the Earl gave him a shadowed, troubled smile.

'It is good to see you, Simon,' he said, but without his usual heartiness.

'And you, my lord,' Simon replied politely.

'I see you are quite the polished courtier now.'

William refused the offer of more wine by placing his hand across the top of his cup. 'Simon gives me excellent service, Earl Waltheof,' he said. 'I trust him implicitly, because I know that my trust will never be betrayed.' He spoke without inflection, nevertheless the comment was barbed.

Waltheof flushed. 'I am doing my best to make amends,' he said in a low voice. 'I make mistakes, I admit I do.'

'There are mistakes, and mistakes. It is no use admitting to them if you do not also learn from them. And a mistake such as treason is not the same as dropping a cup or carving a haunch into uneven slices.'

Simon moved down the board. He did not want to appear to be lingering, and it was obvious that the conversation was going to be hard and filled with recrimination. For Waltheof's sake, he knew he should close his ears. Yet, he wanted to hear what Waltheof had to say in his own defence.

'I have not committed treason, sire. Indeed, I have come to you so that you can truly gauge my loyalty.'

'Is that what I am to gauge from your presence here?'

'I would hope so, sire. Indeed, Archbishop Lanfranc has sent you letters to back my plea.'

'Archbishop Lanfranc has sent me letters saying that you confess and repent, which is not the same.'

'I confess to having been foolish – not to treason, sire. I have brought gold with me, and it is to you that I give it, not to your enemies.'

William grunted. 'Blood money – isn't that what you English call it? Wergild?' He spat out the word like a piece of gristle.

'It is a peace offering, sire.'

William frowned. 'A peace offering,' he repeated. 'I am cautious of letting you off so lightly. Am I to have this doubt of your character every time that the Danes set out to raid our coasts? Gold does not buy trust or restore innocence.' He rubbed his hand over the blue stubble-shadow on his jaw. 'For the moment you will oblige me by remaining at court while I decide what is to be done with you.'

Waltheof sat upright, his eyes flashing. 'You make me a prisoner?' he bridled. 'I came to you in good faith.'

'Over a matter of bad faith,' William said curtly. 'And be relieved that I am merely putting you under house arrest. Earl Roger of Hereford has a less comfortable captivity that he would willingly exchange for yours.'

The flagon was empty. Simon descended the dais to fetch a fresh one, but he had others to serve and there was no opportunity to hear any more of the conversation.

Later, however, William summoned Simon and told him that for the duration of the Earl's stay in Normandy he would be assigning him to Waltheof's entourage. 'You know him, you are comfortable in his presence, and as I said, I trust you.'

'Yes, sire.' Simon gazed at a wood louse toiling through the deep layer of rushes beneath his feet.

'What is it lad, look at me.'

Simon raised his eyes to meet the King's. 'Earl Waltheof trusts me too,' he said. 'If I had to break his confidence in order to serve you, then I would, but it would leave a bad taste in my mouth.'

William nodded. His lips curved the merest fraction. 'I know your worth, lad, and I am glad of your honesty. Unless Waltheof tells you that he intends to murder me in the dead of night – which I am sure he will not – then you may keep your own counsel as you see fit.' He waved his hand in dismissal.

'Sire.' Simon bowed and, feeling slightly less apprehensive, went on his way. Some young courtiers stood jesting in a group. As Simon passed, Robert de Bêlleme stuck out a leg elegantly encased in red hose and deliberately tripped him.

Simon went sprawling in the rushes and felt a jolt of pain slash through his damaged limb. His assailant's tough, calf-hide boot had caught him directly across the area of the old break.

'You'll never be fast enough, De Senlis,' scoffed De Bêlleme. 'I could pull the legs off a crab and it would move better than you.'

His jaw tight with suppressed anger, Simon struggled to his feet. The pain was like the point of a knife blade winkling between his bones, but he refused to show by so much as a blink how much it hurt. The others in the group watched but said nothing. While someone else was being victimised they were safe.

'At least my mind is untainted,' Simon said, knowing that he should hold his tongue but unable to stop himself.

De Bêlleme turned fully towards him, his hand going to the dagger at his hip and a slow smile spreading across his saturnine features. 'Indeed?' he drawled, 'you seem somewhat of a lackwit to me.'

Simon swallowed. 'Think as you will,' he said, 'that is your undoing.' Turning on his heel, he walked stiffly away. His leg was throbbing fiercely but he forced his will through the pain so that although he limped the impairment was no worse than usual. His shoulder blades twitched and he half expected to feel De Bêlleme's dagger blade prick between them, or a hand on his shoulder, grasping and spinning him round. But there was nothing. De Bêlleme muttered something disparaging to his cronies, though, for a burst of laughter followed Simon from the room and he knew that it was at his expense.

Waltheof was in the small chamber that had been allotted to him. The fact that he was under house arrest meant that a guard was posted nearby. His huscarls had been given space in one of the timber guardrooms in the ward, and their weapons confiscated.

Waltheof welcomed Simon with open gestures and smiles; it was obvious to the youth that they were false and that the Earl had never felt less like smiling in his life. He set down the flagon of wine and the platter of honey wafers he had brought and poured a goblet for the Earl.

'I have been a fool,' Waltheof said bitterly. 'I should never have attended Ralf de Gael's marriage.' He seized on the goblet and drank the contents in several swift gulps. Simon concealed a wince. Drowning sorrows did not make them disappear.

'Then why did you?' Simon trimmed the candle and lit another one beside it to brighten the room.

Waltheof exhaled harshly. 'Because he was my friend. Because his company was better than my wife's. Because he knows what it is to have English blood and be a stranger in your own land . . .' Waltheof shook his head. 'I knew he was ambitious, but I did not realise how high he was aiming until it was too late. He asked me to help him . . . and in my friendship and folly I did not refuse him straightaway. Now I am trapped in a noose of my own coiling and I do not know how to escape.'

Simon said nothing. He admired and liked Waltheof, but not for his political abilities, which were dire.

'Has the King said anything about how long he intends keeping me here?'

'No, my lord. Only that I am to serve as your squire in all things.'

Waltheof studied him closely, as if seeking the truth behind the words. 'And I'm glad to have you,' he said, but his voice was flat and he drank his wine with the swift desperation of a man eager for oblivion. 'I only wish that the circumstances were happier.'

'I too, my lord,' Simon said uncomfortably.

Waltheof rested the cup on his knee. 'I do not think that there has ever been a time when I have not been someone's hostage or prisoner,' he said, 'save perhaps when I was very young and my father intended me for the Church. After he died I became a ward of the Godwinssons, and when they fell in battle your king took their place.

It was telling to Simon that he said 'your king'. He frowned at Waltheof.

'Why do you look at me like that?'

'I wondered why you did it . . . why you became embroiled in a plot with Ralf de Gael?'

'I was a prisoner trying the door of my cell.' Waltheof smiled humourlessly. 'Someone offered me a key and I took it, only to find that it led to another cell, deeper and darker than the first.' He grimaced at Simon. 'I do not expect you to understand what it is like to live every day of your life like a yoked ox – to have the power of an earl, which is no power at all when versed against that of Norman sheriffs and officials. To be an unwelcome stranger in your own hall.'

'But you are kin by marriage to King William himself,' Simon pointed out. 'Surely that must count for something.'

Waltheof sighed. 'My marriage is like the great battle of Hastings, with no mercy shown and no prisoners taken,' he said bleakly.

Simon shook his head, not knowing what to say.

'Although, I admit I have my daughters,' Waltheof added softly. 'I would never regret giving them life. And in truth, I once loved their mother, and still do after a fashion, although I doubt that she has anything left in her heart for me but contempt. Ah, enough.' He made an impatient gesture. 'I do not want to talk of the ruin I have made of my life. What of you lad? How soon will you be a fledged knight?'

Simon politely spoke of his own life, but not as eagerly as he would once have done with Waltheof, and although the earl appeared to be listening with eagerness Simon could tell that his inner ear was closed.

CHAPTER 19

In December William prepared to return to England to keep the Christmas feast at Westminster.

Simon was buried under a mountain of preparations; there were errands to run, itineraries to organise, chests to pack. In between dealing with William's demands, he had Waltheof to attend. The Earl was allowed from his chamber but confined to the Tower precincts. The nearest he came to the outdoors was to stand in the window splays and breathe the wind. Simon saw how he bridled at the constraint and sympathised with him. He could still remember with painful clarity how it felt to be hemmed in for weeks on end.

He played chess and dice with Waltheof and advanced his rudimentary knowledge of the English tongue until he was moderately fluent. He brought Guinevere to Waltheof's chamber and let the Earl perch her on his wrist. They spoke of the art of falconry and the beauty of the prized white Norway hawks whose price lay in the realm of kings.

Simon no longer had time for dalliance with Sabina and in his absence she transferred her affections to a young serjeant from the Vexin who was staying behind in Rouen.

Sometimes the Conqueror's sons and their cronies would visit a brothel in the city, but on the rare occasions that Simon was free of duty he chose not to accompany them, for Robert de Bêlleme was always among their number. The youth baited Simon at every opportunity, calling him 'lameleg' and 'clodhop'.

Simon refused to show how much he was wounded by the taunts, but shrugging them off became increasingly difficult.

On the day that the court embarked for England, De Bêlleme made one of his barbed remarks and stuck out his foot as Simon was bearing a dish of hot frumenty to the high table. This time, however, Simon was prepared. He avoided De Bêlleme's boot but pretended to stumble and deliberately tipped the steaming dish of stewed wheat over De Bêlleme's head and down the back of his immaculate tunic.

De Bêlleme roared and shot to his feet. The hot, glutinous grains clung to his hair, skin and clothes, making it look as though he were being devoured by maggots, and he danced and flailed as the heat scalded his flesh. Blobs of wheat porridge flew everywhere and the other diners cursed. 'You crippled son of a whore, I'll kill you!' De Bêlleme howled and whipped his knife from its sheath.

Simon flashed his own blade from its scabbard. 'You tripped me. It is your own fault!' he spat, and knew that although revenge had been sweet it was also short. There was not a chance in hell that he could match the physical prowess of Robert de Bêlleme. Nor could he run.

'Leave him, Rob!' cried the Conqueror's son, also named Robert. 'It was an accident.'

'Accident my arse!' De Bêlleme bared his teeth and made a slashing movement with the knife. By leaping violently backwards, Simon was able to avoid being gutted, but he landed on his unsound leg and went down.

De Bêlleme kicked him, landing him a blow in the ribs hard enough to crack bone. The breath tore out of Simon's lungs on an agonised whoop of air. He saw the foot draw back for another assault and prepared to roll away, but the blow never descended. De Bêlleme was lifted off his feet and the knife twisted out of his hand by a furious Waltheof.

'You shame your knighthood!' the Earl roared. 'You so much as go near the lad again and I will rip your head from your neck and use it to kick around for sport on the sward!'

'Hah, since when have you had the right to speak of shame?' De Bêlleme sneered, wrenching himself out of Waltheof's grasp.

Waltheof rammed the young knight's knife into the trestle. 'Since I witnessed your own shameful behaviour towards one of your own,' he said harshly. 'I meant what I said. Touch him again, and you will reckon with me.'

De Bêlleme's fists opened and closed. He said nothing, but the intensity of his gaze on Waltheof was worth a thousand words.

As the men faced each other there was a flurry at the dais end of the hall and William arrived to break his fast. Amidst the rising and bowing Waltheof dragged Simon to his feet and bore him out of the hall.

'Are you all right, lad?'

Clutching his ribs, Simon nodded. 'I should not have done it, but I lost my temper,' he said with self-reproach. 'You should not have intervened, my lord. Robert de Bêlleme is a bad enemy to make.'

Waltheof shrugged as if ridding himself of an irritation. 'One more will make no difference,' he said with a bitter smile. 'He will not touch you again while I am by, I promise you that.'

Simon shook his head. 'No,' he agreed. 'He will bide his time. Robert de Bêlleme does not care whether he sticks his opponent face to face or in the back.'

'But at least you ruined his tunic,' Waltheof said.

'Oh yes,' Simon said, and suddenly, despite or perhaps because of the shock he had just received, he began to grin. 'I struck him in his vanity, which is his most vulnerable part.'

The sea crossing was cold and uncomfortable, but although the waves were choppy the voyage was swift. From their landing in Southampton, the court rode on to Winchester and the prospect of good hunting in crisp air.

Once they were in England, though, William's mood changed. Before, he had only had access to tales of the thwarted revolt against him through letters and messengers. Now he could see and hear for himself, and what he saw and heard was not to his taste. Those of his barons with English interests whispered in his ear, speaking of the need to guard against further treachery and punish wrongdoers. Waltheof was kept under close house arrest, all hopes of returning to his earldom dashed, although the King relented enough to say that there was no reason why the Countess Judith could not come to him at court. To that end Simon was dispatched to fetch her.

The weather was sharp and clear, and the roads hard with frost. Simon made good time, arriving in Northampton on the third afternoon of his journey.

He was welcomed to the hall, given food and drink while he waited, and presently was summoned to the Countess Judith's private chamber.

She was seated at a tapestry frame, two vertical lines set between her eyes as she attempted to sew by candlelight. Her daughters sat with her, Matilda labouring over a piece of simple stitchery using a large needle threaded with brightly coloured wool. The child's tongue peeped out from between her teeth as she strove to co-ordinate hand and eye. How old was she? A little beyond three years old, Simon thought, and Waltheof's paternity evident in every curve, line and nuance of her body. Her little sister was occupied in sorting scraps of material into piles of different colour under the watchful eyes of Sybille and another maid.

'My lady.' Simon bowed.

Judith beckoned him forward and he came into the ring of candlelight. She was sewing a scene from the life of Saint Agnes, who had chosen martyrdom above marriage. Not an encouraging sign.

'I understand you bear a message for me?' Her tone was formal, warning him not to expect to be treated as a guest, and her lips were pursed, revealing that she was not delighted at her uncle's choice of messenger.

'The King requests your presence at Winchester,' he said, 'and Earl Waltheof asks that you come also.'

She bent her head to her embroidery, sewing the stitches with a steady hand. 'My husband does not return to Northampton then?'

'No, my lady,' Simon said in a neutral voice. 'The King prefers to keep him by his side.'

'You mean he is a prisoner?' She looked up. 'Wrapping the truth in silk will not make it any prettier. Tell me the whole.'

Simon was not encouraged by her peremptory tone. 'The King is undecided what to do about the Earl,' he said. 'I think he is keeping him hostage while he makes up his mind. There are those who say that he should be restored to favour, and others who counsel His Grace to have a care. They say it but takes mention of a Danish invasion to send the Earl hurtling into rebellion.' He did not add that those against Waltheof's release had the loudest voices, chief amongst them her own stepfather, Eudo of Champagne, and Roger de Montgomery, who was the sire of Robert de Bêlleme.

The Countess sewed until she reached the end of her thread, snipped it with a set of silver shears, then sat back and sighed. 'These last few months I have been at peace,' she said bleakly. 'I do not think that I could bear the strife.'

'My lady?'

She gave a small shake of her head. 'When I married Waltheof of Huntingdon, I believed that I could change him, but I might as well have been drawing water with a sieve. He is what he is – and I am what I am.' She rose from the tapestry frame and eased the small of her back with the pressure of her palms. 'Very well. I will come to Winchester, and I will have my say.'

'Is Papa coming home?' Matilda demanded, clearly having understood some of the conversation. Her little face was suddenly bright and eager.

'Papa home, Papa home,' echoed her little sister.

'We shall see,' Judith said in a curt tone that put an end to the matter.

*

In the private royal chambers at Winchester, King William raised his niece from her deep curtsey and formally gave her the kiss of peace. Judith faced him. Although her expression was calm, her stomach was almost clamped to her spine with apprehension. They were not alone. Apart from the usual quota of servants, the room was occupied by her stepfather, her mother, Lanfranc of Canterbury, and several magnates high in her uncle's counsel. A formal gathering . . . or a court preparing to sit in judgement.

William gestured her to be seated. 'Have you seen or spoken to your husband yet, niece?' He gave her an interrogative look as she took her place on the oak bench beside her mother, who drew in her skirts to make room.

She shook her head. 'No, sire, and I do not wish to,' she said. William eyed her thoughtfully. 'Why not?'

Judith had been debating her reply to this question all the way to Winchester and was still no nearer an answer. If she said that she did not wish to see her husband because he upset her equilibrium, her uncle would think she was being ridiculous.

'Well?' William demanded.

She looked down at her hands. When she had sat down, they had been folded in her lap. Now they were clenched. 'Our marriage ended on the day he returned from Ralf de Gael's bride-ale, and told me what he had done,' she said.

She was aware of her mother's sharp glance, and the sudden heightening of tension among the others.

'And what did he tell you?' William asked gently.

Judith swallowed. She could feel the words sticking in her gullet. Should she speak or hold her silence?

'Your duty is to the house of your birth,' her mother muttered under her breath. 'You betray your blood if you do not speak out.'

Her husband or her blood. It was simple when couched in those terms, but still she hesitated. When she opened her mouth to speak, her voice locked in her throat and she had to cough to clear the way. 'He said that Roger of Hereford and Ralf de Gael were plotting with the Danes to overthrow you and that he had taken an oath not to stand in their way.' Now her hands were not only clenched, but her nails were digging half-moon marks in her skin.

'You are sure of this?' William said.

'Yes, sire, I am sure. I told him that he was a fool and that he had been used, but he did not want to listen. When I took him to task, he threatened to beat me. Even so, I told him that he must come straight to you and seek forgiveness, but he said that he could not because he had given his oath to Ralf de Gael. After that, I knew that I could no longer be his wife.' She bowed her head and felt the heat of tears behind her lids. But she did not shed them. 'It is true that he went to Abbot Ulfcytel of Crowland Abbey and Archbishop Lanfranc in troubled conscience, but I believe that he was also biding his time and waiting to see if De Gael's rebellion would succeed. When it did not, he came to you to confess.'

There was silence except for the soft settling of charcoal in the brazier and a shutter cracking in the wind. Then William slowly exhaled. 'It is as I thought,' he said, 'although I would leif as not believe it.'

'No backbone,' Adelaide declared scornfully. 'I knew that from the beginning. He is like that great bear pelt he wears. All shine and glamour, but no substance.'

'Rather a weak reed, madam, easily led astray.' Lanfranc's tone was conciliatory.

'The words make small difference,' she snapped. 'It is the deeds that count.'

'I have no place for a weak reed.' William rose to pace the chamber, his tread heavy and deliberate. 'Once again he has proven untrustworthy and my patience is frayed.'

'What then will you do with him?' asked Eudo, thumbing the cleft in his chin. 'Clearly, you cannot restore him to his lands. By all accounts he has committed treason. You cannot hold Roger of Hereford in a dungeon and let Waltheof of

Huntingdon go free. From the lips of his own wife, your niece, you have received the words of his guilt.'

Back and forth, William paced, restless with the anger that did not show on his face. 'I have no choice but to punish him,' he said.

'Is that wise?' Lanfranc spoke out. 'He is popular with the English people, and the rebellion has been nipped in the bud. Waltheof claims that he was not intending to be an active participant.'

'Do you take his part?' William rounded on the churchman.

Lanfranc spread his arms, showing the full linen sleeves of his under-tunic. 'No sire, I merely point out that you should consider carefully. I do not deny that he has caused you much trouble, and that he should be punished . . .'

'Agreeing to stand aside makes him as guilty as being a participant,' William growled. 'I know full well that if the Danish ships had come sooner, he would have been on the shore helping them to beach their keels.' His regard chopped to Judith. 'Is that not so, niece, or do you say differently?'

Judith bit her lip. 'It would depend how much he was swayed by others. I think that he has tried to live by our ways, but has found it difficult.'

'If Waltheof is so beloved of the English people,' said Eudo silkily, 'then let him be judged by their laws, not our Norman ones. That would show how willing you are to compromise and not impose upon the English way of justice. Of course,' he added, 'Roger of Hereford must be judged by Norman law because he is a Norman.'

William bit on his thumbnail. 'That seems sensible,' he said slowly. 'How does English law deal with such cases?'

Since everyone gathered was Norman, no one knew offhand, although Judith thought that from the gleam in his eyes her stepfather might have an inkling. However, he said nothing.

'Then let Earl Waltheof be imprisoned the same as Earl

Roger until we have the details,' William said. 'For it is not fair that the one languishes in a dungeon and the other enjoys the hospitality of our court.'

'You could unfasten Earl Roger's shackles and confine him to house arrest,' Lanfranc suggested.

'I think not,' William said curtly. 'Indeed, the more I consider the matter, the less forgiving I become. If this rebellion has not succeeded it is only due to the vigilance of my loyal supporters.'

There was silence, although of the relieved and pleased kind. A decision had been reached, apparently to mutual satisfaction. Guards were sent to apprehend Waltheof and put him in a cell.

'I knew no good would come of this marriage,' Adelaide muttered. She and Judith had retired to the women's quarters, where Judith had ordered her maids to see to the repacking of her travelling chests ready for her return to Northampton.

'You cannot claim outstanding success for your own, Mother,' Judith retorted.

'At least none of my husbands ever committed treason,' Adelaide replied. 'Eudo and I understand each other's needs very well. That it involves separate households is by mutual agreement.'

Judith compressed her lips. Pre-empting the maid, she snatched a gown off the clothing pole and folded it, giving her hands something to do.

'You are leaving without speaking to your husband?' Adelaide's expression was filled with disbelief.

Judith thrust the folded gown at her maid. 'I have nothing to say to him.'

'If he were mine, I would have much to say. I would tell the traitor what I truly thought of him.'

Judith faced her mother. 'Don't you understand?' she said impatiently. 'All that is behind me. I have already told him what I truly think. While he is confined, I am free, and that is all that matters.'

Adelaide folded her arms. 'That remains to be seen.' Her tone was ominous.

Judith shook her head. 'My uncle will banish him from England as he banished Edgar Atheling. He can do no other.'

'That will depend on whose word prevails with your uncle. Lanfranc is too tender in this matter, and if your uncle listens to him Waltheof may yet be released.'

Judith looked at her mother with burgeoning fear. 'I pray not,' she said. 'I could not bear it.'

'That is foolish talk. You could and you would.' Adelaide made a dismissive gesture. 'I will do what I can to defray Lanfranc's word, and so will your stepfather. It is a pity he did not give you a son,' she said with a glance towards the apple of her eye, who was playing in a corner with a painted wooden horse.

Judith grimaced. It was ground so often covered that it was staler than trencher bread.

'You must be very careful with your own daughters,' Adelaide warned, wagging an instructive forefinger. 'Do not let them yearn after men who are unsuitable. You must mould them while they are young. You must not let the taint of their father's blood gain dominance.'

'No, Mother,' Judith clenched her jaw.

'The older one. Already she is too much like her father. She needs a firm hand or you will have cause for regret.'

'Grant me leave to deal with her as I see fit.' Judith knew that if her mother said one more word, she would hit her. Mercifully, Adelaide seemed to realise the danger in which she stood.

'Indeed, daughter. I can only warn. The discipline must come from you.'

Adelaide departed, taking her son, and Judith sat down on the small, truckle bed, her legs trembling. The maid pretended not to notice and busied herself securing the hasp on the travelling chest.

Slowly Judith regained her composure. She sent another

maid to tell the grooms to ready the horses. The sooner she was gone from Winchester, the better she would feel. It was as though a great dark cloud was engulfing her, robbing her of her faculties. Had anyone suggested it was guilt, she would have denied it furiously, but denial was not enough. She shied from the vision of Waltheof in a cell. He had always so loved the open air and sunlight.

His misfortune was of his own making she told herself – and she was his misfortune as much as he was hers.

'Well?' Adelaide demanded of Eudo as he drew the curtain across their chamber door. 'What did my brother say?' The men had remained to discuss Waltheof's situation and other matters of state after the women's departure.

Eudo hitched his chausses and sat down on the bench squeezed against the side of the room. Their son was asleep on a feather-stuffed pallet on the floor, his small body covered with a fur-lined blanket and his blond hair softly gleaming. 'Your brother is still of half a mind to let Waltheof go free for that payment in gold.'

'That is foolish!' Adelaide's light brown eyes kindled with wrath. 'Waltheof of Huntingdon cannot be trusted. I won't have my daughter . . . my own flesh and blood yoked to such a one. A traitor once is a traitor for ever!' Her voice was pitched low to avoid wakening their son, but there was no mistaking its venom.

'Lanfranc suggested that Waltheof should be banished from England,' Eudo said, watching her warily. 'Your brother seemed interested in the notion.'

'Lanfranc is an old fool!' Adelaide snapped. 'Waltheof would go straight to Ralf de Gael in Brittany to stir up more rebellion, or to Denmark to rouse his barbarian kinsmen.'

'That is what myself and Montgomery told William.' Eudo rubbed his palms together nervously.

'And?'

'William said he would think on the matter.'

Adelaide made an impatient sound. 'There is naught to think upon. Waltheof is a traitor and should be dealt with as such.' Eudo looked at her, still rubbing his palms.

'What is it?' she demanded. 'What are you not telling me?'

He cleared his throat. 'I spoke to a cleric versed in English law. He tells me that treason carries the death penalty – so if Waltheof is judged by the laws of his own country . . .' he let the words tail off.

Adelaide stared at him. A red flush began at her throat and crept gradually into her face. 'Does my brother know this?'

'Not yet, but he will do soon.'

They looked at each other, and although nothing was said ambition flared between them like a flash of lightning.

'It is our duty,' Adelaide murmured after a moment, 'to support the decision he makes.' She stooped to watch her sleeping son breathe softly in and out. 'And to make sure that it is the right one for all concerned.'

CHAPTER 20

Winchester, Spring 1076

The guard took Simon away from the warmth and light of Winchester's hall and brought him into the darker regions where brightness and sunlight did not reach. A single torch flared in a bracket on the wall and a musty smell pervaded everything – like the soil dug from a grave pit. Simon's nape prickled and an involuntary shudder ran down his spine. Behind a door on the right someone moaned, but the guard paid no heed and led Simon further into the darkness until they arrived at another door of iron-bound oak. A narrow grille was cut in the top for observation, and there was an opening at the base to admit and retrieve food bowls and the slop pail.

The guard peered through the grille and, taking a large key from the ring at his waist, turned it ponderously in the door lock. 'Go on, sir,' he said to Simon with an ushering gesture. 'I'll be outside if you have need. Shout when you are ready to leave.'

Simon nodded, pressed a silver penny into the man's hand, and entered the cell. It was large enough to contain several prisoners but confined a single occupant. The floor was thickly strewn with new rushes and instead of a straw pallet the prisoner had a proper bed with linen sheets and a coverlet of red and blue wool. Wax candles burned with a clear, yellow glow, chasing shadows into the deepest recesses of the walls. The prisoner, being an earl, could afford to pay for such luxuries.

'My lord?' The door closed solidly at Simon's back and the key bolt shot home. He advanced into the cell. Waltheof was kneeling before a crucifix that had been nailed into the wall; either side of it, on a narrow bench, two candles flickered, forming a makeshift altar. He turned at the sound of Simon's voice and his features brightened with pleasure. He did not, however, bounce lithely to his feet as once he would have done, but rose rather gingerly, as if he had been kneeling for a long time. 'It is good to see you, lad. What are you doing here?' Hobbling forward, he embraced the youth.

'I asked the King's permission for leave to visit,' Simon replied. In the confines of prison, Waltheof's vigorous musculature had diminished and it was like clasping a gaunt-boned stranger – a man already halfway to the death that was his sentence under English law.

'And I suppose he gave it so that you could bid your farewells to a condemned man.' Waltheof broke from the embrace with a barren smile.

Simon did not reply, for Waltheof had spared him the need.

'Still, all visitors are welcome for whatever reason.' The smile grew bleaker yet. 'Guests to my cell have been somewhat lacking and in truth I have not expected them. Ulfcytel and the Bishop of Winchester, of course. My soul has its comfort to take to the next world. I had thought that Judith might . . .' He grimaced and thrust his hands through his hair. Uncropped in captivity it gleamed on a level with his jawline. 'I have not seen her since the day I left for Normandy. I was told that she came to Winchester at Christmastide, and it was about the time of her visit that I was cast in here to rot. I wonder if this is any of her doing. I know her strong enough . . . but I cannot bear to think that she would do this to me . . .'

Still Simon was silent.

'Do you know the truth?' Waltheof asked. 'You are a party to much of what is said in the King's chamber.'

Simon lifted his head. 'Indeed I am, but I would not break the King's trust in me by repeating anything that I happened to hear.'

'Even to a man who will take the tale nowhere except to his grave?' Waltheof's expression was bitter. 'Am I not entitled to know who betrayed me?'

'You betrayed yourself at Ralf de Gael's bride-ale,' Simon said. He felt uncomfortable at the turn the conversation had taken, and began to wonder if he should have made this visit at all.

'If I had not been arraigned for my part in Ralf's rebellion, it would have been for something else,' Waltheof retorted. 'I had too much power, too high a standing to be allowed to keep it and prosper. Men are covetous, especially of that which could be theirs for the sake of a push.'

Simon began to feel queasy. The walls of the cell seemed to press in on him. He wondered how Waltheof bore day after day in the gloom, knowing that the only light at the end of the tunnel led to the executioner's sword. 'I can say nothing,' he replied.

'Not even about my wife? Is it because she was responsible that you will not speak? You have to tell me.' He took an agitated pace towards the youth, his hand outstretched to grab at Simon's tunic, but even as he touched the cloth a look of misery and self-loathing crossed his face and he spun away. 'I almost struck her,' he whispered. 'And I would not have hurt her for the world.' His shoulders shook.

Simon was at a loss. He had known plenty of pain in his life, and constant challenge. He knew what misery felt like, but when its cause was this deep he was not sure that his arm was long enough to reach down and rescue. 'Lady Judith had naught to do with your imprisonment,' he said. 'It is true that she came to Winchester at Christmastide, but not in order to seek your death.'

'Then for what? Certainly, it was not to see me!' Waltheof said in a grief-drenched voice. 'Not once has she been near . . . nor my daughters.'

The way he spoke the last word left Simon in no doubt what was hurting Waltheof the most. 'The Countess came to tell the King what you had said about the bride-ale because he demanded it of her.'

'What else? There must be more.'

Simon drew a deep breath. He knew that he was treading on dangerous ground. Unlike Waltheof, he could dissemble when he had to, but it was not a role that he enjoyed. 'She said that she did not desire to see you because your marriage was over . . . but that was all. And she left your daughters at Northampton – out of a care for them I think, not to slight you.'

'A care for them,' Waltheof repeated and his mouth twisted. 'Oh yes, no one could accuse her of being neglectful in her "duty".'

Simon winced, knowing that whatever he said would not ease Waltheof's torment.

Wiping his eyes, Waltheof made an effort to compose himself. 'I should have remained in the Church and taken the tonsure all those years ago. Of all the mistakes I made, that is perhaps the worst one.' He bent a reproachful look on Simon. 'Still, I will go to my God with a clearer conscience than those who remain.'

'I am sorry,' Simon swallowed. 'I came to make my farewell, but I do not know how to do it.'

Waltheof smiled sourly. 'I can lie down on my pallet and we can pretend that it is my deathbed. Would that help?'

'You should not jest, my lord.'

'Why not?' Waltheof shrugged. 'Jesting will avail me more than misery in my hour of reckoning.'

There was an uneasy silence in which Simon cast around for something to say. 'The ordinary folk are disturbed by the rumour that you are to be executed.'

'Are they indeed?' Waltheof's smile broadened and grew a little savage. 'I may yet cause a rebellion then with my dying breath . . .'

'Which William will suppress and swiftly.'

'Oh indeed.' Waltheof paced to the end of the cell and turned. Simon noticed that there was a path worn in the straw. 'Strange how English and Norman rules have suited him,' Waltheof said. 'Roger of Hereford is sentenced to remain the rest of his life in prison because he is a Norman. However since I am English the penalty for me is death, and there is no one willing to stick out their own neck and argue for my freedom.'

'Abbot Ulfcytel has done so, my lord,' Simon objected.

'And he too is English and so his word carries small weight with those who would see me deprived. I should have died in the wasting of the North, fighting with an axe in my hand, not in this dark and shameful way.'

'And I should not have come,' Simon said, and turned to the door. The hand he raised to knock for the guard was trembling.

'No, wait.' Waltheof strode to Simon and grabbed his sleeve. 'I don't want you to leave like this.' Pulling the youth against him, Waltheof smothered him in a second embrace, harder and more desperate than the first. The bone of mortality on bone.

'I know there is nothing you can do. I know that I should not waste my last hours in bitterness, but it is hard,' Waltheof said, his voice tearing. 'Once I gave your life to you. Now live it for me. When you look out on a ploughed field or the women bringing in the May, remember me and see with my eyes as well as your own. When you take a wife and hold your own firstborn child in your arms, think of me.'

'You know I will,' Simon replied, his own voice constricted by the force of the embrace and the emotion that Waltheof was squeezing out of him.

'Do not just say it, swear it.'

'I swear it, on the cross,' Simon gasped as Waltheof's grip tightened.

Waltheof relaxed his hold and Simon dragged a deep gulp of air into his lungs and dropped to his knees.

Going to his bed, Waltheof swept the bearskin cloak off the end. 'I want you to have this,' he said. His large hands caressed the thick, white fur.

Simon stared. His throat ached and he could not speak, but he managed to shake his head.

'You always admired it as a child and it will mean more to you than anyone else. I have no doubt that when they sever my head from my body someone will appropriate this garment to themselves in naught but greed. I would rather you had it.' With a final parting stroke, Waltheof handed the cloak to Simon.

The young man took it across his arm and felt its weight settle – nearly as heavy as a mail hauberk, for as well as the weight of the pelt the outer layer was thickly woven, fulled wool, and the bordering braid was twined with thread of gold. The garment of a magnate, an earl. He was moved and awed. For as long as he could remember he had admired and coveted this mantle. Now he would have done anything to see it back in its rightful place billowing from Waltheof's shoulders as he strode through his life.

'I will treasure this . . .' he said in a tight voice.

'Do not be so precious as to make of it an object of worship. It is meant to be worn – and worn with pride.' Taking back the cloak, Waltheof opened it out and swung it around the squire's shoulders. It drowned his slenderness and the hem almost swept the floor. Borrowed robes that did not fit, Simon thought with an inward grimace.

'You will grow into it,' Waltheof said. His mouth twitched in a painful smile. 'In more ways than one.' He thrust home the enormous silver pin with its thistlehead decoration.

Simon departed shortly after that, and was not ashamed of the tear streaks on his face as the guard led him back through darkness towards the light. He had to hold the cloak above his ankles like a woman holding her skirts to prevent himself from trampling on the hem.

'Worth the meeting then,' the guard said with an envious nod at Simon's acquisition.

'Without price,' Simon said in a choked voice. They passed an alcove redolent with the stink of a latrine hole – a crude wooden seat set over a shaft in the wall. Simon dived sideways and hung over the foul pit, retching dryly. He could have told Waltheof that his betrayers were none other than his mother-in-law and her husband aided and abetted by the Montgomery family, who never forgot a slight, but he had kept that information to himself. He felt as though he had been drinking poison for a long, long time, and finally it had made him sick. Was there a difference between good treachery and bad treachery? Was Waltheof's rebellion against William worse than the calumny practised against him by the venomous tongue of Adelaide of Champagne and Roger de Montgomery? He had no answers, only reaction.

'As bad as that?' the guard said.

'Worse,' Simon gasped, and forced himself upright. No matter how much it sickened him, he was a straw on the flood and there was nothing he could do.

In the morning, the final one of May, Waltheof, Earl of Huntingdon, Northampton and Northumberland, was brought from his cell and escorted by mailed guards to the top of a hill outside the city walls. It was a beautiful dawn, a flushed apricot horizon uplighting the growing blue of the new day. Waltheof's last footsteps left their trail in grass that was silvergreen with dew and starred with the clenched buds of daisy and dandelion.

Simon stood amidst the small crowd that had followed the soldiers to witness the execution. Most were Normans and the majority wore the mail and gambesons of knights and soldiers. There was only a handful of English folk, drawn from the community of castle servants. The executioners had

deliberately chosen the early hour so that few of the townspeople were about or free of their labours. The Normans did
not want a riot on their hands.

Simon saw Waltheof stumble and winced for him. How
long it must have been since he had seen the light and stretched
his legs. At least they had given him access to clean raiment
and he must have washed his hair, for it had a metallic sparkle
in the sunshine and the filaments floated on the breeze like
the finest threads of copper and gold.

The beheading was to be done with a sword, for he was
highly born, an earl, and even those who wanted him dead
for their own base reasons, respected the privileges due to his
high birth. Simon had watched the swordsman sharpening
his blade on a whetstone the night before and the sound of
the brightening of the steel had sent chills through him with
each long rasp. Had he not owed Waltheof his life he would
have fled the slaying, but it was his duty to bear witness so
that he could look Waltheof's executioners in the eyes when
they could not look him in his.

On the crest of the hill, facing the dawn, the guards thrust
Waltheof to his knees. As Walkelin, Bishop of Winchester,
prayed over him, the swordsman approached, the blade
shining with the reflection of the rising sun.

Waltheof's eyes widened in panic and Simon saw that they
were full of the desperate need to live. That even now Waltheof
could not believe that he was about to die. 'For the love of
Almighty God!' he cried in a choked voice. 'At least let me
say the Lord's Prayer one more time . . . for your sake, and
for mine.'

The swordsman hesitated and looked round at the gathered soldiers for instruction.

'So be it,' growled Eudo of Champagne with an impatient
flurry of his hand. 'But make haste.' At his side Robert de
Montgomery scowled, clearly irritated by the delay. He set
his hand to the hilt of his own sword as if he would do the
deed himself.

Waltheof spread his hands, bowed his head, and his voice rose above the prelate's in recitation of the Lord's Prayer. '*Pater noster qui es in caelis, sanctificetur nomen tuum. Adveniat regnum tuum . . .*'

Simon prayed too, clearing his throat and raising his strong young voice. Folk either side who had been murmuring their own responses looked at him askance, but he did not care. This was for Waltheof, an affirmation of support and belief.

Waltheof raised his head and followed the sound until his eyes met Simon's across the sward. They held him, nailing him to the promise he had made the night before and filled with a terrible entreaty that Simon was powerless to aid.

'*Et ne nos inducas in temptationem.*' Waltheof's voice died away and his gaze left Simon's and struck on the group of nobles whose pressure had brought him to this place. Roger de Montgomery, Robert of Mortain, Eudo of Champagne. He looked until their image blotted the gold and blue of the new morning from his sight. '*Sed libera nos a malo.* But deliver us from evil.' The crowd around him stirred restlessly and the bladesman's eyes flickered with apprehension. At a nod from Eudo the man laid both hands to the sword, drew back to gain impetus and struck round and down in a lightning movement that clove flesh and vertebrae in one crunching slice.

'Amen!' Simon's voice finished alone, then died in appalled silence. Some members of the crowd turned aside to vomit. Simon had done that yesterday. Now, dry-eyed, he bore witness as Waltheof's crumpled, blood-spattered body was lifted onto a bier and the head placed beside it. Some of the crowd tried to push forwards and the soldiers held them back with spears. Simon, being a royal squire, was permitted through the cordon. Already a servant was swilling the bloody grass with pails of water, removing all trace of the deed. The bier was lined with absorbant hides to soak up the blood that still leaked from the body. The corpse had been covered by a blanket and this too was slowly reddening as the bearers carried it towards the grave that had been made ready.

Simon stood by the deep pit they had dug. Waltheof was permitted neither the dignity of a coffin nor even a shroud, but was tumbled from stretcher to pit in a single motion. One man leaned down to take the head and set it against the severed neck. Immediately labourers began shovelling earth into the grave, their haste as unseemly as the manner of Waltheof's death.

'Is the Earl not to be brought home to Huntingdon for burial?' Simon asked one of the monks attending the Bishop at the graveside.

The man shook his head. 'Our instructions were to bury him at the place of execution,' he said, clasping his hands and joining the others in chanting a litany for the dead.

Listening to their intonation, Simon knew that their prayers were a waste of time. Waltheof's soul would not rest easy in this soil. His ghost would walk and cry out – if not for vengeance, then for proper reverence and peace.

The soil was packed down and covered with fresh green turf. Dry-eyed, burning within, Simon turned on his heel. A small girl and her mother had been watching from a distance. The woman was a servant from the palace kitchens. Her gown of natural brown wool was patched and her braids were bundled up in a simple working kerchief. Her daughter had flaxen braids and deep blue eyes set in a dainty face. Her arms were occupied by a mass of spring flowers, early campion, daisy, dogrose and mingled with them the greenery of young wheat, cut long before its harvesting time. Given a gentle push of encouragement, the child ran over to the raw mound of earth and scattered the flowers on top. Then she crossed herself, curtseyed and hastened back to her mother.

Simon's throat tightened. He looked at the woman, intending to smile, but that died as he saw the hostility in her eyes. 'Norman bastards!' she hissed and, taking her daughter's hand, hastened away towards the timber service buildings.

He paced slowly to the graveside. The breeze stirred the petals on the delicate flowers, already beginning to wilt from their untimely cutting. After a while, Simon too, crossed himself, bent his knee, and limped rapidly away.

CHAPTER 21

Crowland Abbey, October 1087

S omewhere a skylark was singing. The bubbling song drew Simon's gaze away from the space between his horse's ears and upward to the expansive sky, deep autumn blue swept with a feathering of high white cloud. After a moment, he located the tiny warbling speck halfway to heaven. He wondered what it was like to look down on the world from the height of angels, to be a bird and feel cool air streaming against feathered pinions and see everything from a different perspective.

The song ceased and the lark plummeted towards the pasture, sere-gold at summer's end and autumn's beginning. Meres and pools glittered like a reflection off armour. Placid white cattle grazed on the higher ground, taking a final fattening before the days shortened too far and the grass ceased to grow. On the still, clear air the bells of Crowland Abbey tolled the hour of terce, summoning the monks to worship.

Hearing the sound, seeing the church rising from out of the flat, fenland landscape, Simon felt a flickering in his gut but whether of anticipation or unease, he could not have said. It was eleven years since he had made his farewells to Waltheof. Now he came to don a mantle bestowed upon him by the new king. But first he had a pilgrimage to make.

William of Normandy, known to some as the Bastard and to others as the Conqueror, had died in Rouen at the beginning of last month, mortally wounded when his horse trampled on a burning cinder and threw him so hard on to the pommel of his saddle that his bladder ruptured. During several days of lingering agony he had bequeathed Normandy to Robert, the eldest of his three surviving sons. England went to his middle son, William Rufus, and he had given young Henry five hundred marks of silver from his treasury.

Many thought that Robert, as the eldest, should have inherited England. Robert thought so too, and trouble was brewing faster than yeast froth on new ale. Hence Simon's presence in these parts at the head of a seasoned troop.

As he and his men drew closer to the abbey they passed a steady trickle of folk travelling in the same direction. Some were wealthy enough to be mounted, others rode in ox carts, but the majority were either on foot or had used the extensive waterways surrounding the abbey to arrive by barge and punt. Simon saw a small, golden-haired child walking beside her mother, a bunch of late wayside flowers clutched in her hand. The image reminded him of Waltheof's execution so vividly that his hands twitched on the bridle and his mount danced sideways. The child looked up with sudden fear and the mother's hand shot out in protective alarm. Simon drew the rein in hard, bringing himself and the horse back under control.

'I am sorry,' he said in English.

The mother's eyes flashed and then lowered. He felt the hatred and knew that, despite the passage of time, nothing had changed. Slapping the reins on the dun's neck he rode on at a faster pace. His troop followed, the hooves of their mounts churning the dust. The woman covered her face with her wimple and used the edge of her overdress to shield the child.

Near the abbey gates, hucksters had set up stalls selling chaplets of greenery, small wooden crosses and metal tokens to hang on leather belts. There were pie booths, a baker's counter and even a cobbler, industriously mending shoes that had not stood up to the road. Fascinated, one hand on his swordhilt, the other on the reins, Simon turned in the saddle and stared around.

'What's all this for?' demanded Aubrey de Mar, the serjeant in command of Simon's troop. He fiddled with the nasal bar of his helm.

'The English have made Waltheof of Huntingdon a martyr,' Simon replied. 'They say there have been miracles at his tomb.'

Aubrey grunted. 'Do you believe it?'

Simon shrugged. 'Stranger things have happened. It is rumoured that when the monks opened his grave at Winchester in order to bring his body back to Crowland, they discovered that his head had been miraculously restored to his torso and that the corpse was as fresh as the day it had been placed in the earth.'

Aubrey curled a sceptical lip. 'I heard a dragon was seen in York last month. Turned out to be a runaway bullock that overset a cauldron of fat and began a house fire.'

Simon gave a wry smile. 'It would be a barren world without wonders. What matters is that the people believe it.'

'Old King William must be rolling in his own grave. Look at 'em all.' Aubrey jerked his head at the pilgrims.

'He knew the risks when he agreed that Waltheof could be brought from Winchester to Crowland. He need not have given his permission for the reburial, but he did.'

'To ease his conscience you think?'

'Quite likely. Even before the Rouen campaign he was ailing. I believe that his past deeds had begun to burden his conscience.' Simon could still remember the morning that Abbot Ulfcytel and the Countess Judith had come to ask William's clemency and beg that Waltheof's body be exhumed and brought to Crowland Abbey for burial. It had been incongruous to see them together; the balding little churchman shabby and farmer-like despite the new robes he had donned for the occasion, and the Countess Judith, sombrely clad in charcoal-grey, her face wan and bloodless. She had knelt at William's feet, kissed his hand and pleaded with him to let her have Waltheof's body for Crowland.

'I thought you would banish him,' she had whispered in a choked voice. 'I did not believe that you would command his execution.'

'Treason is treason,' William had growled. 'And he was fairly judged by the law of his own land. If I had banished him, where do you think he would have gone? Straight to Denmark or Brittany, to organise more rebellion.'

Ulfcytel had stepped forward and added his own plea to Judith's petition that William at least grant Waltheof the grace of being laid to rest in Crowland Abbey, where once he had been a pupil. After a brief deliberation William had consented. Indeed, Simon had thought that there was a certain degree of relief in his manner, as if he were atoning for a sin and finding the price not too high.

Looking at the gathering around the abbey gates, Simon wondered if William had been right. Waltheof was viewed as an English martyr to Norman ambition and greed. Pilgrims came not only out of hope for a miracle, but as a way of defying their Norman overlords in a manner that could not be contested.

Simon gave his name at the porter's lodge, rode into the courtyard, and dismounted. He had been on the road for several days, and his left leg was aching ferociously. Through long habit he concealed the pain but nevertheless it prodded at him. Turstan, his squire, took the dun in hand, and lay workers arrived from the stables to help with the horses. The abbey was prospering on the proceeds of martyrdom, Simon thought, studying the fresh, bright paint and the ornate carving over the doorway. The little girl and her mother walked past, following the procession of pilgrims in what was obviously the direction of Waltheof's tomb. Simon ungirded his sword belt, handed it to Turstan, and bidding his men wait, took the path to the church.

The hushed whispers of the pilgrims rose and echoed around the sturdy barrel vaulting of the roof. Geometrical designs were painted on the columns in colours so bright that they almost hurt the eye. Grass green, blood red, lapis blue. Jewelled light from the stained glass window over the altar streamed down upon the pilgrims so that it seemed they were standing at the foot of a rainbow.

Simon's spurs scraped softly on the swept earth floor as he limped up the nave. A young monk was swinging a censer and the scented smoke drifted on the air and settled its heavenly breath on garments, skin and hair.

Waltheof's tomb stood in the Chapter House, the carved wooden housing covered with a pall of dark-red silk bordered with gold embroidery exquisitely worked. Above the tomb a ceramic oil lamp supported in brass chains sent out streamers of scented smoke.

Two older monks stood by the tomb, keeping a close watch on those who filed past and lifted the pall to kiss the dark wooden side. Simon supposed that a piece of the silk, surreptitiously cut away by a palmed knife, would fetch a high price from relic seekers. Among the flowers, the silver pennies, prayer beads and lighted candles placed as offerings around the base of the tomb were the sticks, crutches, bowls and cups of the sick who had been cured or improved by their pilgrimage.

The little girl laid her flowers among the other gifts, thus completing the image in Simon's memory. She dipped a curtsey, kissed the pall and with her mother was ushered on by another monk whose task it was to keep the file of pilgrims moving.

Simon knelt on his good leg, crossed himself and said a silent, private prayer over his clasped hands. A part of him half expected the pall to surge or the lamp to come crashing down on his head, but there was nothing, only the shuffle of the people waiting their turn and the soft jingle of the censer as the monk swung it back and forth, fumigating the crowd with its holy fragrance.

Perhaps Waltheof approved of what Simon had come to do. Comforting himself with that thought, he rose to his feet and followed the pilgrims out of a side entrance. His departure took him past another relic in the form of the skull of Abbot Theodore, who had been martyred in a Danish raid two hundred years before. Stripped of flesh, the cranium bearing the mark of the killing blow, the sockets stared Simon out into the bright morning air where the current abbot was waiting for him, not Ulfcytel, as he had expected, but a taller, thinner monk with patrician features and a neatly clipped silver tonsure.

Once again Simon knelt. He kissed the ring of office on the Abbot's extended fingers. 'Father,' he murmured, managing to keep the note of surprise from his voice.

'I have sent your men to the guesthouse in the company of two brethren who will see to their needs,' the monk said pleasantly as Simon rose. 'I am Abbot Ingulf. Forgive me, it is not often that we see Normans at Crowland.'

Simon thanked him for the care of his men. 'My pilgrimage is a personal one,' he said, adding after a brief hesitation, 'Forgive me but what has become of Abbot Ulfcytel?'

'You knew Ulfcytel?' The Abbot's brows rose towards his tonsure. Simon could see him struggling with the notion of a Norman courtier and soldier having such an acquaintance.

'Not well, but I met him on occasion and he seemed to me a good and holy man.'

'And so he was, God rest his soul.' Ingulf crossed himself and beckoned Simon to walk with him towards the low timber building that housed his private solar.

Simon signed his breast. 'I am sorry.'

'He is buried in Peterborough Abbey, where he finished his days as an ordinary monk.' Ingulf looked sidelong at Simon. 'Three years ago he was removed from the abbacy.

His duties were becoming too onerous for his mind and body to perform.'

'It had nothing to do with the way he stood up to the King over Earl Waltheof?' Simon said neutrally.

The Abbot clasped his palms together. 'Yes, that too.' He gave a sorrowful shake of his head. 'Ulfcytel's mind took to wandering and he became outspoken – as a result of senility I believe, not out of any great desire to make mischief, but it was clear he was no longer fit for his duties. They sent him to Glastonbury, but I asked that he be permitted to return to Peterborough, which he knew and loved. He died there shortly after. We pray for his soul every day.'

Ingulf ushered Simon into his private solar and bade him be seated in a cushioned chair near an unlit brazier. Sunlight poured through the window arches and shone on the scattered bundles of floor rushes. 'I see that prayers are said daily for Earl Waltheof too,' Simon observed.

'Indeed.' Ingulf's expression was bland. 'He is in our care, and we honour our obligations.'

'Do you think he is at peace?'

Unsealing a leather costrel, Ingulf poured mead into two earthenware cups. 'As I understand, he was always at peace here,' he said gently. 'The difficulties began when he had to leave. Now he is home again – not in the manner that Ulfcytel would have chosen for him, but fitting in its own way.'

Simon took the cup that Ingulf handed to him and drank. The mead was dry and golden, with notes of autumnal crispness.

'And what of the Countess Judith?' Simon tried to make the question casual but saw from the sudden sharpening of the Abbot's gaze that he had failed.

'Despite her estrangement from the Earl in the months before his death, she has mourned him with great dignity and genuine . . . remorse,' Ingulf said.

Simon noted the use of 'remorse' not 'sorrow'. He had not seen Judith in more than ten years. What would she be like now? Although his expression remained unconcerned, his stomach churned.

'The Countess has given much time to the founding of her nunnery at Elstow,' Ingulf continued. 'God has become her solace. She and Waltheof may have had their differences, but they were united in their love of the Church. She has remained a chaste and dutiful widow.'

Simon almost grimaced but managed to lose the expression in his cup.

Ingulf studied him. 'Mayhap it is not my business to ask, but what brings a soldier of the Norman court to these parts? Surely not for the purpose of praying at the tomb of an English earl executed for treason?'

'Is it so obvious?' Simon asked wryly.

Ingulf gave a wintry smile. 'Not until thought about,' he said. 'If we see Normans at Crowland it is either because they are travellers in need of a night's shelter or sheriff's men keeping an eye on our pilgrims.'

Simon inclined his head. 'You are right, Father Abbot. Indeed, had I followed my purpose and no other considera- tion, I would not have come to Crowland at all. What brought me here today was honour and memory.' He hesitated and turned the cup in his hand, contemplating the decorative zigzag design.

Ingulf said nothing, but his silence was one of encourage- ment. Simon gnawed his lip. Here in the Abbot's solar it was almost like a confessional and he found himself letting down his guard.

'I loved Waltheof,' he said. 'When I was a child, I thought of him as a heroic warrior. He saved my life and I worshipped him. Even when I grew out of the adoration, I cherished the image of the first time I saw him, striding out as though he owned the world with that red hair flowing and that cloak of his pinned at his shoulder with silver and gems. That is how I remember him. I have seen him with feet of clay many times, but those are not the occasions that hold my mind.'

Ingulf smiled and nodded gently. 'Ulfcytel told me that he always saw Waltheof as a young boy, learning his Psalter with the other lads in his care. He said that he saw the child standing at the side of the tomb, staring in bewilderment at what became of the man.'

'A vision you mean?'

The Abbot shrugged. 'So some would say, and I would not deny them.'

Silence fell again. Simon gently swirled the mead in his cup. 'You asked my purpose, Father. When I leave Crowland, my journey is to Northampton . . . to the dowager Countess,' he said. 'On the new king's command.'

'Ah,' Ingulf said, and the way he spoke told Simon that there was no need to say more; the Abbot understood perfectly. 'You will not necessarily find a welcome,' he warned. 'The Lady is strong-willed and accustomed to governing by her own hand. Nor has she made a pig's ear of the task. Harsh she may be, and not well loved as Earl Waltheof was, but she is fair. And she has the support of her family . . .'

'I have not been remiss in asking about such matters,' Simon said evenly.

'Then you will know what to face, my son.' The Abbot gave him a look that was almost pitying.

The last two words made Simon feel gauche and juvenile. For a seasoned courtier and battle commander it was ridiculous. He set his mead cup on the Abbot's trestle. 'I should be returning to my men,' he said abruptly, and rose to his feet. A pain, sharp and dull by turns, throbbed across his shin.

'Of course.' Ingulf saw him to the door and when Simon refused the services of a lay brother to show him the way to the guesthouse, Ingulf pointed him in the direction. 'You are always welcome here.'

Thanking him, Simon joined the stream of pilgrims, easing his way through them until he came to the guesthouse situated near the porter's lodge. He sluiced his face and washed his hands in the laver provided. His men had made themselves beds along one wall with straw palliasses. Listening to them joke as they assembled and sorted their gear, Simon briefly wished that he was one of their number, with nothing more pressing on his mind than obeying simple orders and looking forward to the next meal. And then he thought of the prize and realised that being one of their number had never been his destiny.

CHAPTER 22

The tree was heavy with apples, green flushing with pink and gold as they ripened, and the size of a strong man's clenched fist. In the thirteen years since Matilda had planted the pip it had grown into a sturdy tree, kept compact and shapely by careful pruning and loving attention. Matilda had grown with it. She towered above Sybille and Helisende and was a good handspan taller than her sister and mother.

Stooping to the water jug at her feet, Matilda poured a silver libation around the base of the tree and murmured a blessing. The water elf still dwelt in his well, but now she was old enough to draw the lid herself. She always carried a quarter penny in her pouch to pay him. Her mother would have called the custom pagan and bid her cease, but what her mother did not know could not be a source of friction.

The garden belonged to Matilda. Ever since the planting of that first apple core, it had been her source of pleasure and refuge. She relished the feel of the crumbly dark loam in her hands. There was nothing more satisfying than setting seeds and watching them thrust their way into the light, in nurturing them and harvesting their fruit.

Her mother often rebuked her for spending so much time among her plants, but she never prevented her outright.

The tending of the garden was a suitable task for a female, and since Judith did not enjoy the pursuit herself she was glad to leave it to her daughter. Matilda delighted in the solitude and the breathing space, much preferring the vagaries of the elements to the hencoop of the women's chamber.

She scattered the last glistening droplets around the roots of the tree and watched them soak into the ground. The garden gate squeaked, announcing Helisende's return. Matilda had sent the young woman who was both maid and companion to the solar with a basket of lavender for strewing among the rushes, thus giving each of them the excuse for a few moments alone.

'We have visitors,' Helisende announced, cheeks pink and eyes sparkling with excitement. 'A whole troop of them.'

Visitors to Northampton were frequent. Northumbria had been taken away on her father's death and given to the bishop of that diocese to administer, but Huntingdon and Northampton remained beneath her mother's vigorous rule. However, while stewards and administrators, merchants and soldiers came and went in a constant trickle, an entire troop was a different matter.

'Do you know who they are?' Matilda's first thought was that they were her grandfather Eudo's soldiers from his lands of Holderness. He brought them to Northampton several times a year, usually with his son Stephen in tow. But then Helisende would have said so.

'No,' Helisende shook her head, 'but I saw my father and their leader giving each other a handclasp and smiling like old friends. They were speaking English too.'

Matilda's curiosity sharpened. English noblemen were rare these days. What one was doing at Northampton, where Norman ways were encouraged, was intriguing. Glancing down, she realised that there was soil on her hands and bits of leaf and twig festooning her gown, which was her oldest one of plain grey wool. Hardly the garb in which to greet a visitor whatever his status. Whilst not overly vain, Matilda well knew that first impressions were often lasting ones. Nor with her mother's strictures ringing in her ears could she fail to be aware of her duty to keep up appearances.

Leaving the garden, she hastened towards the women's solar. There was no sign of the visitors, although several fine horses were being turned out in the paddock beside the stables. 'Was he old or young, this lord?' she asked the maid.

Helisende's flush deepened. 'There was no silver in his hair,' she said.

Hastily Matilda exchanged her old grey gown for one of sky-blue linen with a yoke and sleeve trim of darker blue that brought out the colour of her eyes. Although as an unwed daughter of the house she was not forced to wear a wimple, her mother preferred her to cover her hair in formal company. Matilda settled a veil of plain cream linen over her copper-bronze braids and secured it with a woven band stitched with tiny seed pearls.

'You've a smut of soil on your cheek.' Helisende dabbed it away with the end of a kerchief dipped in the laver jug. 'You should pinch your cheeks and bite your lips to give them colour.'

Matilda laughed. 'Why should I do that? Whoever our visitor is, I doubt that he's come courting.'

'You never know,' said Helisende.

'No,' Matilda said. 'My mother does not like men. She founded the nunnery at Elstow for her spiritual comfort, and she wants this place to be like a nunnery too.'

'She will never manage that,' Helisende replied stoutly.

'It does not stop her from trying.' Matilda smoothed her palms over her gown and adjusted the side lacings so that they flattered her trim waist and full bosom.

'Perhaps you should elope,' Helisende suggested.

'Find me a suitable mate and I will,' Matilda retorted, going to the door.

When she arrived in the hall, it was to find the visitor's troop supping at trestle tables with the soldiers of her mother's guard. Her sister Jude was seated at the dais table in their mother's place, playing host to a quartet of knights. Matilda assessed them. Two were grey, one was going bald and the other had a beard. There was also a handsome squire, but he was in mid adolescence and in no wise a man.

'He's not here,' muttered Helisende out of the side of her mouth.

'Neither is my mother,' Matilda said. Jude had seen her and was making frantic eyes for help. Lifting her chin, Matilda walked down the length of the hall and tried to remember to keep her steps small. Her mother was always taking her to task for striding out like a warrior.

The men rose to greet her and she inclined her head and smiled graciously. Jude stammered out introductions. She had a quiet nature and playing hostess was daunting.

The men all had Norman names, none of which Matilda recognised, and they spoke French, not English. 'You are most welcome to our hospitality,' she said formally as she took the high-backed chair her sister had vacated. 'Has my mother greeted you also?'

'Indeed, Lady Matilda, she has,' said the one named Aubrey de Mar. 'If the Countess is not here now, it is because our lord desired to have words of a private nature with her.'

'Your lord?'

'Simon de Senlis, my lady. He is here on the orders of King William.'

'For what purpose?' The question was surprised out of her before she could phrase it more courteously.

The men looked at each other and she could see them thinking that Countess Judith's daughter was cast in the same autocratic mould as her mother.

Outwardly calm, Matilda signalled an attendant to refresh the goblets and directed another servant to place a dish of honey cakes before the men. Food and drink always served to appease and mellow.

'Forgive me if I was brusque,' she said. 'But it is not every day that we receive a visitor with orders from my cousin, the King.'

She saw grudging humour light in the eyes of Aubrey de

Mar as she reminded them of her rank while apologising for her lapse of grace.

'Not at all, my lady,' he responded in a hoarse voice that sounded as though he had eaten the road rather than ridden on it. 'Indeed, you will learn my lord's purpose soon enough. But it is only proper that he informs your mother first.'

Matilda inclined her head and took a sip of wine from her cup while she recovered her composure. Simon de Senlis. The name echoed in her memory, but was too distant to recall. If she had met him, it must have been a long time ago.

'Tell me,' she said, 'does your lord speak English?'

'He does, my lady, and taught by your late father.'

Matilda's stomach leaped and she looked at the knight with widening eyes. 'He knew my father?'

'Indeed, my lady, he did. It was before I entered my lord's service, so I know few details, only that they were master and pupil. Doubtless, my lord will tell you himself. He prefers to do his own speaking.'

Matilda's hand shook as she took another drink of the wine. She might not be able to remember Simon de Senlis, but the image of her father was still as sharp and clear as the day on which he had ridden out and not come back. Shining hair of deep copper-red, a soft golden beard, the smile that was for her alone, and the sadness behind it. She had prayed so hard for him to return – and eventually he had. Now he lay in his shrine in the chapter house at Crowland. So near and yet so far. They never spoke of him in this household – or at least not in front of her mother, who would not stand to hear the mention of his name. Sometimes she and her sister would whisper together, or Sybille would talk of him, or Toki spin memories, but all in a clandestine fashion to avoid detection by Judith. The ordinary folk had more access to her father than she had ever done. Now, with this visitor from the past, this Simon de Senlis, she had a chance to strengthen the fragile memories and build a solid edifice worthy of him.

'Do you know how long you will be staying?' she asked

when she was sure that her voice was steady. 'I need to ensure that the household is provisioned.'

'No, my lady.' De Mar spread his huge hands. 'My lord has not told us, and it will depend on how matters progress . . . If it helps you, I would say that you could plan for a week at least.' He reached for a honey cake, bit into it, and smiled. 'Mayhap longer if this is any indication of the fare on offer.'

Matilda returned the smile, but in a preoccupied manner. It was all she could do not to leap from the table, rush to her mother's apartment and seize hold of this Simon de Senlis. The knight said they would be staying at least a week. There was time enough. She just wished that it were now.

Simon stood in Countess Judith's private chamber, and took in his surroundings with a feeling of unease that raised the hair on his nape. An embroidered frieze depicting the lives of various female saints relieved the plainness of the lime-washed wall. There was also a wooden crucifix nailed above a small prie-dieu. The Countess's bed spanned a scant body-width and was made up with coarse blankets, not a fur in sight. She was living the life of a secular nun, he thought, and that did not bode well for what was to come.

The Countess did not invite him to sit. Nor did she offer him wine. Both should have been courtesies extended to a guest, but it was already clear that she viewed him as an intruder.

Facing him, she lifted her chin. 'Well, my lord, are you going to inform me of the reason for your visit and why it is better told in secret than in the open company of the hall?'

At six and thirty she was still an attractive woman, although her features, like her nature, had sharpened with the years and he could see that in old age she would be a replica of her fearsome mother.

'Not in secret,' he said, refusing to be intimidated. 'But in private. Since the matter is somewhat delicate, I thought it best discussed between us without an audience.'

'I cannot see that I have anything to discuss with you, witnesses or not,' she said.

She had not offered him a seat but he took one anyway, settling himself on the cushioned bench that ran along the far wall. Irritation and resentment sparked in her eyes and Simon sighed. He could see that his purpose was already doomed. She might listen, but she was determined not to hear. He reached into his tunic. Secured between it and his shirt, held in place by his belt, was a letter bearing the royal seal. 'King William Rufus has entrusted me with the care of the earldom of Northampton and Huntingdon,' he said. 'His instructions are here.'

She stared at him, her body stiffening as if she was turning to stone. 'I am the Countess of Northampton and Huntingdon,' she said icily. 'He cannot do this.'

'The dowager Countess,' Simon corrected, 'and the lands are within the King's gift. He can bestow them where he chooses.'

Her complexion was ice-white. 'It is ten years since my husband's death. I have ruled these lands competently. He has no reason to issue such a command.' She almost snatched the packet from him.

'The King needs them to be held with military strength.'

'Hah!' she snapped. 'If that is so, then why has he sent a cripple?'

The words were intentionally cruel. Simon had learned in boyhood not to flinch, and he matched her gaze stone on stone. 'That is unjust of you, my lady. I thought you above casting cheap insults.'

Her cheeks reddened and her dark eyes glittered. She was beautiful in a strange, hard way that made Simon want to shiver. How many brittle layers had she grown since Waltheof's death, each one more frozen than the last?

'And is it not "unjust" of you to come and take these lands when I have ruled them competently since my husband's death?' she demanded. 'Is it not an insult to me, to my governance?'

'No my lady, it is not,' Simon said evenly. 'No one is disputing your administrative abilities or your judgement. But you cannot lead men in war or make military decisions based on the training of experience. You can only appoint deputies.' Even as he spoke, he knew that his words must sound like the greatest insult of all. How could he not offend her when he came to remove her authority?

'Neither can you, my lord,' she said, sweeping his slight build with a disparaging look.

'In that you are wrong, Countess,' he said quietly, for he had long since learned that keeping his temper was more than half the battle. 'If I were a boastful man, I could present you with a list of campaigns and military services to the house of Normandy that would take the day to recite. I may not be capable of swinging a battleaxe like your late husband, but no one has ever found me lacking. You are a wealthy widow of childbearing age and you have young daughters. This earldom is a plum, and in plain terms the King wishes to secure it to a man of his choosing rather than those who would profit at his expense – including your mother and stepfather and their son. I am sorry for your distress, but rail as you will, Countess, you can change nothing.'

'The people will never accept you,' she spat.

'They accepted you,' he pointed out, 'despite the rumours that you had connived at your own husband's death.'

That blow hit home and Judith recoiled. 'I did not!' she gasped and drew herself up. 'I went to my uncle on bended knees to beg that my husband's body be allowed to rest at Crowland.'

'But that is guilt,' Simon said softly, 'not sorrow. You may not have connived at your husband's death, but neither did you plead for his life.' Suddenly he felt as exhausted as if he had fought a day-long battle. Making the effort, he rose to his feet and forced himself to go to the door. Each step burned, but his pride would not let him limp.

The maidservant Sybille was seated outside on a stool,

awaiting her mistress's call, her ear inclined towards the heavy, studded oak. 'I would appreciate a flagon of wine,' Simon said courteously.

Sybille curtseyed. A smile curled her mouth corners. 'You have changed since last I saw you, my lord,' she ventured.

Simon returned the smile and felt some of his tension dissipate beneath the warmth in her tone. It had always astonished him that someone as proper and glacial as Judith could have a maid who was earthy, mischievous, and completely lacking in the propriety of which the Countess seemed so fond. 'Whether for the better I do not know,' he murmured ruefully, 'and I could say the same for your mistress.'

'She is hard on everyone.' Sybille darted a glance at the door to make sure that Judith was not within hearing range, 'and twice as hard on herself.' She looked at him. 'I do not think that you are here to cushion that hardness, my lord.'

'I am here,' Simon said, 'because the King has given me orders, and because I would have to be without ambition to ignore them. I cannot help your mistress if she will not help herself.'

'I doubt that she knows how,' Sybille said. Her eyes gleamed with curiosity – too much of it.

'Will you go and bring wine, or do I have to summon one of my men to do so?' Simon said, more curtly than he had intended.

A glimmer of resentment flared in Sybille's eyes. 'No,' she said, 'I will fetch it. But just remember that I once swatted you around the ears for filching fig pastries from Countess Adelaide's table.' Her nose in the air, she left on her errand.

Rubbing his brow where a headache was beginning to throb, Simon turned back into the room.

Judith was standing near the embrasure, gazing down at the sheets of vellum in her hand. She had obviously read the contents for her expression would have crusted hell's cauldron in ice.

'It is not to be borne,' she said with controlled fury.

Simon lowered his hand and wrapped it round his belt. 'I can see that this news has come as an unwelcome shock, my lady,' he said. 'But I urge you to reconcile yourself to what has to be.'

'Never,' Judith said vehemently.

Simon knew it was futile, but still he spoke out, because he had promised. 'If you wish to remain in your position, there is nothing to prevent you, should you consent to be my wife.'

The words struck the air like fire. Rufus had set the condition when bestowing the earldom. See the women safe and provided for. Give Judith the opportunity of remarriage while there was still sap in her body, while she was still young enough to bear more children.

'Should I consent to become your wife?' she repeated, and looked him up and down as though he was some loathsome thing that had just crawled out from under a stone. 'If you are not jesting, then your wits are deranged.'

'I am neither in jest, nor lacking in wit,' Simon said quietly. 'Marriage to me would vouchsafe your status and enhance mine. You are still of childbearing age. I can fulfil the military obligations that Rufus requires. It would suit us both, if you could find it within you to swallow your pride and be civil.'

'I can find nothing within me but contempt,' Judith said. In her face he saw a revulsion so strong that it cut him to the quick. He was not accustomed to that look from women.

'You think me beneath you?' he asked. 'You think me damaged goods and lacking in the esteem by which you set so much store?'

Judith's lip curled. 'I swore when my first husband betrayed me that I would not wed again. I lusted after Waltheof Siwardsson, and it gained me naught but grief. No man is worth the price. I put my faith in God.'

'So you refuse my offer?'

The curve of her smile was thin as a whip. 'I throw it in your face,' she said.

Sybille entered the room bearing a flagon and two cups. 'Here we are,' she said cheerfully.

'Messire Simon is leaving,' Judith said without looking at her maid.

Simon narrowed his eyes. Crossing to Sybille, he took one of the cups and the flagon and poured himself a measure of wine. 'When I am ready,' he said, 'and only as far as the hall. What you do is your decision, my lady, but what I do is your cousin's. By all means keep this chamber, I will find one of my own, but let us be in no doubt as to who has the reins of governance here from now on.'

Judith glared at him and he knew that if looks could have killed he would have died there and then. He returned her stare, his expression impassive, but his heart was bumping in his throat. Without taking his gaze from hers, he raised the cup to his lips and drank with slow, symbolic deliberation.

Judith held her ground, but she was trembling with the effort – or perhaps it was just with anger. He finished the wine, set the cup down on the coffer and sauntered to the door. 'Think on what I have said, my lady,' he said. 'Swallowing pride may be difficult, but living off it will be more difficult still.'

'You have my answer,' Judith said stiffly. 'I would rather go forth in rags than pledge myself to you.'

'Let us hope it does not come to the test,' Simon said with a bow and left the room.

Her control had the strength of iron. He was half expecting to hear a cup or a candle stand crash against the doorpost or whistle past his head, but there was only silence.

As Simon walked away he was hit by the same reaction that came upon him after facing the danger of battle. His legs turned to water and his vision blurred. Pivoting from the walkway, he braced himself against the wall and vomited until his throat was on fire and his stomach aching, but although he had rid himself of the wine the sensation of malaise remained and intensified.

Gasping, he leaned against the wall and closed his eyes. He would have slumped down against the welcome support of the painted timber, but he dared not lest Judith emerge from her chamber and find him thus. He was in no condition to face the crowd in the great hall and impose his will. First, he needed to gather that will and hold it together.

A cool draught blew across his face, chilling the sweat on his brow. He opened his eyes and glanced out of the narrow embrasure. The walkway faced an inner courtyard and he could see the greenery and floral colours of a well-tended garden. With lurching steps, one hand pressed to his aching stomach, Simon sought the respite of its sanctuary.

CHAPTER 23

Matilda was beginning to feel anxious. There was still no sign of her mother and she had exhausted all topics of conversation with their visitors. The flagons had been replenished and the griddlecakes were a memory of crumbs. There was no sign of Simon de Senlis either, and the knights at the high table were growing restless.

What should she do? Matilda had no precedent. She also had no idea why Simon de Senlis was here. Amid the polite conversation, there had been no hints beyond that first comment that they would be in Northampton for at least a week.

She turned to Aubrey de Mar. 'If you and your lord are to remain here for a week, then sleeping arrangements must be prepared. By your leave I will go and attend to the matter.'

The knight made an open-handed gesture. 'By all means my lady.' His expression was an odd mingling of relief and anxiety. She could see that he was glad to relinquish the burden of polite conversation and plainly concerned by the absence of his lord.

As she left Jude scrambled from her own place on the bench, agitated at the notion of being left behind to continue the entertainment. 'Where's Mama?' she hissed, seizing Matilda's arm. 'What is she doing?'

Matilda shook her head. 'Likely in her chamber talking to Simon de Senlis about the matter that has brought them here,' she said.

'What do you think it is?'

'I do not know, but it must be important. From what I could glean from Sir Aubrey, Simon de Senlis is one of the new king's most trusted men.' She gave Jude's hand a reassuring squeeze, as much for her own benefit as her sister's. 'If these men are to spend several nights here, the most important will need beds making up. I must have the keys to the linen coffer, and Mama keeps them on her belt.'

'She will be angry if you disturb her,' Jude warned.

Matilda shrugged. 'She is always angry for one reason or another. What difference will it make?'

They had been passing a window embrasure as they spoke. Matilda stopped abruptly and took a back step. There was a stranger in her garden, seated on the turf bench beneath her apple tree. His head was thrown back in a posture of utter weariness and his arms were folded across his chest. A pang of resentment shot through her that he should be in her place but mingled with it were anticipation and sudden breathlessness. It had to be Simon de Senlis. He was no longer with her mother, but for some reason had chosen the solitude of her garden above the company of the hall.

Matilda gave her sister a gentle push in the direction of their mother's chamber. 'Go to Mama, and ask her about the linens,' she said. 'I will join you presently.'

Jude looked alarmed. 'Why? Where are you going?'

'To speak with Simon de Senlis,' Matilda replied, and, before the impulse could desert her, she turned towards the steps that led down to the courtyard.

Her sister gnawed her lip, hesitated, and then continued towards their mother's chambers, where the very worst that could happen was a scolding.

At the garden gate Matilda hesitated. The need that had carried her thus far suddenly flickered and turned to apprehension. She should not become embroiled. She should be a dutiful daughter of the house and seek her mother's bidding.

What was she going to say to the man who was occupying the shade of her apple tree? However, the double measure of stubbornness and courage inherited from both parents drove her forward. She opened the gate and fastened the rope latch behind her with resolution.

Her tread was purposeful but it was also quiet, for she wanted the advantage of observing him before he should notice her. Simon de Senlis had not stirred from his position on the bench beneath the apple tree. His arms were still folded and his legs were stretched out, barring the path. She noticed that the waxed thread on one of his shoes was coming unstitched and that his chausses, although of excellent quality, bore the dusty appearance of hard travel. Whatever had happened between him and her mother, the Countess had not seen fit to offer him the courtesy of refreshing himself.

His eyes were closed, the lids lined with dense brown lashes tipped gold at the ends. Matilda could not tell if he were asleep or just resting, but she took the opportunity to examine him. His jaw was outlined in dark stubble and his brown hair was sun-bleached to blond on top, revealing that he had spent the summer months outdoors. Unlike the sheriff and the blunt men of his garrison, he did not resemble a Norman reaver. There was evidence of neither bulk nor breadth. A courtier, perhaps, she thought. But he was not dressed like a courtier either.

It was only after she had perused him thoroughly that she noticed he was sitting on his cloak and belatedly realised at what she was looking. The lustre of white fur against a background of blue wool trapped her eyes and filled them until they overflowed. Through a blur of moisture, she remembered being wrapped in the warmth and security of that garment, remembered being encompassed in her father's love. It was a memory as sharp as it was distant, and made all the more powerful in her life by the fact that it was one of the few she had of him.

She must have made a small sound, for De Senlis stirred

and opened his eyes. His arms unfolded and he instinctively groped for his sword, then relaxed as he realised there was no danger. Matilda swallowed against the tightness in her throat. De Senlis stood up, and through her tears she caught the hint of pain in his expression before he schooled his features to careful neutrality. A trifle hazy, but clearing fast, his eyes were a clear fox-gold.

'My lady, you surprised me.' Given the slightness of his build, his voice was deeper and more certain than she expected. One hand rested on his swordhilt, but she thought it was a customary gesture rather than a sign that he was about to draw it on her. It spoke oceans of her mother's reception that he had not removed it, though. She saw that he leaned on one hip, slightly favouring his left leg.

'Your men are wondering where you are, my lord,' she said breathlessly.

He raised a thin, interrogative brow. 'They sent you to find me?'

From the way he was studying her, Matilda knew that he was trying to place her within the household hierarchy – maid or mistress. 'No, my lord. I was seeking my mother for the keys to the linen chest when I looked from the embrasure and saw you seated here.'

'Ah.' He gave a half-smile. 'Would I be right in assuming that your mother is the Countess Judith?'

'Yes, she is.'

'And yet you diverted to talk with me rather than going directly to her?' He spoke as much to himself as Matilda and seemed to be weighing something in his mind.

'My sister was with me. Our mother will give her the keys.' She licked her lips, feeling tense beneath his scrutiny.

'And which sister are you?' Without taking his gaze from her, he reached to a low hanging apple, cupped it in his hand and gave a gentle tug. The fruit came away with scarcely a bend of the bough. Dappled green, gold and red, it shone in his hand, reflecting the late glow of the sun.

'I am Matilda. My sister is Jude.'

He nodded. 'You were named for King William's queen, God rest her soul,' he said and crossed himself. 'I saw you once when you were a small child – little more than a babe in arms. I was a squire in the King's service then.'

Matilda's gaze darted to the cloak on the bench and her stomach turned over. 'Your men said in the hall that you knew my father.'

He shrugged. 'I thought I did, but now I believe that only God truly knows any of us and what we will or will not do.' His coppery gaze was assessing. 'You resemble him.'

'I remember him wearing that cloak,' she said in a choked voice. 'I always wondered what had happened to it . . .'

'He gave it to me when he was imprisoned in Winchester.' He turned the apple in his hand, lightly running his thumb over the glossy surface.

Matilda lowered her eyes and fought the wave of jealousy that swept her. This man was a link with her father. It should not matter that the cloak had been given to him, not her. Even had it been returned to Northampton, she knew that her mother would never have allowed her to keep it. She longed to reach out, to thrust her hands into the thick, white pelt, to press her nose against the tickly fur and be four years old again. But not in front of De Senlis.

'Why are you here?' she asked brusquely. She wanted to snatch the apple out of his hand too.

If he was taken aback by her tone he concealed it well, although he hesitated before he spoke. 'King William Rufus has bidden me take the earldom of Huntingdon and Northampton into my custody.' He glanced towards the embrasure of the Countess's apartments. 'Your mother has no choice but to yield.'

Matilda stared at him. The words played across the surface of her mind, too new and strange to be absorbed on the instant. 'You are to take my father's lands?' she heard herself ask.

'His Midland shires, yes,' he said. 'I am under royal orders to do so . . . and I will brook no resistance.' His voice grew harsh on the last statement.

It was on the tip of her tongue to ask what resistance he expected to receive from mere women, but from his manner it was plain that he had not emerged unscathed from the meeting with her mother.

She raised her chin. 'What is to become of us? Are you under royal orders in that matter too?'

He gave her a brooding look. 'Yes, I am under orders,' he said curtly, 'and in truth I am of half a mind to disobey them.' Raising the apple, he bit into it. His teeth were sound, for there was no hesitation, no attempt to find good ones with which to chew.

Matilda stared at him, afraid to ask what he meant and filled with indignation.

He inclined his head to her in the barest deference and, without clarifying his statement, left the garden.

She gazed after him. His walk was slightly lop-sided and she could see that he was striving not to limp heavily in her sight. He had left the cloak strewn on the bench and she wondered if it had been as deliberate a ploy as taking and biting the apple. Matilda sat down upon the pelt, and, as she had been longing to do, filled her hands and buried her face in the cool, glossy fur.

The feel brought the distant memories of her father flooding back. She could see the laughter in his dark blue eyes and sunlight sparkling on his ruddy hair. She could hear the rumble of his voice, speaking in English, and experience the delight tingle through her body as he swung her aloft in his arms. Tears burned her lids. Wrapping herself in the folds of the cloak, she was both comforted and desolated. An odour clung to the wool – of sun-warmed fabric and dust, and something else. The individual scent of the man to whom the cloak now belonged. The hair rose softly on her nape and she gazed in the direction of the garden gate, her lips slightly parted.

Hearing the click of the latch, she thought for a moment that he had returned to claim the cloak, but it was Sybille who came hurrying down the path, cheeks flushed and wimple askew. 'Your mother wants you immediately,' the maid panted.

Matilda rose and the older woman's eyes widened at the sight of the blue mantle.

'Sir Simon left it behind,' Matilda explained. 'I was about to return it to him.'

Sybille shook her head. 'No time for that, sweeting. And best not take it into your mother's presence,' she counselled. 'She's already fit to burst.'

'Sir Simon told me that he is here to take the earldom into his hands.' Matilda removed the cloak and draped it over her arm. It was almost as heavy as a mail shirt.

'Did he tell you anything else?'

Matilda smoothed her hand over the soft, midnight-blue wool. 'Should he have done? Is there more?'

Sybille gave her a dark look. 'Enough to shake the walls to their foundations,' she said with a certain grim relish. 'I won't say more. The mood your mother's harbouring, one word out of place would be cause for a whipping.'

Outside her mother's chamber, Matilda paused to lay the cloak in a chest standing against the wall. Straightening her skirts, tucking a stray wisp of hair back under her wimple, she braced herself and entered the room.

Judith was pacing the floor, a deep frown scored between her brows. Her mouth was tucked in upon itself, making her look shrewish and old. When she saw Matilda, she ceased pacing and faced her, fury brimming in her eyes.

'Your sister informs me that you went to speak to Simon de Senlis,' she said icily. 'Do you want to tell me why?'

Matilda cast about for an explanation that would satisfy her mother. 'I saw him in the garden and from the way he was sitting I thought perhaps he was injured.'

'Well, he is not,' Judith snapped, 'and you are to stay away from him. He is a wolf in sheep's clothing.' Her voice shook on the pronunciation. 'What did he say to you?'

'Very little,' Matilda said, beginning to feel resentful of her mother's stance. 'Only that he had come to take my father's lands into his care.'

'Your "father's lands",' Judith sneered. 'Your beloved, blessed father could keep neither his lands nor his head. It is I who have maintained them through all the years of your life, and I will not be replaced by some upstart knight.' The tremble in her voice increased.

'But if it is the King's command . . .'

'I will appeal against it. William Rufus is a fool, and Simon de Senlis is no more an earl than I am a serf. I will not wed him and let him make of me his chattel.'

Matilda gasped and clapped one hand involuntarily across her mouth.

'Oh yes,' declared her mother with a vicious nod. 'He wants to legitimise his claim by marriage, the traitorous thief. I knew Simon de Senlis when he was a snivelling brat. I will not be subject to his rule now.'

Matilda's stomach roiled with shock, anger and a strange unsettling stab of feminine jealousy. When she had stood in the garden and looked upon the vulnerable figure of Simon de Senlis, she had certainly not been viewing him in the guise of stepfather.

'At first light we will leave and take refuge at Elstow while I decide what is to be done,' Judith said.

'But if we leave, surely that will be granting him the victory.'

'No. It will show that we spurn him, and his authority will be diminished.' Judith curled her lip. 'My family will not stand quietly by and see this happen to me, and nor will the people of these shires. I am Waltheof's widow, and not without influence.'

And I am Waltheof's daughter, Matilda thought, but she held her tongue. Across the room she caught her sister's eye.

Jude looked frightened. It was obvious that the keys to the linen coffer had not been given and that there was no point asking for them. The only beds that her mother intended Simon de Senlis and his men to lie upon were made of thorns.

It was late evening. The Countess and her daughters had appeared in neither the hall nor the guest chamber. Not that Simon had expected them to do so. The mother hen had swept her chicks beneath her wing and was cooped up in the women's bower clucking in high dudgeon. The notion brought the slightest of smiles to his lips, but it did not linger. Countess Judith was not a hen and he did not believe that she would sit and cluck for long.

Rubbing his leg, he eased himself down onto the bench and lifted the cup of wine that his squire had left to hand. Since the Countess had originally had the chamber built to house important guests, it was spacious and well appointed – which he doubted she would have wished for him. A cosy burial casket was probably the accommodation she currently had in mind.

He thought of his encounter with the daughter in the garden. The girl possessed her father's strong bones, although the features were refined to feminine delicacy. There was a look of Judith about the arch of her brows, but instead of being glossy black they were a rich copper-bronze and made him want to smooth his thumb across them, and then down the line of her cheek to the soft curl of her mouth corner.

It was many years since he had played at love and lust with Sabina the falconer's daughter. Long too since he lost his virginity in a hayrick with a cowherd's young widow. He knew about attraction, the excitement of the chase, the pleasure of gorging on the kill. Knew also about the brothels that Waltheof had once warned him against.

How old was the girl? He was tired, his leg was paining him, and his mind was woolly. Fifteen, sixteen summers? Of an age to be bedded, and she had Waltheof's blood in her veins.

His musings were disturbed by the return of Turstan his

squire and several attendants bearing a large oval bathtub and pails of hot and cold water. Late it might be, but Simon could not bear to lie another night in his own sweat and dirt. It was not that he was particularly fastidious, but there came a time when the itch and prickle of unwashed skin and hair became unpleasant. Besides, a hot tub would soothe the ache in his leg.

The attendants, albeit that they belonged to the Countess and kept their heads down, were swift and efficient. He laboured to his feet so that Turstan could help him unarm. On retiring to this chamber, Simon had removed the grinding weight of his mail shirt, but he still wore his padded tunic and swordbelt. A show of constant vigilance was prudent.

Once the tub was filled the attendants were dismissed. The last one out closed the door but did not latch it, and as the squire knelt to unfasten Simon's hose bindings it swung open on a draught of air that sent the flames guttering in the two hanging lamps. Instinctively Simon reached for his sword, and the squire flashed his knife from its sheath.

Matilda paused, looking from one to the other, alarm flaring in her eyes.

'My lady.' Simon uncurled his grip from the hilt of his sword and motioned the squire to put up his knife. 'You are brave to enter the lion's den,' he remarked, the imagery suggested to him because she seemed like a young doe, poised for flight.

She blushed, but advanced into the room, although he noticed that she did not close the door. There was no sign of her maid; she was without a chaperone.

'I am not brave at all, my lord,' she replied. 'I know that you are honourable and that you will not harm me.'

Simon gave a humourless smile. 'I doubt you have imbibed such sentiments from your lady mother,' he said. 'And I wonder if you are right to trust your source of information. Any man can turn from his honour in the dark of night if given the opportunity.'

'You are not any man, my lord,' she said.

Her answer surprised a snort of genuine amusement out of Simon. What might have sounded arch and flirtatious coming from an older woman in a different tone was made comically touching by the plain innocence of the girl's. 'Am I not?' he said.

'The King would not have sent "any man" to this task.' She gave him a clear, steady look. 'You knew my father. He would not have given you his cloak unless he thought highly of you.' She held out her arms like a handmaiden, the garment draped across them. 'Since we are leaving in the morning, I am returning this to you now.'

With a gesture and a nod Simon dismissed the squire, following him to the door and ensuring the latch fell behind the lad. Then he approached Matilda and removed the cloak from her outstretched hands.

'Do you still trust me, girl?' He could not control the hoarse note that had entered his voice, nor the speed of his breathing.

'Yes, my lord.' She stared back at him and he saw that although her gaze was steadfast her breathing was as rapid as his own.

'Well, you should not. Even a tame beast will turn wild of tooth and claw if provoked.'

'Have I provoked you, my lord?'

He went to lay the cloak on the coffer, giving himself time to gather his wits and his control. 'In ways you cannot begin to know,' he said with a short laugh. When he was more certain of himself, he turned to her. 'It is courteous of you to inform me that you are leaving on the morrow. I suspect that your mother does not know you have done so – or that you are here in my chamber.'

'No,' she said, biting her lip. 'She does not know. Will you prevent us from going now that I have told you?'

He steepled his hands beneath his chin. 'Where does your mother intend to take you?'

She hesitated, her eyes slipping from his.

Dwelling at court, observation of expressions and bodily actions had become second nature to Simon. 'Lies may help you get over a small slope, but eventually you will come to a mountain and the burden you have accumulated will be your ruin,' he said.

Her chin jutted. 'I was not going to lie to you. If I paused it was because I was unsure how you would respond to my answer.'

'Which is?'

'To the nunnery at Elstow, and then to my step grandfather's estates in Holderness.'

'Ah,' Simon said, and lowered his clasped hands. 'I thought your mother might seek her sanctuary there. After all, your step grandfather has a vested interest in these lands – and a son.'

She made no attempt to deny his words.

Unlatching his swordbelt, he turned to lay it across the coffer beside his discarded hauberk. 'Do you want to go with your mother?'

Although his back was to her, he felt her surprise at the question. The breath she drew was audible.

'Do I have a choice?'

The tone of her response told him she was already ahead of the conversation, that she knew where it was going – and perhaps that was why she had come to him in the first place.

'I think you know the answer to that.' Facing her again, he bent double and extended his arms. 'If you could help me, it will save me calling my squire . . . unless you wish me to do so.'

She shook her head and, coming to him, peeled the gambeson off with nimble efficiency. 'We keep to the custom in this household that honoured guests should be served personally,' she said, and a rueful smile lit in her eyes. 'Most of the time, at least.'

'Your mother considers me neither honoured, nor a guest,' Simon replied, equally rueful. Then he grimaced. 'God's Life,

I stink like a midden pit,' he apologised. 'Too many days in the saddle and on the road.'

She looked at the gambeson in her hands, its outer layer streaked greasy black from his hauberk and its inner layer giving off a staggeringly concentrated aroma of man. 'I'll put a broom pole through the sleeves and hang it to air in the wind,' she said. 'The laundry maids can tend to your linens if you have fresh raiment in your baggage. I will see that your tunic is brushed and aired.'

He nodded, both amused and impressed by her efficiency. He wondered if she was using it as a shield. Or perhaps she was showing him how advantageous it would be for him to let her remain.

He pondered while she folded his tunic to one side and cast his shirt into an open willow basket for taking to the maids. Chausses and leg braids followed. With great diplomacy, or perhaps a sense of self-preservation, she ensured that her back was turned as he removed his braies and cast them into the same basket as his shirt.

Simon stepped into the water. It was still hot and sufficiently deep to reach to his mid-chest. 'You still have not answered my question,' he addressed her spine. 'Do you want to go with your mother?'

She turned around, a dish of soft soap in one hand and a linen washcloth in the other, her blush now fiery. 'You said I had no choice.'

'Not exactly.'

'In so many words.' She came to the tub. A servant had left a jug at the side. She filled it with water from a spare pail and doused his head.

Simon spluttered beneath the deluge. Twice more she did it and then he felt the coldness of the soap and the kneading touch of her hands as she lathered his hair. 'No,' she said. 'I do not want to go with my mother. Why do you think I came to your chamber when I could as easily have sent a servant with your cloak?'

The pressure of her fingers set up opposing sensations of languor and lust. It might be the family tradition for the women of the household to bathe honoured guests, but usually it would be in full public with servants present. He doubted that she had ever been in this situation before. Raising his knees, he concealed his arousal.

'I asked your mother to marry me,' he said.

Again she doused him, this time to sluice the soap from his hair. 'I know,' she replied. 'And she refused you.'

He took the cloth that she handed him and dried his face. The water rippling around his torso was rapidly turning a scummy grey. 'My own fault for asking the wrong woman.' He put deliberate emphasis on the last word. 'I always thought of Waltheof's daughter as a little girl, but while my imagination has remained still, the reality has moved on.' He gave a wry shrug. 'Your mother has made it plain what she thinks of a match with me. Indeed, if we were to wed, it would be a marriage made in hell for both of us.' Reaching back, he took her arm in a wet grip and drew her round to the side of the tub where he could look at her. 'If I ask you now, it is not because you are second best, but that I had not seen you then and I did not realise.'

Her complexion might be flushed but she was in full control of her mental faculties. 'I know that in many ways I have lived a sheltered life,' she said, 'but my mother is a dowager countess and she has raised neither me nor my sister in ignorance. I know that to truly make yourself lord of my father's lands you must seek a marriage alliance either with his widow, or with one of his daughters, who bears his blood in their veins. I recognise that this is a bargain of the market place, not of the scented bower.'

He gave her a pained smile. 'That is a speech inspired by your mother and delivered with the honesty of your sire.' He extended a hand to touch her cheek. 'You are right in most of what you say, but even in a market place there is space for a seller of rare jewels.'

She rose to her feet and moved away, but only to fetch more soap. 'And if I refuse you, will you go to my sister and ask the same of her?'

He heard the challenge in her voice and had to bite back a smile for fear of offending her. 'I might,' he admitted, 'but it would be a great pity. But I say again, you would not be here in this chamber except by your own will. And I have not forced you to perform the services of a bath maid.'

'No, my lord, you have not,' she agreed.

'So, what say you? Shall I send Turstan to fetch my chaplain while I dress?'

She looked startled and a little apprehensive and he saw her throat ripple as she swallowed.

'There is no stepping back from this point,' he said softly. 'Either stay, or remain the night – as my wife. That is my ultimatum.'

Although she trembled like a leaf in the wind, she held her ground. 'I will remain,' she said, lifting her chin.

He nodded. 'Good. I hoped you would agree.' Taking the dish of soap, he washed himself, not trusting his reaction should she offer to perform the task. After all, he thought with grim humour, they were not yet wed, and it would not be proper.

Matilda's stomach was queasy with fear, but she knew that she had made the right decision. It had been her choice to come to him in his chamber, no other's. To do so she had crept from the room where her mother and sister were sleeping with a murmur that she was visiting the privy. She had lied and used subterfuge. She had not screamed and pounded upon the door that he closed, and of her own volition she had ministered to him in the bathtub. Come hell or high water, she was not going to lose her courage now. He needed her, if not for herself then for her blood; she was Waltheof's daughter and the Conqueror's great niece. From the moment she saw her father's cloak, she had known that whatever happened she was bound and beholden to Simon de Senlis.

To keep her apprehension at bay and occupy her hands, she fetched the rough linen towels that had been warming on a stool near the brazier. Laying one on the floor, she held the other out to him. He rose to his feet in a surge of dirty water and took the towel from her. He was slender and wiry, but there was muscle nevertheless, firm and compact, closely following the line of bone. His chest and stomach were flat and hard, and a crucifix of curling dark hair ran from nipple to nipple and from the hollow of his throat to his crotch. The latter he covered smartly with the towel before she had taken more than a startled glimpse.

Taking a third towel from the stool to dry his hair, he went to the door and pulled it open. The squire was leaning against the wall, arms folded, but immediately came to attention.

'Fetch Father Bertulf and Aubrey de Mar,' he told the lad and looked back at Matilda. 'Do you have a female companion you wish to stand witness?'

Matilda frowned in thought. 'My maid Helisende, if you can rouse her without waking my mother,' she said.

The squire nodded and without question disappeared on his errand.

Simon closed the door and, rubbing his hair, came back into the room. 'I am sorry it is to be like this,' he said. 'Most women like to have a fuss made of their wedding day. I promise you a full mass and a feast to follow as soon as I can.'

Matilda shrugged. 'I have never been very fond of ceremony,' she said.

'No?' he sounded sceptical. 'Not of wearing fine clothes and being the centre of attention?'

She shook her head. 'I enjoy celebrating. I like great gatherings, and it is true that fine clothes are appealing. But the glitter swiftly tarnishes when you are forced to it day in and day out. My mother says that I should never forget my rank. I am the great niece of a king and the daughter of an earl and I should live accordingly.' She screwed up her face. 'In truth I am happiest on my hands and knees in my garden, with a piece of sacking tied around my waist and my hands dark with soil. The importance lies beneath. When we are dead, we become naught but bones, and then who is to tell the difference between a beggar and a king?'

It was grave wisdom for one of such tender years and Simon was touched, intrigued, and saddened. 'Indeed,' he said. 'However, for my own sense of ceremony and to show the value I set by your consent, I will still give you a wedding day to remember . . . and, I hope, a wedding night.'

Matilda was immediately flustered. Her mother's protection meant that to a great extent men were an unknown territory. Helisende, giggling, had told her what happened on a wedding night and Matilda believed her because, although protected, she was not blind to what went on around her. She had often pondered the matter. What it would be like. How it happened. Thoughts she had kept to herself because they were immodest and unseemly and if her mother had known of them she would have marched her straight to confession.

She went to a wooden coffer against which his large green and gold kite shield was propped. 'Is this your baggage?' she asked a little too swiftly. ·

He told her that it was and, although her back was to him, she did not miss the note of rueful amusement in his voice. 'You need not be afraid,' he said. 'I will not harm you.'

'I am not afraid,' Matilda said stoutly, and it was almost true. Her greater fear was that this was all a dream and that in the morning she would be forced to go to Elstow with her mother, and from there to Holderness and the tyranny of her grandmother's household. That thought led on to another. 'If my sister wishes to stay here too, will you let her?' she asked with a swift look over her shoulder. 'Jude is quieter than me, more likely to do my mother's bidding, but out of obedience and duty rather than desire.'

'Of course,' Simon said gravely. 'I will be pleased to offer her my protection.'

'Thank you,' she murmured and turned to his baggage

again before she was trapped in that knowing, golden gaze. He did not have many garments, but those he possessed were of excellent quality. There were two shirts of soft linen chansil, bleached in the sun to the colour of ripe barley. His braies were of chansil too – both luxurious and sensible since the fabric was soft and would not chafe.

Simon's spare hose were fashioned from wine-red wool in close-woven diamond twill with bindings of red and blue braid. He had two tunics, one blue, one soft tawny, and both trimmed with the red and blue braid at neckline, hem and cuffs, garments that would take him from palace to castle to manor and be appropriate for all.

He donned the braies and shirt and sat on a stool to draw on the legs of the hose. Matilda saw him wince as he pulled the left one up his leg.

'What's the matter?'

'Nothing. An injury I have had since boyhood. It pains me now and again.' A defensive note entered his voice.

From the way he had been limping earlier, and his grimace now, Matilda thought perhaps that it was more than nothing. 'We have some marigold salve if that will help,' she offered.

'There is no need,' he dismissed. 'It is only painful because I have been standing on it for too long. If I support it with leg bindings, it is not so bad.' As he spoke, he rapidly wound the length of braid from ankle to calf and tucked it neatly in the top. Matilda sensed that he was vulnerable, that he did not wish to pursue the matter.

She took a hesitant breath. 'Will you . . . will you tell me about my father,' she said.

He raised his head. His eyes were as clear as the best mead, but totally unreadable. 'What do you want to know?'

She clasped her hands, looked down at them, then at him.

'Is it true that he was a wastrel and a drunkard?'

He considered her for so long that she began to grow afraid that he would confirm her mother's opinion, but as she was about to break the silence and say that it did not matter, she would rather keep her dreams intact, he spoke.

'Your father was a man with faults like any other,' he said. 'Not a saint, even if that is what folk are trying to make of him now. Yes, he could drink an alehouse dry, and yes, he would rather go out hunting than sit down with his steward and a heap of tally sticks, but there are worse failings than that. He had generosity and courage in abundance – and if I am here now, it is because of him.'

Matilda listened with rapt attention as he told her how Waltheof had saved his life in Fécamp. She could see the scene vividly in her mind and the image of her father snatching Simon to safety and wrestling a wild horse to a standstill gave her a queasy feeling of pride and pleasure. 'He was always so strong,' she murmured, tears prickling her lids. 'I knew what my mother said of him wasn't true.'

Watching her, Simon wondered if by telling her the tale of Waltheof's prowess he had tipped the balance too far the other way. Then again, he suspected that she would be selectively deaf. For the moment she only wanted to hear the good and heroic things. And who could blame her?

There was a light tap on the door, heralding the return of his squire with Father Bertulf, Aubrey de Mar, and a wide-eyed Helisende.

Simon gestured to the maid. 'Attend your mistress,' he said.

Matilda had few preparations to make. Helisende helped her to remove her wimple and hair net. Her braids were unpinned and her hair combed down until it shimmered at her hips like a river of molten bronze shot through with fire.

'Are you sure you know what you are doing?' Helisende whispered. There was fear in her voice, but also an incorrigible glint of relish.

Matilda gave a tremulous laugh. 'Not in the least,' she whispered back, 'but I know that it is right.' She was still resonating from Simon's words about her father. She felt elated and dizzy.

'Your mother will not see it in the same light.'

Matilda's expression grew stubborn. 'That is my mother's choice,' she said, 'not mine.' As the words left her lips, a sense of power stirred in the pit of her belly. Her choice. Hers. Mayhap brought about by circumstance, but she had selected the path . . . and the manner of its treading.

With head high, she went to join Simon and the waiting chaplain.

CHAPTER 24

The ring Simon had given her fitted Matilda's finger perfectly. It was one of his own, for he had small hands and hers were a feminine version of her father's, large and square. She examined it by the light of the night candle, for it was unlike any ring that she had seen before; set in the gold band was a circle of blue-grey stone that had been expertly worked to show two clasped right hands surrounded by a border of leaves.

'I believe it is Roman,' Simon said, looking over her shoulder and handing her a cup of wine. 'I bought it from a trader in Rouen who had it from a man who found a cache of coins and jewels buried in a field. There is not another like it . . . that's why I wanted it to be your marriage ring, for you also are a rarity.'

Matilda blushed at the compliment, unused to such flattery. Once again, they were alone. The chaplain had officiated at the taking of their wedding vows. Simon's squire, his knight and Helisende had borne witness. Now all that remained to make the marriage indissoluble was the consummation.

For a second time Simon started to undress in front of her. She averted her glance, but he caught her arm and gently turned her around.

'No,' he said softly, 'do not look away. I want you to know my body as familiarly as I will know yours. Since we are united in marriage, it behoves us to be two halves of one whole from the beginning.'

Matilda swallowed. 'I do not know what to do,' she whispered. He had unfastened his belt and removed his tunic. Shirt, hose and braies remained.

Capturing a handful of her loose hair, he drew her towards him. 'It is an easy thing to learn,' he said.

She was nearly as tall as he was, and when he set his arm around her waist and pulled her against his body they were a match. Matilda caught her breath. She had never been this close to a man in her life before, except her father. No one until now had had the right or the audacity to touch her as Simon de Senlis was touching her. She could smell the soap of his recent bathing, and mingled with it the masculine tang of his skin.

'Be my squire,' he said softly, bringing his face close to hers, so that their lips were almost touching, 'and I will be your maid.' Taking her hand, he set it against the tied lacing of his shirt.

Matilda felt weak and hot. She was afraid, but intoxicated too. With trembling fingers she unfastened the knot, and was fascinated to watch her own hand at the task, adorned by the new wedding ring. The shirt fell open exposing the wiry curl of hair at his throat and an expanse of summer-tanned skin.

'Now my turn,' he said, unpinning the round brooch securing the neck of her gown. With hands that were as steady as hers were trembling, he unplucked the drawstring of her chemise. Matilda shivered but raised her arms obediently so that he could draw her overgown over her head.

'Now you.' He placed her hands on his waist. For a moment Matilda was unsure what he meant, but then she realised and tugged his shirt out of his braies and off over his head. The scent of freshly washed linen and the warm smell of his body beguiled her senses. He was naked to the waist, and she was a mere breath from his flesh. A crucifix of garnets set in gold glittered on his chest, the jewels and metal flashing each time he inhaled.

He took her lightly by the hips and pulled her against him, angled his head and nuzzled beneath her ear. 'Now me,' he said, and while one hand held her against him the other moved up her body and cupped her breast.

Matilda gasped at the sudden jolt of sensation. He nipped and sucked at her throat and she shivered. Without stopping what he was doing, he guided her to the fastenings that held his hose to his braies. 'Now you.'

Matilda fumbled, unsure without looking, and the back of her hand brushed against his erection. Simon hissed through his teeth and Matilda recoiled, torn between a worry that she had done wrong and her fear of the unknown. But he drew her back and placed her palm and fingers against the front of his braies.

'It is how all men are made,' he said, and there was a smile in his voice. 'Granted you may not have encountered one in quite this condition before, but there is nothing of which to be afraid. And your touch does not hurt . . . Indeed, it is a source of great pleasure.'

Matilda swallowed and dared to close her fingers around his length. Under her hand she felt something like a drop spindle full with woven yarn, springy, yielding, but bone-hard at the core. He made a sound of pleasure and pushed against her hand and kissed her on the mouth.

His lips were warm, smooth, not in the least how she had imagined a man's lips to be. His tongue circled her lips and then thrust gently back and forth, echoing the motion of his hips. He slipped the loosened chemise from her shoulders and it dropped to the ground, leaving her clad only in her knee-length hose.

Matilda shivered at the cool air on her naked skin, and at the same time was scorched by the expression in his eyes as he drew back to look at her. 'I am dazzled by your beauty,' he said hoarsely.

No one had ever told her that she was beautiful. Everyone considered Jude the pretty one with her daintier size and bones. 'Truly?' she whispered.

'Truly . . .' His hand followed his eyes in a slow caress down the length of her body and Matilda trembled beneath his touch. He drew her to the bed and, laying her down upon it, gently removed her hose and completed the unfastening and removal of his own. Matilda felt the coolness and warmth of fur at her back, and realised that she was lying across the bearskin cloak. She dug her fingers into the gleaming pelt and wondered if he had placed it there deliberately.

Simon lay down beside her and moved his hand over her thigh, circling upwards. At first his touch tickled and made Matilda giggle, but that sort of sensitivity very swiftly gave way to another that made her gasp and arch. Higher still. Her eyes widened. She was not quite certain where his fingers were now, but she didn't want him to stop, and if that was being wanton she did not care.

When he drew her hand to his braies, she was more eager to touch and stroke this time. He slipped his thigh between hers, nudged them apart and mounted her. Matilda gasped and gasped again as he moved upon her. He twisted his body and kissed and sucked her breasts, and the first cry was torn from her. She dug her fingers into the flesh of his arms. Her legs widened and she returned his rocking motion in a rhythm that came from instinct. His own breathing was ragged now, his heartbeat swift. Lifting himself from her, he was in haste to untie the drawstring of his braies and pull them off. For the first time Matilda was gifted with a view of a man in a full state of arousal.

'It is not as frightening as it looks, I promise you,' he said breathlessly.

'I am not afraid,' Matilda replied, determined to be brave. With great daring she willed herself to touch him and found the feel not unpleasant. Smooth and warm, hard and yielding.

'I am,' Simon gave a congested laugh. 'If you continue to do that, I might gain great pleasure, but not the consummation we need to make this marriage binding.'

She looked at him curiously, not having the least idea what he meant.

He pushed her hand aside and moved over her. She felt the solid hot nudge of his flesh, felt him enter a fraction, then held her breath. She heard him swallow and through her own body felt the tremors of his restraint. He fondled and stroked her until she clutched at him. Instinctively she bore down and he eased further inside. And still he held off, continuing to pleasure and caress. The stimulation became unbearable. Matilda felt a swelling tightness in her loins. Suddenly she didn't care about anything but the feeling building within her pelvis. Whimpering, uttering little cries, she bore down on the pain of his invasion, because behind and above it there was a pleasure so huge that she would do anything to be a part of it.

His hands delved to her buttocks, tilted them upwards, and with a groan he thrust into her full measure, once and then again. The pain blossomed in a raw, red starburst, but so did the pleasure and she sobbed, her body drawing each pulse of his seed deep within her womb.

He groaned softly against her throat and continued to rock gently upon her, the first violent surge spent. Gentler waves of pleasure followed each other through Matilda's loins and she shifted, seeking the echoes of the wild delight she had just known.

Slowly, with much greater effort than it had taken to mount her, Simon withdrew. 'I am sorry if I hurt you,' he said. 'I would have given you greater joy but . . .' He made a shrugging gesture serve for the rest.

Greater joy? So there was more than this? The bed, being intended for guests, was large enough for them to lie side by side and not even have to touch unless they wanted to, but Matilda needed the closeness. 'It is true that I am sore,' she said. Indeed, now that the throb of pleasure had diminished, she was aware of the tenderness of bruised tissues, 'But I do not know how you could have given me greater joy than you did just now.'

The faintest of smiles curved his narrow mouth. 'By not giving you pain,' he said. 'I am not accustomed to deflowering virgins.'

Matilda raised her eyebrows at that. 'No?'

'Very few men are, whatever tales you hear,' he said wryly. 'The only virgins that have come my way have either been heavily chaperoned by their families or spoils of war. And since I am not a man given over to rape and debauchery, the latter fruit has never appealed to me – unlike some.'

'So all the women you have known have been experienced?' Matilda felt a pang of jealousy, followed by fear. How was she, who knew nothing, ever going to measure up?

'That is so.'

'Have there been many?'

His lips twitched. 'One or two. Several in my youth who were more use to me than I was to them.'

Matilda lowered her gaze from his face, not wanting to read his expression. Her eyes happened upon his member. Before it had seemed an enormous thing, quivering with a life of its own; now it was much diminished, curving towards his thigh. The sight fascinated her and she realised anew how ingenious God was.

'What?' he said, tilting her face on his forefinger so that she had to meet his gaze.

She caught her underlip in her teeth. 'I was thinking that it is a good thing that a man's part is able to diminish as it does,' she said. 'Otherwise it would be a great hindrance to every activity but mating.'

He roared with laughter at that, and Matilda's heart fluttered. This morning she had not known of the existence of this slender, unprepossessing man. Now she wore his ring on her finger, was naked by his side, and had taken his seed into her womb. Already she could be with his child.

'A man would say that it is a good thing for both sexes that it is able to rise as it does,' he commented. Pillowing his hands behind his head, he yawned hugely. 'Not that mine will do any more rising this night, unless you are truly a worker of miracles.' He glanced at her, his lids heavy and dark smudges beneath them. 'However, that is because weariness outstrips lust on this occasion. It will not always be so.'

She was not sure what he meant so she just gave him a smile and made a resolution to find out as much as she could from Helisende. Sybille was the usual font of such wisdom, but being her mother's maid was unavailable to ask. The thought of facing her mother in the morning caused her to move closer to her new husband, seeking the comfort of his body.

His eyes had closed, but with obvious effort he opened them. 'You will never regret this marriage, I swear to you,' he mumbled, and tucked a wild strand of her hair tenderly behind her ear. 'You need give me no assurances,' she whispered in reply and pressed herself against him. 'I know in my own heart that I could have done no better for myself than this.'

He kissed her fingers and did not speak. Moments after that he was asleep, his breathing deep and even, with a slight catch at the top of each breath. Matilda lay against him, watching the glitter of the garnet cross in the light from the single candle. She whispered his name like a talisman. Girls dreamed of love and talked of it with their maids and companions. They flirted with the squires and knights of their fathers' retinues; they set their fancy on passing troubadours. But love had come to Matilda in a single hammer blow, and its image was not that of a tall, fair young man bearing gifts and songs, but of a slightly built soldier with a damaged leg and a baggage wain full of cares.

Laying her cheek against the smooth curve of his bicep, feeling beneath her the soft prickle of her father's bearskin cloak, she was content.

CHAPTER 25

The instant Judith opened her eyes she knew that something was wrong. Too overwrought to rest, she had dozed throughout the night, such sleep as she had managed beset by dark, unpleasant dreams. Now, jerked to awareness by a stealing sensation of unease, she sat up. The large night candle had burned low on the wrought-iron pricket, but more lights were blossoming in the doorway and she could hear Sybille's swift murmur.

Judith flung back the covers and stood up. Whatever was happening, she would go to meet it, head on as she always had. She more than half expected the disturbance to be that of Simon de Senlis' soldiers, coming to imprison her. It would be their shame, not hers, if they were to take her in her chemise, her hair uncovered.

'What is happening?' She raised her voice imperiously. Hearing it cut across the air, as it had always done, gave her a boost of confidence. And then she saw Matilda and she froze. The girl was wearing yesterday's blue gown. Her hair was decorously concealed beneath her wimple and, at first glance, there was nothing untoward about her appearance. However the fact that she was entering the room gave Judith cause for concern because she could not recall her leaving. She must have crept from the chamber very circumspectly indeed. A swift glance at Matilda's pallet revealed the girl's subterfuge; the bedclothes were mounded in the shape of a sleeping body. What disturbed Judith most, though, was the look on her daughter's face. The heavy lids, the flushed cheeks told their own vivid story.

'Where have you been?' she demanded. 'If you have been conniving behind my back, I will never forgive you.'

Matilda lifted her head in defiance and Judith saw Waltheof clearly in the line of jaw and thrust of chin. 'I have done no more conniving than you, Mother,' she said. 'Simon de Senlis knows of your plans, but he will not stand in your way if you wish to leave.'

Judith gave her daughter a look filled with disdain. 'I do not need his yeasay to do as I please.' Her voice was deadly with control. 'I am mistress here yet.'

Matilda drew a deep breath and clasped her hands in front of her breasts. 'No, Mother, you are not. Last night I was married to Simon de Senlis. I wear his ring on my finger and the match has been witnessed and consummated.'

The words poured over Judith like an icy drench. 'That is impossible. I have given no consent to the match.'

'But I gave mine,' Matilda said. 'Our vows were taken in the presence of Father Bertulf. He's not only Simon's chaplain, but also an ordained priest of St Stephen's in Caen. I was not forced. I agreed to the marriage of my own will.'

'You have been duped!' A red mist hazed Judith's vision. 'All that Simon de Senlis wants is the sanction of your blood to bolster his position. This marriage would not stand up for one moment in a court of law.'

'Why don't you test it and see, my lady.' Simon emerged from the gloom of the doorway. He was wearing a fresh tunic of tawny wool that reflected his eyes. His sword was girded at his hip, and his left hand lightly grasped the buckskin grip. 'I doubt you will find it other than watertight.' He went to stand beside Matilda and possessively took his bride's hand. He raised it to his lips, pressed a kiss in the palm and curled her fingers over it.

Judith felt sick. 'You have betrayed me!' she hissed at her

daughter. 'In truth, you have your father's blood, for he was weak and unsteady of purpose too. It was his downfall, and now it will be yours.'

'No, Mother, you were *his* downfall,' Matilda retorted.

'You were just a child, how could you know?' Judith spat bitterly. 'All you had were his kisses and adoration. You did not see his indecision and the way that he would take refuge from it in drink. You did not see the times I had to follow him like a parent, clearing away the debris of his mistakes.' She stabbed her forefinger. 'You did not see his fecklessness and stupidity. It was I who had to live with that.'

Matilda had flushed beneath Judith's onslaught as if each word were a slap across the face. 'No,' she said in a trembling voice, 'I did not see, because he was my father and I loved him. But I do not believe he ever received love or even respect from you, Mother. Sometimes . . .' she swallowed. 'Sometimes I think that you hated him.'

'I hated his weakness.' Suddenly Judith's eyes were stinging. 'Think what you will of my feelings for your father. It will not alter the truth.'

De Senlis laid his hand on Matilda's shoulder. 'Enough,' he said gently. 'You will tear each other to pieces. Lady Judith, if it please you, my men will escort you wherever you wish to go. I do not think it appropriate that you remain here for the moment.'

Judith flashed him a glare of utter loathing, which was met by an implacable wall of courtesy. She had spoken of her husband's errors of judgement, but now she wondered if she had made one of her own in refusing De Senlis. It had been an instinctive choice, born of the memory of seeing him as a child at the royal court, and then as an invalid, his handicap the indirect result of her carelessness. She had not wanted the humiliation of yielding her personal governance to him. If she had quashed her pride she could at least have had half a loaf. Now there were not even crumbs, and in one fell swoop her daughter had snatched the title of Countess for herself.

'I would not stay even if this was my last place of refuge,' she said scornfully. 'At least her father, whatever his faults, did not come like a thief in the night.'

The remark bounced off his blank expression like a blunt spear off a hardwood shield. It was her daughter who flinched as if wounded. De Senlis was right. They were tearing each other apart.

She turned to summon Jude, who had been watching the proceedings with widening eyes, but De Senlis pre-empted her.

'I am desirous that your younger daughter remain with her sister,' he said in that same, quiet tone that left room for neither discussion nor argument. 'She is more easily protected under my jurisdiction – and I believe that she will be the happier for remaining here.'

Judith's knees almost gave way. 'And if I refuse to yield her?'

His shoulders twitched in a shrug. 'There is little you can do to gainsay my will, my lady. Accept it with a good grace, and in return I will be gracious too.'

Nausea churned Judith's stomach and the taste of defeat was in her mouth. He was right. She could do little until she reached her family – save perhaps salvage her dignity.

'You have stolen my daughters from me,' she said, lowering her own voice to match the tone of his. 'And the lands that I have cared for since my husband's death. Perhaps it is God's way. Perhaps this is my penance for that day of heedless pride in the stableyard at Rouen. I will pray God to forgive my many sins, and I hope that I can find it in my heart to pray that he forgive you yours . . . for I am mortal, and I cannot.'

She did not have to push past Matilda and De Senlis, for they stood aside to let her go and neither spoke to call her back. Judith stumbled in the darkness of the corridor. Her cheeks were wet with the first tears she had shed since Waltheof's body had been borne to Crowland. If this was God's will then she did not know how she was going to reconcile herself.

Biting her lip, Matilda made to go after her mother, but Simon gripped her arm. 'No,' he said. 'Leave her. You have come to a parting of the ways and whatever you said now would only make things worse. Let her grieve awhile in peace. There will be time enough later to make things right between you.'

'Things have never been right between us,' Matilda said desolately. 'As my mother says, I am my father's daughter, and that alone is unforgivable in her eyes.'

'Then it is she who must change, not you.' He gave her arm a small shake to bring her attention fully to him. 'You are chatelaine of this place now. The care of its people falls to you.'

Meeting his gaze Matilda encountered a will as implacable as her mother's but differently channelled.

'I need you by my side, not just as a decoration or a seal to my rule, but as a true wife and helpmate.' He claimed her lips in a kiss that drew a collective gasp from the Countess's women.

Simon raised his head and glanced at them. 'Those of you who wish to follow your mistress are free to go with her,' he announced. 'Those who wish to remain may do so.' His arm around Matilda, he left them to their decisions and withdrew to the hall.

While Simon was speaking to his knights, Jude grabbed Matilda's arm. 'It is true then?' she whispered, her glance darting towards Simon.

Matilda's lips twitched. 'Is what true?' she teased.

'That you and he are married – is it binding?'

'As a piece of thrice woven braid. There will be no annulment.'

Jude lifted Matilda's hand to the growing light from the shutters to look at the ring.

'He tells me that it is Roman, and very rare.' Matilda's smile deepened.

Jude looked over her shoulder to make sure that Simon was

not listening and gave her sister a little nudge. 'What was it like?'

'What was what like?'

Jude dug her in the ribs again. 'You know . . . Are the things that Sybille says true?'

Matilda giggled. 'I am not sure that it is decorous for me to tell you!' She cast her own gaze towards Simon and felt her cheeks grow hot. 'But if you were to press me, I would say that Sybille was restrained.'

Jude's eyes sparkled with curiosity. 'Did it hurt?'

'Not beyond bearing,' Matilda said, and gave a small shiver, thinking that what had been almost beyond bearing was the pleasure and the alchemy between man and woman that changed everything in its wake. Gold was dross. Dross was gold. The burden of love was light as a feather and heavy as lead – if love it was, and not the glamour of the night dazzling in her eyes. She could not explain such things to her sister. Instead she smiled and squeezed Jude's hand.

'My heart is gladdened,' she said. 'I cannot pretend to be cast down when I am not . . . although I could wish that the circumstances were different.'

'You mean Mother?' Jude bit her lip. 'I . . . I did not want to go with her,' she confessed. 'When Lord Simon said I was to stay, I felt glad . . . and then I felt guilty because I was glad.'

Matilda embraced her sister. 'I feel that way too; but if we had gone with her it would have been to no avail. Simon would have sent men after us before we had gone half a mile. Indeed, I doubt he would even have allowed us out of the gates.'

'Is that what you were thinking when you went to him?' There was a note of admiration and a tinge of envy in Jude's tone. 'That it was better to play by his rules than Mother's?'

Matilda looked down at her hands, and then at her new husband. Her heart swelled. 'No,' she said softly. 'I went to return his cloak . . . and it became my marriage bed.'

CHAPTER 26

Northampton, November 1087

A cold winter rain slashed against the walls of the palace. It had been dark all day, for the shutters had been closed against the inclement weather and the only chinks of light came from angled windows high up near the roof beams of the hall.

In their private chamber Matilda approached the bed where Simon lay. Beneath his left leg was a linen cloth to protect the winter coverings of Norwegian furs. The cold, wet weather and his own restless energy had caused his old injury to trouble him. Not that he had admitted as much, but after two months of marriage Matilda was becoming more adept at reading the language of his body. It was difficult, because he gave so little away. He was either good-humoured or impassive – as controlled as her mother, but without the coldness. She took the glimpses of his true self he yielded to her, but was unsatisfied and ravenous for more.

She did at least know that he abhorred being confined. He refused to stay abed longer than it took his body to rest in sleep, or to lie with her in the act of love and procreation. She was also discovering that the latter might as easily take place in a stable, under a tree in the woods, or in the arbour of her garden as in their chamber.

Today's vicious weather had confined them to quarters,

though, and she had insisted that rubbing his leg with a soothing balm made from the herbs in the garden would give him ease.

'I ought to be out on the walls,' he said.

Matilda hiked up her skirts to climb on the bed, making sure that he got a glimpse of thigh above her gartered hose. 'Why?' she asked. 'No one else is. It is true that folk can work in the rain, but not when it comes down like arrows and is so cold it is almost ice. One day will make no difference.'

He gave an impatient grunt. 'But one day will become two, then three, then four. I promised the King I would make all haste to secure this place with a keep and strong walls to protect the town. I want to give him a good report of the work's progress.'

'And so you shall, but not if you push yourself beyond your endurance and become too sick to make your answer.' Straddling him she took a dollop of balm onto her fingers and applied it to his leg. There was a misshapen lump where the broken edges of bone had fused together. She knew that he suffered more pain from the old injury than he was prepared to admit. Late in the day, if he had been particularly active, she would see the tension in the skin around his eyes and his gait would become progressively uneven and stilted. A comment that he should rest would draw forth the reply that he was not an invalid. If she pushed further, he would become quiet and self-contained, effectively shutting her out.

With firm pressure, she rubbed the balm into his leg. He had condescended to remove his hose, so she knew that while his conscience dictated that he should be elsewhere it was not strong enough to override other considerations. The aromatic tang of chamomile, meadowsweet and warm undertones of bay filled the chamber as she pressed and smoothed with long strokes of her thumbs. She felt his body relax beneath her ministrations. His lids grew heavy, but they did not close.

A fresh burst of rain spattered against the shutters like a handful of flung shingle. He pushed his hand beneath her skirt and stroked her thigh with a languid hand. Matilda gasped at his touch then gasped again as he quested further.

'I fear,' he murmured lazily, 'that in trying to ease me you have only made the situation worse, indeed much worse.' Cupping her buttocks he pulled her up his body and raised his tunic. 'The stiffness has moved, and if you do not relieve it then I will go mad.'

He filled her with such heat and strength that she felt as though she were riding upon a burning brand. Her mother would have been horrified at the notion of fornicating in almost broad daylight, when anyone could have walked in on them but Matilda cared not. It was not a holy day when the priests said that a couple must not join, and if it were a sin to take her pleasure above her husband she would confess later.

It did not take long, for both of them were fired by the piquancy of what they were doing. In moments, Matilda was shuddering in the throes of pleasure, her teeth clenched to muffle the cry that might bring Jude or Helisende hastening in upon them. Seizing her hips, Simon lunged up into her body, and she felt the frantic surge of his release.

For some time there was no sound but the harshness of their mingled breathing. Then Matilda sat up, pushed loose strands of hair from her face, and giggled. 'Have I then saved your sanity?' She rocked on him, enjoying the last flickers of pleasure.

He laughed and she felt the humour tremble through his body into hers. 'No, you have rendered me witless.' The rigidity of lust had departed his expression to leave it soft and tender. He ran his hands up the long bones of her thighs and stroked her skin gently.

Matilda shivered. 'I think it would take more than this to render you witless,' she murmured. 'Indeed, I am the one who is in danger of losing myself.'

Outside the weather lashed at the shutters. 'Imagine if you had married my mother,' she said as she regained her breathing and climbed off him. It was a thought that visited her on odd occasions – usually ones like this. Judith had retired to her nunnery at Elstow and they seldom spoke of her, but her shadow still lingered.

He caressed her braid as she lay down at his side. 'I do not dwell on it,' he said quietly, 'because I married you. I openly admit that from the moment I saw you in the garden at Northampton, I wanted you in my bed. I did not have the same reaction to your lady mother.'

'But if she had said yes, you would have taken her to wife?'

'Yes, I would have done it. I doubt we would have made each other happy, but we would soon have arranged separate households.'

'And do I make you happy?' She played with a loose thread on his tunic.

'Have I not just given you the proof of that?' he said and kissed her.

It was an answer and it was an evasion. But she was afraid to push him, lest his pleasure in her was indeed no more than masculine lust for a nubile female body. What she had was enough. It was greedy to seek more. But she had never been good at suppressing her appetite.

The next morning the rain had stopped and the work could go forward again on the new walls and castle of Northampton. Matilda rode out with Simon to observe the progress of the builders. Workmen's huts and shelters were clustered on the site and straw had been thrown down to absorb the worst of the slurry from yesterday's heavy rain. The sky was grey and there was a cutting wind from the north. Matilda blew on her fingers and watched Simon go among the men. He had a way with them, was swift to comprehend, and allowed neither his rank nor his disability to stand in his way – especially the latter. She winced as he began climbing the scaffolding with one of the masons. Small wonder that his leg required so much tending when he would not rest it. Indeed, he seemed determined to prove that he had more power of endurance than any man in his retinue.

What her father would have made of the Norman keep rising above Northampton town, or of the encircling walls, she did not know. In the ten years of her mother's widowhood, Northampton had grown as the presence of the dowager Countess and the frequent visits of her illustrious family attracted traders. It had been much smaller when Matilda was a little girl and her father alive. Now the place warranted a castle. Simon said that the King had sanctioned its building because he did not feel secure on the throne and was ensuring that men loyal to him had every means of holding their lands. Castles were the Norman method of exerting control over each other and the English. They were here to stay, no matter the opposition to their building. At least, she thought, Simon had compensated the occupants of the twenty-three houses that had been pulled down to make space for the foundations of the keep. She had made sure of that by encouraging him when he had seemed in doubt. He had accepted the conscience-nudging with patience, the sexual bribery with enthusiasm and finally admitted with a grin that both were superfluous since he had been intending to compensate the people from the start.

Matilda spoke to her groom and he helped her to dismount. Holding her gown above the mud, she moved among the workmen at the foot of the scaffolding. One eye cocked to the antics of her daredevil husband, she joined the masons' wives who were standing around the warmth of a cooking fire. Broth and a pease pudding in a cloth were boiling in the same cauldron over the flames, and one of the women was frying griddlecakes. The savoury, smoky aroma made Matilda's stomach growl. Tentatively one of the women offered her a cake, and seemed both delighted and surprised when Matilda gratefully accepted.

At first Matilda was puzzled by the woman's attitude, but when she thought about it realised that until recently her mother had been the highest female authority here and would not have deigned to dismount from her horse, let alone join a group of artisans' wives at their domestic fire. Matilda, however, had an affinity for such gatherings. They gave her a sense of companionship, of belonging. All the affection she had ever received in her life had come from folk of lesser degree than her exalted mother and she instinctively gravitated towards them.

The griddlecake was smoking hot with a crisp brown outer crust and a tender white centre. Matilda did not think she had ever tasted anything so wonderful, lest it be the fried fat bacon and toasted wheaten bread that the gardeners shared with her on early summer mornings outside their hut.

'The changes come quickly, my lady,' ventured a woman whose husband was one of the trench diggers. She spoke in English but Matilda understood her well enough, for she had her father's ear for language and although her mother had disapproved of Matilda speaking the tongue she had recognised the usefulness of comprehension.

'Indeed they do,' Matilda said between mouthfuls.

'Your mother was a fair mistress, I'll give her that,' the woman said, holding her hands out to the warmth of the fire. 'Exacted every penny that was her due, but we always received justice.' She tilted her head to one side and studied Matilda out of rheumy eyes. 'But it was your father we loved, God rest his martyred soul.' She crossed her scrawny bosom. 'And since you are his daughter, we love you also.'

Matilda had crossed herself too at the mention of her father. Now she blinked to stem a sudden rush of tears. 'You are my people. I will do my best for you . . . and so will Lord Simon.'

The woman pursed her lips. 'He will do his best for himself,' she said boldly but without insolence. 'But a woman of English blood who can gentle him and who understands us is a boon. Some say as you are overly young to the task, but you have been well schooled, and you have learned to shoulder burdens early.'

'And what do the people say of my husband, other than

that he will do his best for himself?' Matilda asked, a note of
challenge in her voice. She was nearly but not quite offended.

Her companion shrugged. Taking an iron poker leaning
against the spit bar, she riddled it among the flames. 'That
he is a Norman and one of the new king's supporters. That
he is like a cat and that folk should not think that just because
he treads softly he has the gentle ways of the old lord.'

Matilda thought that the assessment was probably right,
although she was stung by the way the woman said 'Norman'
as though the word alone was an insult. She drew herself up
and dusted the griddlecake crumbs from her hands. 'My
father loved Lord Simon as a son,' she said. 'He gave to him
his own cloak on the eve before he died, and it is a sign of my
husband's right to this earldom that he has brought it back
to me. Lord Simon will make this place great and prosperous.
The town walls will protect you all. More people will come
and trade will flourish.'

The woman smiled and rested the poker back against the
spit bar. 'Aye, my lady,' she said. 'I am sure that it is fitting.
May you always look upon him the way that you do now.'

Was that a word of warning? Matilda narrowed her eyes,
but the woman had lowered her gaze and would not meet
Matilda's scrutiny.

There was a sudden flurry of curtseying among the other
women. Turning, Matilda found Simon standing at the
entrance to the shelter. His hands and clothes were muddy,
stone dust smeared one cheek and his eyes were bright with
relish.

'Well?' she said, holding out her arm so he could curve his
around it and lead her out among the buildings. 'What will
you have to report to the King?'

He looked smug. 'That this town will be the equal of York
in size when it is done – which is fitting, since York bears
tribute to your ancestors, does it not?'

'My grandfather Earl Siward is buried there,' Matilda said.
'Your white bear cloak was originally his.'

'Well then, I will lay another York at your feet.' He glanced at her sidelong. 'Why do you smile like that?'

Matilda walked carefully through the mire, trying not to slip while keeping the hem of her gown from trailing in the mud. 'Because I have never seen York to know what it would look like at my feet.'

Simon's gaze widened in astonishment. 'Never?'

She shook her head. 'Indeed, I have never seen any place larger than Huntingdon or Northampton. When I was a child, if my mother travelled to Winchester or London she would leave Jude and me with our nurse. This is our world.' A defensive note crept into her voice. She knew how strong Simon's desire was for new experiences and places. The only time he was still was immediately after making love. Even in sleep he was restless and as often as not would steal all the covers. Matilda, however, was as happy toiling in the tranquillity of her garden as she was going about grander business. 'You have been the companion of kings,' she said. 'You are accustomed to the large towns and grand palaces. I may be the daughter of an earl, but my life has been simpler.'

'Mayhap so,' Simon said, 'but I would enjoy showing you different places.'

'And I would enjoy seeing them,' Matilda said, and felt a qualm of excitement and a larger surge of misgiving at the notion.

He smiled. 'Good, then you can attend the Christmas court at Westminster with me.'

'The court!' Matilda's voice became a squeak.

'Why not? It is true that the King is a bachelor and keeps other bachelors around him, but at Christmastide there will be barons present with wives and daughters. After all, you are the King's kin within the third degree. It is only fitting that you should be seen at court . . . and Jude too.' He gave her hand a squeeze. 'It is time you saw something of the world around you.'

*

'Well?' Simon grinned. 'What do you think to the royal palace of Westminster?'

Matilda's eyes were at full stretch and still she laboured to take everything in. They had arrived as a frosty winter dusk was falling over the city, whitening the buildings with a glitter of silver rime. The cold weather had gripped for several days, and the air burned as she drew it into her lungs.

'It is big,' she said inadequately, as she faced the many buildings that made up the precincts of palace and church. Here the English King Edward was buried in the cathedral that had been his life's work. Here too were his royal apart-ments, now the domain of King William Rufus, blazing with torches to light the way of visitors and guests.

Simon grinned. 'Is that all you can say?'

She dug her elbow in his ribs. 'Does it have a garden?' she asked sweetly.

'I . . . umm . . .'

'You don't know,' she pounced, and her own lips curved at having jolted him out of his smugness.

'I was always too much occupied on my lord king's busi-ness,' he said loftily.

Matilda laughed and wagged her finger at him. 'In that case you might as well have been anywhere, and you have no advantage over me.'

Simon was spared from finding a suitable answer by the arrival of the grooms to attend to their horses and a steward to show them where to pitch the tents they had brought with them. The sward outside the King's hall was already a mass of coloured canvas, but a space had been reserved among the ranks that were closest to the hall.

As Simon's men set to work with canvas, rope and tent pegs, a fair-haired knight emerged from one of the erected tents. He had large hazel eyes and a look of natural good-nature.

He greeted Simon with a hefty slap on the back and an ear to ear smile. 'Well, my lord,' he said, 'is an English earldom to your taste?'

'Very much,' Simon replied and, drawing Matilda forward, introduced her to Ranulf de Tosny. 'A friend in arms and in wine cups,' he said ruefully.

'My lady.' The knight bowed to her, and Matilda encountered admiration and amusement in his eyes. 'Simon has ever managed to land on his feet. I had heard rumours of his marriage, but not that his wife was quite such a beauty.'

Matilda reddened. Until she had wed Simon compliments had seldom come her way, and she was still unaccustomed to dealing with praise and to seeing open appreciation in men's eyes. Her growing awareness of her feminine power was only matched by the fear that she was climbing too high too swiftly. Her husband said, 'Dare.' She obeyed him, and then was terrified to look down.

'And he did not tell me that he had such gallant friends to call upon,' she responded, finding the words from the uncertain depths of her new confidence.

Ranulf de Tosny laughed. 'Mayhap he does not want too many rivals,' he said. Then his gaze fell upon Jude, who was standing modestly at Matilda's side. And the focus of his attention changed.

'This is my younger sister, Jude,' Matilda said.

Jude dipped a curtsey and De Tosny bowed. 'You didn't tell me that your wife had a sister either,' he said softly to Simon.

'A good shepherd is always prudent when wolves are sniffing around,' Simon replied with a smile but a warning note in his voice.

'Is that an insult?'

'Common sense when I remember some of our days and nights at court – or should I say some of your days and nights?' Simon retorted.

Ranulf snorted. 'Then you do not remember your own now that you stand on the other side of the stockade?' He winked at Matilda and Jude. 'I could tell you some tales.'

Simon cleared his throat. 'Tales would be all they would

be,' he said, although Matilda was fascinated to see that his colour was high. Thinking of their marriage bed, knowing his penchant for exploration, she was certain that there was no smoke without fire.

Ranulf de Tosny fiddled with the handsome buckle of his belt. 'Tales are the language of the court,' he said. 'A whisper here, an insinuation there. Always in the background, no matter the loudness of what you hear on the surface.'

Simon raised an eyebrow. 'And what tales would be rife at the moment?'

De Tosny shrugged. 'I will leave the tellers to spin their stories themselves. Suffice to say that Bishop Odo is stalking the court and casting his web as he goes.'

'Ah,' Simon nodded. 'The old spider is still at his tricks then?'

'More than ever. The old king was his brother, but that did not stop him from intriguing. Now he has nephews to manipulate, and he thinks them considerably more malleable than his iron fist of a brother.' De Tosny looked around. There was no one to hear, but still he drew in his horns. 'I will talk to you later once you have settled in.' He slapped Simon on the shoulder. 'I would not like your sheep to freeze. Lamb always tastes sweetest when it is warm.' He bowed again to the women, smiled incorrigibly for Jude's benefit, and, blowing on his hands, vanished into the deepening blue twilight.

'You keep some interesting friends,' Matilda said with amused curiosity. 'Does he really have such a bad reputation with women?'

'Only with women who have a bad reputation themselves,' Simon answered – 'but he is known to play outrageously close to the knuckle with the chaste wives and daughters of barons who attend the court. Fingers may not have been burned, but there have been some narrow escapes.'

'Is he betrothed or married?'

'Not as yet,' Simon said blandly.

Matilda nodded and said nothing, but she missed neither her sister's furious blush, nor the tone of her husband's reply. Everyone cast webs she thought, only some did it with more subtlety than others.

Matilda was accustomed to comfort and luxury. Even if her mother had leanings towards a religious life, she had also believed in maintaining the dignity of her status and the hall at Northampton had been as well appointed as any in the land. However, nothing had prepared her for Westminster's great hall. Charcoal burned in decorative wrought-iron braziers, giving off waves of glowing red heat. The walls bore the smell of new limewash, and gleamed, as yet unblackened by successive layers of smoke. Embroidered woollen hangings ran in horizontal bands along the walls, and colourful shields and banners decorated the higher reaches. Lower down, obscuring some of the hangings, great swags of evergreen had been hung to enhance the festive season and resinous forest scents added to the melange assaulting Matilda's nose. The floor was thickly strewn with dried reeds and scattered with herbs that gave off a pleasant aroma as they were trampled underfoot. The gardener in Matilda identified lavender, bergamot and rue.

There were one or two women in the hall, but they were vastly outnumbered and, to Matilda's astonishment, outdressed by the men. She had to prevent herself from staring as a plump baron traipsed past. His tunic of salmon-pink wool with yellow silk sleeve linings was wearing him rather than the other way around. His ankle boots were of goatskin dyed green with silk lacing and he was wearing green and yellow striped hose. Luxurious dark-brown hair tumbled to his shoulders and caught glints of red in the candlelight.

'Close your mouth, sweeting, it is not seemly to gape,' Simon murmured in her ear.

'You must have thought us very dull when you came to Northampton,' she said as another man passed, every finger

adorned with gem-set rings and his tunic sparkling with
hundreds of seed pearls and little gold beads.

'The old king's court was somewhat more staid, I agree,
but this is the Christmas feast and an opportunity for all to
dress in their most exaggerated finery.'

Matilda's own finery consisted of a gown of dark green
wool embellished with a necklace of irregular polished amber
beads that had once belonged to her paternal great grandmother. Jude wore wine-red with a cross of gold. Dowdy by
no means, but they resembled two nuns in comparison with
the garish butterflies surrounding them. Even the bishops
and archdeacons were part of the display, their silk copes stiff
and glittering with thread of gold.

'Your father would have enjoyed this,' Simon remarked.
'He would have outshone them all . . . and I mean that in a
praiseworthy sense.' He squeezed Matilda's hand. 'Although,
truth to say, his daughter is a more than worthy representative.'

She laughed. 'You do not need to play the courtier with
me. Male birds always have the brighter plumage, do they
not?'

Simon grinned at her retort and tweaked one of her braids.

'But I think you are right about my father,' she added softly.
'I remember he wore gold bracelets at his wrists. I can see them
now . . .' For a moment she was a tiny child, watching her
father push aside the well housing. She had a clear image of
his hands, the long fingers, the red hair growing strongly on
their backs, the cunningly worked bracelets and the way they
slid together and clinked musically on the bones of his wrist.
'My mother hated them, but I thought they were beautiful.'

'He wore them at his marriage,' Simon said. 'He had cropped
his hair and shaved his beard for your mother. He was going
to remove his bracelets too, but I said he should keep them.'
He smiled wryly. 'I was thirteen years old, what did I know?'

'Him,' she said with lucent eyes. 'You knew him.'

'Perhaps.' Simon shrugged and bit his tongue on the

comment that Waltheof had probably had more in common with a thirteen-year-old boy than the woman he had been about to wed.

An usher arrived to lead them to a long dais at the end of the hall where the new king sat with a gathering of courtiers. The sight of William Rufus at close quarters almost caused Matilda to stop walking but a quick prod from Simon restored her pace. She lowered her eyes, swallowed the urge to giggle, and, once they reached the foot of the dais, sank in a deep curtsey.

Above her, she heard the creak of the high-backed seat as Rufus rose. She was engulfed in a powerful embrace, set on her feet, and brought eye to eye with the King, who was built like a barrel and not overly endowed with height.

'Cousin Matilda, welcome to Westminster.' Rufus' voice was as loud and harsh as the call of a crow and hurt her ears. His hair was pale sandy-blond, with a centre parting exposing a broad forehead and framing the ruddy, wind-burned complexion that had given him his nickname. He wore a tunic of clashing bright red splashed with green embroidery that reminded Matilda of a whoremonger whom her mother had once whipped from the parish.

'I am pleased to be here, sire,' she replied.

'God's Holy Face, but you resemble your sire – does she not, Simon?'

'Indeed, sire,' Simon answered gravely. 'She has his courage and his joy in life.'

'But let us hope not his judgement, eh?' Rufus laughed, and his barrel belly shook.

Matilda went crimson.

'She resembles her mother too,' Rufus continued tactlessly. 'She too could give you a look that would shrivel your cods in your braies. Although I warrant she does not shrivel yours, eh Simon?'

'Not in the least, sire.' Simon's tone was level, revealing neither amusement nor anger. The courtier's mask, Matilda thought. Was this how he survived at gatherings like this?

'Aye, well she's got the hips on her to breed you some fine sons.' So dismissing Matilda, Rufus turned his attention to Jude. 'Now this one looks more like her mother, although I hope she doesn't have the temper to match.' He chucked Jude beneath the chin. 'A pretty little doe, aren't you?'

Jude blushed and looked down. Rufus let her go and turned to Simon. 'What did you do with my sweet cousin, their mother?' His tone suggested that he considered Judith anything but sweet.

Simon cleared his throat. 'The lady expressed a preference to retire to her devotions with the nuns at Elstow, sire.'

'Hah, I should think you were overjoyed. I doubt she has mellowed with the years.'

'Her leaving was to our mutual agreement,' Simon said with quiet dignity.

Rufus snorted. 'I used to wonder what my father saw in you – until that time you came to my aid when everyone else stood back. Not all that glitters is gold, is it?'

Smiling ruefully, Simon plucked at his plain reddish brown tunic. 'I most certainly do not glitter, sire.'

Rufus gave Simon a punishing blow on the shoulder. 'When you do, I will have cause to worry.' An imperative gesture furnished Simon and the two women with a place at the side of the main trestle. Goblets were set before them and expensive wine poured to the brim.

Matilda strove to keep her revulsion from showing on her face but the effort made her tremble. She felt as if she had been pawed over and besmirched.

Simon lightly laid his hand over hers. 'Let it slide from you like water off a duck's back,' he cautioned, murmuring in her ear so that it looked to a casual observer as though he were speaking love words. 'It is the only way.'

Matilda had an opinion on that, but a sense of self-preservation held her from voicing it. She took a long drink and prepared to endure.

Rufus demanded to know how the building work was
progressing at Northampton and Simon gave him the relevant
details. Quietly observing the King, Matilda saw that he
could not be still for a moment, that he had to twitch and
gesture and interject comment. He belched and farted as if
he lived on a diet of onions and cabbages, and he laughed
aloud at some of the riper sounds and stenches.

How, she wondered, could her mother and this man have
sprung from the loins of the same grandparents? And how
could Simon bring himself to serve such a sovereign? And
yet, as she watched and listened, her hands folded in her lap,
she began to see glimmers of a different personality beneath
the crude and garish façade. William Rufus was acting the
fool, but acting was not the same as being one.

Later, when the King had retired to an inner chamber with
two handsome young attendants, Simon led Matilda and Jude
among the other barons to make introductions. Matilda
quickly learned that the swirl and current of court politics
was as deadly as a river in spate. There were men whom
Simon called friend with open smiles and relaxed manner,
others he treated with wary courtesy, and sometimes, beneath
her hand, the muscles of his arm grew as hard as iron and she
could almost see the hair rise on his nape.

Roger de Montgomery, Lord of Shrewsbury, and his sons
were one such group. Matilda curtseyed to them as Simon
bowed. As she straightened, her gaze was trapped by the most
handsome of the four men. He had hair as black as midnight
water, eyes of pale, crystal grey and features that were so
chiselled and clean that a stonemason would have wept. His
dark colouring and strange eyes were set off by a magnificent
court tunic of dark blue silk lined with the deep purple-red
hue that only the richest in the land could afford. His name,
she learned, was Robert de Bêlleme, and from the way Simon
was standing she understood that her husband disliked him
intensely.

'We heard that you had wed at the behest of England's

new king,' declared Montgomery. His tone indicated that congratulations were not in order. 'And that you are to be invested with the title of Earl of Northampton.'

'You know better than I how the mill wheels of court gossip grind the corn of destiny,' Simon replied and made to move on.

Montgomery caught his sleeve. 'If I listen closely to what is said, it is because I am a prudent man. It may be that your title is not worth the air of its speaking. William Rufus has been anointed king, but some say that it is not his right to inherit the crown.'

Simon raised one eyebrow. 'Someone once said that it was not his father's right to take England's crown, but I see few of them at court today. Still,' he shrugged and smiled, 'it is a fact of life that gossip-peddlers – like whoremongers – will always be amongst us.' He drew his arm from beneath Montgomery's clasp and moved, ushering Matilda and Jude before him.

'So will halfwits and cripples,' said Robert de Bêlleme in a voice that was as precise and balanced as his features. 'But I know which have the more value to me.'

For a moment Matilda thought that Simon was going to turn round and lash out at his tormentors, but with formidable control he continued to walk away. His complexion, however, was ashen, and his eyes fierce gold with fury. Matilda's own anger, slow to kindle, burned hot at the core for the insult that had been cast at Simon like a spear.

'How dare they,' she said through clenched teeth.

Simon strode blindly. Near the door he paused in a draught of icy air and drew several slow, deep breaths.

'Trouble?' enquired Ranulf de Tosny, detaching himself from another group of courtiers and joining them.

Simon shook his head. 'Only my own,' he said. 'Take care of Matilda and Jude will you?' Without waiting for a reply he went outside, his stride swift and uneven with the anger that still gripped him.

'It seems that he does trust a wolf with his sheep after all,' De Tosny said, but in a preoccupied way, his eyes on Simon. He turned to the women. 'What happened?'

Matilda told him and De Tosny glanced towards the Montgomerys, distaste apparent in every line of his face.

'Their blood is tainted,' he said. 'Not a good one among them.'

'They seem to be in like company,' Matilda said angrily. 'I used to wonder why my mother shunned the court, but now I see that she had good reason.'

De Tosny grimaced. 'It was not always as dangerous as this. You have come at a time of change and turmoil. There is a new king on the throne, but some here believe that his older brother has the better right to sit there.'

'Meaning the Montgomerys?'

De Tosny's gaze slipped from hers. 'Among others,' he said warily. 'Robert of Normandy would not hold the reins of government as tightly as Rufus, and certain lords would be able to take their chances.'

From his behaviour, Matilda judged that he did not want to name the 'certain lords' and was anxious not to be pressed. It was of no consequence. She would ask Simon. The thought of her husband drew her eyes to the night sky framed in the doorway.

'He needs a moment's stillness to regain himself,' De Tosny said as he saw her look. 'He will return soon enough.' A wry smile lit in the depths of his eyes. 'Even if he has left you and your sister with me, he is still a diligent shepherd.'

His words were intended to soothe and reassure, but Matilda's nurturing instincts remained perturbed. Murmuring her excuses, she went in search of her husband.

Outside the air was freezing and the frost had grown a coat of silver-white fur. Matilda shivered and folded her hands together inside her mantle. It was double-lined wool, but still it did not entirely protect her from the bite of the winter evening.

She found Simon not alone, as she had expected, but deep in conversation with the hugest man she had ever seen. He must have stood around two yards tall and his girth was such that it almost blotted out the horizon. His face was so fat that it resembled an inflated bladder of lard. Beside him Simon looked like a scrawny waif from the gutters.

Seeing her, the enormous baron ceased talking. The look he sent her was shrewd and for a moment lustfully apprecia-tive. Simon turned. A frown flickered briefly and was gone. Holding out his hand, he drew her to his side.

'May I introduce my wife, Matilda, daughter of Waltheof of Huntingdon. Matilda, this is Hugh Lupus, Earl of Chester. Hugh's mother and your grandmother Adelaide are half-sisters, so you are cousins of a degree.'

Leaning forward, Hugh Lupus kissed Matilda loudly on both cheeks. 'And delighted I am to greet you . . . cousin,' he said a trifle salaciously.

The smell emanating from the man of sweat and scented oil in equal proportions was so overpowering that she almost heaved. His lips were wet and red and slightly obscene.

'A rare beauty you have there, Simon, look at those Viking bones.' Stepping back, Hugh Lupus eyed her up and down as he would a brood mare at Smithfield horsefair. 'You must be glad her mother rejected you, eh?'

Simon paused, but Matilda did not sense any anger as there had been when confronting the Montgomery clan. Indeed, there appeared to be a glint of wry amusement in his eyes. 'Overjoyed,' he said dryly.

'And you should count your blessings too, lass,' Hugh Lupus added, wagging a sausage-thick forefinger at Matilda. 'Simon is one of the best.'

'I only have to look around me to know that, my lord . . . with all respect,' she said a trifle tartly.

Hugh Lupus threw back his head and gave a great, wheezy laugh. 'Beauty and spirit,' he said. 'Nearly makes me wish I had been sent to Northampton in your stead, Simon.'

'Since you're her cousin, and a man already wed into the bargain, I doubt you would have had much success,' Simon retorted.

'I seldom let such trifling matters stand in my way.' Slapping Simon on the shoulder with sufficient force to make him stagger, and winking broadly at Matilda, he went on his way.

Matilda gave a small shudder of relief. Her cousin or not, she thought she would prefer him to keep his distance. 'I was worried about you,' she said.

He turned to her, his breath a coil of white vapour in the freezing air. 'Without cause. All I needed was a moment to recover.'

'You didn't get it though.'

He pulled her against him and slipped his hands beneath her mantle to find and grasp hers. 'Mayhap not, but Hugh Lupus is an old acquaintance. We understand each other, and he too has no love for the Montgomery clan.'

'Why do they bait you?'

He twitched his shoulders. 'I have never been at odds with the father Roger de Montgomery – until recently, but I have always had small tolerance for his son Robert and he for me. He takes men's weaknesses and mocks them. From boyhood, it has ever been his pleasure to inflict pain.' His eyelids tightened. 'I have been on campaigns with him and seen what he does to prisoners. Where there is war, there is death, I accept that; I am not a soft-hearted fool. But sparing men on the battlefield in order to torture them at leisure and for sport is a different matter.'

'Robert de Bêlleme does that?' Matilda remembered the arresting pale-grey eyes and shivered.

'And more. Your father stood up to him once on my behalf, and after that De Bêlleme did everything in his power to harm your father's standing with King William.'

Matilda bit her lip. 'And now will he harm your standing with the new king?' she asked

Simon shook his head and began to walk along the pathway

between the buildings, the way through the shadows illuminated by star and torchlight. 'Not in the least,' he said. 'Rufus views the Montgomery family with suspicion, and rightly so. The Conqueror might have bequeathed this kingdom to his namesake son on his deathbed, but his eldest, Robert, claims that it should have been his.'

Matilda nodded. 'And the Montgomerys support Robert's claim. Ranulf de Tosny told me.'

Simon sighed. 'They have been reticent on the matter thus far, but their leanings are common knowledge. It is also common knowledge that Odo of Bayeux supports his eldest nephew's claim. I do not believe he is at court now to make peace with Rufus, but rather to stir up support for Robert. I have no doubt that before the twelve nights are out I will be approached and asked to change my loyalty. That was what Hugh and I were talking about when you came upon us.' He rubbed his palms over his face and pressed his fingertips against his lips.

'What is Robert of Normandy like?' Matilda gave him a look filled with curiosity.

'Pleasant, good-humoured, indolent. He is skilled with a sword and lance – a fine soldier, if not a fine general.' He returned her look. 'What are you thinking?'

'I was wondering if he would make a more fitting king than Rufus,' she said. 'After all, Robert is the eldest son, and Rufus is . . .' she paused, searching for a diplomatic word.

'A buffoon,' Simon finished for her. 'A coarse, loud clown with a weakness for handsome young men and the clothes of a quean.' They paused at the river's edge to watch the lapping sparkle of black water, reflected torchlight quivering on its surface. 'You are not alone in your wondering,' he said, 'but anyone who has glimpsed beyond the first impression will know that Rufus is by far the better choice for England. Robert talks, but Rufus acts. Robert can fight, but Rufus is the better general and he has a superior grasp of the day to day task of ruling. Robert would promise all to everyone, do nothing and this land would dissolve into chaos.'

'So why do such as Bishop Odo and the Montgomerys support him?'

'To their own ends. Chaos and the wherewithal to go their own way would suit them very well. They would be able to create their own little kingdoms.'

Matilda absorbed this and eyed her husband thoughtfully. 'But do you not desire a small kingdom for yourself too?'

'I have as much as I need and at the King's gift,' he said. 'To take more would only be biting off more than I could chew. Believe me, my love, Rufus is by far the better king. Hugh thinks so too, and since his lands border those of Montgomery he will be a check to their ambition.' He stooped to pick up a stone from the path and throw it into the water. There was a splash and torchlit ripples shimmered towards their feet.

'You become accustomed to negotiating the difficult waters of the court,' he said. 'The rules for survival are to say little and observe everyone – listen to what they say, both with their voices and their bodies, watch with whom they associate, and talk with the servants who are in a position to know what goes on behind locked doors.'

'You do all this?'

'When I am at court – yes.' Matilda made a face.

'It is a skill to be learned like any other.' He faced her. 'Those who master it prosper, those who do not struggle. When you dwell at court for a long time it becomes a part of your nature. My father was King William's chamberlain and I learned the skills early. Your father did not have them, nor did he wish to learn. He took every man and woman as he found them, and in the end his trust was his downfall. He had no shield and they cut him down.'

Matilda shivered. The words found a hollow place within her stomach and lodged there like a leaden weight.

'And what if Robert's faction prevails?' she asked. 'What if they cut you down too?'

He raised his hand to stroke her cheek. 'Robert's faction will not prevail,' he said. 'And much as I loved and respected your father, I am not him.'

Matilda laid her fingers over his, but she could take no comfort from his warmth, for the winter evening had set a bone-deep chill over everything and her flesh was numb. She remembered her father telling her that all would be well, and that it had been a lie, because nothing had been well from the moment he rode out. Now Simon, in his own way, was asking her to trust him. But if she did, would she be paid in false coin and one day find herself abandoned to face the world alone?

Simon looked at her shrewdly. 'Come,' he said, 'let us go within. At least, whatever the company, the braziers are warm. Besides,' he added, trying for lightness, 'I would leif as not leave your sister in Ranulf de Tosny's care for too long a time.'

Matilda smiled, but it was only a token stretching of the lips. The sooner they were away from court, the better, she thought and for the first time in her life she found herself sympathising with her mother.

CHAPTER 27

Nunnery of Elstow, July 1088

The nuns were harvesting raspberries in the gardens beyond the west wall of the chapel. Matilda itched to join them and indulge in the satisfaction of plucking the ripe red fruits from the bushes, but that was servant's work, and since she was on her mother's territory she was doing her best to abide by her mother's rules. Relations between her and Judith were tepid, but Matilda had made the effort to bridge the chasm opened up by her marriage to Simon, and to her surprise her mother had built the foundations of a bridge on her own side of the divide. They would never be close, but at least they were on speaking terms.

She was not the only visitor to Elstow on this bright summer afternoon. Her grandmother, the formidable Countess Adelaide of Aumale, had been dwelling in the guesthouse for the past month, attended on by a host of servants and nuns. She was suffering from severe joint ache in her hipbones and could only get about with the aid of a walking stick and the support of a sturdy maid. The pain and the inconvenience had sharpened her naturally irascible temper until it was like a new blade.

'So then,' she said, looking Matilda up and down, 'all praise be to God that you carry a child in your belly. I

was beginning to wonder if De Senlis had empty seed
sacks.'

Matilda flushed and pressed the flat of her hand against
her stomach. 'I am glad for your concern, grandmère,' she
said, 'but there is no cause.' She was entering her fourth
month of pregnancy. The sickness had recently abated and
the exhaustion of the early weeks had been replaced by a
feeling of wellbeing and energy. Hence she had felt suitably
fortified to pay a visit to Elstow whilst Simon was absent on
the King's business.

'Hah, being forced into marriage with a cripple is more
than enough cause,' Adelaide snapped.

'Simon is not a cripple, and I was not forced,' Matilda said
with angry indignation. 'Indeed, I was very willing, and I
have not a single cause for regret.'

'Doubtless they will come later,' Adelaide retorted sourly.
'Look at your mother. Hot with lust for your father she was,
burning up with it. Nothing would please her but that she
had him, and look what happened. Ended up they could not
bear the sight of each other.'

'Mother!' Judith said sharply. She had been listening to the
exchange though taking no part, but now she launched a
protest. 'You are raking over old coals. It is in the past and a
matter I would rather you did not discuss.'

'Because it shows your weakness,' Adelaide said. She
wagged an admonitory forefinger at her daughter. 'You could
have had the cream of the young men of Normandy, but you
chose that wastrel Waltheof Siwardsson instead. I always
knew it would end in grief.'

'Grief or not, grandmère, his name is revered,' Matilda
said fiercely. 'Pilgrims swarm to his tomb, and even Normans
say that he was falsely executed. King William himself
repented of the deed after it was done.'

Judith rose to her feet and walked away from the conversation, distancing herself. Matilda remained and faced her
grandmother, determined to hold her ground.

'He was executed for treason,' Adelaide snapped. 'For plotting against the King and attempting to set a Danish pirate on the throne.'

'The men who instigated the plot were not executed,' Matilda pointed out. 'One still rides free, and the other languishes in prison, but they both have their lives. What about the barons who are in rebellion against William Rufus? Will they face beheading if they are defeated? I think not.' She spoke in the deliberate knowledge that her grandmother's half-brother Robert of Mortain was one of the rebels, and that it was only by the slimmest of decisions that Adelaide's husband and son had opted to support William Rufus.

Two spots of colour like badly applied rouge blossomed on Adelaide's cheeks. 'You were a small child when your father turned traitor, you could not know.' Raising her walking stick, Adelaide pointed it at Matilda. 'He ruined your mother's life with his drinking and his irresponsible ways. He could no more rule his lands than could an infant in tail clouts.'

'That was still no reason for him to die.'

'Reason enough,' Adelaide said harshly. 'He did not deserve to live, and I made sure he did not.'

There was something so chilling in her tone that it raised the wisps of hair at Matilda's nape. A creeping silence grew, and with it a terrible sense of foreboding.

Judith turned from the embrasure and paced back across the room, the hem of her gown swishing the rushes. 'Mother, what did you do?' Her voice was quiet but its cadence could have sliced stone.

'Nothing of which I am ashamed.' Adelaide clutched her stick like an unsheathed sword. 'When that weakling husband of yours was arrested, you came to court and said that you disowned him because he was a traitor. Your uncle was disposed to be lenient for your sake and merely banish him, but I knew that could not be allowed to happen. Banishment would not have meant banishment for such as him. Come a

year or two, he would have returned – likely in the company
of Danish pirates to judge from his previous behaviour.' She
paused to draw a breath, the gold cross she wore around her
neck flashing erratically. 'I persuaded my brother that where
there was leniency, there would be regret.'

'You sealed his death warrant,' Judith whispered. Her
complexion had turned the unhealthy hue of parchment.

Matilda stared between her mother and her grandmother,
icy prickles running up and down her spine.

'Don't be so foolish!' Adelaide's light brown eyes glittered.
'Your uncle would never have changed his mind on my word
alone. Those of whom he sought counsel were all agreed. Your
uncles Odo and Robert for certain, and Roger de Montgomery.'

'All who had their axes to grind,' Judith said harshly.

'You had your own axe to grind as well, daughter. Or
perhaps sealed up in your nunnery you forget how desperate
you were to be rid of your husband. You begged me to help
you, and you were content when I said I would see what could
be done.'

'I wanted him banished, not dead. Jesu God, Mother!' The
oath burst from her and she clapped her hand to her mouth
too late.

'Hah! For ten years you dwelled as mistress of his earldom.
Not until your uncle died did you relinquish your grip – and
only then out of your own folly.' Adelaide's face was pinched
with malice. 'Does not the Bible say that a man should not
remove the mote of sawdust from his neighbour's eye until
he has removed the plank of wood from his own? You are as
guilty as I am, daughter – more so because you could not bind
Waltheof to your side and prevent him from folly. He was
weak, you should have moulded him. When you could not it
was left to me to do the only thing possible and make sure
we were rid of him for good!'

'No, Mother, you did it for yourself,' Judith cried. 'For
your precious son, because you wanted to see him Earl of
Huntingdon!'

'And you complied, daughter . . . do not missay me, for you are only looking at your own reflection.'

The cold prickles down Matilda's spine worked inwards to her belly. Suddenly she felt so sick that there was scarcely time to leap to her feet and reach the corner where she retched violently into the rushes. Her vision turned speckled black at the edges and her knees buckled.

'Now see what you have done!' she heard her mother snap. 'If she miscarries, you can add another murder to your tally.'

Dimly Matilda felt her mother's arms fold around her, and she tried to thrust her away. 'Do not touch me!' she gasped. 'I want none of you.'

Judith avoided Matilda's half-fainting efforts at rejection and gripped the harder. 'Whether you do or not, you have no choice,' she said grimly. 'Now calm yourself. You do not want to harm the child.'

The last words reached Matilda's mind and anchored her by a thin thread to reason. For the sake of the baby she managed to draw a steadying breath. Through her struggle for composure, Matilda realised that Judith too was fighting for balance. Her mother's breathing was as harsh as her own, and she could feel the tremors pass through her flesh as though they were one body.

Behind them there was a rustle of straw as Adelaide pushed herself to her feet and, leaning heavily on her stick, limped from the room without another word. Judith started to pull away but Matilda would not let her go and clung to her fiercely. Digging her fingers into the dark wool of her mother's sleeve, she forced her to meet her gaze. 'Swear to me that you had no part in my father's death,' she whispered. 'Swear to me.'

Her mother's throat worked. 'That I cannot do,' she whispered, 'although I wish to God that I could.' She closed her eyes. 'You were so young, and you adored him as much as he adored you. You never knew the other side of him – the feckless fool who would drink himself into a stupor at the slightest excuse and had less than a child's grasp of politics.'

'So you ended his life for that?'

Judith's eyes flashed open. 'I did not know that my uncle would execute him. I thought that he would be banished. The guilt torments me. No matter how long I pray on my knees to God, the burden does not ease. Yes, I wanted him gone from my life, but not at the cost of his life . . . If I had known what was to happen, I would have begged my uncle to spare him.'

Matilda released her grip on Judith and sat back, tears streaming down her face. Cold, proud, unyielding as granite her mother might be, but an accounting of the truth had always been essential to her, no matter how bitter the fruit.

Judith rose to her feet and stepped away from Matilda, gathering her own composure around her like a cloak. A swift brush of her hand across her lids, a slight sniff was as much as she yielded. 'I tried,' she said, 'but it was not enough. You might as well have mated fire and ice and expected one to survive.'

'And what of me, Mother?' Matilda demanded in a choked voice. 'If I am a mingling of your blood and my father's, how am *I* to survive?'

Judith's expression assumed its customary frozen composure. 'Perhaps, out of all the women in this family, you will emerge the most unscathed because you have the ability to bend rather than break. That at least your father has given you to your advantage. Besides, whatever differences I have with your husband, he is a man of ambition, familiar with the ways of the court. And he is Norman. The challenges of your marriage will not be the same as mine.'

'Then what will they be?' Matilda whispered.

Judith shrugged. 'Simon de Senlis is like a tomcat,' she said. 'He seeks a warm hearth at which to curl up in the winter and all the comforts that home provides. But come the spring, when there is prey to pursue and territory to explore, you will not keep him. That is why I am glad that you have the ability to bend.'

Matilda knuckled her eyes again and rose clumsily to her feet.

'I could have had him for my husband,' Judith said. 'The babe growing in your belly could now be growing in mine. Remember that. He wed you out of ambition and necessity. You accepted his offer because it was convenient, because you were attracted to him as you are to all waifs and underdogs, and most of all because he was wearing your father's cloak.' She looked at Matilda, her brown eyes hard but not hostile. 'I say these things for your own good. Bear them in mind and do not let yourself become carried away on a surfeit of minstrel's tales of love. That is the way to survive.'

Hooves clattered in the guesthouse courtyard alongside the sound of male voices. Smearing away her tears, Matilda went to look out of the double-arched window and saw her husband dismounting with an escort of knights and serjeants. They were all wearing either mail or quilted tunics and the horses were sweating and hard-ridden. She saw her grandmother hobble over to Simon and speak to him, using her stick for emphasis as usual. Simon smiled, bowed and answered her with a courtier's polish.

Her mother's words had made Matilda feel wretchedly queasy because they struck at the core of her fear. They had been cruel too, even if they did have an element of truth. Despite, or perhaps because of them, her heart turned over. She needed Simon. Needed the strength of his arms, his re-assuring words, and most of all she needed him to take her away from here. Spinning from the window, she hurried to the door, flung it open and ran down to the courtyard.

Simon turned, a broad grin spread across his face, and he opened his arms. Matilda flung herself into them like a desperate fugitive grasping a sanctuary knocker. Adelaide sniffed scornfully and stumped away in the direction of the church.

'Tears?' Simon brushed his thumb across her cheek. 'What's all this?'

'Nothing.' Matilda shook her head, although it was a great deal more than nothing. 'I will tell you later.' She squeezed him fiercely. 'It is so good to see you. When can we go home?' Her voice shook.

He held her gently at arm's length and looked her up and down. 'It is too late in the day to ride for Northampton,' he said, 'but there is nothing to stop us from spending the night at Oakley . . . if that is your wish.'

Matilda rested her forehead against the cool, metal rivets of his hauberk. 'Yes,' she said. 'If you are not too tired from the road.'

'Nothing that a cup of wine and some food will not refresh,' he replied as a couple of squires led the horses away to the trough in the yard. 'We have ridden hard, but not so much that a few more miles will make any difference.'

Matilda nodded, sensing that he had no more desire than she did to rest tonight beneath her mother's roof.

Moonlight spilled through the open shutters and cast silver-grey light on the bed and the naked flesh of the entwined man and woman. In the aftermath of lovemaking, Simon had been telling Matilda about the fighting in the south. Bishop Odo and the Montgomery family had raised rebellion against King William Rufus, declaring that the Conqueror's first son, Robert, should be king. Rufus had mustered his supporters and hastened to deal with the insurgents. Montgomery had surrendered, but Odo had had to be prised out of Rochester like a winkle hooked out of its shell with a silver pin, only instead of a pin Rufus had used thirst and starvation, his endeavours aided by a plague of flies.

'The garrison had to take it in turns to eat while their comrades brushed the insects from around them,' Simon said with a grimace. 'We could smell the city rotting from our positions outside the walls. Men, horses, dogs . . . Once you have experienced such a stench, you never forget it.'

Matilda, whose own knowledge of bad smells was confined to memories of the days when the gong farmers emptied out the cess pits, shuddered at his words. Yet, she did not try to stem them. She understood his need to speak rather than have the memories fester within him.

'Montgomery went to negotiate with them. At first they wanted their liberty and their lands in exchange for their surrender and oath of homage, but Rufus could see that he had them in a cleft stick and he refused. He said that they might have their lives and their weapons. Those who still had horses could keep them and ride out.' Simon was silent for a moment, threading his fingers through her hair.

'They came in double file,' he resumed, 'holding on to their dignity despite the fact that they stank of the midden, their lips cracked with thirst and their bodies covered in sores. Rufus had the victory trumpets sounded from our ranks, as loudly as the heralds could blow. The common Englishmen who had been drawn from their fields to serve in Rufus' ranks jeered and poured scorn on them, crying out that they should be hanged.'

'What did Rufus do?' Matilda asked.

'He stood back with a smile on his face and let them give tongue,' Simon said. 'What more proof did he need that he was King of the English than to let the English scream his name in approbation and bay for his enemy's blood? I think that he is a cunning general and a shrewd politician.' He spoke without admiration.

'So the danger is over now that Bishop Odo and the Montgomerys have been brought to heel.' She moved closer to him.

'For the moment. Odo may continue to scheme, but he is growing too old to involve himself in the strain of battle. When he rode out of Rochester on the surrender he was carrying his years like a heavy sack on his shoulders. I do not believe that he will return to England – unless in the aftermath of an invasion if Robert prevails – which I doubt will happen. As to the Montgomery faction, they surrendered and survived by a whisker this time, but their powers in England will be checked by the likes of Hugh Lupus and Fitzhaimo of Gloucester . . . and me.' He gave a humourless smile. 'Now there's a task to relish.'

Matilda pressed her nose against his flesh and felt the tickle of his chest hair. She did not want to think of him being involved with the Montgomerys in any way. 'But you will be staying at home a while?' Hearing the anxious note in her own voice, she bit her lip. She knew that he hated to be fettered, and yet she needed a modicum of security – and following the revelations at Elstow she felt terribly vulnerable.

He spread his fingers, webbing her glittering hair across them. 'A while, yes,' he said in a soothing voice. 'I have a castle to build, and a son to see born. Enough for any man.'

Matilda hugged him in gratitude for a moment, but then her head came up. 'What if I should bear a daughter?' she demanded. 'My mother bore two girls, and her mother before her. My uncle Stephen did not arrive until my grandmother was past her fortieth year.'

Simon shifted position to look at her. Raising his thumb, he brushed the furrow from her brow. 'If you should bear a daughter, then no matter. I will still cherish her, and she will be but the first. You do not have to follow the pattern laid down by your mother and her mother before her, do you?'

'I will never follow their pattern,' Matilda vowed fiercely. 'Never.' She clenched her fists. 'If our child is a daughter, she will grow up loved and valued and the only duty I will impose on her is that she love and value others the same.'

Simon stroked her back. 'That seems a fine notion to me,' he said soothingly. 'Pride is no bad trait to possess, but too strong a measure can taste of bitter grief. I do not believe your grandmother was ever happy in her triumph, or even satisfied. And you have seen how it is with your mother. She has grown a shell to shut out the hurts of the world, and now it has so many layers that she is trapped within it.'

Matilda lay against him and gazed out of the shutters at the swollen white disc of the moon. She had not had to tell him much about her grandmother's part in her father's downfall. He had been a squire at court, and knew already. When she had asked him why he had not told her, he had shrugged.

'The art of keeping silent is one I have learned to value,' he had said, and would not be further drawn.

As always she was left with the worrying feeling that she did not know him at all, and the knowledge that in contrast he knew her very well indeed. Perhaps he understood about her mother's shell, she thought, because he dwelt inside one of his own, and the art of silence was part of that carapace. If only she could breach the defences and truly know him as he seemed to know her. If only she could prove her mother's words wrong.

The moon sailed across the unshuttered aperture and disappeared, leaving a dark blue sky ablaze with stars. Matilda watched the night, and for the first time felt the flutter of new life within her womb.

CHAPTER 28

Northampton, Spring 1090

Simon had put all of Northampton's wealth on show to honour the marriage of his sister-in-law Jude to Ranulf de Tosny of Conches. The trestles in the newly completed great hall were draped with bleached linen cloths. On the high table the napery was embroidered with English gold-work, and the flagons and cups set out for the guests were fashioned of silver gilt and rock crystal.

Seated beside her husband on the high dais, Matilda watched the bridal couple sip from the loving cup and eat off the same trencher. Jude's silky dark hair was uncovered in token of her virginity and fell in two thick plaits to her waist. A bridal chaplet of daisies, may blossom and fresh greenery was bound at her brow and she wore a gown of red wool with sleeve linings of blue silk. The bridegroom seemed much taken with his wife, as well he might, Matilda thought. Jude not only looked lovely but had a sweet nature, and the lands that she brought to her marriage were enough to make any man rush to make his vows.

'I would have liked our own wedding day to be as great an occasion as this one,' Simon said and briefly covered her hand with his own.

Matilda gave him a startled look. Had she seemed wistful? She thought not. 'Mayhap,' she said, 'but I do not miss gilding the lily. When we were little, Jude would plunder our mother's coffer, try on her finest veils and most elaborate girdles. It was always my task to keep watch and make sure that she was not caught!'

Simon laughed. 'But surely you enjoy gilding the lily just a little? That shade of blue suits you well.' His gaze wandered appreciatively over her figure, as slender as if she had never borne a child.

Matilda blushed. 'A little,' she admitted, 'but I do not yearn.'

He looked amused. 'Most women of my acquaintance would sell their eye teeth to be the centre of attention tonight.'

'Indeed. And with how many women are you acquainted?'

'Enough to count my blessings.' He kissed her hand.

'Spoken like a true courtier,' Matilda said, smiling, but with an edge to her voice.

Their banter was curtailed by the arrival of Helisende, who had managed to make her way down the side of the hall, threading through servants bearing flagons and steaming platters.

'My lady, your son is awake and crying fit to bring down the rafters.'

'I have never known a child so greedy,' Simon said, looking pained.

Matilda smiled and as she rose, tugged a lock of his hair. In the more relaxed atmosphere of Rufus' rule, the short crops of the Conqueror's reign were giving way to longer styles, and Simon's tawny brown hair now rested level with the neckband of his tunic. She liked it that way, for the depths of her mind harboured a dim memory of her father's hair at that length, sweeping against his cheek as he played with her in the garden. 'He takes after you,' she said.

Simon gestured at his trencher. 'I do not know how you can say that,' he declared with a glimmer of amusement. 'I am no glutton at the board.'

'I was not talking of food,' Matilda retorted pertly. She left with the sound of his chuckle chasing the shadows from her heart, and went to feed their son. At seventeen months old he was well on the way to being weaned, but still woke on occasion and nothing would content him but the comfort of suckling at her breast.

His birth had been easy, for Matilda had the large bones and wide hips of her Norse ancestors and the baby, although healthy and vigorous, was of Simon's build. He was placid and good-natured, with abundant copper-red hair and eyes of deep sea-blue. It had been only fitting to christen him for the grandsire he so clearly resembled.

She watched him as he nursed and felt a surge of deep and tender love that was almost a physical pain. He was walking; his vocabulary was developing rapidly and soon he would not need the security of her breast. The time of dependency was fleeting and, cling tightly as she might, nothing could prevent these moments from slipping through her hands like silver into the darkness of a well.

'It is a great pity that your grandmother is not here to see what a fine child he is,' Judith remarked from the doorway.

Matilda looked up with a start. She had been so absorbed in tending to her son that she had not seen her mother arrive. 'It is an even greater pity that my father is not here to see his first grandchild,' she replied, and the generous curve of her lips was suddenly tight.

The birth of a son had forever changed the relationship between them, for in producing a boy Matilda had accomplished what Judith had not, and the balance of power, already in Matilda's favour, had shifted further. Indeed, following that terrible day at Elstow Judith's manner towards her daughter had changed. She had become more conciliatory, more willing to listen, and much less critical. Mention of Adelaide was still enough to strain the atmosphere, though. Adelaide had died of a flux shortly after little Waltheof was born. Matilda had not attended the funeral, for she had still been recovering from the birth, but she had been more than glad of the excuse and it bothered her conscience. She should be able to forgive, and it disturbed her that she could not.

'Indeed it is,' Judith said with a sigh. 'He loved small infants – far more than I ever did. But then perhaps that was what attracted me to him in the first instance – his joy and innocence.'

Matilda looked down at the suckling infant and kept very still. It was the first time that her mother had ever spoken of her marriage to Waltheof in less than disparaging terms.

'He was not afraid to laugh or weep,' Judith said, 'and I had been raised in a household where to do either was unseemly. I thought that your father could teach me how to do both, but it proved beyond both our capabilities.' Her voice stumbled, and looking up Matilda was disconcerted to find her mother's eyes filling with tears. Perhaps it was because the season was so close to the anniversary of his death. The morrow's eve.

Judith blinked, clearly irritated with herself. 'I came to remind you that we should begin the bedding ceremony – before the men grow too drunk to stand.' She made an abrupt gesture. 'I did not mean to speak of your father. Perhaps I have drunk a goblet too much myself.'

The baby gave a milky belch, and a white dribble appeared at the corner of his mouth. 'Full to the brim,' Matilda said, aching to see her mother retreat behind the familiar wall of frozen dignity. 'I am glad that you did,' she said softly. 'I have so little of him to keep.'

'You have the best parts,' Judith said. 'I do not know whether to envy or pity you.'

Matilda gestured the nurse to take the baby, and repinned the deep neck opening of her gown. 'I want neither your envy nor your pity. They won't make any difference, will they?' Rising to her feet, she shook out the folds of the dress in a gesture designed to end the conversation and smooth her ruffled emotions. 'Come, or else they will begin the bedding ceremony without us.'

The air of constraint between mother and daughter was swiftly banished as they exchanged the peace of the women's chamber for the hall where the wedding celebrations had developed a raucous edge. Women and men had separated off, the former surrounding the bride, the latter the laughing groom.

Matilda paused briefly at Simon's side and gave a worried glance towards Ranulf de Tosny. 'I hope he is not too far in his cups that he hurts Jude,' she said.

Simon squeezed her waist. 'You need not fret on that score. 'It is mostly high spirits. After the first two cups I made sure that the wine was watered. Cheaper for me that way too,' he added flippantly. 'Besides, I didn't want to be in my cups either.' His hand moved briefly over her buttocks, revealing that he was not quite as sober as he claimed.

Matilda laughed and pushed him away. 'We shall see,' she said with a look through her lashes, and went to join the women.

Jude was brought to the main bedchamber. Usually it was reserved for Simon, Matilda and their immediate attendants, but tonight they had vacated it in honour of the bride and groom. A new crisp, lavender-scented sheet had been spread tightly over the feather mattress. In the morning, stained with the bride's virgin blood, it would be hammered to the wall behind the dais table as proof that her husband was the first man to touch her and that any child born nine months from this time would be of his loins. There was a covering sheet of bleached linen, a woollen blanket, and a counterpane of embroidered silk that was part of the wealth that the bride brought to her marriage, silk being literally worth its weight in gold.

With great ceremony the women stripped Jude of her garments and combed her hair until it lay in a shining skein down her back. Seeing how much she was shivering, Matilda folded her in a wrap of beaver fur while they awaited the men.

'It will be all right,' she murmured and kissed her sister's temple.

'I know it will,' Jude said with a tense smile. 'Sybille told me everything . . . the way she told you. If it were left to Mama, I would be as innocent as a spring lamb. And if I had believed everything that Ranulf told me before the wedding, I'd not be a virgin now!'

That broke the tension and Matilda started to giggle. So did Jude. The raised eyebrow of disapproval they received from their mother only increased their mirth.

Footsteps sounded outside the chamber door, and the wood resounded to the thump of a fist and loud voices craving entrance, with many jests about 'forcing portals' and 'turning keys in greased locks'. Judith's frown deepened and her lips started to purse. Pushing aside the maid who had been about to admit the men, she raised the latch herself and, throwing the door wide, blocked the threshold with her body.

'I thought dragons were supposed to be hot, not cold,' slurred Ranulf's brother Roger, wavering where he stood.

Ranulf flourished a bow in Judith's direction and managed to stand upright again without falling over, revealing that he was reasonably sober. 'Madame belle mère,' he saluted her. 'I have come to claim my bride, if you will but yield her to me.'

Matilda saw that he was wearing Simon's bearskin cloak – useful because it draped him from collar to ankle, the surplus length folded like a cape around his shoulders. Beneath it, he was naked save for his shoes.

Judith inclined her head in return. 'Treat her well,' she said in a voice that cut across all their jesting and merriment like a whip, 'or you will answer to me.' She gestured stiffly for the men to enter the room then stepped back.

'I will cherish her all my days,' Ranulf replied, although his eyes were now on his bride, not his mother-by-marriage. 'Why should I not when she has beauty and lands and she sets my heart alight?' He took Jude's hands within his own, his expression soulful, laughter dancing in his eyes.

'You would be surprised how many men find reason once they have grown bored of the taste of the fruit,' Judith retorted. Her spine as rigid as a broom handle, she returned to the middle of the room, determined that a degree of propriety should be maintained.

'Not me,' Ranulf said confidently.

Judith gave him a hard stare. 'I hold you to it,' she said, and ushered forward the priest to bless the couple and the waiting bed.

That ritual performed, Ranulf swept his bride up in his arms and placed her amid the sheets to a chorus of halloos and yells of encouragement.

'I need no help this night,' Ranulf retorted cheerfully and tossed the bearskin cloak back to Simon.

'Well, just call out if you do,' Simon grinned.

Ranulf's teeth flashed in response. 'If you hear me shouting, it will be for a different reason entirely!' he quipped, causing Jude to blush fire-red.

More whistles and bawdy comments followed, but the wedding party took the hint and trooped from the room on a final volley of advice and good wishes.

The wine continued to flow and the kitchens continued to supply bread and small pastries, stuffed figs, honey sweet-meats, and tender slivers of lamb marinated in wine, cooked on a griddle and served on beechwood skewers.

Simon and Matilda mingled among their guests who showed no sign of flagging. Matilda danced with Earl Hugh of Chester and fended off his determined attempts to flirt, finally escaping on the arm of her uncle Stephen. The latter was only two years older than she, with a mane of thick flaxen hair, ice-blue eyes and his father's cleft chin. Folk said he was one of the few members of the house of William of Normandy who actually looked suitable to wear a crown.

'Do not you dare call me uncle,' he said as they moved and turned in the pattern of the dance. 'It makes me feel like an ancient greybeard, and I'm scarce old enough to grow a whisker. Cousin will suffice.'

'I would not dream of giving you grey hairs,' Matilda said sweetly, and playfully tapped his arm. 'It was good of you to come.' She liked Stephen. Her mother had been avoiding him rather grimly all evening.

He bowed. 'It was good of you to invite me,' he said gallantly. 'There was a time when my parents cultivated notions of acquiring your lands for my inheritance. I would have understood if you had chosen to keep me at arm's length or even barred your gates.'

Matilda warmed further to his charm and candour. 'You are welcome whenever you choose to visit. My husband is sure enough of his own abilities not to feel threatened. Besides,' she added with a swift glance around to make sure that her mother was not within earshot, 'we are neither of us our parents.'

'Thank sweet Christ for that!' Stephen declared, adding hastily, 'I will say nothing against my mother, God rest her soul, nor against my father, because he is not here to defend his reputation . . . but I do not have their eagerness to saddle up a horse named Ambition.'

'Everyone has ambitions,' Matilda said. 'But of different kinds. Perhaps if you had not had everything given to you on a golden platter, you would be hungrier.'

He frowned at her for a moment, but then looked thoughtful. 'I suppose that is true. My mother was always fleeing from the fact that her mother was a laundress and my father was deposed of his own lands in Champagne. But I have what I want. If I strive, it is only to please them.' His eye corners crinkled attractively. 'What of your own ambition, cousin?'

Matilda smiled. 'That is easy,' she said lightly. 'To stay awake long enough to see these nuptials to their close.' She was learning from Simon, she thought. How to fend off probing questions. How to hide what she did not wish to reveal.

The dance ended and they parted. Hugh of Chester was ensconced in a corner, a girl on each ample thigh and his legs spread to allow breathing space for his crotch. Matilda avoided that part of the room. Simon was deep in conversation with Abbot Ingulf of Crowland, and her mother was talking with members of the Tosny family. Unobtrusively, Matilda slipped among the crowds, a word here, a murmur there. Her eyes felt gritty; she was tired, but she bolstered herself with a cup of wine. What *was* her ambition? Her brow furrowed at the thought. To live without looking over her shoulder to the past. To be surrounded in the warmth of a love as deep and thick as a winter pelt. Whether or not such ambition was attainable was another matter.

Had she known it, ambition was also the subject of Simon's conversation with Abbot Ingulf.

'Indeed, I have seen strange and changing times,' the Abbot said, shifting his leg to try to ease the gout that was plaguing him. 'I was a clerk in the household of the Holy King Edward and it was there I first learned my trade. Got to know Normans too.' He bestowed Simon a wintry smile. 'It stood me in good stead because I learned that we are all the same in the eyes of God.'

'Indeed,' Simon said politely. Abbot Ingulf was garrulous and the evening was growing late. Although Simon had never needed a great deal of sleep, the length of the day was beginning to tell. He clenched his jaw to suppress a yawn.

'When King Edward died, I left the royal service,' Ingulf continued and refreshed his goblet, obviously prepared to settle into a long, enjoyable monologue. 'Harold Godwinsson had his own preferred clerks and I was still a young man with a young man's restlessness. It is true that I had travelled many roads with King Edward's court and seen more of England in my youth than most men see in a lifetime . . . but that only increased my wanderlust.' He took a swallow of wine and washed it round his mouth. 'Serving the King, there had been little time for God, so I packed my satchel, took up my staff, and went on a pilgrimage.'

Simon forgot to be bored and turned to the Abbot with a new gleam in his eyes. 'Where did you go?'

'To the Holy City of Jerusalem,' Ingulf said, a ring of pride in his voice. 'And there are not many men who have done that in a lifetime either. Some say they will go, but by the time they are ready it is too late and their bodies are not strong enough to withstand the journey. Certainly I could not do it now. I doubt that my legs would permit me as far as the Narrow Sea.'

Simon gazed at him. The spark of interest had rapidly become a flame. 'What was Jerusalem like?' he demanded and poured wine into his own cup, all notion of sleep thrust aside.

Ingulf smiled. 'Not paved with gold, as some will tell you, but golden in its own way, with the sun shining on the stones and all the candles gleaming within the Sepulchre. To walk in the dust where Christ walked is the most humbling and exalted experience a man can have. I have seen Gethsemane, and the rock of Golgotha, and the very place where Our Lord was entombed.'

Ingulf spoke on and Simon listened, rapt, as the Abbot told him of the great Byzantine cities with their cisterns and fountains, of lands perfumed with exotic spices and heat and dust beyond imagination.

'Of course you would have to go yourself, to truly know what it is like,' Ingulf said in a voice that was growing creaky and hoarse. Two further cups of wine had disappeared down his gullet and he was starting to slur his words. 'And while you are still young enough to do so. The way is arduous and there are many dangers.'

'I intend to,' Simon replied fervently. 'Even as a child I relished setting my feet on different ground.'

The Abbot smiled sceptically. 'Mayhap you will, and mayhap not,' he said. 'I have known many men – and some women – swear to see Jerusalem when the fire is in their eyes, but it goes no further because it is easier to dream than to do. It was simple for me. I had no master, and I could not return to royal service. But others have harder shackles to break.' He lifted his gaze and swept it meaningfully around the hall. 'You would have much to leave behind, my lord.'

Simon nodded, and some of the brightness went from his eyes, but a glimmer remained. 'Indeed I would, and I know that the time is not ripe, but the seed is a fruit and it is still growing. I will get there.'

The Abbot tilted his cup to his mouth, found it almost empty, and set it ponderously aside without refilling it. 'The drink does as much talking as the man,' he said. 'It is not always wise to pay heed to an old fool whose tongue has run away with him.'

'Not always,' Simon agreed, 'but is it not also said *In vino veritas?*'

'Ah, you know your Roman proverbs?' Ingulf smiled. 'Truth in wine. Perhaps after all you will succeed.' He levered himself to his feet, wincing as the gout gnawed at his toes. 'I'm afraid I have a pilgrimage to make of this moment – to the privy pit.'

When he had gone, Simon sat for a brief time alone. The Abbot's tales had stirred the old restlessness, which had been lying like sediment at the bottom of a deep pool. Now it swirled through his blood with the wine, infusing him with desire.

It was late in the night, much closer to dawn than dusk, when everyone finally settled down for the night. Since Matilda and Simon had given up their chamber to the bride and groom, they had bedded down in the women's solar with several other guests.

'What were you and Ingulf talking about so deeply?' Matilda wanted to know as she curved her arm around Simon's body in the dark when he eventually came to bed.

'Mmmm?' He turned. 'His life before he was a monk. He used to be a royal clerk, and then he went on a pilgrimage.' Simon's voice was sleepy and deliberately indifferent. He knew that Matilda would not respond with enthusiasm to the notion of his becoming a pilgrim. She would see it as abandonment. Besides, for the moment it was no more than a stirred-up dream. He folded her hand in his and pretended to settle into sleep. Within moments, the pretence had become reality.

Simon and Matilda presided over a somewhat subdued table the next morning. The bride and groom had yet to rise and only the hardiest souls had stumbled to the trestle to partake of bread, cheese and watered wine. Matilda was sleepy, but since she had not overindulged at the flagon was in a reasonable condition. Simon was rather green around the gills and she had given him an infusion of willow bark tisane to dull the worst of his headache.

'I should know better at my age,' groaned Ingulf, and gave Simon a pained look. 'Your wine is too strong and smooth, my lord. I am accustomed only to ale and water.'

Matilda did not believe that for one moment. An abbot of Ingulf's status was bound to keep a fine cellar – his guests would expect it of him.

'You were the one who sent it past your lips,' Simon retorted with a wry smile. 'I think you are annoyed at your own inability to resist temptation.'

The Abbot raised his hands, admitting culpability.

Matilda rose. 'I will go and brew a cauldron of headache remedy,' she said. 'Likely there will be many in need.' Especially Hugh of Chester she thought. By her reckoning he had sunk nearly two gallons of their best wine.

She set off down the hall but was apprehended by a mud-splattered messenger. Her steward hastened to intercept the man, but she gestured him aside, signalling that she was content to deal with the matter herself.

'I am Matilda, Countess of Huntingdon and Northampton,' she said. 'Whom do you seek?'

The messenger bowed and Matilda's nostrils twitched, for he stank of smoke.

'Abbot Ingulf, my lady,' he said and showed his teeth in a grimace of distress. 'He is needed immediately at Crowland; there has been a terrible fire.'

'A fire?' Matilda pressed her hand to her throat and felt her pulse leap against her fingers. 'Dear sweet Christ . . . How much has been lost?'

'Many of the buildings, my lady. The guesthouse, the dorter, the library . . .'

Matilda swallowed. 'What of the chapter house? What of my father's tomb?'

His gaze slipped from hers. 'There was some damage to the chapter house, but the tomb of Earl Waltheof is intact.'

Relief flooded through Matilda, adding to the shock and almost buckling her knees. Somehow she remained on her feet. It was the discipline of duty, so forcefully instilled in her by her mother, that carried her through the next moments. She brought the messenger to the dais; she sent servants to prepare Ingulf's mule and baggage. She murmured the right words, but it was all a façade. Behind the mask she was a little girl screaming hysterically as her father rode away.

'A rush dip was left unattended in the dorter when the brothers went to prayer at matins the day before yesterday,' the messenger said as a distressed Ingulf demanded information. 'It tipped among the floor rushes and caught alight, then set fire to the straw sleeping pallets. By the time the alarm was raised the place was ablaze and the flames had spread. We saved what books we could from the library, and we managed to stop the fire before it had done much damage to the chapter house.' Here the messenger darted a tense look at Matilda, who was ashen. 'I say again, my lady, your father's tomb was in no way damaged.'

Matilda nodded and clenched her fists in her gown. *But it might have been*, she wanted to cry.

'It is indeed a shock and a great pity,' Simon said, and set his arm around his wife in support. 'We grieve with you.' He gave a practical shrug of his shoulders. 'But there has been no loss of life, and dwellings can be rebuilt. Indeed, it is an opportunity to do so on a finer scale. I agree that the loss of the books in the library is a tragedy, but many can be replaced, and you have monks among your brethren who are skilled illuminators. You could have lost so much more.'

Ingulf left soon after, armed with a promise of funds from the earldom to help rebuild the abbey. In a state of shock, Matilda saw that the wedding guests were attended to, suckled her son, conversed sensibly with all, and later was not to remember a single thing she said or did. Had there been no nuptials to supervise, she would have ridden back to Crowland with Ingulf in order to see for herself that her father's tomb was undamaged.

'He did not burn, and therefore you should not torture yourself,' Simon said, looking so sincere that she knew he was wearing his courtier's mask and humouring her.

Matilda bit her lip. 'It is with me all the time,' she said. 'I cannot help but wonder. You would do so too, were it your own flesh and blood.'

'Your father was as close to me as my own kin,' Simon said sombrely. 'My blood is mingled with his in our son. It is no use dwelling on what might have happened. You are building a castle of woe for yourself out of a single grain of sand. Ingulf says that he will have your father's bones translated to the church and buried with reverence beneath the altar. They will be safe from all harm there.' He took her arm. 'God has him in his care. You should lay your own burden down.'

She shook her head, for, although she understood what he was saying, the very authority of his reason made her want to rebel. She did not want to lay her burden down, because while she had it the connection to her father remained strong. She carried it out of love, she guarded it jealously, and the notion of relinquishing it was too frightening to contemplate.

CHAPTER 29

Crowland Abbey, Spring 1093

'You are sure you are strong enough for this ordeal?' Judith asked.

Matilda nodded and valiantly swallowed a retch. She had eaten a dish of mussels the previous day and it had severely disagreed with her. They had all wanted her to remain at her manor of Ryhall rather than making this journey to Crowland, but she had insisted. Her father's coffin was to be opened so that his bones might be washed in holy water and reinterred before the altar of the repaired monastery church of Crowland Abbey. 'I am all right,' she said. It wasn't true, but she was determined to do what she must.

Judith raised a sceptical eyebrow.

Matilda turned her head from her mother's shrewd gaze and stared at the landscape through which they rode. It was late spring, and the wetlands had begun to dry out. Sheep grazed the higher ground of the reedy marshland and goats nibbled at the scrub and brambles. There was money to be made from wool. The weavers of Flanders paid good silver for the fleeces that came out of these marshlands and were shipped on galleys from Boston to Ghent.

In front of her Simon was talking with animated pleasure to his brother-in-law. She thought that they were discussing hunting, for she had heard hawking terminology mentioned several times, then Ranulf said something about a girl called Sabina and Simon laughed and lowered his voice over the reply.

Feeling hot and sick, Matilda glowered resentfully at his spine.

'It is to be expected of men,' Judith said with a superior curl to her lip. 'Their ways are like children. Few of them ever grow up.'

'Perhaps it is better to be a child than an adult.' Matilda glanced wistfully at her son, who had fallen asleep on Sybille's shoulder. She would have carried him herself had she not felt so unwell.

Judith made an irritated sound to show what she thought of such reasoning.

Matilda eyed her mother. Judith had said nothing about her own feelings towards the opening of Waltheof's coffin. Perhaps she did not have any. Or perhaps the walls she had built around herself were too strong to be broached.

'Did you never miss him?' Matilda asked. 'Don't you ever feel guilty about the manner of his death?'

For a moment she thought that her mother was not going to answer, that she was going to retreat further behind her defences, but Judith sighed and drew the reins through her fingers. 'Of course I felt guilty about his death,' she said. 'And I mourned him too – because he was a child, and the death of a child always comes harder than that of an adult.' She turned in the saddle to face Matilda. 'But he was the one who made his bed, no matter that others laid the covers. I come here out of duty, not to fall weeping over what has happened in the past.'

She dug her heels into her palfrey's flanks and rode on ahead, her back as straight as a rod, her hands competent on the reins.

'Has she been upsetting you again?' Jude joined her. Since there was only room to ride two abreast on the path, she had been hanging back.

Matilda gave her sister a wan smile. 'No,' she said. 'We were in need of a respite. We curdle in each other's company like milk and vinegar.'

Jude stroked her mare's neck. 'How do you think it will be to look on our father's bones?'

The words sent a flash of queasy heat through Matilda's belly. 'I do not know,' she whispered. Every time they came to Crowland, they would see Abbot Theodore's skull displayed with the deep bite of the sword cut in its cranium. The sight had seldom bothered her. She was accustomed to saints' bones and relics as an everyday part of her life, but Theodore's skull was two centuries old, was not of her flesh, and Theodore had not tossed her in the air, or sat her in his lap, or walked with her in a garden, his warm strong hand enclosing hers. To see those hands bereft of flesh, and the dark eye sockets . . . 'It has to be done,' she said. 'And I have to see it done . . . but I will be glad when this day is over.'

'I too,' Jude said sombrely.

Matilda shivered. With no break of trees or hills between Crowland and the North Sea, the wind was frozen and punishing. There were kindly days in the fens, but this was not one of them.

The fire-damaged parts of Crowland Abbey had been demolished and rebuilt in timber as a temporary measure. Stone had been cut from the quarries at Barnack and brought to the site in preparation for some serious rebuilding, and a French mason had been employed to oversee the work. The church itself was intact, and it was here that Waltheof was to be laid to rest, but first his remains had to be washed and wrapped in a fresh shroud of purple silk, provided for the purpose by Simon, who had bought it from an Italian trader in London.

Matilda had been sick twice since entering the abbey precincts. Her stomach was still rolling and the ginger in wine that the infirmarian had given her to abate the nausea had had little effect. It was as much the tension that was affecting her now as the bad mussels. Gripping Simon's arm, she clenched her teeth and held herself rigid as the inner coffin was carried to a linen-covered table and set down with great care.

Simon surveyed her white knuckles and fixed expression with troubled eyes. 'Do you want to go outside?'

Matilda shook her head. It was beyond her to open her mouth and speak. Cold sweat dewed her brow, and her vision swam in and out of focus. The voices of the monks, softly intoning in Latin, echoed off the walls. The infirmary had been rebuilt after the fire, and the resinous scent of new wood hung in the air. Matilda hardly dared to breathe, for even the tiniest movement upset her precarious stomach.

The wooden lid was carefully removed with the gentle levering of crowbars to reveal the inner wooden coffin. Fluid filled Matilda's mouth. She forced herself to look, although her eyes were dry and stinging. Her father was never going to ride through Northampton's gates because his soul was in heaven and what remained of his body was here . . .

Between them the monks carefully eased the lid from the coffin, and to Matilda it was like the occasions when she slid the wooden cover from the well in her garden. She still threw silver to the elf because it was a tradition ingrained, but if an elf really had popped out of the well she would have run screaming. Now she was hemmed around. Could not run, could not open her mouth to scream.

They had reburied him in the robes of a Benedictine monk, dark within the darkness of the coffin, strong cloth unrotted by the years, and knotted about the body by a girdle of rope. Within the confines of the deep cowl shrouding the skull there was a glimmer of rich copper-red. Fierce, vital, still gleaming with the life that its owner had left behind. Flesh upon brow ridges, bony dark sockets sealed with sunken lids. Not entirely a skull, but not full-fleshed either.

Matilda gulped and strove to inhale, but her chest was empty of breath. A sound of swarming bees filled her ears, and although she stretched her eyes as wide as she could there was still no light. She felt Simon's arm tightening around her like a vice, thought she heard a voice calling her through the buzzing, but it was too far away, too distant for her to respond, and the darkness was stronger.

She woke up in the guesthouse, the scent of lavender strong in her nostrils. Jude was pressing a cloth to her brow and Simon was chafing her hands. Matilda stared at them, her focus blurring and clearing by turns.

'It's all right,' Jude murmured. 'You fainted away when they opened our father's tomb.'

Matilda heaved and Simon quickly thrust a bowl beneath her, but her retching was dry. Shudders tore through her body. Simon cast the bowl aside and drew her against him, holding her hard until the spasms eased.

Although she was exhausted, Matilda willed herself to sit up and look at him. 'I . . . have they washed the bones?' she gulped. Her mind filled with the image of the coffin's dusky interior, the gleam of hair, the hint of features sunken within the recess of the cowl.

Simon drew his forefinger gently across her eyebrows. 'No, my love,' he said with a look at Jude. 'They have left them as they are.'

Matilda stared at Simon and her sister in bewilderment.

'It was thought for the best.' Simon took her gently by the shoulders. 'There is still some flesh on the bones,' he said, 'and as you saw his hair remains bright. He has been buried before the altar in the same state that they found him.' He did not need to add that the word would spread among the pilgrims and become exaggerated in the telling. Waltheof would be spoken of as an incorrupt, and a candidate for sainthood. Crowland's fame and wealth would increase with the size of the story. The abbey would be rebuilt on a grand scale with the coin from the pilgrimages and Waltheof would indeed rise from the dead with a vengeance.

'It is proof that he should not have died, isn't it?' Matilda searched Simon's face. 'Like when the slain bleed in the presence of their murderers?'

'Mayhap,' he said. 'But I rather think that the embalmer who dealt with him before they brought him from Winchester knew his art.'

Matilda rose from the bed. Her legs were shaking, but at least they supported her as she tottered towards the door.

'Where are you going?'

'To pray,' she said. 'To welcome my father to his new resting place.' She gave Simon a shadowed look. 'I can at least hope that he will sleep better than I do.'

He let her go. Turning to Jude, he dug one hand wearily through his hair. 'I wonder if she will ever be free,' he said wearily.

Jude shook her head to show that she did not have an answer. 'No,' Simon sighed, 'I do not know either.'

CHAPTER 30

February 1096

I t was the third morning in a row that Matilda had been sick. Staggering back to bed she dabbled with the notion that she might finally be with child again. Her fluxes had always been irregular, but she thought that her last one must have been before she attended the Christmas court at Windsor. Her son was seven years old and she had begun to believe he would be an only child. There had been other symptoms too, when she thought about them. Recently she had been lethargic, sleeping longer in the morning, retiring to bed early. Ordinary tasks that she usually took in her stride had seemed inordinately difficult. She had put it down to the feeling of malaise that would begin to creep up on her as the anniversary of her father's death approached. Since the opening of his tomb it had intensified; that it had begun sooner than usual had perturbed her, but she had thought it due to the distance that had recently sprung up between her and Simon.

She had tried to identify a cause but nothing came immediately to mind. It was true that she had not wanted to attend the winter feast at Windsor, but that was because of the state of William Rufus' bachelor court. Desiring to be with Simon, she had swallowed her prejudices. He had been away from home all summer on campaign against the rebellious Earl

Robert of Mowbray. Rufus had insisted that all his tenants-in-chief be present for the Christmas court, so there had been no option but to endure if she wanted to be with her husband.

The visit, she conceded, had not been entirely dreadful. Ranulf de Tosny had been at the gathering and had brought Jude with him, so the sisters had been able to spend time in the pleasure of gossip and plundering the market stalls that had sprung up with rapid efficiency around the encampment of the court. The latter had been more to Jude's taste than hers, but still, she had emerged with several bolts of Flemish wool to make tunics and gowns, a fine oak coffer decorated with wrought-iron work for the main bedchamber at Northampton, and a beautiful ivory figure of the Virgin for her private chapel. Not to be left out, Simon had acquired a fine dappled riding horse and a new belt for his sword. And between them, it seemed, they had finally conceived a second child.

Gingerly Matilda sat up. Her stomach rolled but she was able to leave the bed without retching. It had been good between them at the Christmas gathering, but something had happened there to change things. It was not that they had argued, more that since their return Simon was preoccupied and distant. Her first thought was that he had taken a mistress, but discreet enquiries and her own observation had shown it not to be the case. She had begun to worry that a grave situation was brewing. Was this how it had begun when her father had contemplated allying himself with the Danes? The long silences, the sense of being shut out? Simon had talked much with the other barons at the Christmas gathering, sometimes long into the night. At the time it had not bothered her, for she had Jude to keep her company and they had their own matters to discuss. Now, in hindsight, she wondered and worried.

Helisende helped her to dress and brought her honey-sweetened wine and dry bread. Matilda sipped the former, nibbled the latter and gradually began to feel better.

'Good for all sorts of stomach upsets,' the maid said know-ingly. 'Even those that take nine months to resolve.'

'Is it as obvious as that?'

'Well, some of the women have been whispering since you were ill yester morn, and now they're certain. And the laundress says she hasn't seen your flux linens since before the feast of Saint Lucy.'

'I should have asked them before I asked myself,' Matilda said irritably. 'Well, tell them to say nothing until I have broached the news to Earl Simon. I would rather he heard it from me than the laundress!'

'Of course not, my lady!' Helisende looked affronted. 'They're good souls, they wouldn't say anything – and if one did, I'd use a bridle to bind her tongue.'

Matilda found a weak smile. She had no doubt, knowing Helisende, that the words were more than just picturesque. 'Is Earl Simon still in the hall?' she asked. 'Or is he about his business?'

'He was in the hall when I fetched your bread and wine, my lady.'

Matilda nodded. Now was as good a time as any to tell him about the child, she thought. Smoothing her gown, checking that her wimple was straight, she went to the curtain separating the bedchamber from the solar and wondered why she felt like a soldier girding up to do battle.

The March morning was already advanced enough for full daylight to be streaming through the open shutters and her women were busy at their spinning and needlework. Of her son there was no sign, by which she knew that he was at his lessons with the chaplain. Simon's former squire Turstan was using the attraction of his new knighthood to flirt with one of the younger maids, but when he saw Matilda he came smartly to attention, and, approaching her, bowed.

'My lady, Lord Simon said to inform you that the Lord of Aumale has ridden in with his troop and is hoping to speak with you.'

Matilda stared at the squire in dismay. 'Are you sure?' she asked out of her astonishment and concern.

'Yes, my lady.' He gave her a puzzled look.

Thoughts panicked through Matilda's mind. Last year there had been a plot to overthrow the King – and Simon had spent half the year in the field helping to put it down. Her step grandfather, Eudo of Champagne, had been implicated. There had been a strong rumour that the intention of the rebels was to put his son Stephen on the throne. The rebellion had been quashed and Stephen had indignantly professed his innocence. Some of the rebels had been imprisoned; others, including Eudo, had been dispossessed of their English lands – in Eudo's case the spit of land on the eastern seaboard known as Holderness. Stephen himself had escaped punishment, but he had been lying very low ever since.

As she followed Turstan to the hall, her unsettled stomach surged and churned. What if he wanted succour? Giving it would surely be dangerous? She wondered if Simon had become embroiled in some scheme. Certainly, it would explain his recent preoccupation. And yet his loyalty to Rufus had never been in doubt and he had nothing to gain from changing sides. Reason told her that she had nothing to fear, but her instinct said differently.

Stephen was warming himself at the fire in the hall and talking with Simon. Considering that he was living under the threat of arrest he looked inordinately relaxed. The wheat-blond hair he had inherited from his father was neatly trimmed and sleeked behind his ears; his eyes were bright, there was a smile on his lips. Simon seemed to have taken his mood, for he was smiling too. Then he caught sight of Matilda, and wariness entered his gaze.

Matilda's misgiving increased, and she found it very diffi-cult to put on a welcoming expression as she advanced to greet their guest.

Stephen turned to her and, with a glimmer of shock, she saw the large white linen cross stitched to the left front of his tunic.

'Cousin!' Grasping her hands in his, he leaned left and right to kiss her cheeks. 'It is good to see you!'

'And you,' Matilda said less enthusiastically. 'A surprise too.' She gestured a servant to bring wine. 'To what do we owe the pleasure?'

Stephen gave an incorrigible grin. 'You sound the way my mother used to when she was gathering herself for a tirade. Do not worry. I am not here to inveigle Simon into turning against the King. Indeed, quite the opposite. You are to be rid of me for some time, and I have come to make my farewells.' He touched the cross on his breast.

Matilda eyed him while her suspicions grew. At the Christmas court there had been vague rumours about a crusade being called to rescue Jerusalem from the infidels. She had paid little heed at the time, but now she wished she had.

'So the cry has gone up in earnest?' Simon said, and there was a note of anticipation in his voice that set up a fresh wave of anxiety in Matilda's breast.

'Ten days ago at Clermont Ferrand. Duke Robert has sworn himself to the cause, and my uncle Odo. It is to be a great undertaking.'

The servant returned with the wine and poured it, red as blood, into three silver goblets.

'And a diplomatic way of keeping out of Rufus' way until the dust has settled.' Simon gave their visitor a knowing look.

'Oh, indeed.' Stephen tilted his head in acknowledgement. 'Not only that, but a crusader's lands are sacrosanct. Any man who dares lay a finger on them while their owner is absent fighting for Christ lays himself open to excommunication.'

'Then you have nothing to lose.'

'Except your life,' Matilda said more curtly than she had intended.

Stephen shrugged. 'But if I lose it in the service of God my place in heaven will be assured. For the moment, there is nothing for me here save exile and suspicion. I may as well spend that exile profitably. Besides,' he said, 'I have a desire to tread the ground that Our Saviour trod and to cleanse my sins at the church of the Holy Sepulchre.'

Matilda could see Simon absorbing the words as though they were liquid gold. As the wanderlust gleamed in his eyes, her fear grew. 'It seems like vanity to me,' she snapped. 'It won't be like a week's hunting in a forest lodge . . . you might be gone for years . . . You might never return.'

'I know the risks,' Stephen said nonchalantly. 'That is why I have come to say goodbye.' He tilted his head and gave her a puppyish look. 'I was hoping that you would see me on my way with a Godspeed and a smile.'

Simon folded his arms. 'You should know by now that the women of the Conqueror's line seldom do anything with a smile.'

Matilda drew herself up. Simon's comment was unfair, even if she had been teary and out of sorts of late. 'Because the men we marry give us more cause for weeping than joy,' she retorted. 'Of course I will wish you Godspeed. It just seems a rather drastic measure to take to keep out of the King's way.'

'Not as drastic as the consequences of remaining,' Stephen said. 'I'd prefer to keep my freedom and my head.'

The words, spoken with a broad, unthinking grin, fell into silence. And in that silence a look of horror and contrition spread across Stephen's face. 'I . . . didn't . . . I'm sorry.'

'If you are to stay the night, you will need a chamber prepared,' Matilda said through stiff lips. She hardly dared open them because she felt so sick. 'You will excuse me.'

Somehow she managed to leave the hall before the spasms seized her and she doubled over, retching violently.

'Matilda?' Simon had followed her out. She felt his arms go around her shoulders. 'It was an unthinking mistake on Stephen's part. You should not take it so badly . . .' There was a note in his voice that was almost impatience.

'You fool,' Matilda gasped as she struggled to control the

heaving. 'It is naught of my father.' It wasn't quite true, but her reaction was still much less about Waltheof than Simon believed.

'Then what? Are you ill?'

She shook her head. 'No,' she said, and managed to stand up, although her stomach was churning. 'I am with child.'

His eyes widened and he silently repeated her last two words. He looked her up and down. 'You are certain?'

She nodded. 'But I cannot tell you when it will be born . . . late summer or early autumn, I think. Are you not pleased?'

For answer he folded her in his arms and held her against him, as though she were made of glass. 'Of course I am pleased! How could I be anything else when it has been so long?'

Matilda wondered if she was imagining the note of reserve in his voice and decided that she was. Why should he not be overjoyed at the news? Unless, like a swallow, he was preparing to fly. She thrust the thought aside, as if ignoring it would be enough to make the possibility go away.

'Perhaps you should lie down a while until the sickness passes,' Simon suggested tenderly. 'Helisende can see to organising a chamber for Stephen, and I can keep him entertained.'

Matilda had no strength to argue. The retching session had left her feeling as limp as wrung-out linen, and her stomach was still threatening rebellion. Besides, she knew that she would be unable to listen to Stephen's tactless enthusiasm with any degree of courtesy. She was glad to retire to her chamber and lie on the bed.

'I am sorry,' Stephen said, looking chagrined. 'I am always being told that I open my mouth without thinking. I regret that she took my words so badly.'

Simon grimaced. 'She is with child,' he said, 'and thus more susceptible to women's moods.' It was not the entire tale but it was easier to explain it to Stephen thus. To describe

Matilda's insecurities since the fire at Crowland Abbey would have been pointless and painful.

'Ah,' Stephen said. 'Congratulations.'

Simon smiled wryly. 'Perhaps more than congratulations are in order. I was beginning to think that little Waltheof would be the only arrow to my bow. Unfortunately Matilda finds the carrying a trial. Last time she was beset by sickness and bouts of weeping, and this occasion looks set to be no different.'

'Mmmm,' said Stephen, acknowledging Simon's words whilst obviously at a loss how to respond to them.

Recognising the younger man's discomfiture, aware that he was not the right person to burden with his domestic troubles, Simon slapped Stephen's shoulder. 'Enough of such business. Tell me more about your plans for your journey.' Drawing Stephen to a bench, he sat down with him, and was soon deeply engrossed in the subject of the crusade.

A bitter wind whistled around the keep walls. Late in the day, it had begun to snow and the flakes could be heard sifting against the latched shutters. In the candlelit bedchamber, its corners warmed by braziers, Simon swirled the heated wine in his goblet and paced the room. Sitting in bed, Matilda looked at him with fear and misgiving. He had scarcely spoken since they had retired, and because of it, because of his pacing, she knew what he would say when he opened his mouth. She could not bear the tension, and taking the battle into her own hands she pre-empted him.

'Tell me that you are not considering following Stephen and the others on this wild foray,' she said.

His brows twitched. 'It is no wild foray, but a call from the Pope on behalf of the Holy Land,' he argued. 'All men from the Christian world are being called upon to go and do their duty.'

'There is duty, and duty,' Matilda said, and vigorously rearranged the bedclothes around her.

'Sweeting, I know there is.' He took a long drink from the cup. 'Indeed,' he said pensively. 'It is my duty that has been warring with my conscience.' Going to the flagon he poured her a measure of wine too and brought it over.

Matilda did not want the wine; her stomach was curdled enough as it was. Yet she took the cup because he had given it.

'My duty as Earl of Northampton, or my duty as a man in the service of the Lord Jesus Christ.' He gave her a wry look. 'If I have had a thorn in my hose, it is because I have been pondering the matter since Christmastide.'

Cold panic ran down Matilda's spine. 'The King gave you this earldom in good faith,' she said as steadily as she could. 'If you take the cross with all the other rebels who are doing it to keep out of his way, you will be betraying him.'

'And if I stay, I will be betraying God.'

Matilda laughed, but the sound was not pleasant. 'Let us have this out in the open. What you want to do is go adventuring,' she scoffed. 'I know you, Simon. You want to pick flowers on the other side of the hill. You are never content. When you came to this earldom, it was all to you in the world, because it was a challenge and it was new. And so was I. Now that your position is secure, you crave new experiences. God is your excuse, not your reason!' She set her cup down on the stool at her bedside with a bang that sloshed the wine over the brim and glared at him.

Simon glared back, his brows drawn tightly down and his tawny eyes ablaze. 'I used to think that you had your father's nature, but now I begin to wonder if you are not every bit the bitch that your mother is,' he retorted. 'A less patient husband would not tolerate such words from his wife.'

'A more considerate husband would not cause such words to be spoken in the first place,' Matilda snapped. 'You must have a high opinion of yourself if you believe that you have the patience of a saint. I have bedded with you and borne you a child. I carry another in my belly. I have loved you well, and if you repay me in false coin, then I swear that I will never forgive you.' Her voice trembled and it was not just the cold that made her shake as she faced him. 'Simon, think well before you make your choice . . . think very well.'

Their eyes met and held. Neither looked away. 'I have been thinking ever since the Christmas feast,' he said evenly. 'Stephen's visit only confirmed my decision. The call has gone out and I have to follow it.'

She shook her head. 'You have to follow your own selfish desire,' she said. 'That is all I see.'

'Then you are blind.' Breaking eye contact, he drank his wine and returned the cup to the trestle. 'At the Holy Sepulchre, I will say prayers for your father's soul and bring back a stone from Jerusalem to lay at the foot of his tomb.'

'Do not tell me that it is for my father's sake you are considering this venture!' Matilda cried in furious astonishment.

Simon raised his hand, palm outwards. 'Listen to me. If your father were alive today he would have been one of the first to sew a cross onto his tunic. Since he cannot, I am taking his banner to Jerusalem.'

'How can you say what my father would have done?'

'Because I knew him.'

The words struck Matilda like a slap across the face and abruptly terminated the conversation. Cruel but true. Simon had known him, and she had not. And if she thought about it in a rational way she knew that Simon was right. Her father would indeed have been one of the first.

'You will follow your intention whatever I say.' She made a weary gesture of capitulation. 'Do as you will.' She lay down, her back to him, and drew her knees up to her chin. She was so cold. It was as if a lump of ice was lodged in her stomach. If Simon went on crusade, then it would fall to her to take up his position at the centre of the wheel and she did not know if she was strong enough. *You have no choice*, said a bossy internal voice that sounded suspiciously like her mother's. *It is your duty.*

She heard his heavy sigh and, for a moment, was afraid that he was going to bang out of the room. However, he muttered an oath beneath his breath and, raising the bedclothes on a waft of cold air, joined her. His arm came around her waist, turned her over and drew her to him. He pressed his lips against her temple, her cheek, her mouth.

'I am afraid,' she whispered, and clung to him, her fingers gripping his shirt. 'I am afraid that I will bid you farewell and never see you again.' At the back of her mind was the hazy but terrifying memory of watching her father ride away to see King William. His promise to return; the emptiness of that vow.

'We cannot let fear stifle us,' he said, 'otherwise we might as well dwell in a cage.' He rubbed his hand up and down her back in a soothing motion. 'I fear the cage more than I fear the unknown.'

'So it is your fear that spurs you,' she said. 'It pushes you onward without thought for what you leave behind. Because you are lame, you must prove that there is no horizon you cannot conquer.'

His hand stopped. She heard the sharp hiss of his breath and realised with a jolt of triumph and pain that she had succeeded in thrusting past his guard. 'It is true, is it not?'

She half thought he would remove his hand, but he did not. Rather his grip tightened. 'We are all ridden by demons,' he said. 'We live with them as best we can and hope one day to throw them off.' He cupped her cheek on the side of his hand and kissed her. 'We live with each other's demons too,' he added softly. 'And perhaps that is the most difficult endurance of all.'

CHAPTER 31

Crowland Abbey, October 1096

The chanting of monks soared heavenwards on wafts of incense. Crowland Abbey's chapel was awash with liquid autumn light, burnishing the fair-brown hair upon Simon's bent head and gilding the embroidered purple pall that lay over Waltheof's resting place.

Outside the abbey gates a crowd of pilgrims waited to file past the tomb, but on the point of setting out on his journey to Jerusalem Simon was granted a moment alone with his father-by-marriage.

'I ask you to watch over Matilda and our children while I am gone,' Simon murmured, his hands clasped and his gaze fixed upon the pall with its surroundings of pilgrim offerings, both the grand and the tawdry. His expression tightened as he spoke of his wife. Matters had been strained between them for several months, each of them avoiding confrontation. He had spent much of his time away from Northampton, raising funds for the journey, discussing the venture with others who were committed and dealing with outstanding business. Matilda had taken to her garden with a vengeance until she was as brown as a peasant woman with rough work-worn hands. Advancing pregnancy had curtailed her frenetic activity, and in the two weeks before the birth she had merely sat beneath her precious apple tree with her sewing and her maids. Simon was not sure how either of them could bridge the distance without warping their natures out of true.

A cloud drifted across the sun and for a moment the light ceased to stream across the tomb. Simon decided that it was an act of nature, not an omen, but his mood was pensive as he crossed his breast and rose to his feet. 'I will see through your eyes as I promised,' he said. 'I will live each day as you asked.' He hesitated by the tomb, but the words that came so easily to him at court remained locked and tangled in his brain. 'Rest in peace,' he said with a swallow, and walked swiftly up the nave towards the daylight.

At the door Abbot Ingulf was waiting for him. 'God speed you on your journey, my lord,' he said with a deep bow. 'We will pray for your wellbeing daily.'

Simon returned the gesture. 'Your support is welcome,' he said. 'If it is God's will that I return from Outremer, I will not forget Crowland in my benefactions.'

Formal speeches over, the men clasped and embraced. In his way Simon had grown as fond of Ingulf as Waltheof had once been fond of Ulfcytel. He saw in the Abbot something of what he wanted for himself. Ingulf had been a courtier, a man of the world. He had wandered far and wide, seen all that he desired and had found his inner peace.

'Have a care, my son,' Ingulf said, a tear in the corner of his eye. 'Come back to us whole.'

'I will do my best.' Simon gave the coarse woollen shoulder a final squeeze and left Ingulf for the abbey guesthouse, where Matilda was waiting to make her own farewells.

The birth of their daughter a month ago had been hard, and although she had travelled to Crowland with him she was still not fully recovered. The weight she had gained during the pregnancy had melted from her bones following the birth, but she did not look well.

Holding the baby in the crook of her left arm, she came to him. Named for her mother, the infant had a fuzz of dark gold hair and eyes of kitten-blue. She was a fractious scrap, with the loudest squawl Simon had ever heard. Another one in the mould of Judith and Adelaide, he had decided. The blood of the Conqueror was at its strongest in the women bred from its line.

Simon took the baby into his own arms and, praying that she did not begin bawling, leaned over to press a kiss on her smooth, small forehead.

'This will be the last time that you see her as a babe in arms,' Matilda said, her voice cracking. 'When you return she will be walking and talking . . . and she will not know you.'

'There will be time enough,' Simon said, his voice impassive to hide the discomfort he felt at her words. 'While she is so little, she will not miss me.'

'There is never enough time,' Matilda said, and then stopped herself by drawing a swift, shaken breath. 'I will not send you away with recriminations . . . I made a promise to myself. But go now, swiftly, before I break that promise.'

Simon gave his daughter to Helisende and swept Matilda into his embrace, kissing her hard. Then he stooped to his son, who was watching the proceedings with solemn deep blue eyes.

'Be a good boy for your mother,' he said, 'and a fine soldier for me.'

The little boy sucked his lower lip and nodded. 'I am good,' he said indignantly.

Simon's lips twitched. He ruffled the lad's fluffy red-gold curls and stood up. 'Then be angelic,' he said, and turned to mount the horse that Turstan was holding. Drawing the reins through his fingers, he nudged the grey with his heels, clicked his tongue and, with a final salute, rode out of the abbey gates.

Some of the children who had come as pilgrims with their parents ran alongside the cavalcade, keeping pace, cheering and waving. Matilda stood where she had bade farewell, rooted to the ground. In her mind's eye she saw herself running after him, stumbling on her gown, screaming at him not to leave her. She had a vivid recollection of fighting to prevent her father from going away with his friend. Of being torn from his arms and thrown down in a pile of straw to shriek and thresh until she was exhausted.

'My lady, are you all right?'

The gentle touch on her shoulder; Helisende's concerned voice brought her around with a shudder. 'Yes,' she said, 'I am all right.' It wasn't the truth, but she could put on a brave face. After all, she was her mother's daughter.

The last horse rode out of the abbey gates, and the procession dwindled to the occasional glint of armour on the horizon. Her eyes grew dry from staring and then began to water.

'Will Papa be home soon?' Her son looked up at her, his eyes anxious with the need for reassurance.

Matilda steeled herself. 'When he has done what he must,' she said in a soothing voice that did not reflect the emotions roiling within her. 'Come, we will go and pray for him at your grandfather's tomb.' She placed a gentle hand on the child's shoulder and turned away from the road towards the abbey. For the benefit of the gathered pilgrims, she smiled. She bade an attendant take a purse of silver pennies and halfpennies and distribute them among the crowd with the exhortation that they pray for her husband's success. She gave Ingulf a smaller pouch of gold for the benefit of the abbey. Serene, courteous, doing her duty. Outwardly the great and gracious lady. Inwardly screaming with grief. Was this how her mother had felt?

'I thought I was different,' she told Helisende as she entered the chapel, its air spiced with incense and the scent of beeswax candles. Streamers of autumn sunshine fell across the purple pall, focusing the eye on the opulence and light. 'But I am not. Simon was right. I am my mother's daughter – how could I not be? And he has in him a streak every bit as feckless as my father . . . and perhaps that is why I love him and I hate him too.'

'My lady, you do not hate him!' Helisende looked shocked. In her arms the baby stirred and made a fretful little sound.

Matilda swallowed. 'I am trying not to,' she said, and knelt at the foot of the tomb, the clay floor tiles striking cold to her knees even through the heavy woollen fabric of her gown.

CHAPTER 32

Port of Brindisi, Easter 1097

Under a spring sun much hotter and yellower than that of England, Simon watched the bustle on the dockside. Brindisi's harbour jostled with all manner of craft, tethered like a herd of horses anxious to gallop across the sunspangled plains of sea beyond the harbour mouth. Gangplanks had been run out to the vessels closest inshore, and sailors, soldiers and labourers toiled to fill the deck spaces with supplies – water barrels, firkins of wine, salt meat, weapons, dismantled tents, horses, harness, soldiers.

The Norman crusader contingent, under the banners of Robert of Normandy and Stephen of Blois, had travelled down through Italy and spent the winter months in Brindisi, assembling a fleet and making the local tavern keepers rich. While awaiting the spring and the right conditions for crossing the Adriatic Sea, many crusaders decided that they had ventured far enough from home and, ripping the crosses from their cloaks, turned back. Others, finding themselves in financial difficulties, sold their weapons and took employment wherever they could find it to earn a crust and a bed for the night.

Beset by neither a waning of enthusiasm nor lack of funds, but filled with a certain degree of impatience, Simon had spent the winter exploring his surroundings, familiarising himself with the region – the handsome dark-eyed people, the food with its warm flavours of olive and citrus. He enjoyed the strange, boiled pastries they made, bland in themselves but superb when blended with meat and spices and washed down with the robust red wine of the area.

Whilst eating and drinking in the various hostelries around the harbour he had picked up a liberal smattering of the language and daily practice had improved his accent and his understanding. Weather permitting, he had ridden out with a guide to explore the countryside and the coastline surrounding the port.

On the days when rain lashed the walls of his lodging house and a bitter wind swirled smoke around the room, guilty thoughts of England and Matilda drove him to send for a scribe and write her letters detailing his progress – or lack of it. On these days too, he would think wistfully of her warmth in his bed and the soothing gentleness of her oiled fingers on his damaged leg. It was with great righteousness and a hint of self mockery that he wrote to her of his chastity. He had slept alone since leaving England. Not that such endurance was entirely the result of an effort to remain pure while engaged in Christ's business. Simon's oath to God was aided by the fact that the available women were less than appealing and free with their favours. He had no desire to sport where a hundred others had sported before him.

A crowd had gathered on the wharfside to watch the first soldiers and supplies embark, their destination the port of Durazzo on the Byzantine coast. A warm breeze was blowing off the sea, and the sailors were using their oars to row the galleys out of the harbour mouth. Each pull and scoop raised small puffs of white water upon the glittering blue. Simon joined the group of onlookers, among them Duke Robert of Normandy and Stephen of Aumale. The latter made room for Simon at his side and Simon found himself standing against a slender man of middle years, with gaunt features and black hair silvering at the temples. Immediately Simon stiffened. He knew that Ralf de Gael was a crusader, had even seen him from a distance, but this was the first time that their paths had directly crossed. While he recognised De Gael, the Breton lord obviously did not remember him, but then Simon had been a green youth at the time of Waltheof's death and beneath De Gael's notice. Twenty years later the boy was long into manhood and the former Earl of Norfolk was growing old.

De Gael smiled at Simon. 'I am not a good sailor,' he said. 'I will be glad when this leg of our journey is completed.'

'So will we all.' Simon forced himself to be civil. 'It has been a long wait through the winter.'

They watched the ships sculling out of the harbour. Gulls wheeled and screamed overhead. Someone made a comment to Robert of Normandy and he laughed aloud. De Gael looked at Simon through lids narrowed with the twin efforts of focusing and remembering.

'Forgive me,' he said. 'I feel that I should know you?'

Simon turned his gaze from the sea to fix it on the man who had trapped his friends in treason and escaped to Brittany to live a full and prosperous life. 'Likely you remember me from the Conqueror's court,' he replied impassively. 'I was a squire of the chamber and my father was one of King William's chamberlains.'

A glint of recognition lit in the eyes and De Gael snapped his fingers. They were elegantly manicured and adorned with fine gold rings. 'Ah, the lad who broke his leg – I remember now!'

'The lad whom Waltheof of Northumberland saved from having his ribs smashed into his lungs by a bolting horse,' Simon said, hunting De Gael's face for a response. The smile that had been about to break vanished. De Gael's right hand closed around his sword belt in a defensive gesture.

'I remember that too,' the Breton said softly. 'It was the most brave and foolhardy act I have ever witnessed.' He fiddled with the tongue of leather folded over the belt buckle.

'I was glad that I had not attempted it myself, but I felt diminished that I had not done so.'

Simon eyed him warily. Part of De Gael's ability to charm lay in his self-deprecating manner. He was ever the first to trample on his own pride and men . . . and women were disarmed by the trait.

'And how did you feel when Waltheof died?' Simon asked, unwilling to be taken in. 'Did you feel diminished then, my lord?'

The dark eyes blazed and dull colour suffused the fine cheekbones. 'By what right do you question me?' he demanded.

'By the right of blood,' Simon answered. 'I am wedded to Waltheof's eldest daughter, and my son is his grandson and namesake. Waltheof did not live to see his daughter grow up and wed nor his grandchildren born because he was foolish enough to trust a man who was supposed to be his friend.'

'You have no right to judge me,' De Gael said hoarsely. 'Only God can do that.'

'And I am sure that God will,' Simon retorted. He made to walk away, but De Gael grasped his sleeve.

'You do not understand. Waltheof was indeed my friend and not a day goes by that I have not regretted what happened. If I could return to my youth and undo that moment, I would.'

'Likely so,' Simon retorted, and steeled himself against the pleading in the other man's tone. 'Since you would still hold the title of Earl of Norfolk too.' He shook himself free. 'My wife carries the memory of her father like a shackle, and there is nothing I can do to free her. Do you know what destruction you wrought with your scheming?'

'Far less destruction than the tyrant who sat on the throne and persecuted from on high,' De Gael snapped. 'It was an ill-conceived and ill-timed idea, but it was born of genuine grievance.'

Simon made a disparaging sound. 'And it died in disaster.'

'I know that. I count myself at fault and, although you will not believe this because I can see you think the worst of me, I took a crusader's vow to atone for my past. In Jerusalem I will pray for Waltheof's soul and make my peace. If I die on the road, my bones will testify my sincerity.'

Simon strove to maintain his contempt for De Gael, but against his efforts found himself warming to the man's candour. It might be false – De Gael had a slick way with words – but there seemed to be a genuine chord of sadness in the older man's voice.

'I am sorry for Waltheof's daughter. She was a pretty little thing,' De Gael continued. 'I know that he doted on her and she adored him.' He grimaced. 'I am afraid that she disliked me. Even then she knew I was responsible for taking her father away from her.'

Simon thought of Matilda's strength and the counterbalance of her terrible vulnerability, most of it brought about by this man. De Gael was not entirely to blame, though. Others had played their part. 'I do not think that time has wrought any change of opinion, my lord,' he said. 'Ask your forgiveness of God, and be content with that. I do not think that we have anything more to say to each other that will be of profit . . .'

De Gael sighed heavily. 'I—'

Whatever else he was going to say was cut off by a loud expletive from Stephen of Aumale, who had been doing his best not to listen to the exchange between Simon and the former Earl of Norfolk.

'God's Holy Bones, the poor bastards!'

Following Stephen's pointing finger, Simon saw that one of the transport ships heavily laden with soldiers had capsized midway between the shelter of the harbour and the open sea. Small figures bobbed briefly in the water before vanishing in the swell. A few fortunate ones had managed to gain a grip on the mast, but, unable to swim and dragged down by the weight of their garments, the majority were drowning. Other vessels coming hard about were rowing frantically towards the stricken ship to pick up those who were clinging on.

'God have mercy on their souls,' muttered De Gael, signing his breast and shaking his head. Among the horrified watchers on shore there were mutters of foreboding, and declarations that it was an ill omen.

'It is a test of our fortitude!' Robert of Normandy bellowed, striking a pose. 'Those of you who are faint-hearted can crawl home with your tails between your legs. Our compatriots are even now in heaven with the Saviour! A ship may be lost, but what is a single one among many?' He strode along the dockside, exhorting and rallying. Watching him at work, Simon could well understand how men had been seduced into rebelling against William Rufus to try to make this man King of England. Robert of Normandy might be small and stout, with receding hair, but he had a certain glamour about him. His character was known to be lazy and indolent, but the crusade had fired his blood and he was proving a more adequate leader now than he had ever done at home.

The few survivors of the sudden, brutal shipwreck were brought ashore together with those bodies that the crews of the other vessels had been able to hook from the water. Robert's chaplain and Archbishop Adehmar came forward to attend the dead, stepping carefully around the drenching pools of seawater that streamed from the corpses.

A woman, her clothes sodden, her black hair dripping around her face, knelt over one of the dead men and howled for him. The sound raised the hair on Simon's nape, and as he stared he was assailed by a chill of recognition. It was nearly twenty years since last he had seen her, but still he knew the oval face and wide, grey-violet eyes: Sabina, the falconer's daughter with whom he had conducted that first affair of innocence and aching, unrequited lust.

Pushing through the crowd to her side he looked down at the dead man whose head she was cradling in her lap.

Time had put a badger-stripe of grey in his beard and given him a paunch to droop over his belt, but Simon still recognised the serjeant who had taken his place in the soft darkness of the mews. Stitched to his tunic was the ubiquitous cross of white linen, its edges frayed and faded from wear and exposure to light. Seawater had made spiky clumps of his lashes, and beneath half-closed lids his eyes were glazed with death.

Someone leaned down to Sabina with a sympathetic word and was batted vigorously away. 'He is my husband!' she snarled like a she-wolf. Leaning over the dead man, she kissed his face and dug her hands into his streaming hair. 'Why didn't God take me as well?' She prostrated herself over his body, kissing and touching him in a frenzy as if her desperation would restore him to life.

Clucking his tongue in pity, Ralf de Gael turned away. Simon stooped to her. 'Sabina?'

The gaze she turned on him was unfocused and wild. Her lips curled back. 'Let me be!' she spat.

'Sabina, look at me. It's Simon.' He touched her shoulder and, like the man before him, was flung off. 'Please, I can help you.'

A glimmer of lucidity kindled within her shock and grief. 'No one can help me,' she wept. 'Saer's dead. I should have died too.' She laid her hand upon her husband's cold throat as though she could conjure a heartbeat beneath her fingertips and rocked herself back and forth, tears mingling with the salt water streaming down her face. 'We were supposed to see Jerusalem together and pray for our children!'

Simon watched her for a moment. Like Ralf he could have turned away and pretended it was none of his business, but it would indeed be a pretence, and one his conscience would make him pay for later. Rising from his crouch, he beckoned to two serjeants from his troop. 'Bring a stretcher,' he commanded, 'and bear this man to the nearest church.' Removing his cloak, he draped it around Sabina's shoulders.

The blue fabric, the white bearskin, gave her complexion the same grey cast as the corpses laid on the wharfside.

The other survivors were being found dry garments and given hot wine to drink. The crusader fleet continued to load up supplies and put out to sea. Ship's horns bellowed out as the vessels communicated with each other.

Robert of Normandy embarked on a large drakkar with round shields overlapped along the side to increase the height of the freeboard. His chaplains and stewards organised prayers for the dead and the hasty digging of graves.

The first terrible wave of grief over, Sabina sat silently by her husband while she waited for him to be taken and buried. She had washed the salt from his hair and beard, had used her bone comb to ease out the tangles, and now she sat with her hands folded and her expression blank.

Simon gave her a cup of wine and she looked at it blankly. 'I did not want to come on this journey, but he thought it would make a difference,' she said hoarsely. 'He thought if only we could petition God at his most holy altar and show how much we loved him that he would forgive us our sins and reward us . . .' She took a hesitant drink from the cup, her hand shaking so badly that she could scarcely hold the rim to her lips. 'Our sins must be greater than we had ever imagined, for look what God has wrought . . .'

'Hush,' Simon murmured. 'It was the work of man, not God, that tumbled your ship. It was laden with too many people and too low in the water.'

'But why was I saved and my husband drowned? Why didn't I die with him?' Her voice rose and cracked. 'Do not tell me that God is merciful, for I will not believe you!'

'I will tell you nothing,' Simon said and touched her hand. 'There is a place for you in my household until you are recovered enough to decide what you want to do.'

'I do not need your pity.' She raised her head and looked at him with angry pride, tears glittering.

His heart turned over. For an instant she reminded him so much of Matilda that he found it difficult to speak. 'It is not out of pity that I am offering,' he replied, 'but out of old friendship. I have lodgings in the town. You are welcome to spend the night while you decide whether you want to go on or return home.'

She continued to look at him and colour burned up in Simon's face.

'It is an honourable offer,' he said. 'To take advantage is not my intention.'

'I know that.' She gave a cracked laugh. 'We always drew back from the edge, didn't we?' Even with his cloak around her shoulders, she was shivering violently.

The chaplain arrived to escort her husband's body to his grave. A low moan rose in Sabina's throat.

'Come,' Simon said gently, and drew her to her feet. 'Let us bury him with dignity.' He gave her hand a squeeze. 'And when it is done, I know an apothecary who will give you something to help you sleep.'

She leaned on him heavily. 'It will take more than an apothecary to help me,' she said.

Sabina's fragile condition led Simon to decide to bring her with him. Despite the dangers waiting on the road to Jerusalem, the way home for a woman alone was more hazardous yet. Even taking a couple of stout serjeants for escort was no guarantee of safety, and Sabina was so engulfed by her grief that she was not capable of looking out for herself.

On the crossing from Brindisi to Durazzo she curled up against the ship's side and hid her face from the sea. When Simon stooped to hand her a cup of wine and ask how she was faring, she shook her head.

'Not well,' she said, but took the cup from him and drank it to the lees. Simon sat down beside her, leaning his back against the ship's side and shifting his shoulder blades until he was comfortable. He said nothing, making it clear that he was content to sit and not make demands on her. Finally Sabina broke the silence.

'It was Saer's notion that we take the cross,' she said. 'He thought that if we showed our devotion to God he would bless us with more children.' Her knuckles whitened around the cup. 'We had three you know – two boys and a girl.'

The 'had' was telling. Simon touched her shoulder in a gesture of sympathy.

'One son and our baby daughter died two summers ago of the spotted fever. Other children in the village died too.' Her eyes were desolate. 'Our eldest son survived, only to cut himself on a scythe blade at harvest time and die of the stiffening sickness . . .'

'I am sorry,' Simon said, knowing that the words were inadequate. It was a fact of life that many children did not survive the journey into adulthood. His mother had lost two sons between bearing Garnier and him, one stillborn, the other succumbing to a childhood illness. But common occurrence was no comfort to parental grief.

'You do not understand,' Sabina said. 'We tried to salve our wounds and comfort our loss by conceiving another child, but Saer . . .' She bent her head so that all he saw was the top of her wimple and a few wind-whipped strands of black hair. 'The loss of his son unmanned him. That was one of the reasons he took a crusader's vow – in the hope of finding a cure. Instead all he found was his death.' She let the empty cup roll onto the deck and, bowing her face into her cupped hands, rocked back and forth.

Simon gathered her in his arms and said nothing, for all words were inadequate.

She clung to him and wept harshly against his breast until she was exhausted. Simon gently eased away from her and tucking his cloak around her body, left her to sleep out her grief.

'A regular champion of waifs and strays,' said Stephen of Aumale, who was one of the other passengers on their vessel. His gaze was speculative.

Simon tried to look nonchalant. 'I knew her and her parents many years ago at court. My conscience would not let me abandon her.'

Stephen raised his fair brows and his lips twitched with amusement. 'A very tender conscience,' he said. 'Matilda would be proud of your devotion.'

Simon gave him an irritated scowl. 'She was an old friend in need,' he said curtly. 'Read no more into the situation than that.'

'Oh, I don't,' Stephen said, but not as if he meant it. 'I am sure it is your Christian duty to succour her in every way you can.'

Before Simon could retort Stephen had moved off down the ship, his tread blithe and carefree. Simon cursed softly beneath his breath. He deliberately avoided looking at the vulnerable huddle that was Sabina and went instead to stand at the steerboard with the helmsman.

CHAPTER 33

September 1097

'Is there really an elf in the well?' Young Waltheof peered into the wattle-lined tunnel with its twinkle of water deep below.

Matilda smiled, reliving her own fascination, remembering how she had scrutinised the mysterious, uncovered darkness with her father watchfully at her side. 'Who can say?' she said. 'Your grandfather told me that the elf was shy and never came out when there were people about, but that he should be paid to keep the water sweet.' Grasping the rope, she drew the bucket to the surface and poured the water into the waiting jug. 'Here.' She gave the child a small silver ring. 'Throw this in to him and make a wish.'

Waltheof screwed up his face to think. 'I want a dog like Hector,' he said. 'With a tail like a curly feather.'

Matilda rolled her eyes. Hector was a menace to all. That the menace was due to sheer friendliness and exuberance rather than malice was no consolation. The 'curly feather' of a tail had a propensity for swishing cups and bowls off tables, while the other end would indiscriminately devour whatever came its way in between slobbering over any human in sight. Hector was the result of an unfortunate meeting between one of the keep's boarhound bitches and a huntsman's spaniel dog and Matilda was in no haste to see the mistake repeated, even for the sake of her son. Fortunately Hector had been the only pup from the mating and Matilda's chaplain had taken him for companionship. The prospect of another such in her bower did not bear thinking about.

The silver ring vanished in a glint of metal and a soft plink as it struck the water far below. Ripples shivered and were still. The boy leaned hopefully over the well opening. 'If I'm very quiet, perhaps he will come out,' he said hopefully.

'Never,' Matilda said. 'The light blinds his eyes.' Her lips twitched slightly. The notion of her son sitting quietly for longer than it took to blink was impossible. Besides, she did not want him lingering beside the open well cover. She knew what fascination it had held for her in her own childhood. 'Drop the bucket back,' she said.

'Won't it hit him on the head?'

'No, he lives too far down in the water.'

The boy nodded acceptance and threw the bucket down with gusto so that it landed with a vigorous splash. Matilda made her own wish as the ripples surged and settled. Gesturing a nearby gardener to slide the heavy well covering back over the hole, she hefted the jug and bore it towards the endive and lettuce bed. The leaves were wilting in the September sun, which in the mid-afternoon still bore the strength of summer. Helisende sat in the shade of the apple tree, her attention on the baby. In the last week little Maude, as they called her, had found her feet and was beginning to totter unsteadily around, her little pink toes plumping intently through the cool green grass.

Matilda watched her daughter pull herself up and use Helisende's knee as a balance before launching herself. Three steps, four, and she sat down with a bump, but only to struggle up again and totter towards her mother, a beaming smile on her face.

Matilda set the water jar down and, making cooing sounds of encouragement, held out her arms. 'Your papa should be here to see you,' she said, and as her throat tightened she felt resentment and longing stir within her. Her son thought it was a great adventure that his father had gone off to war. He would play 'crusades' with the other boys, galloping around on his hobbyhorse, waving his toy sword in the air and slaughtering imaginary Saracens. Sometimes Matilda thought that the only difference between a boy's game and a man's game was that the latter involved real danger and grief and the former could be stopped the moment that injury occurred or the participants grew tired. But one was the training for the other, and that worried her.

The baby staggered the last important step and Matilda swung her up in her arms, welcoming the warm, solid weight. Girls had a different set of worries and burdens to bear, she thought. Her daughter struggled and clamoured to be set down so that she could totter her way back to Helisende. Matilda smiled at her sturdy determination, waited to see her triumphant arrival, then stooped to her water jar.

The last drops were soaking into the soil when a Benedictine monk was brought to her by one of the hall stewards. The man was dusty from travel and the crown of his head shone pink from exposure to the burn of the sun. Matilda greeted him courteously and drew him to the shade of the bench beneath her apple tree. A swift command sent a servant hurrying to fetch water for washing and wine for refreshment.

'You are welcome, brother . . .'

'Matthias,' he completed with a grave inclination of his head. 'I will not trouble your presence long, my lady. My journey is to Crowland, but I am glad of a respite for myself and my mule.'

'Have you come far?' Matilda enquired politely. She was accustomed to visitors but they were usually secular. Monks and priests preferred to rest in the abbeys and convents of their orders.

'From Winchester,' he said. 'I have letters for Abbot Ingulf.' Unfastening his leather travelling satchel, he produced a folded, salt-stained parchment, tied with narrow thongs of rolled leather and closed with a red wax seal. 'This was given into my keeping by a fellow monk who had carried it from Normandy. It has been in many hands along the way, so I am told, but it comes originally from Earl Simon on his blessed mission.'

Matilda began to tremble. A letter from Simon. His hands had touched this as they delivered it to the first messenger in the chain. He had pressed his seal ring deep into the liquid wax to make an impression. He was still alive – or had been when this was written, and he had been thinking of her. Letters had arrived regularly until Eastertide, many from a place named Brindisi, but she had heard nothing since then.

Brother Matthias regarded her with concern. 'My lady . . . are you all right?'

She gave the monk a dazzling smile. 'Yes,' she whispered through a sudden blur of tears and thought that perhaps there really was an elf in the well.

Matilda did not open the letter at once. To do so under the scrutiny of the monk and beset by the surrounding distractions of everyday life would have destroyed the pleasure and unsettled her concentration. She preferred to wait and anticipate.

It was the cool of the evening when she returned to the garden, a lantern lighting her way to the bench beneath the apple tree. Brother Matthias had eaten a large portion of squab pie, washed it down with half a flagon of cider, and then departed for the monastery at St Ives to seek a night's lodging. The children were abed with Helisende to watch over them. A night breeze rustled the leaves and from the direction of the orchard a little owl let out several piercing shrieks. But they were familiar sounds that comforted rather than disturbed her. She had never been afraid of the dark, only of being left alone.

With unsteady fingers she took the small knife from the sheath at her belt and cut the leather thongs binding the parchment. Breaking the seal, she opened the casing and found that it enclosed two more folded sheets of parchment, closely but neatly written in deep brown ink. Simon could read and write, but only when forced. This was the hand of a scribe, elegant and in formal Latin. Judith's interest in the Church meant that Matilda had been taught to read the language. At the time it had seemed a chore, but now she was grateful for her mother's foresight and insistence. She would have hated to summon her own scribe to read aloud the words that needed to be either savoured or suffered in private.

The lantern cast a wavering shadow over the words. Picking it up by its chain, she hooked it over the lowest branch of the tree and angled herself so that the light shone full on the writing.

Earl Simon to Countess Matilda, whatever warm greetings her mind can imagine.

Let your heart be comforted that I have travelled on this blessed journey without harm so far as I have reached. We came to the great city of Constantinople that is ruled by the Emperor Alexius. Although he received our leaders with smiles and gifts, truth to say, he is prudent and jealous of his great and beautiful city. We were not permitted to enter freely and wander at our will, but always under escort in small groups of no more than five or six at a time. Constantinople is a place of great wonder that surpasses anything I have ever seen or that you could imagine. Some say that the streets are paved with gold. That is an untruth, but indeed, there is gold everywhere, and ivory and silk in every bright colour of the rainbow and beyond. The churches drip with wealth and the merchants go clothed in purple like kings. Truly it is a remarkable sight and my eyes have grown sore so much have I stared.

I confess my love, that I have bought you neither silk nor gold from the great capital of Byzantium, for I know such tokens of wealth impress you not. But I have secured something else that I hope will bring you great joy and that, God willing, I will live to place in your hands.

Matilda grimaced as she read this. The only thing that could bring her great joy was Simon's return. She had no difficulty imagining his pleasure at discovering the wonders of Constantinople. What was written here was only the echo of his wonder. A moth blundered in front of the lantern and cast a fluttering shadow as it strove to burn its wings on the dazzle of candlelight. Matilda grabbed swiftly and felt the frantic beating of soft wings within the cage of her fist. Opening her hand, she cast the pale insect far into the dark, and again lowered her gaze to the letter.

We left the city after a sojourn of ten days and sailed across the arm of the sea that surrounds the city and is called the Arm of Saint George. It is said that the sea around Constantinople is cruel to voyagers, but on the day that we sailed it was as calm as a duck pond. After landing, we took horse for the Turkish-held city of Nicaea, and it is from there that I write to you. I have seen hard battle, but through God's great mercy I yet live and with no wounds to trouble my body. The Turkish leader, Quilij Arslan, came upon us in an attempt to relieve the siege, but we scattered his army to the four winds and hope that negotiations will yet win the city for us. We are told that from Nicaea to Jerusalem is but a march of five weeks, and only the city of Antioch between to stop us.

You should know that I have made my peace with Ralf de Gael. He is here amongst us with a company of Breton lords and has spoken to me of his grief and regret over your father's death. I will speak more of this when I return, but I thought that you should know of this detail and think upon it. Lord Ralf has ever been a man of charm and easy words, but I truly believe that the matter of your father's death has lingered on his conscience.

Matilda raised her head from her reading and leaned her head against the rough bark of the tree. She felt a small stab of resentment. Well and good if Simon had made his own peace with De Gael, but she hoped that he had not made it on her behalf too. Her nature might be generous and loving, but in the matter of forgiving Ralf de Gael she was not prepared to be charitable. Indeed, she was irritated that Simon should mention him at all when this letter was all she had of him for months yet to come. He had spoken of hard fighting too, his manner offhand, but she knew that such indifference on the page was not necessarily the truth.

I trust that you are in good health, my love, and that our children are thriving. I hold you all dearly in my thoughts and wish that I could hold you in my arms too. Christ willing, that joyous time will not be too far away. Until then, may God keep you safe.

The last paragraph expressed tender sentiments but in an obligatory fashion, or perhaps she was expecting too much? A letter had to go through many hands on a journey of this length, and it was not unlikely that intimate details might be read by others.

With a soft sigh she folded the parchment and sat with it in her lap. The sky darkened from dusk to true dark, but she remained where she was, wondering what Simon was doing, how he was faring and if he truly was thinking of her the way that she was thinking of him.

CHAPTER 34

Dorylaeum, Anatolian Plateau, June 1097

The night sky was a heavy blue, thickly populated with stars. Beside the small settlement of Dorylaeum on the trade route through Antioch to Jerusalem, the crusader army had encamped for the night – or half of it had. To ease the foraging conditions, the leaders had split the army. The Norman contingent were the vanguard, the southern French and Lorrainers were marching a day behind.

Simon had pitched his tents beside a spring of sweet water and the soft sound it made as it bubbled up from beneath the ground was cool and soothing. The day had been as hot as a bread oven, but with the sunset had come a chill wind and he was glad of the warmth of the white fur cloak. Hundreds of campfires surrounded his position, islands of orange heat and light in the stony darkness. The voices of men, the notes of flute and bagpipe, the high-pitched laughter of women rose and mingled on the night air with smoke and cooking smells.

Four days ago they had marched from Nicaea. The wounded had remained behind, and under the supervision of the Greek army were restoring and repairing the defences damaged during the siege. Absently rubbing his left leg, he wondered if he should have stayed with them. The area surrounding the old healed break was red and inflamed. It had been troubling him for more than a week and was gradually worsening. A physician had told him to wash the area in strong, hot vinegar twice a day, but thus far the treatment was having no effect.

'Your leg is bothering you?'

He turned from his musing to regard Sabina, who had emerged from her small canvas shelter and was studying him anxiously.

'A little,' he said in an offhand manner designed to make little of the difficulty. 'There are times when it has flared up before, but it has always subsided.'

'But usually you have been able to tend and rest it,' she said. She shook out the goatskin rug she held in her hands and knelt down on it before the fire.

'That I can do when we come to Antioch.'

'If you reach it alive,' she said grimly. 'This campaign eats men whole.' She tossed two lumps of charcoal from the supply sack into the small circle of glowing heat and watched the sudden dance of flame.

'Indeed, but no one who set out expected the road to Jerusalem to be easy,' Simon replied and studied her covertly. For the first weeks after her husband's drowning she had moved through the world with as much animation as a child's straw doll, uncaring, interested in nothing. Gradually, however, she had begun to emerge from her trance. It was a slow, painful process. Seldom a day went past when she did not weep for her loss, usually when she was at prayer, but in the between times she had found a kind of balance. Occasionally she even smiled.

In return for Simon's care and protection, she had undertaken the task of laundress and cauldron tender to him and his men. She had her own small shelter, which she pitched beside theirs, and although she mostly preferred to keep aloof she would occasionally join their fire with a piece of mending, or come, like now, to warm herself and contemplate.

'Mayhap, but it is a hard road for a man to travel just to feel righteous about himself,' she said softly. 'You should turn back, before it is too late.'

Simon laughed without humour. 'My leg is not as bad as all that,' he said. 'Besides, I am not just travelling this road in order to feel righteous about myself.'

'Then for what?'

He hesitated. 'I am not sure you would understand,' he said. 'Certainly my wife did not.'

A faint smile curved her lips. 'I am not your wife.'

There was something of her old spirit in the remark, and Simon felt a spark kindle beyond the compassion and pity that had been his response towards her thus far. 'But you are a woman.'

'I see. And more likely to understand your wife than you.' Her smile deepened.

'I suppose so, yes.'

'Then tell me, and let us know for sure.'

The challenge hung between them in the soft night air and Simon realised that if he took it up the level of intimacy between them would change. He needed the diversion. He did not want her to retreat to her shelter and her shell. Taking a stick of kindling, he drew a spiral pattern in the soil. 'I broke my leg when I was a young squire in King William's household,' he said. 'For weeks on end, I had to lie abed while the bones knitted. It was a bad break and, although it did mend, the damage was irreparable. I was left with a limp and frequent pain. Some of this you already know.'

Sabina nodded. 'But you concealed it well,' she said. 'When we were younger I never gave it any consideration. To me you were just the King's squire Simon, with a new hawk to train and a certain way about you . . .' She looked down quickly, and the firelight made shadowy fans of her dark lashes.

'As I remember, you had a certain way about you too,' Simon said softly.

'It was a long time ago.' She plucked at the goatskin on which she was sitting.

'Not so long,' he said. 'I still have Guinevere in the mews at Huntingdon, and she still flies truer than many a younger hawk.'

'She was a good bird, and you trained her well,' Sabina said. 'Even if you were distracted on occasion.' She glanced at him, then down again.

A woman's throaty laugh drifted from one of the other campfires. Simon was aware of a warm heaviness in his groin. If not arousal, it ran the sensation very close.

'You were telling me why you are here,' Sabina prompted.

'It is because of those weeks that I spent cooped in a small room with only the walls for company. I had visitors, I had my lessons and other such joys to pass the time, but everyone and everything had to come to me. I was a prisoner, and even at that tender age I realised how much I had always taken for granted until then.'

She nodded thoughtfully. 'So now you seize every opportunity for new experience that comes your way lest it pass you by?'

He shrugged. 'It is more than that, and less. I cannot bear to feel enclosed by four walls, and that is what happens when I stop. Matilda, my wife . . . I love her dearly, but she is content to dwell within the four walls that I fear. For her they represent security, not imprisonment.'

'That is true, I think, of many women and men,' Sabina said shrewdly. 'The women build nests to raise their children, and the men go out into the world.'

He laughed at first, but as he reflected on her words realised how true they were. 'But you did not remain behind when your husband took the Cross?' He phrased the words as a question.

'No,' she said. 'I followed him because I did not want him out of my sight. Besides, I had no nest to protect and no nestlings to nurture any more.' Abruptly she rose and retired to her small shelter. He heard the swish of the flap dropping, and knew that she had retreated because she was hurt and wanted to cry. For one wild moment he contemplated going after her to comfort her pain, but common sense kept him where he was and the moment passed.

Sighing, Simon tossed more charcoal onto the flames. Recently, a small inner voice had been suggesting that he was a long way from home, and that Matilda had been right to suggest that the grass on the other side of the hill was not necessarily better just because it looked different. His mouth curved as he imagined her in her precious garden, surrounded by the damp, scented blooms of a northern summer. The letter he had written during their rest in Nicaea would not reach her until the leaves were turning to brown and the apples on her tree ripening a speckled red and gold. By the time she cut the seal, he might be in Jerusalem . . . or he might be dead. And all because he had to know what lay over the horizon.

To one side, four members of his troop were playing dice. He considered lecturing them about the profanity of their game but decided not to bother. They would only go behind his back. Even men filled with religious devotion needed their distractions.

He finished the wine and eased to his feet. A throbbing pain shot through his leg, making him gasp and swear.

'My lord?' One of the dice players raised his head, and eyed him anxiously.

'It is nothing,' Simon said brusquely. 'Go back to your sport.' He limped to his own tent and ducked through the flap, waving away Turstan when the young man would have attended him.

'I need nothing else this night,' he said. 'Do whatever you wish.'

'Sir.' Turstan saluted and went to join the dice players.

Careful to avoid jolting his leg, he eased down onto his pallet and closed his eyes. The stuffing was made from several fleeces culled from the flocks that grazed on the fenland at his manor of Ryhall and suddenly it seemed to him that he was standing among the flocks, inhaling their ammoniac smell, and listening to their bleating as they grazed the rich summer meadow. His legs were sound and he went striding among them, seeking the path that ran towards the woods on the far side. The sheep scattered, bleating reproachfully, and he became aware of a figure standing on the edge of the woods, waiting for him. A tall man, copper-haired, blue-eyed, wearing a cloak with a white fur lining. His fist grasped a huge battleaxe, held in a way that said he was on guard but not about to strike. A red line, thin as scarlet thread, encircled his neck.

Simon stared. He was not afraid. He knew that he must be dreaming and that he could wake himself if he chose. But he wanted to see where the dream would take him.

Waltheof smiled at him. 'Just one step further,' he said. 'Is that not what you have always wanted, Simon? One more step to prove that you are as able as any man with two sound legs?'

Simon looked down. 'I do have two sound legs,' he said.

'And I have a head on my shoulders.' Waltheof answered, and turning on his heel walked into the dark forest. Simon hesitated, then followed him. It was what he was meant to do, he was sure of it. Otherwise, why would Waltheof have been waiting for him?

The trees closed around them and Simon's eyes widened to full stretch, trying to pick out the path under the darkness of the branches.

'Where are we going?' he demanded.

'Patience,' his companion said. 'I have something to show you.' He took him deeper still so that light and air seemed little more than memories. The musty, overpowering smell of fungus and woodrot was all pervading. Somewhere a pack of wolves was howling and the hair prickled erect on his nape as he realised that the sound was coming closer.

Waltheof strode on grimly and Simon fixed his gaze to the

flash of white that was the lining of the bearskin cloak because that was all he could see. Behind him he swore he detected the soft pad of paws on the leaf litter of the forest floor. Waltheof stopped and Simon bumped into him. He was solid and alive, not a being without substance as Simon had half expected.

The wolves were very near; the sound of their howling filled the wood, bouncing off the trees, filling his head. Rancid breath heated the back of his neck. Simon groped at his belt but he carried not so much as a knife to defend himself. He looked at Waltheof, at the huge Dane axe in his hand.

'I cannot help you,' Waltheof said. 'You chose to follow me into the unknown. Now you face it.' Before Simon's gaze, his companion's solidity melted away. Something thudded at his feet, and looking down Simon saw the gleam of a skull as it came to rest against the toe of his boot. It grinned at him full stretch, no lips to conceal its mockery. And beyond it he perceived other skulls gleaming, row upon row, filling a clearing in the trees.

'God help me,' he croaked through a parched throat. The wolves attacked. Their howls claimed the hollow of his own skull and although he could not see them he could feel their vicious teeth and claws ripping the life out of him.

'My lord, wake up, wake up!'

Gasping, choking, Simon burst out of his nightmare into the cold, pure air of reality. The mauling of the wolves became Turstan's hands shaking him, but the howls remained. Sharp, loud, ululating.

'My lord, wake up. The Turks are upon us!'

'What?' Simon struggled off his pallet. Pain roared down his leg like a lion, and for a moment he could not move. By the flickering light of a cresset lamp set dangerously on a campstool he saw that Turstan was wearing his armour.

'Quilij Arslan is here with his entire army!' The young man's voice was pitched high and almost breaking with excitement and fear. 'He's surrounded the camp!'

Simon's heart had already been pounding from the vividness of his nightmare. Now it drummed in his ears and his leg throbbed in time with each hard, swift stroke. Turning awkwardly, he reached for his own padded tunic and hauberk.

Turstan helped him with swift efficiency, his fingers nimble despite his high state of agitation.

'They have not attacked yet?' Foolish question. Once witnessed, a Turkish assault could never be forgotten. They sped in on their swift, manoeuvrable little horses, shot arrows from their short but deadly bows, and whisked out of range again, maddening as gnats, constantly biting and darting away. Their swords were so sharp that they could slice off a man's wrist and he would not notice until he saw the blood and his severed flesh twitching on the ground at his feet.

'No, my lord – but it cannot be long. As soon as first light strikes the horizon . . .'

First light, so that the archers could see to mark their targets and the horses would not stumble on the ground. Latching his swordbelt, collecting his helm, his eyes still crusted with sleep, Simon ducked out of his tent, gazed eastwards and saw a thin oystershell rim of dawn on the horizon.

Sabina was already out of her shelter. Sleeves rolled up, she was briskly assembling costrels and pails.

'There is always need of water if there is to be a battle,' she said by way of greeting.

Simon nodded brusquely. 'See if you can find linen for bandages too – raid my coffers if you must.'

She acknowledged him with a wave of her hand, her back already turned as she headed for the spring to fill her vessels.

Simon heeled about and limped towards the tents of the Norman leaders. They needed to organise with unprecedented speed. As soon as the light hit grey, the Turks would attack.

He arrived at the muster point at the same time as Ralf de Gael and Stephen of Aumale, both of them mail-clad and looking pensive and alert. Count Bohemond of Taranto, one of the senior Norman leaders, sat on his horse before his tent, flanked on either side by Robert of Normandy and Stephen of Blois. Bohemond was a tall, muscular warrior with brutal features and a voice that could pierce a shield wall at fifty paces, a man whom others followed confidently into battle, for, although this was a holy crusade, Bohemond of Taranto was graced with the Devil's own luck.

Now he raised that magnificent voice and bellowed their battle plan across the paling sky. 'There are too many of them to face on horseback,' he cried. 'If we ride out to meet them, they will sow our ranks with death from their bows. I have sent a messenger with all speed to Raymond of Toulouse that he may bring the rest of our army to our succour.'

'So if we do not attack, what do we do? Sit here like trussed chickens and let them take us?' demanded a knight standing next to Simon.

Bohemond looked irritated. 'We form a defensive ring until the others arrive to reinforce us,' he said. 'Let the women and the footsoldiers draw in all our tents and pitch them close by the spring. The women and those who are unable to fight will receive the wounded and supply water to the fighting men. Let the knights with the best armour dismount and form a ring of steel around the camp.'

'That is preposterous!' shouted the knight. 'I would rather die charging the enemy than play the coward.'

'No one is asking you to play the coward,' Bohemond retorted, baring his square white teeth. 'By your own words, you play the fool. If you seek to be the most courageous, then take up your shield and join the front line.'

The knight glowered, spat on the ground and shouldered his way back through the gathering.

'Those who want to die for Christ now can go with him,' Bohemond cried. 'Those of you who want to live to see Jerusalem, follow my command.'

A few knights, mostly the companions of the first one,

turned and left, but most men stood their ground and remained to receive more detailed orders.

Ralf de Gael laid a slender hand on Simon's shoulder. 'I saw the way you were limping when you came to the meet,' he murmured. 'I hope that you are not going into the fight.'

Simon stiffened beneath De Gael's concerned touch. By his suggestion, the Breton lord had just made the outcome inevitable. 'I can stand,' he said coldly, 'and likely make a better task of hefting a shield than walking hither and yon bearing pails of water.'

De Gael looked wry. 'It was not my intention to hurt your pride, rather to save your body,' he said.

'My lord, the intentions you have never had have always been the ones that are most damning,' Simon snapped and, turning his back on the Breton, went to organise his troops. Although pain tore through his leg, he forced himself to stride out, full aware that De Gael was watching him.

Just before the sun broke over the horizon the Turks attacked, swooping upon the crusader camp on their light, swift horses. Even while his gut somersaulted with a rush of fear at their assault, Simon still found a space to admire their athletic, languid grace as they shot arrows from the backs of their galloping mounts. Some rode in closer and hurled javelins over the top of the Norman shield wall, seeking to penetrate the closed ranks.

Men screamed and fell as they were hit; others ran into the gap to take their place. Simon's kite shield, blazoned with a simple cross of gold on a red background, protected him from chin to ankle. Even if an arrow did pierce the seasoned lime-wood, it still had to punch through his mail and quilted linen undertunic before it found flesh. However, there was a price to pay for being so well protected. As the sun climbed in the sky, it heated the iron rivets on hauberks until they burned to the touch, and turned burnished steel helms into cooking pots. Sweat poured out of Simon like water from a leaky bucket, and the weight of his shield grew so heavy that it was almost like bearing a full-grown man on his left arm. He gulped hot air through his mouth and gained no respite. Sweat streamed into his eyes, stinging with salt, blurring his vision until he saw everything through a veil of salty moisture he could ill afford to lose. His leg pulsed and throbbed until bearing weight upon it was agony, but bear it he did, for to have withdrawn would have endangered the defensive line.

Every hour the front ranks retired to the back of the line for a respite from the assault of arrows and javelins while the women and non-combatants came amongst them with cooling horns and ladles of water from the spring. Staggering, feeling sick and disorientated, Simon gave up his place to the knight who touched his shoulder, and went to take a brief rest.

Sabina was waiting for him, a bucket at her feet. 'You must drink slowly else you will spew it all back up,' she told him as she dipped a wooden cup and held it out brimming. His hand was shaking so badly that he could scarce unfasten his mail aventail and lift the cup to his lips. More than half of the precious liquid spilled down his chin.

'You are not well.' Her grey eyes filled with concern. 'You should not be among the fighting men.'

'Christ, not you as well,' he snarled. 'I am as fit to fight as any soldier out there. Even if my body weakens, my spirit will hold me to the task.'

'Your stubborn spirit,' she amended grimly, but did not try to dissuade him further. 'Sit,' she said, indicating a campstool. 'And do not say that you have no desire to do so. All I need do is push you and you will fall down.'

Simon tried to glare at her, but his eyes crossed. He tottered the two steps to the stool and slumped down upon it. Not just his hands were trembling, but his entire body. He handed the empty cup back to Sabina and she refilled it. But instead of giving him the cup to drink, she gently removed his helm and poured the water over his head. Simon gasped, as much with pleasure as shock. The cold deluge trickled down the back of his neck and seeped into the sweat-soaked fleece of his gambeson. Twice more she doused him before she let him drink again. Simon was so parched that he thought that however much liquid he absorbed, it would never be enough to satisfy.

Taking his helm, Sabina began binding it with torn strips of wet linen. 'To stop the heat of the sun,' she said. 'And you should wear a tunic over your mail, like some of the Byzantines do.' She handed him a length of silk cloth in which she had slit a head opening. It was a tabard, improvised from some of the cloth Simon had brought from Constantinople. He had intended it as a gift for Matilda, a dress length to make a court robe. The cut had ruined it for such use, but he did not complain. Anything that mitigated the appalling heat of the battlefield was a blessing.

'Do you want food?'

Simon shook his head as he donned the silk over his mail and tucked it down through his swordbelt. The very mention of the word made him want to retch.

'Will we succeed?' she asked, 'or are we going to be massacred here?' Her voice was calm and flat. She had faced death when the galley had capsized, and seen it claim her children and her husband. It had marched as her constant companion, and for the moment she was numb.

Simon shrugged. 'If the second army can reach us in time then all will be well,' he replied, 'but I do not know for how long our men can hold the ground in this heat. Still,' he added quickly, 'the Saracens do not have an infinite supply of arrows and javelins. They must run out if we can only hold them off for long enough.' With an effort he lurched to his feet and swayed. The pain in his leg was agonising. Sabina filled his carrying costrel with water and he drank another cupful before he slipped his left arm through the leather grips on his shield.

There was a yell from the Norman ranks and Simon jerked round. Beside him Sabina craned on tiptoe to see what was happening. A conroi of horsemen forty strong had broken out from the Norman lines and was charging down on a retreating cluster of Saracen archers. Bohemond, who had arrived that moment at the springs to check on the wounded and take a drink, hurled his cup to the ground.

'God's Holy Face, the fools!' he roared. 'I gave no order. Who dares defy me?' He thrust his way through the battle lines like a plough through soil. A horn sounded to call the men back, but went ignored.

The Norman horses were slower than the light desert mounts of the Turks and were unable to catch the fleeing bowmen. A fresh wave of Saracens rode out to support their comrades and intercepted the Normans with a fierce rain of arrows. The knight's charge broke up in confusion as a hail of deadly barbs hit horses and men. Swords flashing, the Turks took advantage and moved in for the kill.

Simon watched one man fall, an arrow in his shoulder. His foot was tangled in the stirrup leather and his panicking horse dragged him across the stony ground at a hard gallop. His screams for help pierced the sky, and then the screams stopped as a rock shattered his spine. Sabina looked away.

'God have mercy,' Simon whispered as he watched swords flash in the harsh white light, and men fall. A handful of knights managed to break out of the ring of death and galloped back to their own lines, their shields quilled with arrows. The wounded were brought through to the water stations by the spring, and Simon recognised the impetuous knight who had been defying Bohemond at the dawn muster. Now his teeth were bared in agony and a black-feathered Saracen shaft protruded from his collarbone, the point forced in so deeply that extracting it would likely be impossible.

It was a high price to pay for folly, Simon thought, and he knew that he was in no case to pass judgement, for he had committed enormous follies of his own and was about to compound them. Hefting his shield, gripping his spear, he limped back into the dusty hell of the battle.

Towards noon Simon's shield took an arrow that punched through the limewood and his mail and sliced a flesh wound beneath his ribs. The impact of the barb made him reel, and because he was unbalanced due to his inflamed leg he went down. He heard the thunder of hooves, and from the corner of his eye saw a Turkish soldier swooping in, spear raised to throw. With a final, tremendous effort, Simon twisted his damaged shield back into position across his body. The spear thrummed home, opening up a jagged hole in the wood and pinning him to the ground through mail and gambeson. The move wrenched his leg and he heard himself scream. Red and black spots danced before his eyes and he briefly lost consciousness.

His awareness returned as he heard Sabina's voice urging him to drink and felt the rim of a cup against his lips. She was supporting his shoulders against her kneeling form and her eyes were swimming with tears. He took a choking swallow of water and a tremor shook him. 'My shield . . .' he croaked. 'Have Turstan find my spare one.'

'Of course,' she murmured. 'He has just gone to look for it. You might as well let me tend you while you wait.'

He knew from the soothing tone of her voice that Turstan had done no such thing, but he was half insensible and in too much extremity to do more than mouth a feeble protest. An almighty roar went up from their ranks and he struggled to rise, certain that Quilij Arslan's men had broken through. The sound grew louder, crashing upon him, filling his ears.

'Be still.' Sabina laid a calming hand on his shoulder and pressed him back down. 'And be glad. The second army has come. We are saved.'

Her words joined the noise of cheering in Simon's head and seemed to swell inside his skull until he thought it would split. His awareness drifted and, although his eyes were open, they saw not the pitched tents and the busy women but a tall man with copper hair and a red ring at his throat, watching him, a poised battleaxe in his hand.

No matter how hard Simon had worked to hold his position during the battle of Dorylaeum, it was after the Turks had been defeated that his own real battle began. As well as the flesh wounds he had suffered, his left leg was now badly infected and he was drifting in and out of delirium.

'We cannot bring him with us to Antioch, the road is too difficult,' said Ralf de Gael when he paid a visit to Simon's camp. The army was due to march on the following morning and head towards Antioch, but the way led across harsh terrain where there was no water and the heat was intense. There was no room for stragglers on the march.

Sabina glanced at Simon, who was dozing feverishly in the shade of an open tent. 'Others have already told me, my lord,' she said softly. 'I know that if he takes such a route it will be his last journey. He must go home, whether he wills it or not.' She turned back to De Gael. 'I am willing to stay with him and tend to his wounds along the way. It was my husband's vow to see Jerusalem, not mine. I have no oath to keep.'

De Gael was silent and she wondered if she had said something wrong, for high colour flooded his narrow cheekbones. With thin, graceful fingers he unfastened the leather pouch from his waist and tossed it to her. 'Here,' he said. 'This will help you on your journey.'

She caught it, and through the soft brown leather felt the solid reassurance of gold bezants. The crusaders who had been capable at the end of the battle two days ago had pursued the fleeing Turks and caught up with their baggage lines. Men who had been beggars at dawn had become as rich as kings by dusk.

'I do not need your charity, De Gael,' Simon croaked from his pallet. He had woken and turned a little to face the Breton, but it was obvious that the move had cost him dear. His complexion was pallid and droplets of sweat dewed his brow.

'I was not giving it to you but to the woman,' De Gael retorted, and stooped over Simon. 'If she is to care for you, then she deserves some reward to keep her loyal.'

Sabina's eyes blazed indignantly at the Breton lord's insinuation.

Simon gave a mirthless laugh. 'You set her worth too cheaply, my lord,' he said hoarsely.

De Gael looked puzzled. 'You mean I should offer her more?'

'I mean that her value lies in more than just gold.' Simon gave Sabina a look that in spite of its fever glaze struck her like an arrow.

'I see,' said the Breton with an arch of his brows.

'No, you do not. You have never seen.' Simon's lips curled in a grimace, but of pain rather than contempt. His eyes squeezed shut.

'My lord, he should be left to rest.' Sabina was swiftly at Simon's side. Wringing out a cloth in a bowl of water, she laid it across his brow.

De Gael nodded. 'I will take your prayers for yourself and Waltheof with mine to Jerusalem,' he said, 'and ask God to be with you on your journey home.' When Simon did not respond, except to gasp, De Gael hesitated then walked away, an air of resignation to his step.

Sabina let out her breath in relief, for his presence had set her on edge. Glancing round to make sure that she did not have an audience, she hitched up her skirt at the hip and tied the purse of gold to the waist belt of her braies.

'I have often heard men say that women keep their greatest treasure under their skirts, but now I have seen it with my own eyes,' Simon murmured weakly. His lids had opened again, but he was barely lucid. She saw the effort it was costing him as pride warred with debilitating pain.

She took the cloth from his brow, refreshed it in the bowl and replaced it. 'You stand need to waste your breath on folly when the journey will take all your strength and endurance,' she scolded. 'You do not have to pretend with me.'

He swallowed, feverish sweat shining on the movement of his throat. 'It is not for your sake that I am pretending,' he said through gritted teeth. 'But my own.'

CHAPTER 35

Biting her lip, Sabina admitted Father Gilbert to the room in Nicaea where Simon lay. Fever had stripped his flesh to the bone, and she was terrified that he was going to die. In the mews she had dealt with the ailments of hawks, had saved the weakly ones from starvation by hand feeding them, had bathed infected eyes, had dealt with parasites and moult, all without difficulty. But she had been unable to save her children from fever and stiffening sickness and her husband from drowning. Now the man who had been her first sweet love was fading before her eyes, despite all that she could do.

The priest was here to confess Simon and shrive him of his sins lest his time was nigh. Sabina closed the door on the chamber and went into the courtyard behind the house. There was a marble fountain – nothing as grand as the marvels they had seen in Constantinople, but pleasing still. She sat down on a bench beneath a fig tree that offered cool green shade from the heat of the day, but she could not settle, and seconds later rose to pace the circumference of the courtyard, which, for all its pleasantness, felt like a prison. The Norman chirugeon who had attended Simon this morning had declared morosely that there was nothing to do but fetch an axe and chop off the infected leg. Simon had been lucid enough to declare that he would rather die than face such an ordeal. Indeed, he would rather be dead than lose his leg and the chirugeon had been dismissed, muttering darkly that only a priest could serve Simon now.

Sabina had heard that there was a Greek physician in the town, but the crusader troops were wary of his remedies and distrusted him as they distrusted all Greeks. It was rumoured that he fraternised with infidels. Aubrey, Simon's master-at-arms, had refused to fetch him, saying that he would not let a foreigner butcher his master. But with nothing left to lose Sabina was growing more inclined by the minute to seek him out.

The sun had shifted a degree on the dial when the priest emerged from Simon's chamber, his expression grave. Sabina saw Aubrey step forward to speak with him, then cross himself as the priest shook his head.

Sabina recognised the signals for they had been part of the preliminaries when her children were dying. 'I will not let it happen,' she said, clenching her fists.

Father Gilbert left the house and she hurried after him, calling out in the hot, dusty street.

He turned, his silver brows raised in question. 'Daughter?'

Sabina wiped her wet palms on her gown. 'Please,' she said. 'Do you know where I can find the Greek physician?'

He considered her thoughtfully. 'If your purpose is to help your lord, I doubt that anyone but God can save him now,' he said. 'He will not agree to the removal of the limb and that is the only thing that might secure his life.'

'Even so.' She made a small gesture serve for the rest.

'Your zeal commends you, daughter, but it is misplaced.'

Sabina drew herself up. 'Mayhap it is, but I will not know unless I try. The Greeks know much of the ancient lore of healing. If this man cannot help then I have lost nothing. And if he can cure my lord, then it will not have been a lost opportunity.'

'You speak boldly for a woman.' Father Gilbert's tone was more speculative than hostile. He folded his arms within his habit sleeves and considered her out of incisive blue eyes.

'I speak as I must. Lord Simon de Senlis was charitable to me beyond measure in Brindisi. Now loyalty binds me to do what I can for him in return.'

The priest nodded. 'You are not then his mistress,' he said dryly.

'Indeed not!' Indignation burned Sabina's face. 'I am a widow of respectable reputation!' The words rang facetiously in her own ears. How respectable her reputation would be by the time she arrived home was open to debate.

'Then your loyalty towards this man does you great credit,' the priest said. 'I am acquainted with the house of the Greek physician and I will take you there.' He raised a forefinger, cutting off her words of gratitude. 'I will warn you that his services do not come cheaply and that he has a contempt for us at least as great as the contempt that we harbour for his kind.'

'I have enough to pay for his services,' Sabina responded, 'and I care not for his nature providing only that he is a competent doctor.'

The priest shrugged. 'That is open to debate, daughter, and a risk you take.' He began to walk, his sandalled feet sending out puffs of dust. Bowing her head, modest in the presence of a priest, Sabina accompanied him through the winding streets of Nicaea until they came to an arched alleyway with dwellings either side, their doors brightly painted and their stone walls fortress-thick. Dark-eyed black-haired children played a ball game in the narrow street. A woman was beating a woven mat out of an upstairs window and a small shower of dust and reed fragments shimmied to the ground. Disturbed from its basking by the debris, a brown lizard shot up the wall and disappeared into a dark crevice.

Pausing at a door that was coloured deep red, Father Gilbert knocked loudly. 'I am looking for Alexius the physician!' he cried, 'I have a sick man who needs his skills!'

The woman who had been beating the mat gave Sabina

and her companion an unfriendly look and, retreating into the dark arch of the room, fastened the shutters with a smart rap. The children disappeared down an even narrower side alley, like the lizard into its crevice.

'Greeks!' snorted the priest. 'Now you understand why it is a waste of time.'

Sabina set her lips. 'I will not give up so easily,' she said and raised her own hand to knock at the red door.

Even before her knuckles had connected, a man appeared from around the side of the house, his expression decidedly grumpy. He was moving his tongue around the inside of his mouth, clearing food from his teeth, and crumbs of bread were trapped within his luxuriant black beard. A loose robe of blue linen with silk borders billowed around his tall, narrow frame.

He looked his two visitors up and down with irascible dark brown eyes. 'Can a man not eat his food in peace?' he demanded sourly. 'You Franks, you are barbarians!' He spoke Norman French with a heavy accent.

'I am sorry to disturb you,' Father Gilbert said stiffly, 'but there is a sick man in need of your services and our errand is one of Christian mercy.'

'Hah, why come to me? You have your own physicians who are quite capable of "Christian mercy".' His tone was scornful. 'I have no desire to interfere with their learned treatments.' Flicking crumbs from his beard, he started to turn away.

'Wait . . . please – they have said that the only way is to remove his leg . . . and I know it will surely kill him,' Sabina cried.

Alexius the physician snorted down his nose. 'That is what your healers always say. They hack pieces off people more readily than common street butchers.' However, his manner thawed. 'I will come,' he said. 'But I will promise nothing. You Franks only send for me in the last resort, when it is usually too late. Wait while I finish my meal and fetch my satchel. A few moments will make no difference.' He disappeared again.

'I warned you, daughter,' Father Gilbert said wryly.

Sabina managed a wan smile. 'In truth I can bear with his manner if he is able to do something for my lord.'

'Only last week, I stood by and watched your Frankish chirugeons kill a man,' said Alexius as he followed Sabina through the large wooden gates and into the courtyard of the house where Simon was lodged. 'He had taken a spear wound to the thigh and I had been treating him with poultices, but your people insisted that he would only recover if the limb was removed.' He gave a snort of derision. 'Needless to say, he parted company with this life almost as swiftly as they parted him from his leg with a war axe.'

'My lord has refused to submit to the knife,' Sabina said. 'He says that if he is going to die, it will be with his body intact.'

'Wise man,' said Alexius facetiously.

They entered the sick room, which was darkened because the shutters had been closed against the hot beat of the sun. Simon was thrashing in the midst of a fevered dream. Turstan, who was keeping watch at his bedside, leaped to his feet and looked anxiously at Sabina and the newcomer.

'It's all right,' Sabina said quickly. 'Master Alexius is here to help Lord Simon.'

'If he is not beyond help,' the Greek confirmed pessimistically and striding to the shutters unfastened the latch and threw them wide to admit a surge of hot, yellow sunshine. 'And that I cannot tell if I cannot see what needs to be done.'

Simon had cried out and thrown his forearm across his eyes at the sudden burn of light. Sweat glistened on his body as if he had just emerged from a pool, and his eyes were opaque and fever-glazed.

The physician approached the bed and, drawing aside the light cover, gazed the length of his patient's body. He made a soft clicking noise between the slight gap in his front teeth and shook his head.

Sabina's stomach plummeted. 'Can you do anything for him?' she asked.

'I can do much for him, but whether he will live is another matter.' Removing his satchel, Alexius pushed back his sleeves.

'I will need hot water and fresh linen bandages.'

Sabina nodded and went to the door.

'And if you have some good, clear wine, then that too.' He stooped over Simon's bandaged, massively swollen leg and once more clicked his tongue.

'You are not taking it off!' Simon gasped and struggled upright against the soaked sheets and bolsters.

'Of course I am not,' Alexius said, his nostrils flaring with indignation. 'I am not one of your barbarous Frankish chirugeons.' He pressed one long, firm hand against Simon's brow. 'Your fever is high, I see, but not so great that you do not know what is happening to you. I am going to give you a drink that will dull your pain, and then I am going to clean and drain your leg and poultice the wound.'

Simon lay back, panting, and bared his teeth in the terrible semblance of a smile. 'Do you then challenge the priest who came here to shrive me in preparation to greet death?'

Alexius mirrored the smile with his own lack of mirth. 'It was the priest and the woman who came to fetch me,' he said. 'Father Gilbert's task is the comfort and saving of souls. My concern is with the flesh.'

Sabina returned with the requested items. She had thought that the wine was a vehicle for mixing the physician's nostrums – indeed, it was, but most of it disappeared down Alexius' throat in very short order and only a scant cupful was left for the patient.

'Drink this,' said Alexius, handing Simon a chalcedony cup filled with hot liquid and herbs. 'It will make you sleep.'

'What's in it?' Turstan demanded suspiciously, his hand hovering close to his sword hilt.

Alexius gave him an irritated look. 'I believe it is what you Franks call a potion of dwale. It contains the juice of hemlock, white poppy and henbane, together with vinegar and briony.'

'Jesu, you will kill him!' Turstan started forward, an inch of steel showing at the rim of his scabbard.

'Put up!' Simon gasped at the young man. 'Think you if he kills me that he expects to leave this room alive!'

'It is the quantities that are crucial, not the contents,' Alexius said, unperturbed. 'A man can kill himself on wine alone if he drinks enough. This will do no more than dull your master's wits whilst I do what must be done.'

Turstan slotted the sword back into the scabbard but his frown remained. Filled with misgivings of her own, Sabina watched the physician hold the cup to Simon's lips. The taste must have been foul, for Simon grimaced, but he drank steadily until it was all gone.

Very soon his eyelids drooped and when Alexius raised Simon's arm and let it drop there was no response. Save for the rise and fall of his chest, the man on the bed might as well have been dead.

Alexius turned his attention to the infected leg and with a dexterity and speed too swift to follow set about draining and poulticing the wound. The stench was appalling and Sabina had to draw her wimple across her face. Turstan visibly paled, but steadfastly held his ground. Alexius seemed not in the least disturbed, all his concentration bent upon his task.

'I can see that this leg has been broken long ago,' the Greek said. 'The ill humour stems from this old injury.' He washed out the crater left by the abscess with warm salt water. 'Now it needs to be poulticed and bandaged,' he said, and snapped his fingers and pointed, indicating that Sabina should pass him the hot water and the bandages.

She forced herself through the barrier of her revulsion and came to the bedside with the items. Even lanced and cleaned, the wound looked so terrible that Sabina did not think it could ever heal.

Alexius tested the heat of the water with his wrist and, with a satisfied grunt, poured about a quarter of it into a wooden bowl. Taking what looked suspiciously like a large hunk of mouldy bread from his satchel he broke it into pieces in the water and mashed it around until it formed a gluey, bluish-grey mass. This he packed into the wound and bound it firmly in place with the fresh bandages.

'So,' he said. 'We replace the dressing twice a day for a week and see how matters progress.' With a grunt of satisfaction he washed his hands in the remaining water and then applied himself to tending Simon's minor injuries from the battle at Dorylaeum. These he smeared with a thick application of honey before lightly bandaging.

'Leave him to sleep now,' he said. 'I am afraid that when he awakens he will have sore need of the pot, for his bowels will void the potion in a vigorous manner.' He gathered up his instruments and returned them to his satchel. 'I will come again this evening before the curfew.'

Sabina saw him to the door and presented him with one of the gold bezants given to her by Ralf de Gael.

Alexius smiled dourly as he took it. 'At least you pay in good Greek gold and not the common silver of the Franks,' he said.

'You do not think much of us, even though your emperor summoned us to help him against the Turks,' Sabina was stung to retort.

'I think you are a barbaric horde,' Alexius said. 'And our emperor asked for a few trained mercenaries, not the rabble of zealots that has washed up against his walls. But I cannot fault your courage, or the endurance of your fighting men and the women who follow in their dust.' Inclining his head to her, he departed, a tall thin figure striding out like an ungainly wading bird.

Sighing, Sabina closed the door and returned to her vigil in the sickroom. She had done her best. Now it truly was in the hands of God and a physician who obviously cared deeply about his craft, if not his patients.

CHAPTER 36

Nunnery of Elstow, Christmas 1097

'Is there news?'

Matilda had known that her mother was going to ask, but even so the question made her tense. 'Only the letter that arrived in September when they were preparing to leave Nicaea.' She shivered. The day was bitterly cold with snow threatening in the raw wind, but her mother had lit only the most meagre of fires in her chamber. Judith could have had grand apartments and as much charcoal on her fire as she desired, but she chose to live a Spartan life, bereft of colour. The embroideries of which she had once been so fond had been banished into one of two plain coffers standing against the side of the room, leaving the walls bare of all adornment save a large crucifix. Even the shutters were plain, with no hangings to exclude the draughts that blew through the wooden joints.

Moving with the stiffness of rheumatic joints, Judith went to one of the coffers, threw back the lid and drew out a green woollen mantle.

'Here, put this on. You are too soft.' She handed her daughter the garment and scooped more charcoal into the brazier with a small shovel. 'Your uncle Stephen wrote that they had a great victory against the Turks at a place called Dorylaeum, but that was in the summer. News takes so long to travel.' She crossed herself. 'I pray daily for their success and their safe return.'

'So do I.' Matilda thrust her head through the embroidered opening of the mantle and shook the folds down over her body. Little Matilda, who had been standing pressed against her skirts, now made a game of hiding under the bottom edge of the voluminous woollen garment.

Sour humour twisted Judith's lips. 'So now, as I once was, you are a Countess with a great burden of responsibility. There are dark shadows beneath your eyes, daughter. Are you sure that the task is not too great for you?'

Matilda shook her head. 'If there are dark shadows beneath my eyes it is because I do not sleep well alone,' she said. 'I do not have your love of solitude.'

Her mother gave a contemptuous sniff. 'Sooner or later, we all must sleep alone.'

'I know that, and I would rather it was later. As to the matter of ruling my lands . . . I watched you do it when I was a child and I learned at your knee. I know which men Simon trusted and I trust them in his stead to see that matters run smoothly.'

Judith's eyes brightened with warning. 'So smoothly that you do not see that they may be stealing from you. It is never wise to trust anyone.'

For an instant her words conjured the spectre of Waltheof into the room. Judith came to stand behind her grandson and laid her vein-mottled hands upon his shoulders, thus suggesting without words that Matilda should have a care for the sake of future generations.

'I am not cheated,' Matilda said with quiet dignity. 'I do not close myself in my chamber and shut my ears. I keep myself busier than a bee in a hive, because only when I am utterly worn out with writs, courts, deeds and accounts, can I snatch a few hours' sleep. I know every servant's duty to me. I do not drive my people the way I drive myself, but they know what I expect of them.' She gave a humourless smile. 'God help me, mother, but sometimes your shadow stands at my own shoulder.'

'I can see how much you resent me,' Judith said. 'Even now, when we have made our peace. But I am not the shadow standing at your shoulder. You must seek elsewhere for that.'

Matilda set her lips, feeling defensive for her mother's words were partly true. Perhaps she would never be free of either parent. 'I do not resent you,' she said. 'We are of the same flesh, that is all. In years to come, I see myself standing where you stand now . . . and it frightens me.'

Judith shook her head. 'Then you fear without cause, daughter,' she replied with what was almost grim humour. 'In my place you would build up the fire and embrace the comfort of a mantle. You do not have the taste for austerity . . . The passions you have are your father's, and they lie elsewhere. Go and live your life . . . not mine, or his.'

The somewhat awkward silence that followed her speech was broken by the sound of the matins bell calling the nuns to worship. It was with a mutual sense of relief that mother and daughter went to join them, each having been given food for thought.

In church, Matilda knelt beside her mother and prayed for Simon's safe homecoming. Little Matilda wriggled like an eel and was only prevented from shouting at the top of her voice by the bribe of a piece of honeycomb to suck. Waltheof behaved beautifully, and seemed totally absorbed in the chants and the ritual. With shining eyes and parted lips, he hung on every part of the service. The sight was so odd in a small boy that it sent a frisson down Matilda's spine. Judith noticed it too, for as they left the church she said, 'It is not usual for firstborn sons to enter the Church, but have you given thought to the notion?'

'I have.' Matilda watched her son skipping along the path, his shoes making scuff lines in the dirt. 'But it is too early to tell, and if I do not bear Simon another son Waltheof will have to live a secular life, whatever his vocation.'

'You had best pray that your husband returns,' her mother said, 'and that you are both still fecund, for the child has a true devotion, and that is rare indeed.' There was such a desolate look in her eyes that all Matilda's irritation vanished, and in its stead she felt a surge of compassion, and gently touched her mother's sleeve. Judith allowed the gesture and after a moment reached over and patted Matilda's hand.

Simon opened his eyes and while his mind roused to the notion of a new day, looked at the ceiling. It was painted with gold stars on a blue background so that it seemed to his waking gaze that he was looking at a night sky. The illusion was marred by a hanging lamp of opaque glass suspended on a chain and giving off a soft, translucent glow from the scented oil burning within. He let his stare travel around the room, taking in the richly coloured frescoes adorning the walls, the bed hangings of iridescent silk, the embroidered covers that had been stitched to mirror the strange ceiling. There had been so many nightmares and strange dreams of late that it took him some time to remember where he was and why.

'Good morrow, my lord,' said Sabina. 'I see you are awake at last.' She came to him across the room, her black hair tightly braided but uncovered in the privacy of the chamber. She was carrying a basket containing fresh bread, its surface painted with honey and slivers of nut, and a cup brimming with wine.

Simon sat up against the bolsters and felt the silk slide sensuously against his skin. 'I think so.' He managed a grin. 'It is difficult to sort dream from reality in a chamber like this.' He took the knife that lay in the basket and carved a chunk from the loaf. The warm, yeasty smell made his mouth water. After nearly dying in Nicaea he had a fresh appreciation of the wonders of being alive. All his senses had been stripped of a dusty layer of familiarity and were now as sharp and new as the colours of spring. Hunger was perhaps the most intense. He had been too ill to eat for weeks and now his body was putting on the flesh it had lost to the burn of fever.

Alexius the Greek physician had known his craft, and it was his knowledge, coupled with Sabina's vigilant tending, that had saved his life. After the draining of the abscess and within a couple of applications of the mouldy bread poultices, the fever had diminished and Simon's leg had begun to heal. Two weeks after Alexius' first visit, they had left Nicaea for Durazzo. Simon acknowledged that, despite his recovery, he was not strong enough to return to the crusade trail. The army was laying siege to Antioch, and conditions were such that anyone who took sick died. If he rode to Antioch, he would become one more mouth to feed, followed by one more corpse to bury. Even if the hills were greener on the other side – which now he doubted – for the moment he no longer wanted to see them.

Sabina sat down on the enamelled coffer at the bedside and leaning over helped herself to a chunk of the bread. Sunlight poked through the slats in the shutters and shone on her braids, putting a rainbow sheen on the raven-black. Her eyes were the soft, violet-grey of a dove's breast and her face the pure oval of a Madonna's, but she ate with the gusto of a soldier. The contrast touched and amused him. When a delicate flush tinged her cheek, he realised that his scrutiny was too intense and he sent his gaze beyond her into the splendour of the room. Astonishing what a gold coin could buy. This dwelling belonged to a silk merchant who was absent on business and it was as magnificent as any palace in England. The walls were painted with figures so lifelike that Simon sometimes thought that he could see them breathing. The colours were deep and rich, and the artist had not stinted to use gold in the paint that delineated embroidery on the fine garments. The effect was opulent and heavy. Exquisite taste, but in the end too much for the eye to take in and the mind to absorb.

'Turstan has gone to the wharves,' Sabina said. Her voice

was hesitant. 'Apparently there is a ship due to sail for Brindisi on the late tide.'

'Ah,' Simon nodded. It was the next step of their journey. He had told Turstan that they would begin searching for a ship today, and the young man was plainly eager to be about the task. Sabina, however, did not share that eagerness.

'The thought of a sea voyage troubles you?'

She forced a smile. 'Of course it does,' she said. 'I cannot help but remember . . . but I have no choice unless it be to stay here.' Abruptly she rose and paced to the window. 'I can endure. I have the strength.'

Simon studied her slender frame. 'I know you do,' he said quietly. 'I owe my life to it. If you had not fetched that physician . . . if you had not stayed at my side and tended me through the fever . . .'

She gave a harsh little laugh. 'That was not strength,' she said. 'That was fear. If I had lost you the way that I lost everyone else who was dear to me . . .' She folded her arms and hugged herself tightly, her back still turned.

'But you didn't lose me,' he said. 'And I am in your debt.'

'You owe me nothing.' Her knuckles tightened against the side seams of her gown. 'I was merely repaying what was owed, and if you offer me your kindness and gratitude I will kick you.'

'Neither of those,' he said hoarsely.

She turned then to look at him. There was a long silence in which the tension built like steam under the lid of a cauldron. One step further. Simon swallowed. His mouth was dry and he was painfully erect, his lust a physical pain made all the sharper for not having been quenched for so long.

She licked her lips and moved closer, drawn by an invisible thread. She paused at the foot of the bed and looked at him. Naked from his sleep, his body was still thin from his illness, each rib delineated, but there was wiry strength in the long muscles of his arms and his flat, firm belly. Face, throat and hands were tanned oak-brown by the burn of the Eastern sun;

the rest was as pale as new milk. She wanted to push her hands through his sleep-tangled hair and lie with him. Touch him, confirm the life force flowing through both of them. It had been so long since she had been held and wanted and loved.

He extended his hand. With trembling fingers she took it, felt sweat leap between them and then the wild, hot burn of longing, and longing assuaged.

CHAPTER 37

Sabina and Simon rode into the convent of Evreux at the same time as the rain. The November skies were grey and heavy with moisture and a bitter wind was blowing from the north. The nunnery boasted a fine timber guesthouse, with feather stuffing in the pallets rather than straw, and wax candles that burned with a clear, yellow light. There was water provided for washing and a deep fire pit in the centre of the room sent out wafts of brazen heat.

Sabina sat on one of the pallets in the guest dormitory. There were twenty in all, arrayed down either side of the room. Someone's travelling satchel and a clean pair of shoes had claimed one of the mattresses, but for now she was the only occupant. The stables were situated beneath and a glance out of the arched window showed her two lay workers busy in the cobbled yard, their hoods raised against the drizzle. She watched Simon cross the yard and speak to one of them. His limp was more pronounced since the old leg injury had flared up and he could no longer make even the slightest pretence of hiding it. However, it had worked to his advantage. The mention he had been on crusade and at the battle of Dorylaeum, coupled with evidence of injury, meant that the doors of abbey guesthouses and castles alike had been flung open to them with effusive welcome.

She watched the familiar gesture he made of pushing his hair back off his face, his other hand clasped around his belt.

Her stomach twisted. She was going to miss him terribly . . .
but it was for the best.

That morning in Durazzo was branded in her memory.
Their lust had been incandescent, so fierce that the first time
it had lasted no more than a dozen racing heartbeats. The
second time the blaze had been slower to kindle, a lazy burn
of pleasure that had grown hotter by steady, calculated degrees
until the time had arrived to free the fire and let it immolate
them.

It had to happen, she thought. In a way, it had been the
closing of a circle that had begun in her father's mews when
they were little more than children. There was no regret on
either side, but they had not lain together again and they had
avoided situations during the journey up through Italy and
France where they might have succumbed.

She heard him climb the staircase to the dormitory and
listened to his steps, alternately firm and hesitant. By the time
he opened the door, she was on her feet and facing it. A
nunnery guesthouse was not a setting to put temptation in
their way, but it was the first time they had been alone in
each other's company since Durazzo.

'You are sure you want to stay here?' he said, casting a
glance around the chamber.

She folded her hands together and faced him squarely.
'Quite sure.'

He cleared his throat. 'You know there is a place for you
in my household, should you wish it.'

She shook her head. 'You mean well, but you are wrong.
Where would I go – home in your entourage to your wife?
What would I do? I have no skill with an embroidery needle,
nor any desire to become a lady of the bower.'

He winced at her assessment. 'Mayhap you are right,' he
sighed, 'but I would not have you think that I intend abandoning you. The least I can do is offer you a roof and
protection.'

'It is noble of you, but I need neither. You took me in when

Saer died and I was grief-wild. I like to think that I repaid your support in full measure when you were sick. There are no debts. We settled the last of them that day in Durazzo.'

Their eyes met. She saw understanding in his, and a renewed blaze of gold like fire. 'You truly desire to become a nun?' he asked. 'After everything that you . . . that we . . .' He made a gesture that served for the rest, a gesture that encompassed the bed.

'After everything,' she affirmed, although her cheeks reddened. 'And not because I have suddenly grown penitent or ashamed. I have thought about taking the veil ever since the road to Dorylaeum.' She looked down at her clasped hands. 'Between then and Durazzo, between Durazzo and now I have done much praying and thinking and my mind is set. If the nuns of Evreux will have me then I will join them – for the peace of my soul, and for the love of God who has taken so much and given it back. For Saer and my children who did not live.' Her voice wobbled but with a supreme effort she steadied herself and found a smile.

He turned to the window, and biting his thumbnail gazed out. The sound of the rain rustled around them and the voices of the grooms floated through the open shutters. 'I have no doubt that the Abbess will welcome you with open arms,' he said. 'A purse of Greek gold and the company in which you have arrived are sure to guarantee you a position.'

'Who knows. One day I may become an abbess myself.'

He made a shrugging gesture. 'If you set your mind to the matter, I do not doubt you will succeed. But to renounce the world . . .' He looked at her sombrely over his shoulder. 'It is a great stride to take.'

She came to the window and, wrapping her arms around him, laid her head on his breast. If the grooms looked up, they would see the embrace, but she did not care. 'No,' she said, with a tremulous smile. 'Like that day in Durazzo – it is but a single step.'

*

Waltheof genuflected, rose to his feet, and carefully laid the garland of evergreen and red-berried holly at the foot of his grandfather's tomb. He loved coming to Crowland, and it was always with great solemnity and sense of occasion that he would enter the chapel and make his offering. His mother visited the abbey several times a year. The last occasion had been late summer and the place had been crammed with pilgrims and dusty travellers, all present to venerate the bones of his grandfather, who, by the ordinary people at least, was viewed as a saint. The blind had been made to see, so it was said, and the lame to walk. Propped against the wall near the tomb were several crutches left by grateful folk who claimed to have been cured by their visit to the tomb. To have such power, even in death, fascinated the boy.

Today, he and his family had his grandsire to themselves. A light snow was sifting down outside, the wind was bitter and most folk were hugging their hearths and waiting out the winter like hibernating animals. Waltheof, however, was warm within several layers of wool and a hooded mantle lined with marten fur. His little sister was grizzling, but then she was a baby and always did. His mother crossed herself and rose from her knees. Briefly she laid her hand on the silk pall covering the tomb housing, her gesture tender and sad.

Waltheof thought that she looked very pretty. She was wearing her best winter gown of reddish-gold wool with little lozenges of gold thread embroidered at the hanging cuff and deep neck opening and her thick, bronze-coloured braids were twined with red ribbons. In a way that he couldn't understand she reminded him of the statue of the blue-cloaked Madonna in the church at Northampton. The clothes and colours were different, but in his young mind some element still drew the two together.

They left the church house and trooped out into the frozen air. Waltheof gazed up through fluttering lashes at the light fall of snowflakes and stuck out his tongue in the hopes of catching one and feeling it melt.

There were riders waiting in the courtyard. Smoky steam

rose from the nostrils of their horses and harnesses jingled as the beasts stamped their hooves on the frozen ground. One of the men had dismounted and was gazing intently towards him and his mother and sister. He looked familiar to Waltheof, but the boy could not quite place him. His mother had stopped, although her gown and mantle still swished gently with the impetus of her last step. She was as rigid as the Virgin statue, and twice as pale.

'Dear, sweet Jesu,' she whispered. Her hands opened and closed at her sides. He watched the movement of her fingers, fascinated by the gleam of light on her gold rings. And then she cried, 'Simon!' in a breaking voice, and ran to fling her arms around the man whom now Waltheof suddenly recognised.

At his back, Helisende lightly placed her hand on his shoulder. 'Your papa is home from his pilgrimage,' she told him, a shiver of emotion in her voice. 'Praise God. Now perhaps all will be well.'

The snowfall grew heavier and more persistent. Although they could have stayed at the guesthouse in Crowland, and Ingulf would have been more than pleased to house a newly returned crusader and exchange stories, Simon was uneasy with the surroundings, and preferred to ride on to the hunting lodge at Fotheringhay.

During the journey he spoke little. He took Waltheof up before him, wrapping the child tenderly in his cloak. Little Matilda clamoured to ride on his saddle too and he obliged, but the novelty quickly wore off and she soon demanded to be returned to the familiar arms of her mother.

By the time they reached the hunting lodge the snow was fetlock deep on the horses and the snowflakes were nearly as large as communion wafers.

'Won't last,' said the cheerful gatekeeper who came out to welcome them, a lantern wavering on the ash pole in his hand. 'Be gone in a couple of days. Will you be wanting the huntsmen to mark some game for you, my lord?'

Simon nodded. 'Some of the men might wish to hunt, and it would be good to have fresh meat for the table.' He gently lowered his son to the ground and then swung carefully from the saddle. His leg was aching with the cold and he was tired, hungry and, if the truth were known, unsettled. Matilda had changed during his absence. Some of the yielding softness had gone from her character, leaving it closer to the bone. Her edge was steelier now, more of her mother's weight in the scales when it had been her father's nature that tipped the balance before. Her manner was brisk and accustomed as she spoke to the gatekeeper and then to the attendants who had made haste to prepare the hunting lodge with only a short advance warning by the herald she had sent ahead. But then, Simon thought, he had left her to her own devices, and she had been forced to stand alone.

A blazing fire had been kindled in the lodge's central hearth and a cook was hastily assembling a cauldron of leek pottage while an assistant mixed dough for savoury griddle-cakes. Simon rubbed his hands and held them out to the fire. Aping him, Waltheof did the same before dancing off to investigate the other rooms in the lodge.

Matilda brought Simon a brimming cup of wine. They had said little to each other since the first, breathless greeting. It was all held behind a dam, waiting for the first breach to be made, and the words to come pouring through in an unstoppable tumult.

He took the cup and their fingers touched in the exchange. A pink flush rose from her throat to her face and Simon felt a responding warmth of desire for her. He also felt a flicker of guilt, but even for the sake of unburdening his conscience he was not going to tell her about Sabina. Some things were better left unsaid.

'What made you turn back?' she asked. 'I thought to be a crusader's widow for a long time yet.'

The wine was a strong Gascon red and made Simon's throat sting. 'You were nearly a widow in truth,' he said. 'My leg became infected and I was only saved by the skills of a Greek physician and some dedicated nursing. By the time I was well enough to leave my bed, our army had moved on. I did not have the health to follow. Had I done so, my bones would be bleaching on a plain in Anatolia.'

A look of alarm widened her eyes but he saw her fight it down. Nor did she insist on finding him a chair or begin to fuss around him. Familiar ground had indeed shifted during his absence.

'Those of my men who wanted to stay have joined the troops of Stephen of Aumale.'

'Not Ralf de Gael?' Suddenly her voice was sharp with challenge.

He shook his head. 'No, I have no Bretons in my troop, and my English knights would never follow De Gael.'

'Yet you made your peace with him?'

'Yes, I made my peace with him. What else was I to do? Challenge him to a trial by combat?' He breathed out hard. 'Every man makes mistakes in his life. God knows I have committed my own share of folly. De Gael took the cross to atone for the part he played in your father's death. I know that he has always been able to charm the birds out of the trees with that smooth tongue of his, but I can tell when a man is lying and when he is telling the truth, and I believe De Gael is genuinely remorseful.' He looked at her. 'Are you so unforgiving and vindictive that you will cling to your past grievances for the rest of your life?'

She gave him a narrow look. 'My English family are fond of their blood feuds,' she said. 'It is a tradition we have clung to time out of mind.'

'You would rather I had put my blade through De Gael's breast?'

'No.' She shook her head. 'He is not worth the sullying of good steel and the damning of your soul. Nor is he worth the bother of my hatred. He is *nothing* to me. Beneath my contempt.' She looked at him. 'Whatever you think, that is one demon that no longer rides me so hard.' She had spoken proudly, but her eyes had grown suspiciously liquid.

Simon's heart moved within him, stirred by compassion and love. Setting his cup down on the hearthstone, he pulled her round and drew her into his embrace. Her own arms swept around his neck and she clung tightly. He buried his face against the soft skin of her throat beneath the veil and felt the beating of her pulse. There was a faint perfume of lavender, and lemon balm, clean, enticing, unbearably erotic. She moved her head sideways and his lips slid across hers. He tasted the salt of her tears and through it felt the leaping response of her need. Her mouth was open, her thighs straining against his.

Their embrace was wild and primitive, no room for anyone or anything else, but eventually they had to surface to gasp for breath and with separation came a modicum of awareness. The servants, heads lowered and eyes discreetly averted, were going about the business of preparing the lodge for the guests. His men were arranging their baggage between the aisles of the hall and unrolling straw mattresses.

Waltheof came bounding back from his exploration and rushed up to his parents, a large deer antler clutched in his fist. 'See what I found!' he cried.

The need to focus on the child further restored sanity. Simon took the antler and admired it. Matilda smoothed her gown and wiped her eyes. While she composed herself, Simon explained to the boy in a less than steady voice that the number of tines on the antler meant that the stag had been six years old when he shed these particular horns.

'I daresay if we search the woods we might come across more sheddings if the huntsmen have not picked them up,' he said.

'Now?'

Simon grinned at his son's enthusiasm and shook his head. 'No, lad. My old bones need to rest first, and while the snow-fall might not be as thick among the trees I have no desire to venture out again in this growing blizzard. Still,' he ran his fingers along the grooved brown stem of the antler, 'this section here will make a fine hilt for a knife, and that can be made beside the hearth.'

The child nodded excitedly and dashed off to show his find to Helisende and his little sister.

Stooping to the hearth, Simon picked up his wine and found that it had grown warm from its proximity to the flames. 'When I was taken sick, I dreamed of your father,' he said. 'He came to me and showed me that the other side of the hill could hold terror as well as freedom. I do not know if it was a true vision or just a fevered dream, but it was one of the reasons I turned back.'

'And what of your crusader's vow?' she asked. 'Will you have a priest absolve you?'

'Mayhap.' He gave an uncomfortable shrug. To be quit of the vow entirely would be to close a door. He had been relieved to turn back – the wanderlust no longer rode him hard – but he still needed to see through the open portal. He watched his small son skip across the room and return to his side, the antler clutched in his hand. 'For now I have a notion to build another church in Northampton and give thanks for my safe homecoming.'

Matilda relaxed and the expression in her eyes grew soft and warm.

'Can I help to build it too?' Waltheof demanded.

Simon smiled and ruffled the boy's red-gold curls. 'Of course you can,' he said. 'Looking after it will be one of your duties when you are a grown man.'

The boy beamed as if he had been given a present of great worth.

'You like buildings, do you?' Simon asked, diverted by Waltheof's enthusiasm.

'I like churches,' he said, and hared off again to show his prize piece to one of the knights who was entering the hall after stabling his horse.

'My mother says that he has a natural vocation, and I believe she is right,' Matilda said. She looked through her lashes at her husband. They were spiky from her tears, but the effect, along with the slight reddening, only served to enhance the blue of her eyes. 'One he cannot fulfil while he is an only son.'

Simon met the sidelong appraisal, and desire flared, hot and ready. 'Then it behoves us to do something about it,' he said.

She looked over her shoulder. The last of the soldiers to enter from outside was just closing the door on a world of whirling whiteness. Candles glowed in all the sconces and the central hearth threw out a cheery red light. 'We have the time,' she said softly, and took his hand in hers. 'For a while, at least, whatever the state of the other side of the hill, you are not going to reach it.'

Matilda looked at the collection of small, innocuous brown bulbs that Simon had tipped out on the bed from their cloth pouch. 'What are they?'

He pillowed his hands behind his head and gave her a smile lazy with the repletion of lovemaking. 'For that you will have to take the word of the man who sold them to me. He says that if you bury them in the garden during the autumn they will produce the first flowers of spring. Milk flowers he called them, and he said that the blooms are white and delicate, but robust nonetheless.'

'I will plant them the moment we are home,' she vowed, and scooped them carefully back into their pouch.

'You see,' he said, 'even when I was chasing my demons I thought of you and your garden.'

Matilda was less than impressed. 'And I thought of you every day,' she said. 'I rubbed my knees raw at first with prayer and lamentation.' Setting the pouch carefully to one side, she faced him. 'But I learned to live with it. It was like grieving. The ache did not go away but it became less in time. My children needed me, so did the people. Much as I wanted to crawl into the darkness and lick my wounds, I could not.'

Aware that her tone was growing accusatory and shrewish, she drew back from further recrimination. She had him now; that was all that mattered. And she could so easily have lost him. The scar on his leg and the hollow where the poison had eaten the flesh away was evidence of that.

'I did not mean to sound clever that I thought of you,' he said softly and unpillowed his hand to stroke a tendril of her hair. 'Perhaps it was more in the way of atonement for the way we had parted . . . and perhaps I was wondering what I was doing so far from home. When I bought them I wanted to imagine you planting those bulbs in your garden.'

Matilda was swept by a wave of tenderness and remorse. Leaning forward, she kissed him. 'You are home now,' she said. 'Let us not brood.' Deliberately lightening her tone, she drew away. 'I have gifts for you, too.'

'Other than the one you have already given me?' he grinned suggestively.

Matilda laughed and blushed. 'I do not think that I could dwell in a convent like my mother,' she admitted.

'Perish the thought.'

She went to her small travelling chest and raising the lid drew out a shirt of fine linen chansil and a tunic of blue Flemish wool, embroidered with a pattern of English inter-laced work at cuff and hem and throat. 'I took the measurements from a tunic you left behind,' she said. She did not add that for a time she had slept with his old tunic clutched in her arms for comfort, or that the act of making him a new one had been a way of adjusting to his absence.

He took the garments and examined the delicate stitch-work with wonder. 'I have never set eyes upon such fine needlecraft!'

Matilda warmed beneath the admiration in his tone and rejoined him on the bed. 'I don't know,' she teased, picking up the leg of one of his hastily discarded hose. 'You seem to have sewn a very neat patch on this.'

The hesitation that followed was infinitesimal but it

changed the atmosphere. What had been warm and intimate was suddenly strained. 'I cannot take the credit,' he said. 'One of the laundresses did our mending.' Suddenly he was very busy, donning the shirt, trying on the tunic.

'One of the laundresses,' Matilda repeated, with narrowed eyes.

'She sewed and washed clothes for everyone,' he said in a muffled voice. When his head emerged through the neck opening of the tunic, his gaze did not quite meet hers.

Matilda said nothing. She decided not to ask if Simon had been faithful to her during his absence. Crusaders might take a vow to be chaste while they were soldiers of Christ, but she knew that many did not succeed in keeping their oath. Simon might not be a sexual predator, but she knew his predilection for pastures new. Still, a laundress was no threat to her position, and there had been no sign of such a woman among his entourage. Thus she spoke no more on the matter, and if she did not dismiss it from her mind, neither did she dwell on it with anguish.

CHAPTER 38

Northampton, Christmas 1097

'Shall I put it here?' Waltheof asked. He wafted a brightly coloured knot of braid at his mother then stood on tiptoe to place it in the bare branches of the apple tree.

'Yes, sweetheart, just there,' Matilda paused in her own decoration of the tree to watch her son stretch out, the tip of his tongue protruding between his lips as he concentrated. She smiled wistfully. Her mother had never held with the ceremony of honouring a tree so that it would be fruitful during the next season. It was as pagan as the elf in the well, she said; nonsense, not to be tolerated. But her father had always permitted his people to 'wassail' the trees and Matilda had encouraged the custom.

Simon lifted his small daughter and helped her hang a row of silver bridle bells along a sturdy twig. 'This time last year I was kicking my heels in Brindisi and waiting for the spring,' he said. 'It seems a lifetime ago.'

'It is a lifetime ago.' Stooping to the basket at her feet, Matilda picked up some false apples carved of wood by one of the knights who had a skill in such things. She handed them to their son and glanced at her husband. 'You regret turning back, don't you?' she said shrewdly.

Simon wriggled his shoulders. 'In some small part, yes,'

he admitted. 'I swore a vow, and I have always prided myself on holding to my word.'

'If you had held to it, you would likely be dead.' Matilda gave a small shiver.

'Yes, but honourably so,' he said with a wry smile. Taking one of the wooden apples he helped little Maude to loop it on a high branch of the apple tree.

Matilda bit her lip. 'Is that why you have not asked the priest to absolve you of your oath – because your business is unfinished?'

Simon pondered for a moment. 'While my vow remains open,' he said at last, 'it means that I have not given up. Mayhap it is more of a sop to my conscience than anything else, but if I go and ask for absolution it will mean that I have yielded.'

Matilda said nothing more. She did not really believe that he would set off again on another crusade to fulfil his oath, but she found it hard not to keep demanding constant reassurance. Hard, but not impossible. She had learned much during his absence, not least that she was strong if she had to be. It was only a matter of time before he would have to leave on the King's business anyway. There was war in Normandy, and Matilda daily expected a summons that Simon would have no choice but to answer.

That afternoon the second part of the ceremony was carried out and all the occupants of the hall gathered in the frosty garden grounds. Cups of steaming mulled cider were ladled out from a large cauldron and everyone joined hands and danced around the tree, exhorting it, as a representative of all the apple trees in the orchard, to grow strong and be fruitful in the coming year.

Dusk encroached, turning the world to silver blue as the first star shone in the sky. Laughing, filled with the pleasure of the moment, Matilda moved among the crowd. The hot cider had filled her with a delicious glow, and it seemed to her that her tree was glowing too, for the lanterns set around its base had gilded it with light.

Waltheof and some of the castle's children were playing a game of chase, winding in and out amongst the adults, their squeals high-pitched and carrying in the twilit air. Little Maude toddled after them, bundled up in various layers of clothing topped by a sheepskin mantle.

Simon curved his arm around Matilda's waist from behind and nuzzled aside her wimple to kiss her throat. Smiling, she turned in his embrace and offered him her lips.

From the direction of the courtyard the sound of a shout and the whinny of a horse carried on the clear, cold air. Simon lifted his head from Matilda's like a hound catching a scent. She resisted the urge to hold him more tightly and turned with him to face the sound of intrusion.

'Surely the King will not summon you to Normandy so close to the winter feast?' She was unable to prevent the note of desolation in her voice.

But the summons was not for Simon, it was for her. From Elstow. Her mother was sick with a fever of the lungs and beyond any help but God's. If Matilda wanted to bid farewell, then she must come at once.

Dazed, she made sure that the messenger was given a cup of mulled cider and bade him to take food from the trestle laid out to one side of the tree.

'I must go to her,' she said.

Simon glanced at the sky, which had deepened beyond turquoise and into sapphire. 'At night?' he asked dubiously. His words emerged on a puff of white vapour.

'The morning may be too late.' She looked at him. 'I have to do this – for my sake and hers.'

He studied her thoughtfully, then gave a nod of acceptance. 'You will need torches for the road and a stout escort. Go and make yourself ready for the journey and I will order the horses saddled.' Squeezing her arm, he left.

The people danced around her tree, singing the Wassail, making merry. It was like looking through a window on a bright and gilded scene from which she had been forcibly expelled. Grimly, she pulled her gaze from the celebration and left the enchantment of the garden for the bleak and practical world beyond.

'You do not have to come,' she said to Simon when she found him in their bedchamber, donning a pair of thick chausses over the pair he was already wearing. He was also apparelled in the quilted tunic he usually wore under his armour.

'I want to,' he said. 'I have never truly made peace with your mother. Besides, you cannot go alone.'

Matilda felt a flash of resentment, keen as a recent wound. She went to her coffer and drew out woollen hose, and a thick pair of socks. 'I have grown accustomed to my own company,' she said a trifle tartly.

He reached for the braid leg bindings to wind between ankle and knee. 'Don't you want me to accompany you?'

She bent her head to remove her boot and draw a sock over the one she was already wearing.

'Matilda?'

She lifted her head. 'Of course I want you to come,' she snapped. 'But at your own behest, not from duty or pity, or because you think I'm a lost sheep who will bleat her way over the edge of a cliff if not supervised.' She turned to the other foot, her movements abrupt and her face hidden by the folds of her wimple. 'And because I want you with me, I feel guilty. I have seen how you have been limping on that leg today because the cold is gnawing your bones.'

Simon's smile was humourless. 'Ah then, my love, you have sealed the bargain. You should know better than to cite my leg as a reason why I should stay at home.' In the absence of his squire, he flipped a leg binding around his own calf with expert speed and tucked in the end. 'Nothing you can say or do will keep me now.'

'Nothing I could say or do could keep you before,' she retorted and with a grimace tried to stamp her way into her boot, the fit now made much tighter by the additional sock. 'God's wounds,' she muttered through her teeth.

Simon came to her, and, bending on his good knee, took her foot in his hands and applied leverage. She felt his grip at her ankle, warm, hard and sure. It was not the touch of a man in a state of weakness. 'Yes, my leg pains me,' he said, 'but it would do so whether I came with you or remained here. I have your father's cloak; I will be warm enough.'

Her foot shot into the boot and he fastened the horn toggle at the side. She touched his hair, and watched the gold strands shimmer among the brown. 'It is your cloak now,' she murmured as he performed the same service to her other foot.

'Is it?' He gave a vexed smile. 'Even now I am not certain.' He eased to his feet. He was adept at controlling the response to his pain, but she saw the betraying tightening of his eyelids and winced for him. There were meanings beneath the words, like rocks under the deception of calm water, or bodies in a shallow grave.

'You have always had your own way of wearing it,' she offered.

He started towards the door. 'You need not sweeten the potion,' he said. 'I knew the burdens when I fastened it at my shoulders.'

'All of them?' She too rose, and followed him. There was a tension in the air, like the quiver after the last note on the harp when a song was ended.

'No, not all,' he admitted, 'but still, I knew what I was doing.'

She believed him. She had seldom seen Simon nonplussed or ill at ease, whatever the situation. It came from being a squire at old King William's court, she thought. That, and a feline degree of self-containment that she had never been able to win past.

He set his arm lightly across her shoulders. 'And I have never regretted it.'

It was Matilda's turn to smile and tighten her lids. 'You do not need to sweeten the potion either.' She drew out of his arm, proving that she could do so, and went down to the waiting horses.

Judith's room at Elstow was nearly as cold as the outside air, where frost was growing on the trees like silver moleskin and the air was as sharp as crystal in the lungs.

Entering on the heels of the anxious infirmarian, Matilda's teeth continued to chatter. 'Why is there no brazier?' she demanded.

The nun shook her head and looked apologetic. 'The Lady Judith said that there was no point in having one. We tried to bring one in and light it, but she grew so angry and distressed that Mother Abbess said that we should respect her wishes.'

Her dying wishes. The words hung unspoken but as tangible as the white vapour that puffed from Matilda's nose and mouth. The room was as bare as a crypt. The walls were barren of all save a crucifix – Christ in hollow-ribbed suffering keeping watch over stark, limewashed plaster. Two plain coffers stood near the bed, one holding a thick candle that burned with a steady golden flame in the midnight deep. Seated next to it, her eyes red and puffy with weeping and the rest of her face pinched with cold, was her mother's maid, Sybille. There was a silver goblet in her hand, half full of some dark-coloured liquid. On the bed itself Judith was propped up high against the bolsters to aid her breathing. Spots of feverish colour stained her cheekbones, but otherwise her complexion was ashen. Her grey-streaked hair lay in a single braid, coiled to the left and lying like a rope over her faltering heart. Within their gaunt sockets her eyes were closed, but she was conscious and aware, for her hands were occupied with a set of prayer beads and her lips were moving as she recited the psalms.

Matilda moved to the bedside, Simon following in her wake. The crackle of their feet on the rushes did not disturb Judith's concentration and she continued to murmur.

'Oh, my lady, thank Christ you have come. I did not know if you would!' Sybille rose stiffly to her feet and embraced Matilda, tears running down her face. 'She has been waiting for you! A messenger has gone to your sister too, but she will not arrive for several days yet and my lady does not have that time to wait.'

'Sybille, hush. You always did have a tongue like a bell clapper.' Judith's voice was weak and reedy, and by the end of the sentence she was fighting for breath.

'Mama.' Matilda pushed out of the maid's arms and knelt at the bedside. She took her mother's frozen, skeletal hands and chafed them in hers. 'You should have sent for me sooner.'

'So that you could watch me die for longer?' A spark kindled in Judith's eyes. 'Where would be the point in that?'

Matilda rubbed her thumb over her mother's icy knuckles. 'To be with you,' she said. 'To offer succour and comfort.' There was a tightness in her throat, but it was more a familiar response to being near her mother than anything of grief. Even at the end, Judith could not be conciliatory.

The sound of the dying woman's struggle to breathe filled the room. 'I need neither succour nor comfort,' Judith gasped. 'I have grown so accustomed to being without that their lack disturbs me not.' Her lips curved in the travesty of a smile. 'Instead I have my pride . . . or I had it.' She swallowed jerkily. Matilda took the half-cup of wine and held it to her mother's lips. Judith took a moistening sip, no more, and leaned her head against the piled bolsters while she gathered strength. 'Still, I am glad you have come.' Her voice was a faded whisper that trailed off as her eyes fixed on a point beyond Matilda's shoulder and widened with a blending of fear and astonishment.

'Come out of the shadows,' she croaked hoarsely, 'I do not see well . . .'

Simon stepped forward, and the candlelight around the bed illuminated the blue of his cloak, glittered on the braid border, and cast a yellow glow on the white fur lining. His shadow wavered on the limewashed wall, fuzzy and distorted so that it looked more ursine than human.

'Madame, belle mère,' he said and, advancing to the bed, stooped to kiss her cold brow.

Matilda felt her mother shudder, and knew without being told that Judith had for a moment believed that the presence of her former husband stalked the room.

'I am guilty,' Judith wheezed. 'I have been shriven, but still I am guilty . . . God might forgive me, but I will never forgive myself.'

'Hush, do not distress yourself,' Matilda murmured. 'You cannot make an end like this . . .' She squeezed the cold hands beneath hers and tried to imbue them with some vestige of her own warmth and life. Softly in the background, she could hear Sybille's choked sobs. 'My . . . my father would not want to see you like this.'

'Of course not . . . your father is a saint!' There was a bitter note in the thin voice. 'He is revered for what I took to be his weakness.'

Matilda steeled herself not to leap to her feet and turn her back on her mother. Not to pour out all of her own bitterness and resentment. Her struggle must have shown in her eyes, however, for she caught Simon's gaze on her in troubled compassion. He gave a slight shake of his head, offering both wordless support and the advice that she should say nothing.

Biting her lip, she held her place, and was suddenly glad that they had not arrived sooner.

'I loved him,' Judith whispered, and two tears suddenly spilled from her eyes and rolled down her gaunt cheeks. 'Despite all, I loved him.' There was no breath in her to cry, and her thin body shook with the rigours of her struggle.

In terror Matilda watched her, thinking that she was going to die of this moment. Shriven perhaps, but far from at peace. However, the spasms ceased, and although Judith gasped like a fish too long out of water, her eyes were yet lucid. She extended one palsied hand to touch the white fur of Simon's cloak. Her fingers closed in the harsh guard hairs and dug through to the snow-softness beneath.

'Then that is all that matters,' Simon said and, unfastening the catch, laid the cloak across her body. 'You have to let all else go.'

She looked at him and seemed slowly to absorb his words, for her breathing calmed a little and her clutch became less desperate on the fur.

'Was Waltheof able to do that?' she wheezed.

'Yes,' said Simon without hint of a stumble or pause and meeting her gaze squarely.

'You tell me what I want to hear . . .'

'I tell you the truth.'

She made a disparaging sound, but her crisis was fought and won and she had regained her control. 'I am glad that you are my daughter's husband and not mine,' she said, and stroked the lining of the cloak.

'So am I,' Simon said.

Judith almost smiled at the remark. 'I hear you have not revoked your crusader's vow,' she said after a pause to gather strength.

'No, belle mère,' Simon said gravely, 'I have not revoked it.'

'Then pray for me.'

'Gladly.' Simon dipped his head in acknowledgement and moved from the bed, leaving the cloak draped across her body. If he was cold without its enveloping warmth, he gave no sign. Matilda was moved by his compassion and filled with pride and awe.

Judith closed her eyes and slept, but even in slumber did not relinquish her grip on the cloak.

From the abbey the matins bell sounded, calling the nuns to stumble from their pallets in the dorter and walk in procession to the chapel. Simon went quietly from the room and returned with his second cloak – an affair of dark green wool trimmed with the contrasting red of squirrel and lined for warmth with sheepskins. He also brought a flagon of hot wine, a small loaf and a half wheel of yellow cheese. 'Food?' he murmured.

Matilda shook her head. Her stomach was tied in a knot and she could not think of eating, but she took the wine with gratitude and drank a warming mouthful. There was ginger in it, and she welcomed the trickle of heat it sent through her frozen body. Sybille drank too, cupping her hands around her goblet and sniffing with cold. She too refused the food that Simon offered. Shrugging, he settled himself on the second coffer and ate a portion of bread and cheese.

'On campaign you eat to keep your strength, no matter if the sight of food revolts your belly,' he said, but made no more effort to force the women.

Twice more as the night drew on Matilda heard the abbey bell summoning the nuns to prayer. The candle burned down on its spike and Sybille brought out a new one from the wall cupboard in the corner. Matilda saw that there were more candles in the recessed cupboard – at least half a dozen of golden beeswax, and as thick as a strong man's wrist.

'Kindle them all,' she commanded the maid. 'We may not have heat, but at least we can have a blaze of light.'

Sybille did as she bade, emptying the cupboard of its contents and seeking out extra wrought-iron spikes. 'My lady would say that it is a terrible waste,' she said with an apprehensive glance at the bed.

'For this once I think that the cost is justified,' Matilda answered. 'Let her path be lit fittingly.' She left the bedside to light a candle from the guttering one on the coffer and from it kindled the rest until the room was huge with light.

From the abbey the prime bell rang out, once more beckoning the nuns to their devotions. Outside the chamber a grey winter dawn was breaking. Simon rose to his feet and, murmuring that he was going outside for a piss, limped stiffly from the room.

As the door closed softly behind him, Judith opened her

eyes and fixed them upon the brightness of the candles, and then with effort, slid to her daughter.

'A profligate waste,' she said in a rusty whisper.

'A fitting salute,' Matilda replied and lifted the cup of wine from the coffer to offer her a drink.

Judith made a feeble gesture of denial. 'Leave be, I am beyond that . . .' Her hand groped and sought upon the coverlet, found the edge of the fur cloak and clutched it. A look of relief softened the lines on her face. 'I dreamed of your father,' she said with a faint smile. 'He was wearing this . . . and unlike me, he had not grown old . . .'

Matilda wondered uneasily if her mother was going to have another seizure of grief, but the smile remained. 'I loved him,' Judith said with her breath, an expression of sad under-standing in her face. 'But not enough.' There was another soft breath that stirred the fur on the white pelt, and one that did not, and then there was silence. The candles flickered, their light glinting in the shine of Judith's fixed stare.

'Mother?' Matilda leaned over the still form on the bed. She took one of the cold wrists in her hand and searched along the delicate blue vein for the pulse of life, but found nothing. Very gently, she pressed the open lids shut.

Sybille rose stiffly from her kneeling position at the other side of the bed and, easing a cramp in her spine, went to unfasten the latch and throw wide the shutters on a grey dawn sky. 'To aid her soul's passage,' she declared. Her face was wet, but then Sybille had always been swift to show emotion, the opposite of the mistress she had served for forty years.

The daylight streamed weakly into the room, taking away some of the glory from the candles' blaze and casting a pallid light on Judith's body. A cold draught guttered the flames and Matilda almost believed that it was indeed her mother's soul leaving its earthly shell and drifting heavenwards. She felt numb. There was no sting of tears, no rush of grief. Nothing, save perhaps a regret as cold and sad as the air blowing through the room.

Leaving the bedside, she joined Sybille at the open shutters and put her arms around the woman's shoulders. The light was steadily paling in the east, and she could see the lay workers going about their business. The smell of new bread from the bakehouse wafted past her nostrils. She saw Simon talking to one of the knights of their escort as the two men trudged back up the path from the latrines. Simon's hands were tucked in his belt in a stance that was so familiar it sent a small leap of emotion through her.

'Only time I ever knew her happy were in the first days of marriage to your father,' Sybille sniffed. 'But they were as different as a cat and a dog. I knew it would end in grief, more's the pity for both their sakes. I pray she finds her peace with God now.' She made the sign of the cross on her breast.

Matilda echoed the maid's gesture. 'I hope so too,' she murmured, but the words came by rote. Sense and meaning would come later – or perhaps not at all.

'I should fetch the priest and the Mother Abbess.' Sybille wiped her eyes on her sleeve. 'My lady will want to lie in the chapel . . .'

'No, let me do that,' Matilda said quickly. 'You knew her the best of us . . . You were her closest companion. It is fitting that you should prepare her for her final resting place.'

Sybille nodded. 'Yes, my lady. I would be honoured to see to laying her out.'

'Good then. Do you make a start and I will join you presently.' She kissed the maid's damp cheek and was briefly engulfed in the choking hold of a fresh wave of Sybille's emotion. In truth she was glad that at least there was someone to weep for her mother.

Descending to the bailey, she went to intercept Simon and bring him the news that Judith had died.

He had finished speaking with the other knight, and now he came towards her, his hands still gripping his belt, his stride stiff and uneven in the frosty morning, but quickening, and his expression filled with concern.

'She has gone,' Matilda said as he reached her, 'And I am glad for her. Perhaps now she will have the peace she never found in life.' The muscles of her face felt stiff, as if the cold had invaded and frozen them.

He folded his arms around her. 'God rest her soul,' he murmured. 'I know it was troubled.'

Matilda pressed her face into the russet wool of his tunic. 'Sybille is composing her body ready for chapel,' she said. 'I must make arrangements for masses to be said for her soul and see that alms are distributed in her name.' She rubbed her cheek against his breast. 'Everything stops while we wait for death to come, and then everything becomes as busy as a beehive.' She gave a little shiver. 'And then everything stops again,' she said softly. 'And that perhaps is a worse silence than the first.'

He rubbed his fingertips gently at the small of her back. 'But only as winter comes before spring. If you can weather the cold, then the season will turn.'

'I am in the winter now,' she said. 'I feel nothing. I am frozen.'

'Well, half of that is because you have been sitting all night in a room so cold that it would turn fire to ice in the snap of a finger,' he remonstrated. 'And you wouldn't eat any food to fuel your belly when I offered. At least ask some hot gruel of the nuns before you set about your tasks.'

'I thought it was women who were supposed to be scolds,' she found the spark to murmur.

'I was caring, not scolding,' Simon retorted.

The words lit the tiniest flicker of warmth at Matilda's core. 'You might have married her,' she said.

'But I didn't.' He sought and found her cold lips with his own. She felt their pressure, the warmth of his mouth, breathing life into hers. Her fingers caught and gripped as a stab of heat shattered the ice encasing her vitals. She made a sound in her throat, half pleasure, half anguish, and it became an integral part of their kiss. She swayed where she stood, locked in longing and a need so great that it almost felled her.

The sound of the draw bar sliding back from the main gate and the entry of a horseman on a blowing bay courser made Simon break the kiss and lift his head. Leaning against him, her body tingling, Matilda watched the rider approach. He wore a thick, fur-lined cloak against the winter cold, and a hood of charcoal-coloured wool. The pommel of a sword shone with a dull steel light at his belt.

Simon tensed, and looking into his face she saw that he was gazing at the newcomer with recognition.

'Beric?' he said. 'What news?' His right arm departed the embrace to extend towards the man; his left remained on her waist and turned her to face the intrusion. 'A king's messenger,' Simon muttered out of the side of his mouth for her benefit.

The man dismounted with a little jump, for his horse was tall and he was not. He was powerfully built, though, and looked as if he knew how to use the weapon at his belt.

'Not so much news, my lord, as a summons.' He reached into the satchel slung from left shoulder to right hip and produced a vellum packet from which dangled the royal seal of King William Rufus. 'He wants you in Normandy. They told me at Northampton's gates that you had come here.'

Simon took the packet from the outstretched hand. Matilda watched the gesture and was transported back to small child-hood with a vivid jolt. She saw Ralf de Gael riding into the courtyard and felt her father's arms slacken around her as his attention diverted to his friend. She remembered the fury and pain she had felt – and the anguish of being punished for her tantrum while her papa rode off to hunt with his friend. And after that everything had changed.

The power of the feeling, coupled with lack of food and sleep and the long, draining vigil at her mother's deathbed, buckled her knees and she sagged against Simon in a half-swoon. He bore her up with an exclamation of concern and she heard him call out across the courtyard. Moments later she found herself being borne away by the porteress and her novice assistant, who murmured over her in concern. To her protests that she was all right and her feeble struggles to be free of them they paid no heed, but brought her to the infirmary and sat her in a cushioned chair by the fire; and it seemed to her that the wheel had turned full circle.

A bowl of hot oat gruel and two cups of sweet mead later, she began to feel better and insisted to the nuns tending her that she did not want to lie down and rest. 'I need to be busy,' she said.

'Aye, it must be a shock, losing your poor lady mother,' clucked the infirmaress, a plump hen of a woman with comfortable, pleated features and shrewd blue eyes. 'Best if your hands and mind are occupied until you're ready to think about matters.'

'Indeed,' Matilda said, but it was not the shock of her mother's death that had felled her.

Leaving the infirmary, she went to the chapel and found that preparations were already afoot to transport her mother's body from her chamber to lie in state before the altar. She spoke to the Mother Abbess about prayers, accepted condolences with appropriate murmurs and downcast lids, and then sped in search of Simon, filled with an irrational fear that he might already have left.

He was in the stables, arranging to have a loose shoe on his horse's off-hind hoof reshod. When he saw her he left his conversation with the groom and she saw the apprehension fill his eyes.

'You are feeling better?' He took her hands in his.

'Enough to do what I must,' she said with a half-smile that was brave rather than possessed of any humour. She gestured to the horse, which the groom was preparing to lead out into the yard. 'You do not need to tell me. I know that you will ride out of here before the bells ring the hour of nones.'

He sighed and released one of her hands so that he could push his hair off his forehead. 'The King desires me to act as one of his commanders in the field and the summons is urgent. I've already sent a rider out to Huntingdon with an order of muster. Now I have to return to Northampton and do the same. Matilda, I . . .'

Quickly she raised her palm and laid it against his lips. 'Do not seek to sweeten the potion,' she said. 'You too are bound to do as you must.'

A look of relief flickered in his eyes. Obviously he had expected her to weep and cling. 'Promise only that you will send word to me of where you are and what you are doing.' She managed to keep her voice level. 'It is the silences that are the hardest to bear.'

The groom clopped the horse into the yard, swung astride, and turned it towards the gates.

'Smith'll have him shod in a cat's whisker, m'lord,' he said.

Simon nodded and flipped the man a silver coin from his pouch. 'I'll be at prayer in the chapel.' Saluting, the groom rode out.

Simon turned to Matilda and drew her into the knee-deep hay of the stable just vacated by his horse. 'I promise.' He pulled her into his arms, and ignoring the toing and froing of servants and grooms kissed her until she was hot and melting and breathless. 'Wherever we are in the field, I promise.'

She rubbed against him with a small gasp. To be doing this while her mother was being prepared to lie in state in the chapel might be wrong, but the need to confirm the life force coursing through her own veins was stronger than censure and abetted by the knowledge of Simon's imminent departure. If they did not make their private farewells now, there would be no other time.

Although it was he who had instigated their lovemaking, it was Matilda who took control. She broke the embrace, but only to draw him into the farthest stall, which was full of clean, fresh hay.

'My mother would be shocked,' she whispered as she pulled him down to her, 'but I will do my penance later.'

'No,' Simon said as he cupped her face in his hands and paused on the threshold of wild lust for a moment of tenderness. 'Deep in her heart, your mother would have been envious. Do no penance, but rejoice.'

CHAPTER 39

Castle of Gisors, Norman Border, March 1098

Removing his helm, shrugging his shield from his shoulders, Simon limped into the Great Hall at Gisors. His temper was close to boiling point, and he was struggling to keep it contained.

The object of his rage was sitting with his boots propped upon the dais trestle, drinking from a handsome silver-gilt cup. Cloak, helm and swordbelt were laid at one side in readiness to ride. Robert de Bêlleme, Simon's *bête noire*, was also a battle commander at Gisors, and indeed the man responsible for the redesigning of what had been an ordinary border keep into what was swiftly becoming an imposing fortress. His skills as an engineer and architect were outstanding. That did not prevent Simon from loathing him. De Bêlleme had changed sides more often than the tables were turned in a busy great hall. While Robert of Normandy was still occupied on the crusade, De Bêlleme was content to serve William Rufus, but Simon doubted the loyalty would last. The baron's nature was too fickle for that. The only light in the darkness was that De Bêlleme was about to leave Gisors for the war that William Rufus was conducting against Helias of La Fleche in Maine.

'Your man Gerard de Serigny has burned yet another village!' Simon snarled as he dumped his helm on the table and slung his gauntlets after it. 'What is the point of building this castle to hold the border if we then lay waste to the area that supplies it and make enemies of the people? Have you no control over the foraging parties you send out?'

De Bêlleme narrowed his eyes. 'If De Serigny has burned a village, then it must have been harbouring French sympathies,' he said. 'It's possible to find lice even in the cleanest hair. And you know how fast they breed.' He made a cracking gesture with index finger and thumb.

Simon snorted in disbelief and reached across De Bêlleme for the flagon, forcing the baron to lean back and inhale a whiff of stale armpit. 'It was no more harbouring French sympathies than you would know honour if it walked up to you and smacked you in the face.' Sloshing wine into a cup, he threw himself down on the bench that ran the length of the dais. 'I trust Gerard de Serigny is leaving with you.'

De Bêlleme finished his own wine, tossed the cup to his squire for cleaning, and rose to his feet. Unlike Simon, who was newly returned from patrol and spattered with mud, De Bêlleme gleamed like a statue in a church, not a speck of rust on his hauberk, not a spatter of mud on cloak or tunic. 'No,' he said with a taunting smile. 'Serigny is remaining here, seconded to Hugh Lupus. I can spare a conroi, and whatever you think, you need men like him. At least they do not get caught by the French.'

Simon's anger bubbled closer to the top of the cauldron. A fortnight since he and Hugh Lupus had been caught on the border by a large troop of French soldiers. Their ransoms had been a formality, swiftly paid by William Rufus, but De Bêlleme had been rubbing it in ever since. 'There is no chance of that while they are raiding villages close to home, is there?' he retorted.

De Bêlleme gave an exaggerated sigh. 'You were an irritating brat, De Senlis, and you've not changed except to grow older and even less competent than you were as a squire.'

'That dish of frumenty I threw down your neck was deliberate,' Simon answered. 'And I count my competence somewhat less rancid than your honour . . . my lord.' He inclined his head to emphasise the sarcasm but there was no deference. These days, being an earl, he outranked De Bêlleme.

'I have neither the time nor the inclination to bandy words with you,' De Bêlleme sneered, and, taking his feet off the trestle, he pinned his cloak and swept together helm and sword.

'Mayhap not, but you will have them with De Serigny before you go, or I will do it myself – with more than words if necessary.'

De Bêlleme glared at Simon. 'Do you know what happened to the last man who tried to tell me my business?'

Simon gave an exaggerated shrug. 'Doubtless you impaled him on a stake in the dungeon or strung him from the battlements by his own guts.' He met the pale gaze calmly, although his heart was hammering and his palm itched with the need to hold a sword between himself and De Bêlleme.

De Bêlleme made an impatient sound. 'I loathe you,' he said, 'but this once I will speak with De Serigny. We will not always be allies, Simon de Senlis. Remember it well.'

His spurs scraped the bench as he stepped over it and strode from the dais. Simon watched him out of the hall with a stare that was fixed and cold, but when the baron was gone, he slumped on the bench, icy sweat in his armpits. Even if his hand was itching to hold a sword his palm was so damp that it would have fouled his grip.

He drained his cup and poured himself a fresh measure, waving away the squire who would have attended him. 'Go and prepare a tub,' he said. 'I stink like a midden.'

The lad trotted off, but moments later and far too soon to have accomplished his errand, he returned to the dais with a sealed parchment in his hand. 'Earl Simon, a messenger asked me to give you this. Says it is a personal matter.'

Simon took the package and squinted at the seal, but it was not one that he recognised. He thought about leaving it until after he had bathed. There were always messengers, always supplicants, always someone wanting something. But he knew that now it was in his hand it would niggle at him. *A personal matter.* He thought at first of Matilda – but it wasn't her seal. 'Did the messenger say where he came from?'

'From the convent of the Holy Redeemer in Evreux, my lord.'

Simon's expression did not change. He thanked the lad and dismissed him to his original errand, then slit the seal and unfolded the package.

When he had finished reading the single page of scribe written brown lines, he threw back his head, closed his eyes, and softly groaned.

Simon drew rein outside the convent and dismounted. Behind him his conroi did the same, but since they did not expect to be admitted they settled down to wait in the lee of the outer wall.

Simon handed his bridle to Turstan and went to rap the lion's head knocker on the nunnery's heavy oak door. The brass ring in the lion's mouth was solid and smooth in his fingers, anchoring him to the reality of why he was here. Above the knocker, a small door opened in the thickness of the wood and a nun peered out at him, her face framed in a white wimple overlaid by a dark veil.

'Simon de Senlis, Earl of Northampton and Huntingdon,' he said to her. 'I am expected.'

A key grated in a lock and a bolt slid back. The nun opened the main door sufficiently to admit him and no wider. Simon suppressed a grimace. The job of porteress was always given to a nun with the mentality of a goodwife guarding her chicken run from foxes. She honoured him with a dip of her head and the suggestion of a curtsey, but only after she had frowned round the door at his men and locked up behind him.

'I will take you to Mother Abbess,' she said. Her mouth was prim and tight. Clearly the reason for him being here was known and not approved – whatever his rank. She led him through the warren of buildings to the Abbess' private solar. Other nuns were about their duties in the space between prayers, indoor pursuits today of spinning, weaving and sewing, since it was not fit weather for gardening. He received swift glances and lowered lids. They would not talk about him behind his back, because they were sworn to speak only as necessary, but he could feel the weight of their speculation.

The Abbess' solar was a pleasant room, warmed by braziers and hung with colourful religious embroideries. The coffers along the side of the room released a scent of beeswax from their gleaming surfaces. It was such a contrast to Judith's chamber at Elstow that it enforced Simon's realisation of how much his mother-by-marriage had mortified herself in her last years.

The Abbess was seated in a high-backed chair, her hands folded in her lap and wrapped around a set of beautiful agate prayer beads. A large gold cross shone on her breast against the dark wool of her habit. Rising to her feet, she greeted Simon cordially, and bade the porteress fetch Sabina.

'I must thank you for coming so swiftly, my lord, and in person,' she said, resuming her seat and gesturing him to a second chair padded with an embroidered cushion. Turning to an exquisite silver flagon, she poured a generous measure of wine into one of two matching goblets and handed it to him.

He raised his brows. 'You thought I might send a proxy?'

'Not to missay your honour, but I thought it likely, my lord. I did not know if you would have the time – or the interest.'

'For this I would,' he said grimly and took a drink of the wine. As he had expected, it was superb. 'After all, the responsibility is mine.'

'Not all men would see the matter in that particular light, my lord. We see plenty of distressed young women at our gates who have been abandoned by their lovers and left to deal with the consequences themselves. And on many occasions the father owns more than a ploughshare.'

'I did not abandon Sabina,' Simon said, his colour rising. 'Indeed, I offered her a place under my roof, but she was set on joining your community . . . I did not know until your letter arrived that she had borne a child.' He met her gaze steadily. 'She is not my habitual mistress, cast off to a nunnery when the arrangement no longer suited. This infant was born of a single occasion of weakness.'

She was not going to let him off the hook so easily. 'And yet Sister Sabina says that you know each other well.'

'We do . . . but not as lovers.'

The nun looked sceptical. He could not blame her. 'He is a fine, healthy baby. We could raise him here and send him for fostering in a monastery when he is old enough, but it is not wise to keep an infant among nuns when one of them is his mother. Even if he is bastard born, he is the son of an earl, and Sister Sabina desires that you foster him in your own household . . . I assume that your very presence here attests that you are willing?'

Simon set his empty cup back on the table and shook his head at her offer of more. 'Of course I am willing,' he said.

The door opened and Sabina entered, a swaddled bundle cradled against her heart. Simon stared at her. She had always been attractive in her ordinary gown and wimple, but the nun's garb made her look like a Madonna. The oval face, the pure features, the grey-violet eyes with their soot-black lashes. He could imagine dumbfounded peasants kneeling at her feet in worship. And he would have been tempted to join them.

Simon rose to his feet, his heart hammering and the words that had always come so easily deserting him. He swallowed. 'Why did you not send to me sooner?' he asked hoarsely.

Her posture was defensive. 'There would have been no point,' she said. 'What could you have done except watch my belly grow? Besides, I did not know that I was carrying a child at first. There had been no signs. In the early months my fluxes had continued. And when I did find out, I had some thinking to do.' She looked down at the baby and gently stroked his cheek.

'You do not have to give him up,' Simon said. 'I would furnish you a place to live, you know that.'

Sabina smiled sadly and shook her head. 'That would serve for his early years,' she replied, 'but the time would soon come for you to take him into your household and train him for knighthood, and I would be left with nothing to do but sit and spin and brood. The parting will be better now than later. I will have my devotions to keep me occupied, and the support of Mother Abbess and the good sisters.' She raised her arm, bringing the child closer to her gaze. 'I may be about to renounce the world, but I want him to grasp it in both hands. He is my healing,' she added, 'a gift from God. I did not think to bear another child after I lost the others. Let him go out and live his life.' Her voice had been steady and calm thus far, but now it developed a wobble and her chin dimpled. 'Take him . . . His name is Simon, for you.' She kissed the baby gently on the brow, and gave him into his father's arms.

Simon looked down at the tiny swaddled scrap. Its eyes were closed in slumber and the wisps of hair peeping from beneath its linen bonnet were dark. Jesu God. He wanted to say that if he had known this would be the result of that moment of lust in Durazzo he would have abstained, but the words stuck in his throat and then dissolved at the feel of the warm weight and tiny skull. Sabina's son was indeed a gift – a wonderful and very disturbing one.

'I have a carrying basket for him,' she said, 'and swaddling bands that I stitched while awaiting my confinement.' She spoke with a swift, almost desperate practicality. 'You will need to find him a wet nurse . . .'

'There are several at Gisors,' Simon said in a distracted voice.

'Some of the soldiers have wives with them, and the Earl of Chester has a woman with a babe in his household.'

'Sister Sabina will see you to the gate,' the Abbess said, granting them a leave of conversation alone.

Somehow Simon took a courteous farewell of the senior nun. He was still reeling, unable to believe that he had a small baby on his arm. Sabina walked at his side, carrying the basket and the swaddling.

'He's a good baby,' Sabina said as they walked. 'He should not trouble your journey . . .' At first glance she appeared composed, but her face was pale and her mouth tight. 'What will your wife do?' she asked.

Simon grimaced. The wind gusted about them and he carefully shielded the infant within a fold of his cloak. 'I will cross that bridge when I come to it,' he said. 'Hopefully her spirit will be generous enough to understand.'

'And if it is not?'

'I promise you that whatever she and I suffer, the child will not,' he said. 'The sin is yours and mine, not his.'

She nodded as though his words had eased her of a burden. 'It is hard to let him go,' she whispered. 'If I seem composed now, it is because I have given myself permission to grieve when you are gone . . .'

'Sabina . . .'

'Say nothing more. Just take him and go. All will be well . . . and better this way.'

At the gate they waited while the porteress again slid the bolt and unlocked the door. Sabina leaned over Simon's arm and placed a final, soft kiss on the baby's brow. 'Godspeed, little one,' she whispered.

For Simon himself there was no embrace, just a single, long look that said everything. Then she turned from him and went back to the abbey. The porteress let him out of the door with the basket and swaddling. 'You take care of that child,' she said sternly. 'God will know if you do not.' The heavy oak swung shut behind him and he heard the lock shoot back into place.

His men came to attention from their positions against the wall and looked at him askance.

'It's a baby!' Simon snapped. 'Haven't any of you seen one before? Here, strap this basket to the packhorse and cover it so that it doesn't get wet.' Handing his son briefly to Turstan he mounted his horse then leaned down to take the infant back in his arms and beneath the protection of his cloak.

No one asked questions, but everyone looked at each other and not at Simon.

'A baby?' Hugh of Chester reddened alarmingly. Laughter brimmed in his eyes, and he was taken with a paroxysm of choking. Hastily he reached for the wine flagon, as usual close to hand, and took several gulps without recourse to a cup. 'Not even I have fornicated with a nun, and I'm reckoned without a shred of moral fibre!' he recovered enough to wheeze.

'She was not a nun at the time,' Simon said stiffly.

Flagon in hand, Chester leaned over the basket to regard the infant. It stared back at him out of the kitten-blue eyes of a newborn. 'You're sure it is yours? You don't think she's foisting a cuckoo on you?'

'No, it's mine,' Simon said, his eyelids tightening. He grabbed the flagon from Chester and took a long drink. 'I have to find a wet nurse among the women.'

'There's Alaise,' Chester said. 'She's weaning young Geoffrey, but she's still got enough milk to float a galley. She'll be glad to feed him. Means she'll not have to worry about conceiving another babe quite yet. Women don't grow big bellies while they're still giving suck.'

'Thank you.' Simon was irritated by his friend, but he was also immensely grateful for his practicality. Chester was a profligate lecher. Alaise was one of several mistresses, but he always returned to her and they had three sons, the most recent being a little over a year old.

'What will your wife say?' Laughter was still flushing Chester's face. His shoulders continued to twitch.

Simon did not want to think about that. 'I would hope that she would be generous,' he replied. 'The child is not to blame.'

'Aye,' Chester snorted. 'She'll take him in and throw you out.'

The baby opened its mouth and gave a small, experimental squeak. Chester snapped his fingers at a squire. 'Take this child to Mistress Alaise and tell her that Lord Hugh bids her tend it as one of her own.'

'Yes, my lord.' The youth picked up the basket as though it held a tangle of writhing snakes rather than a single whimpering baby, and made his way gingerly across the hall to the private apartments.

'It's good to know that you're capable of sinning as much as the rest of us!' Chester slapped Simon on the back. 'Don't you worry. Alaise is a good mother. She'll do for the moment.' He dismissed the subject with a flick of one large, fleshy hand. 'I'm glad you are here. I sent a foraging party out towards Chaumont and they haven't returned. I thought that . . .'

'Who was leading?'

'Who do you think?' Chester said, and now there was no laughter in his eyes. 'Gerard de Serigny.'

Simon swore. De Bêlleme might have flayed De Serigny, figuratively if not literally, but that had been in public. In private Simon suspected that there was a different agenda. De Serigny was, after all, De Bêlleme's man and well placed to keep his master informed about everything that Simon and Hugh Lupus did. Of course he was to be granted leeway. 'You want me to investigate?'

Chester spread his hands. 'You have the skills as a scout as well as a commander. Serigny is no loss if he has been captured by the French – De Bêlleme can pay the bastard's ransom, but he had a full conroi with him and I want to know what has happened. If they've raided a village and got drunk, I'll build a pyre for them myself.'

Simon nodded grim agreement. 'I'll go and arm up.' He was glad to have something to do. It meant he didn't have to think on matters complicated and domestic.

Before he left he paid a visit to the women's quarters. His son was drowsing on Alaise's ample white breast, his lips anchored to her nipple and his eyes closed in bliss. Now and again his small jaws would work, but more for security than sustenance.

'Must have been hard for his mother to give this one up,' Alaise said, her arm curving maternally around the small body. 'Is she truly a nun?'

Simon could see that this was a tale that was going to follow him the rest of his days, adding to his reputation in some quarters, destroying it in others. 'Not yet,' he said, 'And not as a penance for bearing him. And yes, it was hard for her to give him up.'

He left the chamber and went down to the courtyard where Turstan was holding the reins of his grey. Sabina had done what she thought best for the child. Now all he had to do was prove her right. He hoped that he was equal to the task.

CHAPTER 40

Northampton, March 1098

There was a robin on the sundial. Matilda watched it flirt its tail at her. Its breast feathers were the hue of hot embers against the soft brown wing. All around her the garden was showing the colours of spring. The apple tree even had a green suggestion of bud about the carefully pruned branches.

Its base was ringed with the glistening white milkflowers that Simon had brought her from Byzantium. To look at the small brown bulbs, she would not have guessed at the bravery and beauty of the blooms that had opened while the land was still in the grip of winter. They were past their best now, but the last ones to bud still carried their flowers. She wished wistfully that Simon could have been here to see them.

'Are you ready?' Jude asked.

She turned to her sister. Jude's dark brows, brown eyes and warm complexion gave her a strong physical resemblance to their mother and sent a small pang through Matilda. Her sister's arms were folded against her body and huddled under her cloak. She much preferred the warmth of a brazier and the cosiness of her embroidery to the outdoors – at least until true spring had put some warmth into the season.

'Yes,' Matilda said, 'I am.' A frown clouded her brow. 'Do you think I am doing the right thing in going to Simon?'

'Indeed I do. If our mother had followed her heart, she would have been the happier for it.'

Matilda managed a smile, but still felt a twinge of uncertainty. The need to go to Simon had been born out of a gradual feeling of loneliness engendered by the act of clearing her mother's coffers and distributing her garments and effects to the poor. At the bottom of one of the coffers, amid scraps of dried rose petals and lavender stems, she had found a piece of embroidery depicting a copper-haired man on a chestnut stallion and riding beside him on a black mare a woman whose dark hair was shockingly bared to the world. The sight of the token had filled Matilda's eyes with tears. It had confirmed her mother's deathbed words. She had loved Waltheof. The tragedy was that she had never been able to show it, fettered as she was by her duty, by her Norman blood, and by the steep differences of nature that had separated her from her husband. The sight of that hidden length of embroidery had filled Matilda with an overwhelming need to go to Simon. To embrace their own differences of nature and negate them. She was afraid but steadfast. Jude would have custody of the children until her return.

'It is only fitting that you should see Normandy at least once,' Jude said as the sisters turned towards the garden gate. 'After all, we are half Norman, and I think it would have pleased our mother.' Jude had crossed the Narrow Sea on several occasions with Ranulf, and had been very taken with the great stone abbeys and castles that populated the rolling green landscape.

Matilda wondered. For all that their mother was proud of her birth, she had chosen to live out her life in England and had shown no inclination to return to Normandy. However she said nothing to Jude, who was only trying to offer her reassurance and comfort.

The children were waiting in the courtyard with Sybille to bid her farewell. Blinking back tears, Matilda embraced them both tenderly, promising she would be home soon. Waltheof patted her shoulder, offering her grave comfort, his manner more like that of an elderly man than a boy barely nine years old. His sister started to grizzle, but was easily persuaded out of her tears by the present of a sticky piece of honeycomb that Sybille had been keeping in reserve for just such an eventuality.

Matilda accepted a boost into the saddle from the waiting groom, and reined her horse to face the gates. It gave her a strange sense of freedom and fear to be the one riding away. Part of her wanted to turn back, but it was the lesser part, and she responded to it by nudging her mount to a trot.

The new castle of Gisors was a motley conglomeration of stone and wood rising out of a scarred landscape of felled trees and bare earth. A brown and grey wound on a land of bright spring green. Builders and masons toiled on the walls, each freshly mortared slab securing William Rufus' claim to the land.

Matilda drew rein and gazed upon the industry. Recent rain had turned the track to a churned brown glue, but not so wet that the wheels of the wains and ox carts became stuck in the mud. Soldiers were everywhere, all of them watchful and armed to the teeth.

A mile earlier, Matilda had dispatched a herald to give notice of her arrival. She narrowed her eyes upon the men at the gate, but could not see anyone she recognised. No Turstan, no Toki . . . no distinctive blue and white cloak.

Urging her mount, gesturing to the senior knights of her escort, she rode on to the outer gates of the half-grown castle. And saw that she was expected after all. Hugh Lupus, Earl of Chester, came forward to greet her, huge as a bear, light of tread, dark hair swept back from his broad forehead.

'Countess, be welcome,' he said and came to her saddle to lift her down.

Clad in mail, a fur-lined cloak clasped across his shoulders, he seemed more enormous than ever. His two chins had become three since last she had seen him and his paunch strained at the rivets of his hauberk.

'Sire,' she responded with a courteous smile. 'It is good to see you.' She was adept at the social niceties; greased wheels ran better than dry ones.

He drew her into the compound. Timber dwellings had been erected to house the population of the castle while the walls went up, and numerous tents dotted the sward like clusters of mushrooms. She found herself anxiously scanning the banners flying from their posts to see if she could see any of Simon's, but, although there were a few she recognised, his was not among them.

As if reading her mind, Hugh Lupus touched her arm. 'Simon is out with a troop,' he said. 'We expect him back later today, or tomorrow.'

There was an odd expression in the Earl of Chester's eyes, a mingling of speculation, sympathy and grim amusement that caused Matilda's scalp to prickle.

'There is more that you are not telling me, isn't there?'

Without reply, he led her to one of the timber buildings and waving the guard aside, pushed open the door. 'Your husband's chamber,' he said. 'We have not been dwelling in the most princely of circumstances, but I hope it will suffice.'

Matilda shrugged. 'I am not the kind to worry over lack of creature comforts,' she said. 'The peasants survive on far less.' She pinned him with her gaze. 'I hope you would tell me if there is anything amiss.'

He folded his arms across the wide bulk of his chest and looked over them to the layer of thick yellow straw covering the floor. 'As I told you, Simon is out with the troop.' He cleared his throat and rocked on his heels. 'I know your husband's abilities in the field and if I have no fears for him, neither should you.'

Matilda picked her way through what he had said. 'Then if there is no danger to my husband, why do you hesitate in your telling?' she asked.

'It is not every wife would follow her husband across the

sea and to the edge of a battlefield.' His tone was censorious rather than admiring.

Matilda lifted her chin. 'I am not every wife. I have scarcely seen my husband in two years. Even when he returned from the crusade we had no time together. My mother took ill and died, and he was called away to this war.' She flushed beneath Hugh Lupus' scrutiny. 'I have come to comfort him, and be comforted.'

The Earl's expression grew yet more wary. It was clear from the way he spoke and his general stance that he was uncomfortable with her presence and viewed it as an irritation, like something full of little bones that had been added to his already piled trencher. He heaved a sigh. 'Come with me,' he said, and led her out of the building and across the sward to another, similar hall that housed his own retinue. Ducking through the doorway, he brought her to the hearth and gestured to a woman sitting on a stool before the fire, tending a swaddled infant.

'This is Alaise, my mistress,' he said bluntly. 'Since she has milk in abundance, she has agreed to nurse your husband's child until other arrangements can be made.'

Matilda stared. 'My husband's child?' she said blankly.

'I am sorry that you should arrive to such tidings, but . . .' He made a shrug and a down-turned mouth serve for the rest.

'But wives who follow their husbands have to deal with the consequences,' she said in a hard voice.

Chester said nothing.

'How can this be his child?' she demanded with angry bewilderment. 'He has only been gone from me since the Christmas feast.'

Chester nodded. 'And before that he was a crusader. Did you never wonder whether he took comfort along the way?'

Matilda swallowed. 'I . . .'

A young soldier approached the Earl and murmured that he was needed at one of the gates.

'You will excuse me,' Chester said. 'I will speak with you

later. Whatever you need, just ask one of my attendants.' He left at a brisk walk for one so large, his relief obvious.

Matilda's body was rigid with the effort of maintaining her dignity. She looked down at the baby in the woman's arms. Its hair was jet-black, but otherwise it looked very similar to her own children when they had been newborn. Nine months ago, as Chester said, Simon had been returning from crusade. She remembered the way he had avoided her eye when he spoke of the laundress who had so neatly patched his chausses. A suspicion had crossed her mind then, but she had chosen to ignore, if not to forget it. It was in the past. But there was no ignoring this. For how long, she wondered, had this woman been his lover?

'Did you know the mother?' she demanded of Alaise. She made herself speak to the woman, even though she was the Earl of Chester's mistress and such knowledge was hard to swallow in the light of revelation.

'No, my lady. Earl Simon brought the babe here yesterday and I was asked to suckle him.' The woman's look was compassionate, but wary.

'Brought it back from where?'

'The nunnery at Evreux, my lady.'

'God's blood, his mistress is a nun?' Matilda's voice rose. She would kill him. She would take her knife and cut out his heart, but first she would slice off his balls and feed them to the hounds.

The baby gave a little start in response to the raised voice and began to wail. The woman unfastened the drawstring of her chemise to put him to her breast. 'I do not know, my lady. From the talk, I heard she hadn't taken her vows, but she would not leave the nunnery.'

Matilda watched the infant nuzzle and take suck. Simon's son by another woman – a nun. Had they talked tenderly as they lay together, or had it been a transaction of mere lust?

Stumbling from the dwelling, she leaned against the door-post and drew deep gulps of the cold spring air. She had arrived in Gisors with visions of a tender reunion between herself and Simon. Instead she had been confronted by his betrayal. Suddenly she understood her mother's feelings all too well. The bitterness, the anger, the shame. All that remained in the end was duty, and its rigorous enforcing, because it was the only thing over which she had control.

Matilda lifted the cup to her lips and was surprised to find it already down to the lees. She fumbled for the pitcher only to discover that it too was empty.

'Go and fetch more wine,' she slurred at Helisende, who was watching her with a worried expression.

'My lady, the butlery will be closed now. They won't issue any more until the morrow.'

'They will for me . . . I'm a guest. I'm a countess . . .'

Helisende curled her hand around the pitcher's handle. 'Everyone is asleep,' she said. 'It is late in the night. I will have to rouse someone from their bed.'

'Then do it!' Matilda shouted. She rose from the low table where she had been drinking steadily for several hours, tripped on the hem of her gown and sprawled in the rushes. Helisende abandoned the pitcher and rushed to help her.

Matilda tried to bat the maid away but her arms refused to work. She hung her head, suddenly feeling very ill. Helisende smartly tipped some apples out of the wooden bowl on the table and just in time thrust it in front of Matilda's face.

Sobbing, heaving, Matilda was violently sick. She had never drunk even half a pitcher at once before and her body was rebelling in every fibre.

'That's it, my lady, better out than in,' Helisende soothed. 'You'll be all right presently.'

'I'll never be all right,' Matilda wept. 'Never again.'

Grimacing, Helisende went to dispose of the contents of the bowl down the latrine shaft, then she helped her mistress to bed.

Matilda resisted, hanging back. 'Not there,' she said, thrusting out her lower lip. 'Don't want to sleep in his bed.'

'It is better than the floor, my lady. Why should you punish yourself for his weakness? He lay with another woman, she bore a child. Such matters are not the end of the world.'

'He betrayed me,' Matilda flung.

'Perhaps, but where you sleep will not alter things.' Helisende gave her a little shake, trying to impart reason. 'Besides, he could not have lain with her here. Three seasons ago Gisors was less than a stone in Robert de Bêlleme's eye. Come now.' As if dealing with one of Matilda's children, Helisende cajoled Matilda to lie down, removed her shoes and wimple, and drew the coverlet gently up to her shoulders. 'All will seem better in the morning,' she said.

'It won't,' Matilda said. Through a wine haze she remembered Sybille leaning over her when she was a child, soothing her with promises that her father would be home soon. Promises that had lulled her to sleep only to prove hollow in the cold light of day. Her lids felt as though they had been weighted with lead seals, her tongue seemed too large for her mouth, and her limbs belonged to someone else. Tomorrow. She would deal with it when it arrived, but she would not expect anything to be better.

Matilda awoke to a headache so huge that it seemed to fill the room and leave no space for anything but the appalling, drumming pain. Groaning, she pulled the coverlet over her head, but she could not settle back into the dark cocoon of oblivion. Her bladder was bursting, and shifting position made no difference to the urgent demand.

Eyes half closed, she tottered from the bed to the waste shaft, somehow lifted her gown and chemise out of the way, and squatted. Outside she could hear the shouts of men at battle practice and the creak of cartwheels as supplies rolled into the compound. The day appeared to be well under way. Matilda decided she did not want to be a part of it and wandered blearily back towards the bed.

'My lady, you are awake?' Helisende appeared from the

domestic end of the hall, a steaming cup of something herbal in her hand.

Matilda winced. 'If I am dreaming, it is a nightmare,' she said and taking the cup, inhaled the aroma of chamomile. She took a tentative sip and found the astringent taste had been made just about palatable with honey. Walking slowly, she returned to the bed and sat down.

Helisende went away but returned moments later with a ewer of scented water for washing. 'That woman of Chester's was asking me about the babe,' she said as she laid a folded linen towel on the bed.

'What babe?' Matilda asked, and then remembered. Her lips tightened and dark misery filled her mind. 'What of it?'

'She wanted to know if you were going to come and see him today.'

Matilda took another sip of the brew and rubbed her aching forehead. Last night she had told herself that only duty remained, and against that duty had drunk herself into the worst megrim of her entire life. 'I suppose if I must,' she snapped ungraciously and glared at the maid. 'I wonder what my lord would have said to me if he had returned from crusade and found me with another man's child in my arms? Would he have accepted it into his life as I am expected to accept this one?'

'Likely not, my lady,' said Helisende, 'but then men are simple creatures. Rope them by the loins and you may lead them anywhere . . . and they are always too willing to be thus captured.'

'And the women pay,' Matilda said bitterly. 'Either with their reputations or their lives.'

Helisende tilted her head to one side like an inquisitive bird. 'Will you forgive him, my lady?'

'I do not know yet,' Matilda said. 'You are asking me if I will recover from a wound that is still bleeding.'

When the potion had done its work and her head no longer felt as though it was being pounded from the inside by a spiked mace she pinned her cloak at her shoulders and crossed the path to Chester's dwelling. Helisende followed at her heels until Matilda turned.

'Go and find my groom and Sir Walter. Tell them to saddle the horses and have the men ready.'

'We are leaving, my lady?' Helisende looked at her askance. 'Is that wise?'

Matilda gave a bitter laugh. 'I do not know what is wise any more and what is not. What I do know is that I will have no peace until I have been to Evreux and seen for myself.'

'My lady I . . .'

'Do not argue – go!' Matilda's eyes flashed.

Helisende's lips tightened. 'Yes, my lady,' she said, and dipped her mistress a very proper curtsey to show her resentment.

Matilda responded with a glacial stare and the maid stalked off on her errand, her spine stiff with indignation.

Matilda closed her eyes, swallowed, and entered Chester's hall. There was no sign of the Earl, but Alaise was seated before the fire, the baby mewling in her lap as she changed his swaddling. Matilda made herself go and look at him, forced herself to pick him up and hold him along her arm. Whatever the circumstances of his begetting and birth, he was innocent. She had to accept him because he would be raised as part of Simon's household. It would be at least seven or eight years before he went away to be trained as a knight or a priest – perhaps not even then, if Simon chose to raise him at his side.

'Does he have a name?' she asked Hugh Lupus' mistress, who was watching her with wary eyes as though she expected Matilda to dash the baby against the hearthstones.

'I believe he was christened for his sire, my lady.'

Simon. The name slashed Matilda like a knife. What else had she expected? A mistress was bound to name her offspring after the father, to remind him of his obligation.

The baby's skin was as soft as a new rose petal. Although

the tiny features were immature, she could see Simon in them clearly. His chin, the set of the lips. There was no doubting his paternity. Carefully, knowing that she dared make no sudden moves without snapping her precarious control, she returned the baby to the woman's arms.

'Do you ever think of Lord Hugh's wife when you bed with him and bear his bastards?' she demanded.

The woman shrugged. 'Why should I? As long as he don't bring me under the same roof as her, she's content. My lord is a man of strong appetite and she don't have much of one herself. They bide together out of duty.'

Duty, that word again. Matilda shrank from it. Was she more than a duty to Simon? 'And you bide with Lord Hugh out of love?' she scoffed.

Alaise gave a ripe snort of laughter. 'Oh aye,' she said forthrightly, 'I'm fond of the old fool, it is true, and he knows his way around the bedsheets for all his size, but I'd not be as fond if it weren't for this and this.' She plucked the rich red wool of her gown, and touched the gold brooch pinned high at her shoulder. 'We keep each other satisfied.'

Was that why she was looking at a baby and not at a mother and child? Matilda wondered. Was it lack of satisfaction that had driven Simon and his mistress apart?

The only way was to find out. 'Here,' she said to Alaise, and gave her a silver coin from the purse on her belt. 'Add this to your collection.'

CHAPTER 41

'**W**ill you take wine, Countess? You must be thirsty after your journey.' The Abbess lifted a handsome silver flagon.

Matilda did not particularly want to drink wine with the Abbess, but she knew that the courtesies had to be observed before the meat of the matter could be discussed. 'Thank you,' she nodded. 'It is too early for the dust of the road to lodge in my throat, but I have travelled far.'

The Abbess poured the dark red wine into two exquisite goblets of carved rock crystal with silver bases. A wealthy convent, Evreux, not a place to take in common waifs and strays. But noble mistresses, perhaps.

Matilda took the solid weight of the goblet into her hands. She sipped the wine and proclaimed on its excellence. They discussed the state of the roads and the dangers for travellers, and spoke of the turning season. Then the silence fell and the moment came. Matilda set her cup down on the trestle table at the side of her chair. 'You must have an inkling why I am here,' she said.

'The subject, perhaps, if not the reason.' The Abbess inclined her head. 'Indeed, Countess, when your husband visited us he did not mention that you were here in Normandy.'

'That is because he does not know.'

The Abbess' eyes widened briefly before she lowered them to contain and conceal her surprise. Her face remained smooth, expressionless. It was a skill of nuns, Matilda thought, and wondered if Simon's concubine would have it.

'I intend to discuss the matter with him as soon as he returns from his duties in the field,' she said.

'I see,' the Abbess said.

Matilda had the uncomfortable notion that the woman did see – and all too well. 'I need to speak with the child's mother.'

The Abbess started to shake her head.

'I will remain here until I do,' Matilda said determinedly. 'It goes without saying that I am prepared to be a generous benefactor for your support in this matter.' She lifted the travelling satchel she had brought with her onto the table and withdrew a fat leather pouch of silver coins.

The Abbess' nostrils flared. 'You need not resort to bribery, Countess,' she said coldly. 'Even were I to take it, I should tell you that Sister Sabina paid her dower in gold.' She rose to her feet. 'I will ask her if she wants to see you, but if she refuses I will not force her.'

Matilda wanted to withdraw the coin and crawl under a stone, but it was too late for either to be of much use. 'Then give this money to the needy,' she said. 'As alms without condition.'

The Abbess took the bag of coins and carried it to an aumbry set in the wall. She unlocked the triangular door using a key at her belt and placed the coins within the small cupboard. 'I will go and see if Sister Sabina will come to you,' she said. 'There is more wine in the flagon if you wish it.'

When she had gone, Matilda rose and wandered around the room. The walls, for all their limewashed spaciousness, seemed to be pressing in upon her. Taking deep breaths, she went to the open shutters and looked out on a vista of trees, newly clothed in spring greenery. Sabina. Until the Abbess had spoken, Matilda had not known her name. It was of the nobility, or the merchant classes. And she had paid her dower to Christ in gold – her own, or Simon's? Throughout the journey from Gisors to Evreux, she had been pondering what to say, what to ask. How much could she bear to know? How much would she rather abjure? She had no answers, just more questions and uncertainty.

Behind her, the door quietly opened. She was aware of a cold draught on her spine, but she did not immediately look around. One more deep breath. One more moment to calm the thundering of her heart. Slowly, slowly she turned.

A woman stood just over the threshold. Her dark gown was tidy, her rope girdle was neatly tied, and the knotted ends hung at precisely the same level. A string of polished amber prayer beads was looped through her belt, ending on a carved wooden cross. Her wimple framed a pale, oval face with delicate features and arresting, deep grey eyes with soot-black lashes. There were fine lines at her eye corners and the hint of others beginning between nose and mouth. Matilda had been prepared to face a simpering younger woman, all plump curves, and was thrown to discover that this Sabina was closer to Simon's age than her own.

The moment stretched out like a strand of raw fleece spun on the distaff, twirling, pulling out, preparing to snap.

'I wasn't going to come.' Sabina was the first to speak, her voice clear and steady, breaking the tension before it broke the thread. 'But then I thought that if you had ridden so far it would be discourteous and cowardly to refuse this interview . . . and in truth I was curious to see you.'

Her manner was stately and dignified. She neither curtseyed to Matilda nor yielded deference, but she was not insolent.

'Curious?' Matilda raised her chin. 'Well, perhaps no more curious than I have been to see you.'

'He told you about me then?'

Her composure was not as firm as it first appeared. Matilda saw the way the crucifix on her breast shivered to the beating of her heart.

'He told me nothing, nor does he know I am here. But your son and his lies in a basket in Gisors and I am expected to take him into my household.' A coal of anger burned in her voice. 'I came to see what manner of woman you were – pious nun, used innocent, or whore.'

Sabina's eyes flashed and Matilda saw that she had drawn blood.

'I am no whore!' she said proudly. 'I have given myself to no man but my husband, God rest his soul . . .'

'And mine!' Matilda bit out.

'And yours, my lady,' she concurred, 'but not for payment.'

'Then for what – love?' The word emerged raw with pain.

Sabina winced. 'By your mercy I would ask a cup of wine,' she said.

'Perhaps I do not feel merciful,' Matilda said, but after a moment stepped aside and gestured to the trestle.

Sabina lifted the flagon and filled the rock crystal cup that the Abbess had been using. Matilda saw that her hands were shaking. Compassion slipped past her guard, despite her anger.

'I knew Simon many years ago in the time of Rufus' father,' Sabina said. 'I was the daughter of one of the King's falconers and Simon was a royal squire. We were not lovers then, but we played at love for a summer.' She fixed her gaze firmly on Matilda's. 'I came to my husband a virgin, and never looked at another man for all the time we were wed.'

'Go on,' said Matilda flatly.

Sabina bit her lip. 'Saer died on crusade – he drowned when our ship overturned in Brindisi harbour. I was witless with grief. Simon took me into his camp.'

'As a laundress,' Matilda said with a hostile nod.

A pink flush stained Sabina's cheeks. 'And nothing more, my lady. Not until he took sick of the evil humours in his leg and nearly died. They fetched the priest to him twice.' She took a drink from the cup and her composure slipped another degree. 'I had lost my husband and my children. Should I have let the love of my youth die too? I fought for him tooth and nail. It was a bloody battle, but I won.' For a moment the memory of the triumph blazed out of her eyes, but as it faded she dropped her gaze and took another swallow of wine. 'Once he regained enough strength to appreciate his life, we celebrated our survival, and at the time it did not seem wrong. Home was so far away that it had no meaning. We were cast adrift. It was lust, I admit, but it was more than lust too.'

'And the child?'

Tears welled in Sabina's eyes. 'I had not reckoned on conceiving,' she said. 'But then I did ask God for a baby – it was the reason Saer and I went on crusade.'

'And yet you gave him up.'

'I had decided to take holy vows before I knew I was with child. I cannot keep him here for then he would be raised to become a monk. I wanted him to have more choice than that . . . and I thought it was fair that he should know his father and that his father should know him.'

Matilda considered Sabina through narrowed lids. 'But why settle for a nunnery? Did you not want to remain as Simon's mistress? You could have kept your child then.'

Tears spilled down Sabina's cheeks. 'Oh, I thought about it,' she said. 'But where would have been the peace in that? I would have wanted the whole, not the half – and it must be the same for you. It might have been different if Simon did not love you – but he does, deeply. I cannot compete with that.'

Matilda's brows rose. 'He has a strange way of showing it,' she said. Her stomach churned. How did this woman know that Simon loved her when she did not?

A glimmer of impatience flickered in Sabina's eyes. 'I make no excuses for either of us,' she said, 'save to say that given different circumstances it would never have happened. He did not look at other women on our journey. There were brothels aplenty along the way and the only time he visited one was to drag Turstan out by the ears.' She sniffed and blotted her eyes on her sleeve. 'He bought you the bulbs of the milkflower in the markets of Constantinople and he thought of you constantly. Are you going to crucify him for one frail slip?'

Matilda's own eyes began to burn. She would not weep, she told herself furiously. 'I needed to know it was one frail slip,' she said, managing to keep her voice steady by keeping it hard. 'I needed to know why you chose the convent and gave up your child.'

Sabina nodded. 'I would have wanted to know the same,' she said.

Again a silence fell between the women, Matilda studying the smooth dignified features of the woman who had chosen the convent above the castle, and Sabina considering Matilda's statuesque beauty and knowing that her choice was right.

'There is one boon I ask of you,' she said. 'From time to time, will you let me know how my son fares?'

Matilda inclined her head. 'Even had I hated you, I would have done my duty,' she said. 'Your son will be reared to fit whatever station he chooses, be it warrior or monk. And when the time is right, he will be told about his mother.'

'Thank you.' There was gratitude in Sabina's eyes. 'You do not hate me, then?' she said tentatively.

Matilda shrugged. 'I was prepared to,' she said. 'But I cannot. If I do not love you either, you will understand why.'

'And you do not hate Simon?'

Matilda gave a small bitter smile. 'That remains to be seen,' she said.

CHAPTER 42

Simon laid his hand along the grey's arched neck in a soothing gesture, but the stallion still jibbed and sidled, showing the whites of its eyes.

They were entering territory that had been held by the French at the beginning of Rufus' campaign, and was still hotly disputed. He knew that De Serigny had come this way. A couple of villages had already attested to the passage of his troop: horses taken and not paid for, three suckling pigs lifted from a sty, a tavern relieved of a barrel of wine.

'Gently there, gently there,' he murmured, tugging the grey's ears and wondering what was disturbing the beast. To assuage the prickling of hair at his nape, he sent two soldiers forward to scout ahead. Slipping his shield from its long strap on his back, he brought it onto his left arm and thrust his hand through the two shorter leather grips. A gesture signalled his troop to do the same. At his shoulder, Toki ostentatiously unhooked his axe from his saddle and clutched the ash haft in his large, war-scarred fist.

Simon was beginning to wonder if his intuition had played him wrong when he inhaled the taint of smoke on the wind and suddenly a grey veil drifted across the road ahead. The destrier's nostrils flared in alarm and its ears went back. His scouts reappeared at the gallop and drew rein before him in a shower of clods.

'My lord, De Serigny's men have fired a village!' one of

the soldiers panted, thumbing up his helm by the nasal bar. Foam churned his mount's bridle-bit.

Cursing, Simon bellowed to his troop and spurred the grey. The horse lunged into a gallop and he gasped as the high pommel of the saddle butted his midriff. The smoke grew thicker and more acrid and now they could hear the flames roaring through the timber and thatch. The gleeful shouts of men reached them too, and the wild squealing of a pig suddenly cut short. Simon spurred around the last curve and entered what looked like the mouth of hell.

Bodies strewed the village street, felled in the act of running to judge from their sprawled positions. A man with a scythe, his head almost cut through; an old woman, her corpse woven with glistening bloody threads. A baby on a spear. Simon's gorge rose. A soldier ran out of one of the burning buildings, stuffing a leather money pouch inside his gambeson. He turned on seeing Simon's troop and his eyes widened in alarm until he recognised Simon's banner. 'Come to join the entertainment, my lord?' he said with a bow that bore as much mockery as deference.

'Where's De Serigny?' Simon snapped.

'Further in.' He gave Simon a sidelong look. 'Their lord's gone over to the French.' He bared his teeth. 'They deserve what they get.'

A muscle bunched in Simon's jaw and he commanded his men to disarm the soldier of his weapons and spoils. 'Take your horse and go. Be thankful that I do not have the time to swing you from the nearest tree.'

Still snarling, but knowing that escape was better than choking on a rope, the soldier ran to his horse, vaulted into the saddle and galloped off. Grimly, Simon spurred on.

The entire village was on fire. Choking gouts of smoke rose from every dwelling. Not one had been spared. The church still stood, but the priest lay dead against the door, his skull crushed and his blood staining the stones. Half a dozen miserable survivors huddled in the square, roped to each other. Looking at them, Simon saw that they had only been allowed to live because they were useful. Four were young and reasonably attractive women. Two were strong men and would have crafts that could be utilised. Had Robert de Bêlleme himself been present, a few more might have been taken for later sport in the dungeons where the baron stored a terrifying array of instruments of torture.

De Serigny emerged on horseback from the church, a red-stained sword in his fist, a grin dividing his dark moustache from his beard. That grin vanished as he set eyes on Simon and his larger troop. Flourishing the sword, he spurred into the street. 'What's wrong, De Senlis? Don't you trust me to make a thorough job?' he sneered. A jewelled cross bulged from his saddle pack.

'You would desecrate a church?' Simon roared and his own blade flashed. 'Your soul will rot in hell!'

De Serigny snorted with contemptuous amusement. 'Hah! Perhaps marriage to an English wife has softened your brain as well as your sword! The church holds no sanctuary for traitors! My Lord De Bêlleme would not be so squeamish!'

'I well know Lord De Bêlleme's attitude,' Simon said through his teeth, 'but he is not here, and you take your orders from me.'

'I think not,' De Serigny retorted. 'Villages burn, peasants die. Wolves eat sheep – especially the lame weaklings.'

Simon's fury became a white wind, made all the more devastating because he so rarely lost his temper. He spurred the grey, and at the same time swung his sword.

De Serigny was ready and parried the blow, but there was a hint of surprise, perhaps fear in his eyes. Simon was known to be a good general and a fine reconnaissance soldier, but few had ever seen him in active engagement. It was assumed among the men that he avoided conflict because of the weakness in his leg.

Simon turned the grey and turned him again, always pressing the attack. His blows were not heavily landed, but each one was balanced and precise. De Serigny had no room for error, and when he opened up too far Simon struck with the speed of an adder. The sword slipped beneath the protection of hauberk and gambeson sleeve and gouged flesh from wrist to elbow. A rapid twist divided the forearm bones. De Serigny's voice rose and broke on a scream. He tried to retreat, but Simon withdrew his blade only to press the advantage – and did not stop until De Serigny fell from his horse and lay dead in the street among the bodies of the villagers. 'Never mistake a lion for a lamb!' he said contemptuously to the corpse.

There was an uneasy silence. Simon wiped his blade along his chausses several times and gazed around, hard-eyed, at De Serigny's shocked men. 'Does anyone else want to dispute from whom they take their orders?' he demanded. His heart was thudding furiously and waves of nausea were beginning to surge from the hard ball in his stomach that had been the burning core of his rage. He had control of himself again and knew that he must hold them with his words and the force of his stare. He was in no condition to take on more of their number.

'Good,' he said curtly. 'It is settled. Free those people and return to Gisors. I will have words to say later. And do not think to tell a tale of innocence to Hugh Lupus. He knows well enough De Serigny's reputation.'

Scowling, sullen, but not daring to disobey, De Serigny's men did as Simon bade. With bad grace, their second in command took his knife and slashed the rope binding the captives. De Serigny's corpse was slung across his horse like a giant bolster. Simon tugged the jewelled cross from the saddlebag, dismounted and limped into the desecrated church. The damage was superficial. The aumbry cupboards had been ripped open and candles crushed on the floor. A holy vestment coffer yawned open, its hasp hacked off and its contents rifled. A statue of the Virgin Mary had been decapitated and the head flung against the wall so that it had shattered in powdered fragments. There were signs of struggle, clots of blood and hair on the holy water stoup.

Simon returned the jewelled cross to the altar. He bowed one knee in swift reverence and prayer, then eased to his feet.

Outside, hooves thundered and someone shouted. Cursing his lameness, Simon hastened towards the door.

The soldier whom Simon had dismissed earlier was back, wild-eyed. Struggling to control his cavorting horse, he reined to face Simon.

'The French!' he bellowed. 'The French are here, my lord. I've just run into one of their patrols on the road!'

There was no time. Already the thunder of French hooves shook the ground, and Simon knew well how the French would react to this scene of carnage, and it wasn't with sweet forgiveness. 'Christ man, you're mounted up!' Simon snarled. 'Double round and get word to Gisors! The rest of you, to me, now!'

'I still say you should not have come,' said Hugh Lupus testily to Matilda. 'It is too dangerous for a woman.'

Matilda gave him a stubborn look that reminded him so much of her great uncle, the Conqueror, that despite his irritation and anxiety he was almost tripped into laughter.

'You have already made your opinion of the matter quite clear, my lord,' she said primly. 'Besides, you could have prevented me from riding with you had you truly desired. All you needed to do was put me under guard in the bower.'

Hugh Lupus did grin then. 'And have you escape by knotting the sheets together and climbing out of the window? No, my lady. I leave it to your husband to deal with you in a fit manner. I have no desire to handle such a termagant.' Actually he did. His wife was the model of what he expected a wife to be, dutiful, retiring, but capable of running a household. His mistresses were always attractive, flighty baggages with impudent tongues. Matilda of Northampton was an intriguing blend of both, and with more than a suggestion of temper at the moment. He had contemplated making overtures to her while she was reeling over her husband's infidelity. She might be persuaded that sauce for the gander was also sauce for the goose. However, he valued Simon's friendship and prudence had tempered his intention.

'I am no termagant,' she said.

Hugh Lupus snorted. 'That is what your grandmother Adelaide used to say, but I never believed her. The women of your house have always been formidable. But I still do not see why you feel so strong a need to put yourself in danger, my lady. Your presence here will make no difference to the outcome – save that I must spare men to guard you.'

'It is my duty,' she said tightly.

He studied the firm line of her chin, the full lips now pursed, the determination in her eyes. 'Duty my arse,' he said. 'If you were a woman of duty, you would be at home minding your needle. If I did not know your mother better, I would say that she stinted on your training.'

'My mother stinted not one whit on my upbringing,' she said in a scathing voice. 'She stayed at home, minding her needle, and my father rode away to his death. I stayed at home, like a dutiful wife, while my husband rode away to the Holy Wars. I stayed at home nursing my children, tending our lands while he took up with another woman and got a bastard child on her. There is duty and there is duty, my lord. Do not seek to tell me which kind I should follow now for my own good.'

'I would also say that you are your mother's daughter,' Hugh Lupus said wryly. 'A man would never tangle with her out of choice – excepting your father, and look what happened to him.'

Matilda whitened. 'That was unworthy, my lord,' she said.

Chester snorted. 'I am known for my plain speaking,' he retorted, 'not my chivalry.' Raising his head, he narrowed his eyes towards one of the scouts he had sent ahead of them. The man was returning at a gallop, lashing the reins down on his mount's neck.

'Sire, I pray you make haste!' he cried. 'Earl Simon is barricaded in the church and the French have broken through!'

'God's sweet bones!' Hugh Lupus sprang to his feet. He turned to Matilda. 'I have no time to dally behind, nor to protect you,' he said curtly. 'Stay back with the baggage wain until told otherwise! You have no part to play in a battle, but you will be needed later to tend and succour the wounded!'

Mustering his troop, clapping spurs to his mount, he was gone in a shower of clods and stones.

'Best do as he says, my lady,' said the knight in command of the baggage wain, and grasped Matilda's bridle lest she harboured any different ideas. 'If there's hard fighting, no one wants a woman to hamper the swing of their sword.'

'No, but everyone will want one to tend their wounds and warm their beds in the aftermath!' she snapped at him. 'I may be a countess by birth, but I am no wilting flower.' She gave him a proud look. 'My grandfather was an axe-wielding Danish warrior who once fought a wild bear single-handed. I know my own worth.' She flicked her hand, commanding him to let go of her bridle.

He did so reluctantly, but rode his horse close, prepared to grab the rein. Her stomach churned with anxiety, but she steadied herself. Even if she did charge after Hugh Lupus' knights and arrive in the thick of the fray, she could do nothing, and, as the young soldier said, she would only hamper their sword arms.

Ever since the news had been delivered, she had been vacillating between sick terror for Simon's safety and deep anger at him for the situation he had left her to discover at Gisors. Another woman. A newborn child. A side of his life he had concealed and she had not remotely guessed at. Her training ground had been a harsh one and she had maintained her external composure very well, but even the best tempered steel had a breaking point, and she was close to it now. Catching her mood, her mount sidled and flickered its ears.

'How far to the fighting?' she demanded. Her hands twitched on the reins.

'About a mile, my lady,' the knight said, still eyeing her dubiously. 'Beyond that wooded hill.'

They followed the track around the foot of the slope, their horses trotting swiftly in the muddy scored hoofprints of Chester's main troop. There were heavy wheel ruts too, from laden carts. Rounding a curve, the smell of smoke hit them, and when Matilda gazed into the sky she saw the rising grey haze. Within a hundred yards the smoke had thickened and the smell had become a stench.

'My lady, perhaps you should stay back,' the knight cautioned, looking anxious.

'No,' she said, consumed by a desperate fear for Simon's safety and a need to be with him. 'I have to go on!' To give impetus to the bravado, she heeled her mare's flanks and sent her cantering into the village.

The sight that met her eyes was one of utter devastation. Heaps of charred wood marked the areas where dwellings had stood. Some still retained fragments of structure, twisted, black, skeletal. The corpses of pigs and dogs sprawled grotesquely among the debris. A scorched pail lay on its side next to a smashed well housing. Matilda swallowed the fluid that filled her mouth. There was a patch of garden neatly dug and tended. Herbs bordered the edge and new green shoots of onions, garlic and cabbage were growing strongly. Its owner lay in the middle, her kerchief torn off and her legs sprawled wide. A pitchfork pinned her body to the soil.

Matilda leaned over her horse's withers and retched. A garden was a place of nurture and sanctuary . . . not this vile destruction.

The knight grasped her mount's bridle and tried to lead the mare away, but Matilda struck his hand.

'My lady, I beg you. It is not safe.'

The village street was suddenly filled with soldiers on horseback. There was no time to move aside. Caught up in the flurry, Matilda's protectors drew their swords, but they were at a standstill and the oncoming men were at full gallop. Not Chester's, she had time to see, nor Simon's, and then they were too close and the battle closed over her head like a hungry open mouth.

There was a clash of blade on hauberk rivets, a whump of steel meeting flesh. Matilda's guardian lost the hand that had been closed around her bridle. He screamed, the sound stopping short as a lance followed the work of the sword and ran him through. Matilda's mare reared and plunged in terror. Unable to hold her, scared witless herself, Matilda was thrown. She landed hard, struck her head and blackness hit her like a fist and left her sprawled in the road against the wrecked garden palisade.

Toki spared no time for dramatic gestures with his axe: up, round and down in a single blurred arc of steel to swipe aside the French soldier who had run at him down the nave. Beside him Simon used his shield to fend off another two, while he parried and thrust with his sword. They were holding the French, but only just, and for every one of the enemy downed there was a fresh man to take his place. There would be no ransoms taken this time. It was kill or be killed.

Simon's lungs were burning with effort. His shield was a lead weight and he could feel the quiver of overstrained muscles in his weak left leg. Toki was tireless. He was even singing to himself as he swung and struck. Now Simon truly understood what his father and brother had faced on Hastings field.

Three more French soldiers came at them. Simon thrust his shield into the face of one, but the man was swift and strong. His sword found an opening and struck sidelong at Simon's ribs, raising blue sparks from the hauberk rivets. The air gasped from Simon's lungs and fiery pain streaked across his chest, but the heat of battle kept him upright and sheer desperation brought his own sword up to parry the next blow. Blade rasped on blade and slivers of metal flew from the

Frenchman's, which was not as well tempered as Simon's. A shard lodged in the back of Simon's hand and the blood from the wound ran through the cracks in his clenched fist and fouled his grip on his sword. He used his shield to parry and was forced backwards by the Frenchman's greater strength.

A horn sounded frantically somewhere. Simon was in too much extremity to do more than note the sound with a small corner of his mind, but that corner despaired, for it was the attack clarion and he was already overwhelmed. His left leg gave way and he went down, but as he fell he gave one last swipe with his sword. The blow connected with the Frenchman's knee and brought him down too. Lungs wheezing like worn-out bellows, Simon rolled over and with one last effort thrust his blade into his enemy's throat.

Stars burst before his eyes. On hands and knees he scrabbled for his shield, knowing that if he had to face anyone else he was finished. Pushing himself to his feet by will alone, he glanced around. A cursing Toki was wrenching his axe out of the second French soldier, who lay on top of the first. The church suddenly contained only Simon's gasping, exhausted men. Simon staggered to the door. There was fierce fighting in the street and he belatedly realised that the horn he had heard had meant salvation, not death – for some at least.

'If Hugh Lupus wasn't so fat, he might have got here sooner,' Toki panted, seeking to make light of the situation with sour jest. 'Any later and he would have been shovelling earth over our corpses as well as those of the French.'

'You have no gratitude,' Simon said and began to laugh, but as a release from tension rather than from genuine humour.

Toki snorted and clutched his shoulder. 'It is the English blood,' he retorted. 'We are ever ungrateful to our Norman masters.'

Simon sobered. 'It is I who should be grateful to you for saving my life a dozen times over,' he said. 'I can never repay the debt.'

'You could try,' Toki retorted with a grin. 'I would not object.' He pointed at the blood webbing Simon's hand. 'Better get yourself seen to, my lord.'

Simon nodded absently. The splinter of sword was still in his flesh. Raising his hand to his mouth, he gripped the sliver in his teeth and with a sharp tug pulled it out. Fresh blood gushed from the wound, but he bound it up tightly in a strip of linen purloined from the vestment coffer. The church was a total shambles, but the jewelled cross still gleamed softly over all, neither stolen nor dislodged during the intense fighting. That had to be a good omen.

Tottering outside, he became aware of his other aches and pains. Each breath drawn was a sawing ache, but he managed to breathe and he managed to walk.

'God's arse but you get yourself into some situations!' Hugh Lupus declared striding up to him. His mail hauberk and the padding beneath made him look gargantuan. He had removed his helm and sweat poured down his face.

'Serigny burned the village, and a French patrol took exception,' Simon answered, grimacing. 'I was in the wrong place at the wrong time.' He glanced around. 'And so were these poor people.' Suddenly he felt weary to death. All he wanted to do was lie down in a corner and close his eyes, but he was a commander and there was too much to be done.

Hugh Lupus' squire brought two cups of wine. Hugh seized one and drank it to the lees. 'Another,' he commanded the youth.

Simon swallowed his own and wiped his mouth on the back of his good hand.

'You might as well know, your wife is here,' Chester said. 'Arrived at the gates of Gisors as you left on patrol.'

'What?' Simon stared.

Chester repeated what he had said and drank his wine, pausing this time between swallows. 'Your wife knows about your mistress and to say that hell would seem cold by comparison is not an exaggeration. Countess Judith had a way of looking that could shrivel a man's cods in their sack, but her daughter's element is fire. Why any man should desire a mistress when he has such a woman for a wife is beyond me – unless you are a man who lusts after variety.'

'Sabina wasn't my mistress,' Simon said faintly, his wits bludgeoned by the notion of Matilda's presence in all this.

'But the child is yours?'

'Christ yes, but . . .' Simon shook his head. 'It is not what you think.' He hitched at his swordbelt. 'Where is Matilda now?'

'Back with my baggage wain,' Hugh said.

'What, you brought her here?' Simon was incredulous and horrified. 'Are you out of your wits?'

'I had no choice . . . short of binding her hand and foot and casting her in De Bêlleme's dungeon,' Hugh snapped. 'She wouldn't be stopped. It was all I could do to make her stay back. She said that it was her duty.'

Simon groaned and limped into the street. There was no sign of his wife. He wondered what had possessed her to travel from England, across Normandy to the dangerous war-torn lands of the Vexin. She was too responsible to act on a whim . . . or was she? How much did he truly know about his wife? Perhaps as much as he had known about Sabina which was tantamount to nothing.

Anger and anxiety surged through him, holding exhaustion at bay. He saw Chester's covered baggage wain lumbering into the bailey, drawn by two large black cobs. As it turned side on and drew to a halt, he also saw that there was a bay mare hitched to the back – a lady's mount, for no man rode a mare into battle unless he was a Saracen. But there was no sign of his wife.

He hastened towards the wain, uncaring that his limp was pronounced and for all to see. Uncaring that he stumbled. He reached the bay mare and, laying hands to the bridle, saw that it was Matilda's. The silver lozenges at browband and cheek-strap identified it beyond a doubt.

Then he looked in the wain and his heart froze.

'Matilda?' Abandoning the horse, he scrambled up into the covered cart. She lay on a makeshift bed of straw and sheepskins amidst the various items of Hugh Lupus' travelling household, a cooking pot near her head, wooden tent struts at her feet. Her face was as pale as ice, and the jagged cut and swollen blue bruise on her temple stood out in stark relief.

'Jesu God, Matilda?' He shook her shoulder but she was as limp and unresponsive as his daughter's cloth doll. Waves of fear rolled over him.

'She got tangled up with the French troops when they fled,' said the soldier who had been driving the wain. 'Got thrown by her horse.' He sleeved his nose and mouth. 'Can't see any other injuries on her, but she struck her head a heavy blow.' He gave Simon a look in which there was speculation and sympathy. 'She hasn't moved since I picked her up.'

Simon swallowed. Tears prickled behind his lids and he blinked them back. Long ago Waltheof had chastised him for self-pity and he had a morbid fear of becoming caught in its morass again. But if she died . . . He stroked one of her shining red-bronze braids. If she died, his life would not be worth living.

CHAPTER 43

Matilda heard the low drone of a voice intoning in Latin and felt cool moisture on her brow as a gentle finger painted it with the shape of a cross. The click of prayerbeads joined the murmur. She wondered in confusion for whom everyone was praying. Perhaps she ought to join in . . . but she was very tired and her head ached so badly that even considering the notion made her feel sick. Perhaps if she slept first . . .

Simon had been watching Matilda's still face and thought he saw a ripple pass over it as the priest anointed her with the holy oil. But she did not move again, and no one else had seen a sign.

Three days she had lain in this cold trance. They had borne her back to Gisors on a litter and Simon had ridden alongside it, terrified that she was going to die. She hadn't, but he was aware of time trickling away and with it her chances of recovery. They had managed to dribble a small amount of milk down her throat, but she needed more sustenance than that. Already he fancied that the hollows beneath her cheekbones were cadaverous.

Chester gave Simon's shoulder a hearty slap. 'Come away,' he said. 'Leave her to the women. There is nothing you can do here but get in their way.'

'I would rather stay,' Simon said and stiffened his spine. The Earl's bonhomie was well intentioned, but it grated upon him like two ends of broken bone.

'Christ man, you're a soldier, not a wet nurse! She won't know if you stay or leave. Sink a few cups of wine. You'll feel the better for it.'

'She might not know, but I would,' he replied grimly. 'And sinking any more wine than I have done already will only give me a foul head.'

Chester grunted and spread his hands to show that he yielded. 'You are a couple well suited,' he pronounced. 'Both out of your wits.'

Chester left his irritation evident in the heaviness of his footsteps, but Simon barely noticed except to be relieved that he had gone. He took Matilda's hand in his. The fingers were warm and relaxed. He rubbed the pad of his thumb over the carved stone of her wedding ring.

'Matilda . . .' he said softly and stroked her copper hair. 'Whatever I have done to you . . . I am sorry. If I have been faithless, it was out of my own lack . . . never yours. Why in God's name you wanted to follow me to Gisors, I do not know . . . surely there are more worthy causes to pursue than a wayward husband.' There was a tight lump in his throat. 'Unless you wake and tell me, I will never know . . .' Her face remained smooth and slack, the lips slightly parted. The silence stretched out, broken only by the settling of the charcoal in the nearby brazier and the soft murmur of Helisende and the wet nurse beyond the bed curtains.

Simon bowed his head to pray, but the physical and mental exhaustion took its toll. He closed his eyes, intending to entreat God's aid for Matilda, and promptly fell asleep.

Matilda was woken by the sound of a baby crying and someone swiftly shushing it. Her vision blurred and sharpened by turns, making her feel queasy. A fat wax candle cast gold and shadows over the bed. She was aware of a splitting headache emanating from the region of her left temple. Memories swam across her mind like dark-coloured fish and vanished into the murk before she was able to net them. There had been shouting, and battle. The glittering edge of a sword. Blood. Pain. Nothing.

Her mouth was dry, and she could not swallow because she was so parched. She tried to raise her right hand to summon aid and found that she could not, for there was a weight pressing it to the bed. Inching her head round with difficulty, pain stabbing in sharp flashes, she saw that Simon was kneeling at the bedside and that he had fallen asleep against her arm. His fingers were meshed through hers, binding her to him. A three-day growth of golden-brown beard outlined his mouth and his hair needed trimming for his fringe was almost in his eyes. A wave of tenderness engulfed her. And then she saw the bandage wound around his other hand and the brown stains where blood had soaked through and dried.

'Simon?' she mouthed. Her voice was a parched croak. He did not raise his head, but his hand tightened its grip on hers. Making a huge effort, she nudged him and once more breathed his name. His head came up slowly like that of a man being roused from a drunken stupor and for a moment his eyes were fogged and unknowing.

'Simon, I need a drink,' she breathed, and began to cough.

His gaze sharpened and cleared. Reaching for the cup at the bedside, he held it to her lips.

She sipped the watered wine in the cup and the dark fish of memory swam closer to the surface. She had been riding from a convent where she had just confronted her husband's lover. From beyond the curtain, the baby wailed again and the focus of her mind sharpened a further degree.

'Thank Christ,' he said, in a voice that shook. 'I have never prayed so hard in my life as I have prayed these last days . . . When the priest came to shrive you, I thought I would go mad.'

'Then you know my condition,' she murmured. 'For I too have been mad . . . mayhap I still am.' She closed her eyes, feeling sick. Pain hammered through her skull. The world and its problems were too vast to take in. It was easier to shut them out and return to the darkness.

She slept again, and when she woke Simon was still there. Indeed, she did not think that he had moved from her side, for his stubble was now decidedly a beard and even if her eyes had remained closed, she would have detected his presence by pungent smell alone. The candle no longer burned at the bedside and the curtains had been pulled back, revealing that even if the morning was not well advanced, it was beyond dawn. There was no one else in the hall, even by the hearth in the centre of the room where the cooking tripod had been moved to one side away from the direct heat of the flames.

Her head still ached but her vision was clearer, and her stomach no longer made her feel as if she were on the heaving deck of a ship. She tried to sit up and Simon moved to help her, but immediately desisted with a gasp of pain. She managed to struggle upright on her own. Her skull thundered and she was dizzy for a moment, but she weathered the feelings and looked at him in concern. 'What's wrong?'

He sat back down on the bedside stool, his hand pressed to his side. 'My ribs,' he wheezed. 'I took a blade side on and I think I've cracked a couple at least.'

'You fool, why haven't you had the chirurgeon tend you?' Matilda forgot her own discomforts in witnessing his. The bandage wrapped around his hand was as grubby as a beggar's toerag and, although he had removed his mail, his padded tunic was so marinated in the stink of sweat, smoke and blood that it could have stood up by itself and walked around.

He shrugged, then immediately winced. 'I had a vigil to keep.' He took her hand in his and stroked it. 'I realised what I stood in danger of losing.'

Matilda found a bleak smile. 'So did I,' she said.

With his free hand he poured wine, took a drink himself and then put the cup to her lips, the gesture echoing the ritual of the loving cup at a marriage.

He studied her sombrely. The shadows beneath his eyes

were the colour of slate. 'Why did you follow me to Gisors?'

She looked at him and then down at the coverlet. A loose thread poked out of the braid selvage and she plucked at it. 'I came to Gisors because of my mother. And in a way I went to Evreux because of her too.'

'Your mother?' He looked at her, nonplussed.

She pointed to the chest at the bedside. 'Open it,' she said, 'and take out the roll of linen on the top.'

Wincing at the pain from his ribs, he did as she requested. 'What is it?'

She gestured him to unfasten the binding and unroll it. 'An embroidery. I found it when I was clearing her coffer of clothing to give as alms to the poor. She kept it all those years.'

'She had many embroideries,' Simon said as he spread the canvas out on the bed.

'Not in the end. She gave them all away . . . save this one.'

Simon looked at it, following the pattern with his eyes. A young woman on a black horse, a red-haired man on a chestnut, the stitches so skilfully wrought that an observer could almost see the breeze in their garments and hear their laughter. He touched the figures with the fingertips of his good hand and raised his head to Matilda.

'My mother put all her love and longing into an embroidery and then confined it to the darkness of a chest,' Matilda said with a lump in her throat and tears in her eyes. 'I do not want to live my life like that.' She picked up the canvas and traced the lovingly worked red-haired man with her index finger. 'I have dwelt so long in the shadows my father left behind that I am in danger of becoming a shadow myself.' Drawing a deep breath, she raised her eyes to his. 'That is why I came to find you . . . as my mother never came to find her husband.'

Simon swore softly beneath his breath. 'As I remember, she felt he had betrayed her,' he said. 'Have I not betrayed you?'

Matilda's gaze remained steadfast. 'That was what I went to Evreux to find out.'

'You could have asked me.'

'Had you been in Gisors, I would have done – likely with a pair of sewing shears. As it was, I took my fury to Evreux.' At Simon's look of alarm, she smiled a little. 'You need not fear. Sister Sabina is still in one piece. We might not have met and parted the best of friends, but we came to an understanding. She told me what was between you.'

His exhaustion-pale complexion showed a sudden flood of colour. 'I am not proud of what happened, but I will do my best to set it rights. The child is a blameless innocent.' He took her hands in his. 'It is my duty to take him into my household – and into my heart. I will understand if you cannot do the same, but I would ask you to try.'

'It is my duty too,' Matilda said, her smile fading. 'Of course I will do my best.' She had been taught all about duty, and how there were times when the doing of it held the world together. 'Do you still want her?' she asked in a low voice. 'Is there no part of you that regrets she has taken holy vows?'

Simon shook his head. 'It was a fire lit at a single stopping place along the way and doused to mutual agreement. I want you.'

'Do you?' She searched his face.

He took hers between his hands, the good one and the bandaged. 'I wanted you when I saw you in the garden at Northampton, and that wanting has never gone away. Never,' he said. 'And I am not speaking as a courtier or someone trying to ingratiate himself.'

'Then as what?' she whispered. Their lips were almost touching. 'Tell me, Simon. I need to know.'

'As a man who loves his wife to distraction,' he said. 'For her courage and her love and her forgiveness. For everything that she is.'

Matilda gave a small gasp and closed the space between their lips. The kiss was tender and passionate, despairing and joyous, and when they parted they were both breathless.

'Close the bed curtains,' she panted, her eyes luminous.

He looked at her askance and shook his head. 'I don't think I can . . .'

'No, you fool.' She smiled at him through a shimmer of tears. 'Not for that reason! Neither of us is in a fit state. If you tried to stand up you would keel over, and my head is pounding fit to burst. I just want you beside me. Come to bed and sleep.' She flapped back the bedcovers.

He looked longingly at the space she made for him. 'I stink, I need to bathe,' he said with a grimace and a sniff of his armpit.

She shrugged. 'I have no complaint. The morrow will suffice. Come.'

He yielded to her insistence, and the fatigue rushed upon him like water through a burst dam. Somehow he managed to close the bed curtains and shut out the world. Somehow he stripped his gambeson and tunic, his leg bindings and hose. His hands fumbled, and his eyelids felt as though someone had weighed them down with death pennies. Still clad in braies and shirt, he tumbled into bed beside Matilda, pulled her close, and rested his chin against the top of her head. Within moments his breathing was slow and even.

Matilda nestled against him and heard the solid thud of his heart against her ear. She was not so naïve as to imagine that they had faced and defeated all their demons. There would be more quarrels, struggles and misunderstandings to strew their way with thorns. She knew that. But there was also the grace of reconciliation . . . and the light of love. The past was behind them; the future beckoned.

Thoroughly content, Matilda slipped her arm across Simon's waist and fell asleep with a smile.

AUTHOR'S NOTE

Now a note for those readers who are interested to know how much of the history in *The Winter Mantle* is true and how many liberties I've taken. This is quite a difficult question to answer, because some of the research has been contradictory and elusive, to say the least.

Waltheof of Huntingdon was beheaded for treason in 1076. From what the chroniclers of the time report, it would seem that he was foolish and easily led rather than filled with a wild rebellious zeal. He also had enemies at the Norman court who were only too willing to see him fall, and King William seems to have been swayed by their influence and perhaps by the thought that Waltheof had stepped over the line once too often. Judith is reported to have betrayed her husband to William, but after Waltheof's execution she was filled with remorse. Reading between the lines, I think that she expected her uncle to banish Waltheof as he had banished many other English lords who had rebelled against him, and she was shocked when he was beheaded.

Crowland Abbey still stands, partly in ruins, partly as a church in use, but there is little evidence of the abbey that stood on the site in Waltheof's time. It was seriously damaged by fire as mentioned in the novel and was rebuilt in the Norman style early in the twelfth century. Later on it was massively refurbished and it is these fourteenth-century remains that the visitor now sees when they visit Crowland.

Despite the cult that was once attached to Waltheof, there is no mention of his tomb at Crowland, although the visitor can buy postcards of the skull of Abbot Theodore, who was murdered by raiding Danes in AD 850.

The tale of Judith rejecting Simon de Senlis because he was lame is reported in one chronicle, and I had to make use of it because it's just too good a story to pass up. Simon himself is something of an enigma. I found four dates for his birth, ranging from 1046 to 1068. Some sources say he was present at the battle of Hastings, others deny it emphatically. Being as this is a work of fiction, I chose the date that best suited me and that seems to tally with the other known information, and I went for 1058. I also found two different individuals cited as his father. I chose Richard de Rules because he was a royal chamberlain.

Simon was known to have gone on crusade, but he didn't reach Jerusalem because the chroniclers put him in the thick of William Rufus' war in the Vexin in 1098. With this detail in mind I felt free to invent a reason for his turning back. It is also known that he had an illegitimate son called Simon, but so far I've been able to turn up nothing else about the child beyond his name. Again, I felt free to invent a background. Simon's legitimate children are given dates of birth that are all over the place, so I've gone with the story on this and kept them as close as possible to the probability. Amidst all this muddle and vague hints of facts, I came across the positive detail that Matilda's maid was called Helisende. Writing historical fiction can be as surprising and rewarding as it can be frustrating!

For readers wondering about some of the other historical characters who also appear in the novel: Ralf de Gael did not reach Jerusalem but died at Antioch. Stephen of Aumale lived to return and continue with his life. Simon and Matilda had another son, also named Simon, thus enabling young Waltheof to pursue a career in the church. He was later canonised as a saint in his own lifetime.

Simon de Senlis died at the priory of La Charité sur Loire in 1111 whilst attempting a second crusade. Matilda did not remain long a widow but married Prince David of Scotland, later to be King David, and in her forties bore him a son and two daughters.

I welcome responses from readers, and anyone who would like to get in touch with me can do so on Twitter: @chadwickauthor. I also have a website where you'll find more details about me and my work at www.elizabeth chadwick.com.

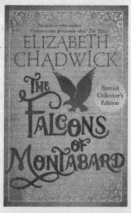

The next 'Director's Cut' edition from Elizabeth Chadwick's bestselling and best-loved novels.

The Port of Barfleur, 1120

Sabin FitzSimon, disgraced son of an earl, finally has the chance to salvage his reputation when renowned knight Edmund Strongfist asks Sabin to join a journey to Jerusalem.

The only thing Sabin must promise is to keep away from Strongfist's beautiful daughter, Annais. Sabin obeys, but his attraction to Annais's spirit, courage and her wonderful harp playing become increasingly difficult to resist.

As Sabin struggles to keep his heart in check, the Holy Land itself is in turmoil from constant warfare and the capture of its King. Simon must take command of the fortress of Montabard, and with it the recently widowed lady of the castle . . .